Hrym harrumph⸱ from doing the ⸱ aware I'm a prisoner for only as long as I *consent* to be a prisoner. Otherwise I'm just a guest in very poor accommodations."

"I am a simple bureaucrat," Temple said. "My talents are organizational, not arcane. Here, Rodrick, catch." She tossed something small and glittering through the bars, and Rodrick snatched it from the air without thinking. He opened his palm and looked down at a ruby the size of his thumbnail.

"Usually I'm the one bribing my guards, not the other way around."

"Burrow," Temple said, and Rodrick screamed as the ruby sank into the flesh of his hand with a sensation like a thousand biting insects swarming across his palm. The gem moved under his skin, and he clamped his other hand tightly around his wrist, but it did no good: he felt the gem slide beneath his gripping fingers and watched as it traveled under the skin along his inner forearm, past the crook of his elbow, scurrying over his bicep and vanishing beneath the sleeve of his shirt. He could still *feel* the ruby moving, like a chip of swallowed ice moving down the throat, but this icy sensation traveled to his shoulder and then down into his chest, stopping in the vicinity of his heart—at which point the sensation vanished entirely.

Hrym was shouting from the bench: "Rodrick! What's wrong? Should I kill everyone?"

"I wouldn't," Temple said mildly. "That gem is . . . let's say . . . an encouragement to good behavior."

"She gave me a ruby, Hrym." Rodrick stared at his palm, which no longer hurt, and which was entirely unmarked. "It crawled under my skin like a burrowing insect and scuttled next to my heart."

"I told you having a heart was a weakness," Hrym said.

"I always thought you meant that metaphorically . . ."

THE PATHFINDER TALES LIBRARY

THE PATHFINDER TALES LIBRARY

Liar's Bargain

Tim Pratt

A TOM DOHERTY ASSOCIATES BOOK
New York

This is a work of fiction. All of the characters, organizations, and events portrayed in this novel are either products of the author's imagination or are used fictitiously.

PATHFINDER TALES: LIAR'S BARGAIN

Maps by Crystal Frasier and Robert Lazzaretti

A Tor Book
Published by Tom Doherty Associates, LLC
175 Fifth Avenue
New York, NY 10010

www.tor-forge.com

The Library of Congress Cataloging-in-Publication Data is available upon request.

ISBN 978-0-7653-8431-7 (trade paperback)
ISBN 978-0-7653-8430-0 (e-book)

Our books may be purchased in bulk for promotional, educational, or business use. Please contact your local bookseller or the Macmillan Corporate and Premium Sales Department at 1-800-221-7945, extension 5442, or by e-mail at MacmillanSpecialMarkets@macmillan.com.

First Edition: June 2016

Printed in the United States of America

0 9 8 7 6 5 4 3 2 1

For Jeff and Katrina

Inner Sea Region

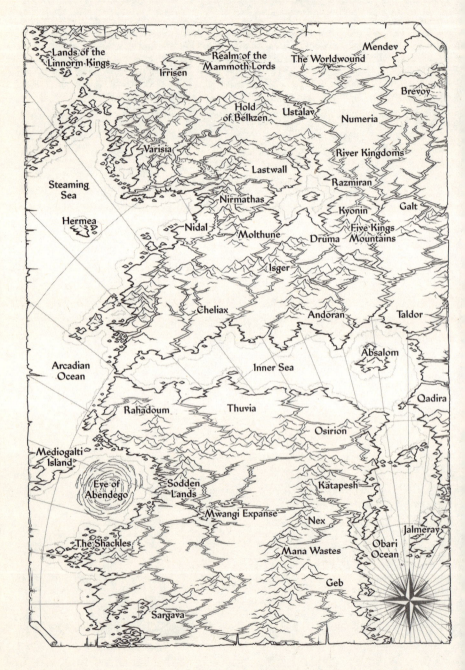

Lands of the Linnorm Kings

Irrisen

Realm of the Mammoth Lords

The Worldwound

Mendev

Brevoy

Hold of Belkzen

Ustalav

Numeria

Varisia

River Kingdoms

Steaming Sea

Lastwall

Razmiran

Hermea

Nirmathas

Kyonin

Galt

Nidal

Molthune

Druma

Five Kings Mountains

Isger

Cheliax

Andoran

Taldor

Absalom

Arcadian Ocean

Inner Sea

Qadira

Rahadoum

Thuvia

Osirion

Mediogalti Island

Eye of Abendego

Sodden Lands

Katapesh

Mwangi Expanse

Nex

Jalmeray

The Shackles

Mana Wastes

Obari Ocean

Geb

Sargava

Story Locations

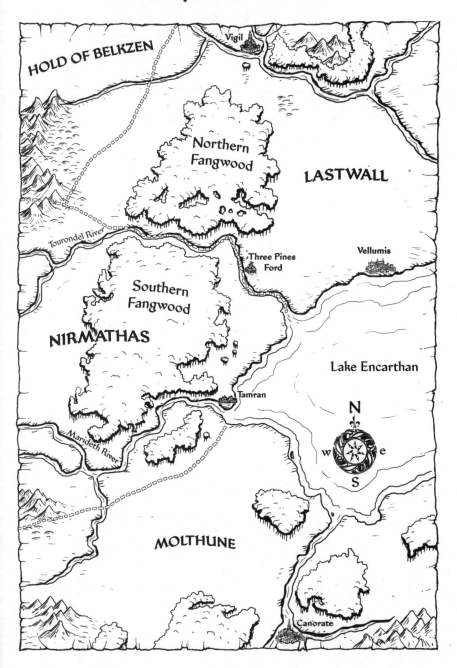

1
A River Crossing

"What I don't understand is why you *believed* her," Hrym said. Rodrick shifted around, trying to find a more comfortable position on his belly under the bush, which was difficult, given all the roots and rocks beneath him and the scratching branches pressing down from above. "We've been over this. She said she forgave me. I thought she was doing me a good turn."

"'Go to Lake Encarthan,' she said. 'Nirmathas,' she said. 'The shores are thronged with wealthy idiots!' And you *believed* her."

Rodrick squinted. Were those feet over there? If they were feet, were they the feet of mere passing foresters of no consequence, or the feet of people who wanted to beat him to death with sticks—or whatever people in Nirmathas beat dishonest gamblers to death with? He shouldn't assume it was sticks. That was probably his city-dweller's prejudice talking. Maybe they used barrel staves, or threw clods of dirt. "I admit my trust in her was misplaced. What can I say? I never took her for the vengeful type."

Hrym chortled. "I am a talking sword, barely capable of telling humans apart, and even *I* knew she was the vengeful type."

"Fair enough. I didn't think she was the *subtly* vengeful type. I thought she might stab me in my sleep, not smile sweetly and send me into the wilderness. You must admit, her argument *was* plausible."

"It's not my job to judge plausibility."

"What is your job, exactly?"

"Dazzling the rubes, and saving your life from rubes who are insufficiently dazzled."

"She said there was gold here. New mines discovered every day, people striking it rich with picks and shovels—she said Nirmathas was full of the *new* rich, who are so much less suspicious and more poorly guarded than the *old* rich. Of course I believed her. Gold must come from *somewhere*. Why not the shores of Lake Encarthan?"

"I did like the parts about gold," Hrym said. "How long are we going to hide under this bush?"

"Until I believe the threat has passed."

"Rodrick. I am a wondrous talking sword of magical living ice, and you are a half-competent swordsman. A few months ago we bested a rakshasa in battle. Half a dozen sawmill workers—"

"And a foreman."

"—and a foreman aren't likely to pose any great difficulty."

"I don't want to kill them, Hrym. They aren't demonic monsters. They're just *people*. Killing them would be murder."

"They want to kill *you*. I think they call it self-defense in that case."

"I doubt the magistrates would see it that way. Besides, if I killed everyone who wanted to kill *me*, the world would be a far less populous place."

"We could freeze them in place, then. My magic isn't inherently lethal."

"If we froze them out here in the dark, they'd be eaten by . . . forest monsters. Wolves. Bears. Whatever they have here."

"So? Doesn't the moral burden fall on the forest monsters in that case? You baffle me."

"We'll make it through the night, Hrym, and then head out in search of better prospects. We're not so far from Cheliax, really. That place is full of rich people."

"Not naive people, as a rule, though."

"True. But at least many of them are evil. We *were* going to focus on stealing from the evil, whenever possible."

"That was your idea, not mine," the sword said. "I don't much care where the gold comes from. I don't suffer from guilt. I'm a sword."

"There's a pragmatic aspect to preying on the villainous, though. The evil are more likely to have lots of money, since they aren't scrupulous about how they get it, and once they have it, they don't go around giving any of it to charity, and so forth. They keep it."

"Excellent. So the current plan is, we hide under this bush until you, a person with demonstrably terrible judgment, decide it's safe to leave, and then we start hiking in the general direction of Cheliax?"

"We'll probably steal a horse, rather than hike," Rodrick said. "Since our old horse is in the hands of an angry mob."

Hrym went *hrmm*. "Seven gamblers don't count as a mob. The horse is probably worth more than you cheated them out of dicing tonight anyway. Why are they still chasing us? They should be glad of their good fortune. A free horse! Why bring violence into it at all? Wait, don't tell me. Morals again, right?"

"Something like that. Or setting a bad precedent. Or beating a stranger to death with sticks counts as an unusually good night's entertainment in this gods-blighted wilderness."

"Wait, you want to steal a horse? Isn't that *evil*? Or is it an evil horse? Or an evil owner?"

"I am prepared to be flexible regarding the horse's moral alignment, so long as it's fast. Or even slow. Just as long as it's faster than walking, honestly."

"Honesty *is* very important—"

"Over there!" someone shouted, which was how you could tell they were workers in a sawmill and not hunters, because hunters knew better than to startle their quarry with shouts.

Rodrick rolled out from under the bush, Hrym in his scabbard digging painfully into his thigh in the process, then leapt to his feet and set off running in a direction that seemed to lead *away* from the voice.

He was so busy concentrating on not tripping over roots or rocks, and avoiding all the tree branches that hung inconveniently just at head height, that he was quite surprised when he fell into the river.

"I could freeze the river, if it would make you feel better," Hrym said. "In a retaliatory way. Unless you think that would be immoral. I'm not sure if it's an evil river or not." The sword was unsheathed, stuck point-first in the earth, helping keep watch.

Rodrick sat under a tree, which would have been an improvement over hiding under a bush, if only he hadn't been soaking wet. He kept his hand on Hrym's hilt, and the sword's magic kept him from suffering the effects of the chill night air, so at least he wouldn't die of exposure. He still squished every time he shifted, and didn't dare try to light a fire to dry himself out, lest the flames give away his position. "Yes, yes, you're hilarious. Do you think they'll keep hunting me, or am I safe now?"

"That depends on whether their desire to kill you is greater than their reluctance to ford a river in the dark. Or on whether there's a nearby bridge we don't know about. With luck they're still searching the other side of the bank for you. Your blundering into the river and floundering some ways downstream *could* be construed as a clever way to evade pursuit—it's hard to track someone after they've gone into the water, and difficult to guess where they might emerge."

Rodrick opened up his pack and poked through it gloomily, looking for something dry to eat. The people of Nirmathas favored jerkies with the consistency of tree bark, and he probably had some stashed away against emergencies. Chewing it would distract him from his other miseries, the same way slamming your fingers in a door could distract you from a stubbed toe.

His hand touched his cloak of the devilfish, one of the magical items he'd acquired—which is to say, "stolen"—during his adventures to date. "Hmm. I could transform into a devilfish and jump *back* into the river, and swim through the night. We could get a long way away from here."

"A marvelous plan. It's a nice, deep, fast river, too. Shame about all the fishing boats and nets strung along its length. When a lucky fisherman hauls an immense, seven-tentacled monster out of nightmare onto his boat, I'm sure you'll have time to explain your secret humanity before he stabs you to death. "

Rodrick found a piece of only moderately damp jerky and began to gnaw on it. He might as well have been chewing on his own belt. "Mmm. You make a good point. Walking might be more sensible. I think I'll wait until daylight, though, as blundering around in the dark hasn't proven very effective."

"Fair enough. Or we could investigate the campfires to the west."

Rodrick squinted into the night. "I don't see anything."

"The fact that you're looking east might account for that."

He grunted and swiveled his head, and in the depthless dark of the forest he did detect a few distant flickers. "Hmm. People. Probably not the ones who were hunting me, either."

"Which means they could offer hospitality."

"Or they could have horses to steal."

"Or that, yes," Hrym agreed.

Rodrick prided himself on his stealth, though for maximum effect he had to keep Hrym sheathed on his belt so his hands remained free for occasional periods of crawling on all fours. He looked like a dashing swordsman (or else a dangerous thug, depending on whether you asked Rodrick himself or someone else) but moved like a sneak thief. He circled around the source of the light, keeping an eye out for sentries, and as he drew closer, counted no fewer than three fires, spaced some tens of yards apart. That configuration suggested a party of some size—which, on the one hand, was a bit daunting, but on the other hand meant they might have lots of horses, and might not notice one little mount missing from the crowd.

He only had one close call, when he went still with his back against a tree while a sentry in a bucketlike helmet walked past less than a dozen feet away, muttering to himself and poking at the underbrush with a pike. Rodrick moved fast after that, hoping to complete his work before the man made his next circuit of the camp.

There were two groups of horses, tethered separately, and Rodrick wondered if they were sorted by disposition. He chose to approach the horses situated farthest from the fires to avoid detection, and since he was no particular judge of horseflesh anyway, selected the one on the outside without much internal debate. The beast was gray or black or brown or who knew what color—impossible to say in the darkness—and looked like more of a pack animal than a racing mount, which suited Rodrick fine. Spirited women had their attractions, but he didn't feel the same about spirited mounts. The animal was sleeping, but Rodrick touched its side gently and murmured reassuring sounds as it woke up, and the horse blinked at him and then waited with every appearance of patience as he untied the tether from a tree branch and slowly led the horse deeper into the forest. The animal wasn't saddled, of course, and riding bareback was even more horrific than ordinary riding, but needs must.

Rodrick wasn't about to ride a horse in the forest at night and risk breaking the animal's legs and his own neck, but the trees thinned out closer to the riverbank, so if he could lead the horse in that direction he should be able to ride safely—

"Thief!" someone shouted, and as usual, it was the second most unpleasant thing he'd ever heard anyone shout. (The first most unpleasant was "My husband's home early!") Rodrick attempted to climb up on the horse's back, because caution was suddenly less important than escape, but the horse failed to cooperate, skittering away—Could horses skitter? He wouldn't have thought so, but this one managed it—in alarm as the camp was roused. Rodrick slid along the horse's side, lost his footing, and sat down hard on a tree root, at which point he decided his feet were the only form of locomotion he needed. The camp was roused now, full of shouting voices, and Hrym was complaining, too, demanding to be let out of his sheath so he could see what was going on, and Rodrick hissed, "Shut up shut up shut *up*" at the world in general as he did his best to run away from the noise.

He tripped on some abominable forest-related bit of the landscape, banged his chin on the ground hard enough to make his teeth snap together, and watched the night become even darker as black stars filled his vision. He pushed himself up on his elbows, lifted his head, and nearly put his own eye out on a spear point. The spearhead was shortly joined by two sword points, all pointed at his face, which was really more weaponry than anyone should require to kill someone like him.

2

A Journey on Horseback

"Thank Erastil you're here," Rodrick said. "I've been in pursuit of a notorious horse thief, and tracked him to your camp—"

"Lie," a harsh voice said. Rodrick risked turning his head, and was alarmed to see a hulking figure with long gray hair wearing a chainmail shirt and no pants, holding a sword so large it seemed like it should be merely decorative—the sort of weapon you might hang on a wall in a castle, not actually *fight* with.

"Our spiritual adviser says you're lying," a milder voice said. Rodrick looked in the other direction, where a younger, dark-haired, more fully dressed woman stood, holding a more reasonable-looking sword.

That giant was a priest? And one who could detect lies, apparently. He'd encountered people with that power before. They were annoying. They forced you to tell the truth *very carefully*.

"Ah." Rodrick stayed flat on the ground, because the armed people around him hadn't invited him to stand. He lined up the words just right in his head, then spoke. "I apologize. I've spent the past few hours being pursued by men who believe I cheated them in a dice game, and during my flight I had various unpleasant experiences, including falling in a river, and as a result I became rather desperate and made the incredibly bad decision to try to steal one of your horses. I deeply regret that."

"True," the big man said.

The woman grunted. "They believed you cheated them, you say? *Did* you cheat them?"

Rodrick winced. "Not on *every* throw."

She laughed. "So you're a cheat and a thief, and confess to those crimes from your own mouth. Very well. By my authority as a captain of the crusaders of Lastwall—"

"Wait, Lastwall? This is Nirmathas!"

The big man grunted. "He thinks it's true. Amusing."

She shook her head. "Nirmathas is on the other side of the river you fell into, I'm afraid. As I was saying: by my authority as a captain of the crusaders of Lastwall, I accept your confession, and sentence you to death by hanging, said sentence to be carried out with all due haste."

"Let us go now, or everyone here dies." Hrym's voice was muffled by the sheath, but he was clearly audible. "Well, not *everyone*. Not me, obviously, and not Rodrick. But the rest of you, most definitely."

"True," the priest said, in tones of wonder.

There were suddenly a lot more swords pointed at Rodrick, and a lot of people frantically looking in every direction. "Who said that?" the captain demanded.

Rodrick closed his eyes. "My sword has a mind of its own. His name is Hrym. Hrym, meet captain . . . something . . . of the crusaders of Lastwall."

"True." The priest sounded impressed.

"A talking *sword*." The captain squatted on her heels, bringing her eyes level with Rodrick's. "Show me this sword. Very slowly."

"May I stand up? Drawing a blade while sprawled in the dirt isn't a skill I've practiced often."

"You may kneel."

"How kind." Rodrick got to his knees and slowly drew Hrym from the scabbard. He got about halfway before the captain spoke again.

"That's far enough." She peered at the glittering, icy blade. "Do you truly speak, sword?"

"Speaking is the *least* of my abilities. Set us free, or I'll show you rather more remarkable powers. Very painful ones."

"Mmm. How did a wandering horse thief come by such a remarkable weapon? Perhaps it's some kind of trickery."

"Would you like a demonstration of my powers?" the sword said.

"Hrym, let's not escalate matters," Rodrick said.

"I'd say they're fairly well escalated already." Icy vapor swirled around the blade. "I'll freeze every one of you into a lump of ice if you don't set us free *right now*."

"True," the priest said. "If it were just a lump of steel, and the thief were throwing his voice or something, I don't think my ability to detect lies would work on it. It's real."

"Fascinating." If the captain feared for her life, she wasn't showing it.

Rodrick wished, not for the first time, that he had a good relationship with any particular deity, because this seemed like an optimal time to pray for divine intercession.

"You aren't listening." The temperature dropped, and frost formed on all the exposed metal in the vicinity. "Let us go, or die in ice."

"We're listening," the priest said mildly.

The captain nodded. "You think we fear death? We're crusaders. We face undead horrors and orc hordes, and we *chose* that life. Death holds no terror for us."

"Horrors and hordes are causes worth fighting, and perhaps even dying for," Rodrick said. "I, however, am just a man who made some bad decisions. No one has to die here. Just let us go, all right? We'll be back across the river and out of your territory within the hour."

"Crusaders do not compromise. Hrym, is it? Let this serve as notice that any act of aggression on your part will lead to the swift death of your wielder."

"You mean a *different* swift death than the one you've already promised him? Death by sword instead of death by rope?"

Everyone was silent for a moment.

Rodrick said, "He makes a good point. If you're going to kill me *anyway*, Hrym's got nothing to lose killing all of you, too."

"I'm vengeful," Hrym said. "And that's one of my *better* qualities."

"I'm still not convinced you can—" The captain gasped and dropped her sword, which was suddenly encased in a thick carapace of ice.

"Unless you think my ability to freeze things is inexplicably limited to swords, you should be able to guess what I can do to *you*." Hrym's tone was insufferably smug.

"I'm so sorry," Rodrick said. "There's no reasoning with him when he gets like this. You should really just let us go."

The captain sucked her frostbitten fingers for a moment and scowled. "Do you think I'm frightened of a little magic? This is Lastwall, boy. When the Whispering Tyrant raised our own dead against us, we *still* didn't surrender. We certainly won't run from you."

"Wasn't the Whispering Tyrant a bit before your time?" Rodrick said. "Oh, wait, I see, you're using the *institutional* we. As a *group* the crusaders of Lastwall never back down, absolutely, understood, but within that institution isn't there some ability for individuals to make accommodations with circumstance? Think of the good you and your soldiers can do against hordes of the undead, or orcs, or both—like vampire orcs, let's say. Certainly *they're* a greater threat than *I* am. Spare me, spare yourselves, and fight more meaningful battles later."

"We're all going to die," the priest said gloomily, but not as if he intended to do anything about it. "As Iomedae wills."

Someone cleared her throat. It was the woman with the spear, the first one who'd pointed a weapon at Rodrick's nose, who hadn't spoken until now. "*Technically*, Captain, since he's a civilian criminal, we don't have to deal with him at all. We could just hand him over to the Bastion of Justice."

The Bastion of Justice. Sounded like a terrible place, thing, or idea—but it was probably preferable to the death of everyone in the camp. Rodrick nodded enthusiastically. "Yes, please, why don't you hand me over to . . . that."

The captain frowned. The priest said, "She makes a good point. The Bastion would be happy to get their hands on that sword, too, and we're going to Vellumis anyway."

The captain sheathed her sword. "Very well. What's your name, thief?"

He almost lied out of habit, then remembered that a limited sort of honesty was the best policy for the moment. "Rodrick."

"Do I have your word, Rodrick, that you will not resist us, or try to escape, or seek to do us harm while we transport you to the Bastion for judgment? Not that the word of a thief is worth much, but the priest will know if you lie."

"Honestly, then? I'll escape if I see an opportunity. But I can promise not to attack any of you."

The captain chuckled. "Very well. Will your sword behave itself, too?"

"Hrym, don't kill anyone, all right? These fine men and women are protecting us from being overrun by blood-crazed orc vampires. They deserve our respect and admiration."

"Eh?" Hrym said. "Oh, fine. I hope this doesn't take long. No killing. But if they try to take me away from you, I'll ice them all."

"All true enough," the priest said.

"Sheathe your sword, please," the captain said. Rodrick obeyed, and then his hands were wrenched behind him by the spear-wielding woman, who tied them together. They wisely left Hrym on his hip, though. A couple of stout crusaders picked him up and draped him facedown across the back of a horse—the same horse he'd tried to steal, which was either a joke or a coincidence—and then tied his ankles, too.

"Well, Hrym, we're traveling on horseback after all."

"Everything always works out for us, doesn't it?" Hrym said. "It's because we're so virtuous."

"So what's this Bastion place, anyway?"

The woman with the spear had apparently been assigned as their minder, for she led the horse along the slow procession out of the woods and onto a well-maintained road Rodrick hadn't realized even existed. A fair amount of dust blew into Rodrick's face, leading him to keep his eyes closed, but that was fine; the view of a horse's side wasn't particularly stimulating anyway.

She said, "Lastwall is a military country. The army maintains watch over the ruins of the Whispering Tyrant's realm to ensure he doesn't rise again, and holds back the orcs in Belkzen. The crusaders are too busy to deal with less important matters—burglaries, drunken fistfights, ordinary murders, and the like. The Bastion of Justice is in charge of crimes committed by and against civilians in and around Vellumis. We'll hand you over to them, give our testimony to the magistrate, and they'll pronounce and carry out sentence."

"Ah. What's the sentence for trying to steal a horse?"

"Death, I assume. Our legal code is fairly simple."

"So, effectively, I've postponed my death. I'm not complaining, mind you. A delay isn't as good as a pardon, but it's better than the alternative."

"When we get to the Bastion, I'll just threaten to kill all of *them*," Hrym said. "They'll let us go."

The woman said, "Mmm."

Oh no, Rodrick thought. "Except, of course, they'll have wizards and the like on hand to try to neutralize Hrym's power."

She shrugged. "I wouldn't know. I've never worked for the Bastion. But the defenders of Lastwall, as an *institution*, do have some experience dealing with magic-wielding enemies."

Rodrick bounced along, thinking dark thoughts. The whole country of Lastwall, as he understood it, existed solely because after a mighty army destroyed the monstrous lich called the Whispering Tyrant, the winners felt the need to keep watch on his tomb to make sure he didn't wake up again. Later they'd expanded their responsibilities to include acting as a bulwark against the Hold of Belkzen, a nation (of sorts) filled with warlike orcs bent on overrunning the Inner Sea . . . or so the stories went. Rodrick suspected the knights had actually found guarding a dead city boring, and considered massacring orcs, and being massacred in turn, a good way to pass the time. The crusaders probably didn't run into many orcs who used magic, since as a people orcs favored hitting their enemies with sharp heavy things, but the crusaders had once upon a time fought an evil wizard-king, and they probably remembered a few tricks from the old days. They might well be able to keep Hrym from using his magic.

Still, all wasn't lost. The sword was a powerful weapon, after all, and in Lastwall, they needed powerful weapons. Hrym wouldn't agree to serve anyone *other* than Rodrick, so perhaps he could offer his services on the front lines, standing against the orcs . . . and escape from there instead. It was an article of faith for Rodrick that he could talk his way out of almost anything.

"How much farther to—what's the place called? Valormouse?"

"Vellumis," the spear-carrier replied. "It's about a hundred miles."

"You expect me to travel a hundred miles tied on the back of a horse?"

"Not at all," she said. "We wouldn't put the horse through that."

"Good."

"We're meeting up with a larger caravan at Three Pines Ford. From there, you'll travel tied up in the back of a cart."

"Luxury," Rodrick said, and meant it.

"I saved the world from a demon lord once," Rodrick announced to the occupants of the cart and the world in general. Well, why not? It was worth a try. The woman with the spear was still there, watching over him, and quite vigilantly, too; if she'd been on guard duty the night before, Rodrick wouldn't have gotten as close to successful horse thievery as he had. The priest was also sitting in the back, nestled among sacks of grain and barrels of salted meat, reading from a volume bound in wood that looked heavy enough to crush skulls. He tore a strand of hair from his immense beard, laid it across the page to mark his place, closed the book, and cocked his head at Rodrick. "Say that again."

Rodrick obliged.

The priest clucked his tongue. "Interesting. You really believe that. Strange. You don't *seem* mad."

"It's true," Hrym chimed in. "Enormous thing like a centipede with a human face. Human-ish, anyway. Name of—oh, what was it? Calamitous?"

"Kholerus." Rodrick shivered. "We stopped a demon cultist from freeing Kholerus from his prison beneath the Lake of Mists and Veils."

"And here *we* are, imprisoned in the vicinity of another famous lake." Hrym made a noise that might have been a laugh. "That's irony for you."

"Are they serious?" the spear-woman said.

The priest nodded. "They're both convinced of their sincerity. And that name, Kholerus . . . I've heard it, but not many have, I think. The son of Deskari, the Locust Lord, driven with his father into the Lake of Mists and Veils by Aroden." He rose and vaulted over the side of the cart—which was moving slowly, but still, he was acrobatic for a grizzled gargantuan war-priest. Rodrick allowed himself to begin to hope. Crusaders hated demons, so surely they'd love him?

Some time later the cart stopped, and the priest returned with the captain, who demanded to hear Rodrick's story. Rodrick told it, with assorted interjections (mostly self-aggrandizing) from Hrym. Rodrick was careful to cast himself in the best possible light *and* avoid any outright falsehoods. Fortunately, there was no harm in leaving certain facts out: the secret to dealing with truth-tellers was to restrict yourself to lies of omission. The captain periodically looked at the priest, who affirmed Rodrick's essential truthfulness with nods and grunts.

Rodrick's throat was parched after the recitation of his great deeds, and the guard tipped a cup of water to his lips and let him drink his fill.

The captain looked at a spot just beyond Rodrick's left shoulder. "A noble act in the past does not erase the stain of a later crime, but it may . . . mitigate your sentence. That's up to the officials in the Bastion to decide."

"He's practically a paladin, really," Hrym said.

"Well, I don't like to boast," Rodrick said. "But only because that's not very paladin-like."

The captain sighed, shook her head, and climbed off the wagon.

3

A Conversation
Through Bars

Rodrick's experience of the nations around Lake Encarthan had given him the impression that it was a land of timbered buildings and towering trees and dirt floors, so he'd expected Vellumis to be basically an immense fort.

It was with great surprise, then, that he turned his head to see a gleaming city of marble domes, immense archways, glistening white walls, and elaborately carved eaves. While Vellumis didn't match the majesty of Absalom, or even his home city of Almas, it was without a doubt a *real city*, and Rodrick felt himself begin to relax for the first time in weeks. Yes, he was a prisoner, and if he couldn't talk his way out of his predicament, Hrym would have to freeze a great number of noble crusaders to allow Rodrick to escape. But still, this was a *city*, the kind of place where he was most at home, the kind of place where great things could happen, the kind of place where fools and their money could be most expeditiously parted.

The cart curved around the outskirts of the city until it finally approached a domed fortress of stone surrounded by a high wall. "The Bastion of Justice," the guard said. "Some of the best dungeons in all of Lastwall down there, I'm told."

Rodrick thought about that. "Best . . . as in . . . most pleasant for prisoners? Or best as in most effective at destroying a prisoner's will to live?"

The guard just smiled.

The gates opened, and the cart rolled into a courtyard full of military bustle: crusaders training, grooms doing things to horses, people running to and fro with urgency. The clash of steel on steel, the clang of hammers shaping metal, the smell of forge fires—Rodrick found it all terribly depressing. They were so *organized*. How could anyone stand it?

A crusader with a round helmet jammed on her head approached, frowning. "Do you have a prisoner for us?"

The captain nodded. "One for Underclerk Temple, I think."

The crusader whistled. "Really? Let me see." She climbed up onto the cart, and instantly drew her sword, leveling it at Rodrick. "Why does the prisoner still have a weapon?"

The captain sighed. "Because his sword is sentient and magical and promised to murder anyone who tried to disarm his master."

"It's true," Hrym said. "Except he's not my master. We're partners. He's the junior partner, really."

"No one needs to murder *anyone*," Rodrick said. "This is just a misunderstanding, and it can all be worked out. I'm a fighter for the side of good myself, mainly, just fallen on hard times lately."

The official nodded slowly, but didn't sheathe her sword. "Yes. One for Temple, indeed. Sir, you *do* realize you're in the middle of Vellumis, a city of battle-hardened crusaders?"

"I've noticed, yes. Lovely city, too. Much nicer than I expected."

"Will you hand over the sword, so we can talk without quite so much . . . tension?"

"It's not up to me, I'm afraid. Hrym, would you like to go with this nice crusader?"

"No," Hrym said.

Rodrick gave an apologetic shrug. "Sorry. He can be very stubborn."

The woman rubbed her jaw with her free hand. "All right, then." She shouted "Clear the courtyard!" in a booming voice, and then sat staring at Rodrick for three full minutes, the force of her attention entirely withering his attempts to dazzle her with a charming smile. After the courtyard had emptied of all personnel, including the big priest and the friendly-ish spear-carrier, the crusader leaned forward and cut the ropes tying Rodrick's feet. She stepped out of the cart and beckoned him to follow. Rodrick struggled upright and climbed out of the cart, his hands still bound in front of him, but both resting on Hrym's hilt.

She led him through deserted hallways of dark stone and down spiraling stairs, deep into the Bastion of Justice. "Not very well staffed, are you?"

"Everyone is avoiding the area until I have you secured, so if your sword does anything . . . inadvisable . . . casualties will be minimal."

"Good for everyone else. Not so good for you."

She shrugged. "Rank has its drawbacks."

"What if I froze you solid and we ran away?" Hrym said.

"Your wielder would be filled with crossbow bolts the moment he poked his head outside," she replied.

"Ah. That's what I thought," Hrym said.

"Here we are," she said eventually, gesturing.

"Ah," Rodrick said. "Yes. Only the *best* dungeons for me."

Rodrick didn't need long to explore his new home: a small room of bare stone with straw thrown on the floor, furnished only by a bench carved from a single piece of wood, so there were no nails to pry loose or legs to break off to use as weapons. Before he had time to become too bored, a guard opened the barred door and let in a gray-haired, sour-faced man carrying a black bag.

"Hello," Rodrick said. "What's in the bag?"

"Tools of the trade."

"You aren't a torturer, are you?"

The man barked a laugh. "Depends on who you ask. I'm a chirurgeon. Mostly I cut off infected arms and legs to keep the rot from spreading, but I'm just supposed to see if you're healthy or not."

"If you try to give him a sleeping draught or harm him in any way, I will bring terrible destruction down on this place," Hrym said.

The man frowned. "A talking sword, they said. I thought they were playing a joke. Oh well. Doesn't matter to me. Swords never need tending on the battlefield, at least not from me. Stand up, would you, and stick out your tongue?"

Rodrick had undergone the occasional physical exam in the past, and this was less invasive than some: the doctor listened to his heart and lungs by pressing an ear to his chest, peered into his mouth and ears and nostrils, made Rodrick cough, prodded at his gums, asked him disgustingly personal questions about his recent bowel movements and whether he had any pain when he passed water. For the most part, Rodrick answered honestly.

"All right, I'm done." The doctor picked up his bag, which he'd never even opened.

"What's the verdict?" Rodrick said.

The man shook his head. "*You* don't pay me. Why should I tell you?"

A guard let the chirurgeon out, and closed the door, and that was all that happened, for a while.

"I could pick the lock, if there was a lock." Rodrick examined the door of the cell. "The door seems to be sealed by magic, which isn't very sporting."

"Rodrick, I can freeze the bars and you can break them with a kick."

"True. A bit loud, though. Might bring the guards running."

"So I'll freeze *them*, and you kick them as well."

"I see a few flaws with that plan."

"You're softhearted, Rodrick. You should be more like me. I don't have any heart at all, soft or otherwise."

"Even if the prospect of indiscriminate murder didn't give me pause, I'm still hoping for a more elegant solution than destroying the Bastion of Justice and bringing the wrath of the entire nation of Lastwall down on us. They can be quite persistent, I understand, and I'd rather not be pursued across the continent. Though I accept that as a tactic of last resort."

The door at the end of the hall opened with a squeal of rusty hinges. Rodrick wondered if the door made that noise naturally or if they'd worked on it with dirt and sand and steel wool to create the right ominous tone.

A short, stout woman of middle age walked down the hallway at a brisk, no-nonsense pace. Her skin was dark brown, her hair curly and cropped short, with a great deal of gray mixed in with the black. She wore vaguely official-looking black robes with baggy sleeves, and carried a burlap sack in one hand. Rodrick thought she looked rather matronly, until she stopped outside the bars and smiled at him; then she looked more like someone who might eat her young, if the need arose. "My name is Underclerk Temple. I am a humble servant of the Bastion of Justice, and I've been chosen to oversee your case."

In Rodrick's experience those who described themselves as humble servants were usually neither—they tended to be zealous priests or power-mad dictators—so he nodded politely. "Very pleased to meet you. I hope we can straighten this out. It's all just a misunderstanding, really."

"Oh? You didn't try to steal a horse from a group of crusaders?"

"I *did*, but there were mitigating factors—"

"You needed the horse to escape the consequences of an earlier crime, yes, I heard. I don't think there's any misunderstanding. It's a simple case, hardly worthy of my attention. I don't usually bother meeting with horse thieves. I concern myself with a better caliber of criminal. But word reached me of your supposed exploits in the Lake of Mists and Veils, and of course about your wondrous sword, and my curiosity was piqued."

"My wondrous sword and I are happy to answer any questions you might have."

"Oh, I may have some later, but I spent much of last night in correspondence with some associates of mine in Andoran and Absalom—we have magic mirrors, much faster than relying on couriers to carry letters—and I think I have a full understanding of your capabilities and history. I haven't found much in the way of confirmation regarding your claim to have defeated a demon lord, but there's a certain amount of circumstantial evidence, and I have assurances that you at least *believe* your story to be true."

"I'm either a hero or a madman, then?"

"The difference between those two can be *very* slight," Temple said. "I don't think you're either one, personally. You're a thief, a confidence trickster, and an opportunist who occasionally does the right thing, when there's no more profitable alternative available. You also have a loyal friend who happens to be a magical sword as dangerous as an ancient white dragon."

"Pleased to meet you," Hrym said.

"Oh, good. I was afraid you might say, 'Ice to meet you,'" Temple said. "I loathe puns. But, yes, it's . . . interesting to meet you, too, Hrym. We don't usually lock prisoners up with their weapons, but I suppose in this case you qualify as a prisoner, too."

Hrym harrumphed. "Are you a wizard, then? Can you stop me from doing the things I do? Because if not, you should be aware I'm a prisoner for only as long as I *consent* to be a prisoner. Otherwise I'm just a guest in very poor accommodations."

"I am a simple bureaucrat," Temple said. "My talents are organizational, not arcane. Here, Rodrick, catch." She tossed something small and glittering through the bars, and Rodrick snatched it from the air without thinking. He opened his palm and looked down at a ruby the size of his thumbnail.

"Usually I'm the one bribing my guards, not the other way around."

"Burrow," Temple said, and Rodrick screamed as the ruby sank into the flesh of his hand with a sensation like a thousand biting insects swarming across his palm. The gem moved under his skin, and he clamped his other hand tightly around his wrist, but it did no good: he felt the gem slide beneath his gripping fingers and watched as it traveled under the skin along his inner forearm, past the crook of his elbow, scurrying over his bicep and vanishing beneath the sleeve of his shirt. He could still *feel* the ruby moving, like a chip of swallowed ice moving down the throat, but this icy sensation traveled to his shoulder and then down into his chest, stopping in the vicinity of his heart—at which point the sensation vanished entirely.

Hrym was shouting from the bench: "Rodrick! What's wrong? Should I kill everyone?"

"I wouldn't," Temple said mildly. "That gem is . . . let's say . . . an encouragement to good behavior."

"She gave me a ruby, Hrym." Rodrick stared at his palm, which no longer hurt, and which was entirely unmarked. "It crawled under my skin like a burrowing insect and scuttled next to my heart."

"I told you having a heart was a weakness," Hrym said.

"I always thought you meant that metaphorically." Rodrick rubbed at his chest, the banter coming weakly and automatically.

"Metaphorically *too*. Let me guess, Underclerk Temple: if Rodrick disobeys, the gem will, what—explode into crystal fragments, shredding his heart?"

"Not technically accurate, but *practically* accurate, yes. Disobedience equals death."

"And if, say, I flung an icicle through your heart right now, and blew a hole in the wall, and Rodrick and I ran off?"

"That would be rude. It also wouldn't help. If I don't speak a particular phrase each morning, the gem will do its work regardless. Killing me now would sentence Rodrick to death tomorrow."

Hrym chuckled. "This is a promising development, Rodrick."

He stared at the sword. "I . . . disagree. Weren't you listening?"

"Yes, but you weren't, or at least, not closely enough. If she's *threatening* you with death, that means they aren't planning to *put* you to death."

"I'm not sure slavery is preferable to death, Hrym." He still had his hand over his heart, trying not to think of crystal shards ripping him apart from the inside.

Temple clucked her tongue. "No, no. You misunderstand. It's not slavery at all. Think of it as community service. In your home country of Andoran, some minor offenses are punished not with beatings or fines or years in a dungeon, but simply by making the guilty party clean up horse dung on the streets or scrape barnacles off naval ships for a few weeks, yes? This is a similar situation. You will assist me with certain projects, and after a certain period, you will be set free, your debt to society paid. The program is quite enlightened and civilized. I have concluded that you'll be more useful to Lastwall alive than you would be dangling at the end of a rope."

"Ah," Rodrick said. "I see. You want to hurl my body into the teeth of some horrible problem you don't dare risk one of your *own* people on. Or is it more interesting than that? Perhaps you want me to embark on some mission that no *legitimate* member of Lastwall's government can undertake. If I succeed, I get no credit, and if I fail in some spectacular way—well, I'm just a rogue criminal, and your government can't be blamed for my reprehensible actions."

"What a marvelous grasp of the situation!" Temple said. "Of course, there's no reason it can't be *both*. I can already tell working with you will be a delight. Would you like to meet the rest of the team?"

"You mean I'm not the only luckless bastard you've roped into this scheme?"

"No, merely the latest. I'll let you out of the cell, but I'll need you to sheathe Hrym in this." She held up a long scabbard made of green crystal.

"I've had less attractive accommodations," Hrym said.

"But not more restful." Temple tapped a ring on her finger against the crystal, which rang like metal. "This scabbard is made of rare skymetal, brought at great expense from Numeria."

"I knew a man with a skymetal chainmail shirt once, and saw it turn an arrow as big as a spear fired from a giant's bow—it would have pierced plate mail." Rodrick frowned. "Of course, the impact still cracked all his ribs, and one of *those* punctured his lungs, but still, I was impressed. The shirt wasn't made of green crystal, though."

"Probably adamantine," she said. "*This* is made of noqual, and though it looks like crystal, it can be forged like iron. Noqual has fascinating properties—mainly the suppression of magic. When we sheathe Hrym here, he'll fall asleep, more or less."

"I don't like the sound of that," Hrym said.

"Nor I," Rodrick agreed.

Temple shrugged. "Consider my situation. I'm trying to make an enforceable bargain with a pair of desperate criminals. I can compel Rodrick's good behavior with that gem, but you, Hrym, are a trickier beast to reckon with. Threatening Rodrick seems to make you behave . . . but can I count on that to work forever? In this sheath, you can do no harm. You'll be returned to Rodrick when you're needed to help him with a mission. In the meantime, you won't be bored, and I won't have to worry about you burying the Bastion of Justice in a mountain of ice because you're offended that Rodrick stubbed his toe."

Rodrick shook his head. "Why should we believe you? What's to stop you from selling Hrym off, or presenting him as a gift to some high-ranking crusader?"

"Know this, Rodrick of Andoran." Temple leaned forward, her dark eyes fixed on his face. "I will *never* lie to you. Our relationship depends on my absolute power over your life and death, and that relationship renders most lies unnecessary. I may not tell you the whole truth, but anything I do tell you, you can believe. If you consent to put Hrym away in this scabbard for now, you will be reunited with him later—sooner than you think—and in the meantime, I'll introduce you to the other recruits, and explain the particulars of your new situation."

Rodrick touched his chest. He couldn't feel the ruby, but he knew it was there. "Hrym, our choices seem to be either going along with the esteemed underclerk's plans, or dying in a courageous but pointless last stand."

"*I* wouldn't die," Hrym said. "But I would be trapped at the center of a mountain of magical ice. Killing everyone would be satisfying, but the consequences would be boring."

"I have one stipulation, Temple. I assume these little errands you want me to run will be dangerous?"

Temple shrugged. "For someone with your skills? Not very. But accidents do happen."

"In the event of my death, Hrym is to be offered retirement on a pile of gold coins, *not* an eternity of dreamless sleep in a magical scabbard."

"And if I refuse?"

"Everyone has to die someday, Temple," Rodrick said. "If my day has come, I would at least have the satisfaction of taking you with me."

Temple nodded. "Very well. I'll make that amendment to your agreement. You'll have a chance to review the contract." She slid the scabbard through the bars of the cell.

Rodrick took it—the sheath was heavier than it looked—and knelt by the bench. "We'll figure something out, Hrym."

"We always do. Worst case, we can just do what she says. Perform a few tasks, and then take our freedom."

"You believe her?"

"I do. She has a trustworthy face."

"I thought all humans looked alike to you."

"Stop stalling," Hrym said. "At least in that sheath I'll get a moment's peace from your prattling."

Rodrick slid Hrym into the scabbard, which was too long for him but otherwise a good fit, and then passed him through the bars.

Temple tucked the scabbard under her arm like it was a rolled-up broadsheet. She spoke a word of magic and the cell door swung open. She beckoned, and Rodrick followed her out. He briefly considered hitting her over the head, grabbing the scabbard, and fleeing, but it was idle speculation. It was possible she was lying about the gem, but it was hardly a risk he was willing to take.

Temple took him down the familiar corridor, then through a nondescript wooden door and down a spiraling stone staircase that descended below the earth, every landing lit with a magical glowing orb. "The Bastion must be quite well funded," he said. "Most places just use lanterns."

"Ah, but with a single word I can extinguish all these lights, or cause them to flare to blinding brightness, or even to explode in cascades of fire. We're very conscious of security here in the Bastion." She didn't sound threatening at all, which was somehow even more threatening.

After taking the rest of the descent in silence, they reached a heavy door of oak banded in iron, also lacking a keyhole. Temple pressed her hand against it, and the door swung inward.

Beyond was something between a spacious apartment and a palatial office. Amazingly, natural light suffused one corner of the room, which at first Rodrick took to be magic, but then he realized there was a light well: a narrow shaft running all the way from the surface to these subterranean depths, shining on a small plot of flowering and leafy plants. The floor was stone, but liberally covered with rugs. The walls were hung with a strange assortment of items: a broken sword, the stuffed head of an orc with unusually prominent fangs, a horned iron helmet with a star-shaped hole in one side. A desk was set up against one wall, beside an apothecary's cabinet full of hundreds of small drawers and a shelf filled with volumes and scrolls. In the middle of the room there were several chairs and settees arranged around a low wooden table. There was even a kitchen of sorts: a woodstove with a teakettle on top, a cabinet full of cups and dishes, another full of dry goods, a large stone basin, and even the handle of a water pump. There was a hallway not far from the light well, with closed doors on either side and one at the end, open to reveal a set of bunk beds. This was a fully contained set of living quarters, then. As far as barracks went, he'd seen worse.

Rodrick took in the surroundings at a glance, but he spent more time looking over the *people*, though he tried not to make his examination obvious. The most striking of the group was a devilkin woman perched on the edge of the desk, looking entirely human apart from her crimson skin and dark blue lips. She was quite shapely, and dressed to show it off in high boots, tight breeches, and a blouse unlaced halfway down her cleavage. She had long black hair bundled into a ponytail, a pretty face, bright eyes, and a smirk that was several degrees beyond "insufferable": she looked immensely pleased with herself, and as if you should be pleased with her, too, if you had any sense.

Standing in a corner behind her was a tall man wearing a heavy brown winter cloak despite the warmth of the room. His skin was the color of curdled cream, and judging by the gauntness of his face, he must be calamitously thin and cadaverous under that cloak. His eyes were the same muddy brown as his clothing, though the whites were more like yellows: Rodrick thought of piss in a snow bank. The man looked *ill*, but also like he'd been ill for a very long time, and was getting along fine despite it.

The others sat by the low table, one lounging in an armchair, and the last sitting stiffly upright on a bench against the wall. The lounger was a woman of perhaps twenty-five with the features of someone from Jalmeray or the Impossible Kingdoms—dark skin, dark eyes, dark hair—but dressed in Inner Sea garb, a pale blue blouse and skirt over dark leggings and boots, with a sheathed dagger at her waist. The last was an old man in a baggy shirt with ink-stained cuffs and the attentive and acquisitive eyes of a crow, wearing a pair of pince-nez spectacles. Even so, he looked less like a scholar and more like one of those hard, sinewy old men you saw in the country, who could heave hay bales and slaughter cows all day long and still have energy left over to chase away perfectly harmless trespassers with a pitchfork.

"Welcome," Temple said, "to the first meeting of the Lastwall Volunteers."

4

THE VOLUNTEERS ASSEMBLED

He's the one we've been waiting for?" The devilkin looked Rodrick frankly up and down. "He's nice enough to look at, at least compared to the other options in the room, but what does he bring to the team that we don't have already?"

Temple stared at her for a moment, sighed heavily, and said, "You're the field leader, Merihim, but this is not the field, so kindly shut up until I solicit your comments." She nodded to Rodrick. "You. Sit."

He shrugged and took a chair beside the Vudrani woman, who looked him over thoughtfully, through lowered lashes, then looked away, biting her lower lip for a moment and contriving to look as if she were blushing even though no discernible blush touched her cheeks. *Aha*, he thought. *She is coquetting at me.* Which meant he should keep an eye on his coin purse in her presence. Oh, to be young and innocent again, and capable of thinking that fetching glances were meant to fetch anything other than his gold. True, pure flirtations were possible, but since the woman was here, she was almost certainly a criminal of *some* kind.

He expected Temple to start talking, but instead she poked Merihim in the ribs. The devilkin slid off the desk—managing to make it look like moving along was her own idea—and sauntered over to lean against the wall beside the cadaverous man, murmuring something in his ear. Whether she was whispering dire threats, hilarious commentaries, vicious insults, or ribald proposals, Rodrick couldn't guess, as the man's expression didn't change at all; he might have been carved from a piece of particularly unappetizing-looking cheese for all the reaction he displayed.

Temple dropped heavily into a chair behind the desk and flipped through several sheaves of paper, muttering to herself and making notations with a quill. She paused to glare around the room. "I'll be with you all in a moment." Then she returned to her notes.

Since they were apparently being left to their own devices, Rodrick turned to the Vudrani woman. "My name's Rodrick."

"Charmed," she said. "You may call me Eldra." It was hard to tell in so few words, but she didn't seem to speak in a Vudrani accent. She must have been raised in the vicinity of the Inner Sea.

"I was in Jalmeray recently. In Niswan, mostly." Rodrick decided not to mention that he'd been a guest of the thakur in his palace: it was true, but hardly plausible.

"Oh?" She brightened. "My family comes from Niswan, but I haven't been back there in, oh, half a lifetime."

Rodrick smiled. "In your case, half a lifetime is, what, ten years?" Probably more like thirteen, but he'd seldom gone wrong flattering a woman about her youth.

She chuckled. "It's been rather longer than that, if I'm honest. I've spent most of my life in these barbarous lands." She looked around the room. "Well. Perhaps not quite *this* barbarous. Absalom, Andoran, Cheliax, Taldor."

"You've traveled a great deal, for one so young."

"And you've traveled farther than any other Andoren I've met. What took you to Jalmeray?"

"A business opportunity."

Her laugh was musical. "Ah. Is that what brought you *here*, too?"

He grimaced. "Something like that." He liked her, which didn't mean he would stop being vigilant or suspicious, but it did make being in her presence more pleasant.

"All right." Temple shoved back from her desk and stood up, but still peered down at the papers. She gestured vaguely toward the devilkin and the gaunt man. "Introductions. This is Merihim. As you may have noticed, she's not entirely human. She was apprehended in the vicinity of the Whispering Tyrant's tower prison with a suspicious array of arcane equipment, and was brought here for adjudication."

Merihim pressed a hand to her chest and said, in tones of outraged innocence, "I was merely taking a walk, and strayed over a poorly marked boundary into forbidden territory. My only *crime* was walking while being devilkin. My continued imprisonment is a terrible offense against justice."

Temple ignored that. "Merihim is your field leader, Volunteers." The devilkin dropped a curtsy. "She has an impressive history of planning and pulling off complex and challenging crimes, and a firm grasp of tactics. We're going to channel those antisocial tendencies into more useful work. The creature beside her is Prinn. I think he's a wizard or a sorcerer, but he's either mute or incredibly stubborn. Loyal to Merihim, at least. I confess, my inquiries didn't turn up *anything* about Prinn, beyond his association with Merihim, but he has demonstrated great skill when it comes to infiltration and subterfuge, which will likely be useful."

"Prinn's not anything at all," Merihim said. "He's just my valet. All women of quality have one."

Temple turned her gaze to the others. "The gentleman with the spectacles is called the Specialist. If he has a name, no one has ever mentioned it to me."

"What does he specialize in?" Merihim asked.

"Everything." The man's voice was harsh and grating.

"Then shouldn't you be called the *Generalist*?" Rodrick said.

"He was apprehended trying to break into a trove of forbidden volumes," Temple said. "My research indicates that he used to be an alchemist with a sideline in the study of dangerous artifacts, and a further sideline in the *retrieval* of dangerous artifacts, but his principal obsession seems to be knowledge. That said, when the guards caught him breaking into the library, he broke one of their jaws and two of their arms before they managed to subdue him."

The Specialist shrugged. "I spent a winter studying fighting techniques at Tar Kuata in Osirion. It's just the application of certain fundamental anatomical principles."

"He'll be in charge of gathering intelligence and materiel, and will assist Merihim in planning as necessary." Temple nodded to the Vudrani. "This lovely young woman is Eldra. Don't let her apparent youth and innocence fool you. She has been a courtesan, a spy, an assassin, a jewel thief, and assorted other occupations. A very talented woman, especially when it comes to making people like her and then relieving them of their valuable possessions. If you need to sweet-talk anyone or worm your way into someone's confidence, I daresay she can manage, and she has other practical skills, too."

Eldra beamed at them all. "Thrilled to be part of the team."

"She actually sounds *sincere*," Merihim said. "That's remarkable."

"That brings us to the newest members of our group." Temple nodded toward Rodrick. "While you are all formidable in your own ways, what we've lacked so far is sheer *muscle*—brute force and destructive capability."

Rodrick scowled. *I'm mere muscle?*

"What, him?" Merihim said. "Prinn could break Rodrick over his knee like a twig. He doesn't look more formidable than any other oafish leg-breaker you could have dragged out of the cells."

Rodrick opened his mouth to object, but Temple spoke first. "Ah, but Rodrick is only half of the equation. Perhaps only a quarter. His good strong arm wields *this*." She drew Hrym halfway out of the magic-deadening scabbard. Everyone leaned forward— the Specialist just a fraction, Merihim and Eldra with a more acquisitive and obvious sort of interest—except for Prinn, who didn't even glance at the blade, but kept staring at a point halfway between nowhere and nothing.

"Hrm?" Hrym said. "What's all this then?"

"Hrym, meet our coworkers." Rodrick pointed them out quickly. "Eldra, Merihim, Prinn, and the Specialist."

"A talking sword!" Eldra said. "I've heard of such things, but never met one."

"We've had bad luck with joining ragtag bands of misfits in the past," Hrym said. "Are any of you secretly demon cultists? You have to tell us if we ask. It's the law."

"That's bigotry." Merihim crossed her arms. "Just because my skin is a bit pinker than Rodrick's, you assume I'm in league with demonic forces?"

"There are no demon cultists here, Hrym," Temple said. "The only gods any of these people worship is the god of naked self-interest. Rodrick, would you like to hold Hrym?"

He rose and crossed the room, taking the hilt and sliding out the blade. *Now* Prinn looked at him, eyes like augers. Rodrick leaned against the wall, sword in his hand. "Hrym and I have worked together a long time."

"Rodrick likes to think he's the brains and I'm the brawn," Hrym said. "Really I'm the brains *and* the brawn and I just keep him around because he has legs."

"His brain won't be particularly necessary on these missions." Temple sat down in the chair and laced her fingers over her belly. "But his legs will be. Merihim, you can now add a suite of powerful ice magics to your tactical toolbox. Hrym can summon blizzards, freeze people in place, make walls brittle enough to smash with hammers, create ice slicks, obscure your movements with freezing fog, and, I'm sure, other capabilities. Ideally you'll use his powers to cover escapes and prevent detection, but if you get into a situation where you *must* fight, he's the best tool you have."

"Why bring Rodrick with us at all?" Merihim said. "No offense, but why not strap Hrym on Prinn's back?"

The ghoulish silent figure behind her smiled. Rodrick shuddered. It was like seeing a corpse grin.

"All of *your* loyalties are secured because you've been infected with poisonous gems," Temple said. "Hrym is rather more difficult to control, but he has an inexplicable fondness for Rodrick."

"If anyone else tries to wield me, they'll catch a nasty cold," the sword agreed.

"No puns," Temple said severely.

"I *also* have a wealth of experience regarding Hrym's capabilities and know how best to use his powers in any given situation," Rodrick said, but everyone ignored him. Oh, that rankled. He was used to running operations, or at least running his *own* secret plans while pretending to be in the employ of others. Being reduced to a sort of mobile sword-stand was not going to agree with him. Perhaps he could arrange for Merihim to suffer some terrible embarrassment in the field—without giving away his own complicity, of course—and position himself to take over as leader of the Volunteers . . .

But what was he thinking? That was like angling to become king of a rat-heap. Why would he *want* leadership of this press-gang? Better to push down his pride and go along quietly until he saw an opportunity to escape.

"I'm not entirely convinced about these gems of yours," the Specialist said. "You could simply be exploiting our fears, using harmless trinkets and illusion spells to make us *think* we'll die if we disobey."

"It's a good thing I anticipated your objection and planned a demonstration. Gather around, children." Temple slid back her chair, reached under the desk, and removed a wooden box with a barred lid. She placed it on the desk, slid back the lid, and lifted out a squirming rat almost the size of a kitten. The animal wriggled in her hand, but she kept a tight grip behind its neck. With her other hand, reached into her pocket and removed a familiar-looking, thumbnail-sized gem. She pressed the gem against the rat, and Rodrick shuddered as the ruby burrowed beneath the animal's skin, making the rat squeal and writhe even more ferociously.

Temple put the rat back into the cage and slid the bars shut. "Everyone move back, hmm? In creatures *your* size most of the gem's destructive force will be absorbed by your bodies, but some of the magic might . . . spill over . . . in something the size of a rat." They all stepped back several feet, including Temple. "Watch closely, Volunteers." She cleared her throat. "*Infadibulum*," she said.

The rat squealed, and a burst of strangely radiant darkness burst forth from the bars of the cage—along with a quantity of blood, fur, and flesh. After a moment, Temple said, "Go on, take a look."

Rodrick and the others gathered and looked into the cage. Where the rat had been there was little more than a smear of gore and fur and shreds of intestines. It was as if the rat had exploded. The crimson gem rested in the center of the mess.

"Why 'Infadibulum'?" the Specialist said.

Temple shrugged. "It's just a word I saw in an old book. I try to make the trigger words things I'm unlikely to say in casual conversation. If words like, oh, 'cabbage' or 'chair' or 'boot' made the gems inside you explode, it could lead to embarrassing mistakes. Of course, there are also words I have to say each morning to keep the gems from going off automatically."

"That's a lot to remember," Eldra said. "But I suppose you have a list."

"Only in my mind, Eldra." Temple reached into the cage and removed the gem from the mess, slipping it into her pocket. "No amount of lock-picking or file-rifling will help you escape your current situation. I know it's hard, since all of you are schemers and chancers and opportunists, but it really *will* be best if you resign yourselves to a year of service and settle down to earn your freedom. All right? While off duty, you'll be kept in these quarters—there are three bunkrooms, and you can sort out your sleeping arrangements—and the pantry is stocked with food. There's a garderobe down the hall. Crusaders doing penance will come in occasionally to empty your chamber pots and carry away your night soil. Don't try to leave the area or go up the stairs. While you're cooped up, I suggest you get to know one another. Complain about me: it will give you a shared enemy and foster group cohesion. Rest up. Tomorrow morning I'll brief you on your first mission."

Temple left the room, pulling the door shut after her, leaving the carcass of the rat behind.

"All right," Merihim said. "Prinn has a bit of healing magic, so let's find a sharp kitchen knife and cut these gems out. He can keep us from bleeding to death in the process. Then I say we find Temple and stuff the gems down her throat."

5

Team-Building

The Specialist went to one of the armchairs and slouched. He shook his head glumly. "A nice idea in theory, Merihim, but it won't work. I wanted to goad Temple into giving us a demonstration so I could determine how the gems operate. The rat was killed by a powerful burst of negative energy—the sort of power channeled by clerics of evil gods." He sighed. "The burst is so powerful, it kills instantly. Not even magical healing could help. If we were vampires, or some other form of undead, the gems wouldn't work on us at all—in fact, the burst of negative energy would *heal* us. But, alas, we are all among the living. Tampering with the gems will almost certainly cause them to release a burst of death magic that no magic can prevent." He rubbed absently at his chest. "There may be a way to *deactivate* the jewels—I will ponder that—but simply cutting them out won't save us."

"It could still be a trick." Eldra looked impossibly relaxed, sprawled on the long couch on her side, one leg crossed over the other knee, kicking her foot back and forth gently. "She might have caused the rat to explode in some other way, and just blamed it on the jewel."

The Specialist twiddled a finger around in his ear, removed it, and peered at the fingertip, entirely without self-consciousness. "The possibility occurred to me, but I've heard of gems like these before. The Whispering Tyrant's generals used them to control important human thralls, and to extort the cooperation of living people in neighboring regions. It's hard to imagine the crusaders of Lastwall using such vile artifacts, instead of merely sealing them away . . . but I suppose Temple is more ethically flexible than her superiors. You can make your own decisions, of course, but I intend to proceed as if my life is indeed in Temple's hands."

"I can't believe the righteous crusaders of Lastwall employ a creature like Temple, someone who's willing to use . . . well, people like *us*." Eldra clucked her tongue. "It's truly a blow to my faith in all that's right and righteous and good."

"I don't think a nation that acted entirely honorably in all situations would survive for very long," Rodrick said. "People like Temple are probably a dirty, necessary secret."

"The muscle speaks," Merihim said. "You could be right. Or Temple might be running this operation entirely on her own, without the knowledge of the Precentors Martial. Most of the nation's attention is fixed on the orcs in Belkzen, and the rest is still fretting over the Whispering Tyrant's restless grave. I imagine a quiet, competent bureaucrat with a knack for rerouting funds could run her own mini-fiefdom without much difficulty. Whether Temple is operating on her own authority or with the blessing of the Watcher-Lord is irrelevant, though. She's got us under her thumb, and we need to figure out how to get *out*."

Merihim paced back and forth in front of the desk, and Rodrick wrinkled his nose at her. She was one of *those* people, who had to incessantly stalk up and down while thinking. She probably waved her arms around and talked to herself, too, just to make sure everyone *knew* she was doing heavy cogitation.

"Why not just serve Lastwall for a year?" Hrym said.

The others turned and stared at Rodrick. He shrugged. "Don't look at me. Hrym has his own mind."

"I have only so many years left to live," the Specialist said. "I doubt I would learn very much doing dirty work for Temple. I'd rather not waste my limited time here."

"I'm not getting any younger, either," Eldra said. "I have business to attend to, anyway, some of which is quite time-sensitive."

"Oh, you short-lived mortals are always so worried about *time*," Hrym said. "But your alternative is exploding like . . . like an exploding rat . . . so it hardly seems like a difficult choice."

Merihim clucked her tongue. "Ah, but Hrym, we're schemers, revolutionaries, thieves, *operators*—we don't get tricked, we do the tricking. We don't get strong-armed, we do the strong-arming."

"If you were all *that* good at scheming, you wouldn't have been caught," Hrym pointed out.

Merihim waved a hand. "No one is perfect all the time. Even gods make mistakes sometimes, so it's understandable that we might do the same. We're problem-solvers, all of us, and this situation . . . it's *intolerable*."

The sword made a snorting sound. "Death is very tolerable, as I understand it. The dead don't seem to mind it at all."

Rodrick sighed. "So we'll pretend to go along, and gather what intelligence we can, and if we see a way to escape, we'll take it. Perhaps we can even make a pact to aid one another? If one of us finds a way to escape, she'll help the others as well?"

"Mmm," the Specialist said.

"What a good and thoughtful idea," Eldra said.

Prinn stared at nothing.

"Don't be an idiot," Merihim said. "Even if we made that promise, what would it mean? We're all here because we're criminals. Why should we believe each other? If you saw the chance to escape, would you waste time helping us out the window after you?"

"Of course," Rodrick lied. "We're a team, aren't we?"

"Not yet," Merihim said. "But I suppose we'll have to become one—or at least learn to fake it. And since I'm in charge . . . Rodrick, clean up that rat."

He considered objecting, but there wasn't a good way to do so without getting into an all-out struggle for power. Since Temple had decreed that Merihim was their leader, and since Rodrick had decided he didn't *want* the job, he decided to acquiesce. "I'll toss it in the stove," he said. "Burning rat doesn't smell good, but it's better than rotting rat."

Prinn moved with the speed of a striking snake, darting toward the cage and picking it up, clutching the reeking box to his chest. He glared at Rodrick, as if expecting him to try to take the cage, then sidled over to Merihim and murmured something in her ear. The devilkin sighed. "Fine, take it." Prinn scuttled off toward one of the bedrooms. "Prinn and I will take the room on the right. He wants to study the effects of the gem on the rat a bit further."

The Specialist rubbed his nose, seemed about to say something, then simply shrugged instead.

After a moment's silence, Merihim said, "So, who here knows how to cook?"

"I do," the Specialist said.

Rodrick sopped up the last of the mushroom sauce with a hunk of bread, swallowed, and sat back, feeling entirely content, apart from the deadly gem embedded in his chest and a year of enforced servitude looming over him. At least he was being well fed. "Where did you learn to cook like that?"

"I spent a year apprenticed to one of the great chefs of Absalom." The Specialist dabbed at his mouth with a napkin. The others were shoving their plates away, too, making appreciative noises, except for Prinn, who'd supped solely on a cup of water and a raw carrot. Did the man have some kind of strange ascetic religion, or did he just hate delicious things on principle, or had he filled up on exploded rat? He seemed an odd traveling companion for Merihim, who seemed the type to live her life with ample (perhaps even excessive) gusto.

Merihim stood up from the table and crooked a finger at Prinn, then headed toward the room they'd claimed. The pale man looked at the devilkin's back before rising to follow, and his blank countenance momentarily spasmed into a look of hateful rage before smoothing out again. Rodrick wondered if anyone else had noticed. Probably Eldra—she seemed sharp—but the Specialist was muttering to himself and drawing designs with the tip of a knife in the gravy on his plate.

The Specialist looked around, scratched at his messy thatch of beard, then picked up his plate and carried it to the middle of the three bedrooms, closing the door behind him. A moment later he opened it again and poked his head out. "I need this room to myself. I have books. And many poisons." Then he closed it again.

"I suppose that means we're rooming together." Rodrick lifted one eyebrow at Eldra. "Unless you insist I sleep out here on the rug? I can assure you, I'm a perfect gentleman."

Eldra smiled sweetly. "I'm pleased to hear it. The alternative would be for you to be a dead blackguard. I have *ever* so many knives. You're welcome to share my quarters, if not my mattress, as long as you don't snore."

"None of those who've shared my bed have ever complained."

"Not true," Hrym said from the corner, where Rodrick had propped him. "I've complained. You're always breathing. And shifting. Sometimes muttering. Flesh is so noisy."

Eldra turned toward the sword. "Tell me, Hrym, is Rodrick a dependable and loyal friend?"

"Loyal? To a point. Dependable? Intermittently. Why do you ask?"

"We're going to be serving together, and we're apparently to be sent on a mission quite soon. It would be nice to know what sort of people I'm serving with."

Hrym humphed. "We're not mysterious. I like resting on piles of gold. Rodrick likes *spending* our gold on women, wine, and velvet cushions. Thus, we never have enough gold, and are forced to leave the comfort of our quarters occasionally in order to obtain more. That is our relationship, and our motivation, in their entirety."

Rodrick groaned. "There's a reason I do most of the talking in our partnership. Hrym is entirely too honest sometimes."

Eldra's smile now was less sweet, but struck Rodrick as more genuine. "I find his frankness refreshing. So it's just avarice and hedonism that motivate you, then? No personal, political, or ideological factors? You're purely amoral beings?"

"Love of gold is a philosophy," Hrym said. "In fact, it's an immensely popular one, with adherents all over the world."

"I wouldn't say I'm purely amoral," Rodrick said. "I'm Andoren, after all. I don't like slavery. I think people should have a say in their governing."

"But you don't go out of your way to fight slavers, or try to spread Andoren principles of government into the heart of, say, Nex?"

"No, but I don't hire myself out to slavers or tyrants, either. I also don't *knowingly* work for cults devoted to evil gods, or for demon-worshipers. I'd rather not see the world overrun by locusts with human faces or enormous slugs with shark's teeth and so on."

Eldra trailed her finger through the gravy on her plate, then sucked her fingertip, looking at Rodrick thoughtfully before saying, "You're not out fighting demons at the Worldwound, though."

"We stopped a cult from freeing a demon lord once," Hrym said. "I'd say we've done our part. Consider our service rendered."

"We believe in leading by example," Rodrick said. The way she'd sucked her finger, staring right at him . . . Rodrick knew when he was being manipulated, but that didn't mean it was ineffective.

"Do you murder people in order to steal their gold?"

"Of course not."

"What if they're *bad* people?"

Rodrick shook his head. "I won't say we've never killed anyone—"

"Mostly me," Hrym said. "If it's bigger than a fly, anyway."

"—but we're not *muggers*." Rodrick made a sour face. "Murdering people to steal from them is inelegant. There's an artistry to taking someone's gold. Ideally you get them to hand it over willingly, and get them to thank you for the opportunity. At worst you take their gold in secret and travel many leagues away before they notice."

Eldra nodded. "I have a similar philosophy. I'd like a long and comfortable life, and I'll go to whatever lengths are necessary to secure it, but I don't look for opportunities to harm others, and I find needless cruelty boring and vulgar. It's pleasant to find a like-minded person—and sword—here. The Specialist strikes me as less a man and more a collection of eccentricities and obsessions, and Merihim and Prinn . . . I have no idea what their goals are, but I don't think they'd hesitate to do murder if it helped their cause. And Temple . . . Well. Temple is a zealot. Zealots are usefully predictable, but I'm never comfortable around them."

"Perhaps we should make an informal alliance, then?" Rodrick said. "Sending us all into the field to work as a team seems like a laughably naive proposition, sure to end in disaster and betrayal, especially with Merihim in charge. But if you and I and Hrym make an agreement to look out for one another, it could greatly increase our chances of survival."

"Hmm." She cocked her head. "That strikes me as acceptable."

"And if one of us finds a way to get rid of these gems . . ."

"Oh, indeed. Share and share alike."

"I feel better already," Rodrick said.

"If the two of you are going to roll around together with your clothes off, please leave me out here while you do it," Hrym said.

Eldra's laughter bubbled. "I don't think there's much danger of that tonight, Hrym. But in the future . . . who knows? Battlefields sometimes forge strange bonds. Give me a quarter hour to prepare for bed before you come in, Rodrick?" She rose and walked, with a doubtless perfectly calculated amount of sway, into the bedroom, shutting the door behind her.

"Is she manipulating you, or are you manipulating her?" Hrym said.

"I'm surprised at you, Hrym. It's disheartening to see that level of cynicism in a sword so young."

"I can't help it. I'm observant."

Rodrick leaned back in his chair, balancing it on the two back legs and putting his feet on the table. "I'm honestly not sure it matters. We're almost certainly using each other, for mutual protection and aid, and I imagine she's as alert to the possibility of betrayal as I am. Of course, if she decides to lure me into her bed in hopes of securing a more lasting sort of loyalty from me, I won't complain. That would make the next year pass *much* more pleasantly."

"You're repulsive. I'm repulsed. If you get to have your carnal pleasures, I demand my metallic ones—I want a bed of gold."

"Wouldn't it be a wonderful world if everyone got what they wanted?"

Hrym seemed to think about that for a moment. "No," he said at last.

6

A BRIEFING

Rodrick was dreaming of fiery red beetles trying to burrow under his flesh when someone nudged him, hard, under the left armpit. A distant woman said, "He hibernates like a bear, doesn't he?"

Hrym's familiar voice replied, "He excels at laziness."

Rodrick groaned and sat up. Eldra was sitting on the edge of her small bed across the room, looking at him innocently as he rubbed the tender spot on his ribs. What had she poked him with? The purple-and-white parasol leaning against the foot of her bed seemed a likely culprit. "What is it? Is something on fire? Why wake me up unless something's on fire?"

"It's morning, and you need to wait outside while I wash up." She inclined her head at the table that held a basin, pitcher of water, and mirror.

Rodrick smoothed down his unruly hair. "Why do you need to wash up again? You washed up last night. You haven't done anything to get dirty."

"She's got all sorts of powders and unguents and things in jars and vials," Hrym said. "I think she must be half alchemist. The mysteries of womanhood."

"Exactly," Eldra said. "As you polish boots and sharpen knives, I too must tend to the tools of my trade."

Rodrick, who had never sharpened or polished anything in his life, groaned again, picked up Hrym, and staggered out into the common area. He went to the kitchen and splashed water on his face, then walked to the lightwell and looked at the little plants growing in pots in the weakly filtered spill of dawn light. He looked around, confirmed he was alone, then poked his head into the lightwell, looking up the shaft. Probably about twenty feet up to the surface. The sides of the shaft were rough stone, and the shaft was narrow as a chimney, so climbing out of it wouldn't be a terrible challenge . . . but there were three different metal grates, set at different intervals, starting halfway up the shaft's length.

"We could freeze the iron and shatter the bars," Hrym offered.

"Not without leaving a mark, unfortunately. If we were actually plotting an escape, that would be an option, but I was just hoping to find a way to slip out unawares and return unobserved. Temple doesn't seem inclined to give us anything to drink down here apart from water, and a year without wine, ale, or liquor will feel like a century. Perhaps when we're sent on missions I can slake my thirst." He closed the window, propped Hrym in the corner, went to the low couch, and sprawled out, hoping for a bit more sleep.

His hopes were not fulfilled. Merihim came out dressed in stylish leathers, whispering with brown-robed Prinn, then sat at the desk and began writing something on a sheet of parchment. The Specialist emerged soon after, wearing the same ink-stained garb as before, and began banging pots around in the kitchen. Finally Eldra emerged, looking fresh-faced and natural, with her long black hair put up in a deceptively simple-looking arrangement of braids, wearing yellow silk trousers and a white blouse. Rodrick considered disappearing back into the bedroom, but by then he was thoroughly awake, so he sighed and sat at the table with Eldra just as the Specialist set out a pot of tea.

The Volunteers were just finishing up breakfast—the Specialist had done something amazing with eggs, sausage, and some local herbs Rodrick had never encountered before; Prinn ate half a turnip—when Temple arrived carrying a wooden scroll case under her arm and Rodrick's bag dangling from her hand by the straps. She was trailed by the tallest woman Rodrick had ever seen, with short dark hair and a hawkish face, dressed in leather and chainmail, with a very large sword on her belt and her hand firmly on the hilt. The edges of an ornate necklace peeked out from beneath her clothing, an oddly decorative touch for someone so otherwise brutally practical.

Temple looked them over and nodded, as if confirming some grim suspicion. "Good, you're all up. I was afraid Rodrick would still be sleeping."

"Would that I were," he murmured. "May I . . . ?"

Temple tossed the bag in his direction, and Rodrick smiled, rising to retrieve it and peer through the contents. Everything seemed in place, including the only items of value: his lockpicks, his devilfish cloak, and the medallion he'd gotten in Jalmeray that allowed him to speak and understand almost any language. He returned to his seat beside Eldra.

"Everyone start paying attention." Temple turned and nodded toward the scowling woman beside her. "This is General Andraste, the highest-ranking member of the Lastwall crusaders you lot are ever going to even *glimpse*. She's been kind enough to support my little endeavor, because she'd rather you lot die on dangerous missions than good soldiers of Lastwall."

"I love your hair," Eldra said, with apparent sincerity.

The general's mouth twisted in distaste. "These Volunteers of yours seem to be everything you promised, Temple."

"All that and more, I'm afraid. But they're more than equal to the tasks we'll set before them. And if they're not . . ." She shrugged. "No great loss. We were going to hang them anyway."

Andraste looked at each of them, hard, as if memorizing their faces. "All of you are scum. The best of you are merely liars and thieves; the worst are far worse. But even the likes of you may be redeemed. There is no nation more noble than Lastwall, and no people with more important work than our crusaders. Your assistance will help balance, to some small extent, the vile acts you have performed in the past. Perhaps if you die in service to Lastwall, Iomedae will smile upon you. Perhaps not. But if you do *not* serve, you will die in a state of disgrace, of that you may be sure. I have my doubts about your worth. I think perhaps it would have been better to hang you. Please do your best to prove me wrong." With that, she turned and stomped out of the room.

Hmm. A general, and a high-minded one at that. Rodrick's suspicion that Temple was a completely rogue element of Lastwall's government seemed a little less likely . . . though it was still possible this was a pet project supported by only one general. He couldn't imagine the entire leadership of such an honor-bound country would possibly get behind an initiative like the Volunteers.

"All right," Temple said. "On to business." She opened the scroll case and removed a large sheet of paper, which she deftly pinned to a wooden wall, one tack per corner. She pointed to the image sketched there in black ink. "This is your mission. His name is Bannerman. Study his face."

The face on the paper was that of a middle-aged human man, with long lank hair, deep-set eyes, a prominent nose that had been broken once or twice, a narrow and stubbled jaw, and a long jagged scar down the right cheek. He looked like a rough and disreputable sort, which didn't mean much. (Rodrick was generally considered to have an open and friendly countenance, which didn't stop him from robbing people down to the soles of their boots.)

"He probably isn't in disguise," Temple said, "though he may have more of a beard by now. His eyes are a sort of muddy brown, and his skin is tanned and leathery from long years on the battlefield. He's in the Fangwood, last I heard. I want you to bring him back, alive and unharmed."

"Should we assume he won't come willingly?" Merihim said.

Temple smiled faintly. "It's fair to say he won't come unless you capture him and *make* him come."

"Why do you want him?" Eldra asked.

"I *need* him," Temple said. "Alive, too, and of sound body and mind. No torture or maiming allowed. You can knock him around a bit if that's necessary to complete your mission, but don't do any serious damage."

Rodrick raised a hand. "I know Lastwall has thief-takers, and more soldiers than you know what to do with, all of whom are more skilled at tracking fugitives than we are. Why send *us*?"

Temple sighed. "You all seem to be under the impression that this is a sewing circle or a conversation in a coffeehouse. I give you a mission, and tell you the requirements, and you do it. You continue to do it for a year, and then you get to go free. Understood?"

"At least tell us if he's dangerous," Merihim said.

"Of course he is. Would I send you after someone harmless? Fine. Some background will help your efforts. Bannerman is a trained crusader of Lastwall, and before he joined that august fighting force, he grew up in the forests of—well, the area now known as Nirmathas. He knows combat, and tactics, and how to use the forest to his advantage." She smiled. "He's quite formidable, actually. It's a good thing there are five of you."

Rodrick glanced around. "Five of us, but none of us is exactly a ranger. I do rather better in cities than among the trees." He didn't mention that he never would have been captured by Temple in the first place if he hadn't been blundering around in a forest, hiding under bushes and falling into rivers. The confession wouldn't have done much to increase the esteem of his fellow Volunteers.

"I spent a year tracking a golden panther cult in the Mwangi Expanse," the Specialist said. "My woodcraft is tolerable."

"I'm good at everything, anywhere." Merihim shrugged. "And Prinn doesn't care. Prinn is Prinn in every environment."

"I quite enjoy the occasional stroll in the country," Eldra offered. "A forest is just a sort of overgrown garden, really."

"I want some gold," Hrym said, presumably because everyone else had spoken and he wanted to contribute too, but no one paid him any attention.

Temple crossed her arms and looked them over. "You'll leave in an hour. I'll have horses saddled and waiting upstairs, along with supplies to keep you going in the field. You have three days to bring back your target. If you're not back by the morning of the fourth day, I'll let the gems do their work. Same if you come back without your target. Oh, and one other thing: I mentioned that you shouldn't kill Bannerman . . . but don't kill any *other* people, either."

Merihim scoffed. "Really, I don't mind a few restrictions— they get the creative juices flowing—but that's too much. What if we're set upon by brigands?"

"Practice your nonlethal skills. I'm sure the Specialist and Eldra both know a few. And Rodrick and Hrym can neutralize a great many threats without drawing blood."

"Sometimes people lose fingers and toes and the odd tip of a nose to frostbite," Rodrick said.

"Acceptable losses."

"What about *monsters*? The Fangwood isn't a park."

"I said don't kill *people*. Monsters are monsters." Temple handed the scroll case to Merihim. "Maps of Fangwood, with Bannerman's likely location marked. Happy hunting." She exited through the heavy wooden door.

Merihim spread out the maps on the kitchen table, and the Specialist joined her in studying them.

"What's the plan, O Great Leader?" Rodrick said.

Merihim shrugged. "I'm like a great architect being asked to build a birdhouse. The plan? Go into the woods and drag this Bannerman out. How hard can it be to capture one rogue crusader?"

"Doesn't that seem like an astonishingly dangerous thing to say?" Eldra sighed. "These slippers won't do for tromping through the forest, will they?" She disappeared into the room and shut the door again.

"I know she can't be as frivolous as she seems, but she certainly plays the part well." Merihim moved to sit in the chair Eldra had departed, beside Rodrick. "Did she make an alliance with you, big man? Or, wait, no—she got *you* to suggest it, didn't she?"

The Specialist snorted, but didn't look up from the map.

"Why do you ask?" Rodrick said.

Merihim waved a hand. "She tried it on me, but I like boys. She tried it on the Specialist, but he likes books. And Prinn doesn't like *anybody*, so he was no help. She made a pass at Temple, even. I think the lady of stone would have been receptive under other circumstances, like if Eldra wasn't a conscripted prisoner under her authority, but our dear underclerk is too law-abiding to take advantage of the situation that way. Plus Temple's smart enough to know Eldra would be taking advantage of *her*. We all figured you were the best prospect for Eldra's come-here-go-away, keep-him-off-balance seduction style."

"Maybe I'm seducing *her*." Rodrick hoped he didn't sound too ridiculous. It was a faint hope.

"Maybe mice eat owls," the Specialist muttered. "But not in my experience."

"They don't take me seriously, Hrym," Rodrick complained.

"So?" Hrym said. "That means they won't expect you to do anything. You just have to be the muscle. Not even the muscle. The hand that carries the muscle. Enjoy it. This year should be very relaxing."

"Impress me in the field, and my opinions about you will change." Merihim smiled, showing off even white teeth. "I'm a reasonable woman. Show me you can do more than carry Hrym, and you'll get to do more than that. And don't let Eldra lead you around by the nose. Or any other part of your body."

Eldra emerged dressed in a top with flowing sleeves and a bodice closed with laces, appealingly tight breeches, and knee-high soft leather boots, all in shades of green. She looked less like a huntswoman and more like someone playing a huntswoman in a piece of musical theater. She spun around, smiling. "What do you think, Rodrick? Am I ready to hunt fugitives in the Fangwood?"

"Evildoers should clearly beware," he said.

"How do you have so many clothes?" Merihim said. "Did you bring a trunk with you?"

Eldra affected a look of puzzlement. "Of course not. Just one? That would hardly do. I have two trunks. Underclerk Temple was kind enough to have them brought down when we settled in these accommodations. I do appreciate her willingness to let us keep the tools of our trades."

Merihim clucked her tongue. "You obviously have many fine qualities. Some of which are shown off to good effect in those clothes. That said, I'm not sure how much good you'll be in the woods."

Eldra dropped a little curtsy. "Oh, I'm a delight wherever I go." Her hand flickered, and a moment later there was a *thump* as the knife she'd drawn and thrown in an instant stuck quivering in the drawing of Bannerman's left eye.

7

FIELD TESTED

They all looked at the knife, and Merihim grunted. "You'd think I wouldn't make the mistake of judging people by their appearance, as often as *I've* been misjudged for mine." She worked the knife out of the wall and handed it back to Eldra, who tucked it back into the sheath at her belt. "You probably shouldn't aim for the *actual* eye, though. Temple will be cross if we blind him."

"It's not my fault there's no picture of his leg. I can hit that just as well." Eldra caught Rodrick's eye and gave him a conspiratorial and friendly wink.

Merihim clapped her hands. "All right, everyone pack what you need to do violence and sleep in the woods."

Some hours later the Volunteers rode along a muddy track through a curtain of thin but persistent rain. Rodrick's horse was a mare with a distracted air that kept stopping to crop grass at the side of the road. Merihim rode an impressive black stallion, probably a crusader's warhorse, and she controlled it expertly while barely touching the reins, somehow conveying her desires psychically, or else with her knees. Eldra's mount was a sprightly white pony that clearly wanted to run, and the Specialist had a plodding gray carthorse of a beast. Prinn was riding the most pissed-off looking donkey Rodrick had ever seen.

It was hard not to think Temple was making some sort of commentary based on the mounts they'd been assigned.

When the rain began hissing down, they'd paused to pull out whatever foul-weather gear they had, which mostly ran to oiled cloaks. Rodrick put on his cloak of the devilfish, which looked rather disreputable with its ragged hem, but it was very much waterproof and rather more durable than it looked, like most garments imbued with magic.

The Specialist drew up alongside him. "That's a cloak of trans-formation, isn't it? I saw a cloak that changed its wearer into a manta ray, once, and this seems similar, but not identical."

"I just use it to keep the rain off." Rodrick wasn't keen to give away his secrets, or let his thieving compatriots know he possessed anything of great value. Hrym could defend himself, but the cloak didn't have opinions about who owned it.

The Specialist nodded gravely, as if Rodrick had told him something of great significance. Water dripped from his broad-brimmed hat. "I was hoping to speak to your sword."

Hrym was presently frozen to the exterior of a leather scab-bard strapped to Rodrick's back. He didn't like to be sheathed when there was sightseeing to be done. "That's up to Hrym. He chooses his own conversational companions."

"What do you want?" Hrym said.

"You must be very old. Do you perhaps date from the era of the Shory Empire?"

Rodrick frowned. That was true, but it wasn't supposed to be *obvious*. According to certain antiquarians who ought to know, Hrym was a type of rare Shory blade called a "spellstealer," made to absorb enemy magics. He'd been left sitting in a dragon's hoard for centuries, though, and had soaked up the dragon's powers— along with its intelligence, and possibly even its personality—over the long years, becoming permanently imbued with ferocious ice magics and an equally ferocious mind.

"I've seen a few winters come and go," Hrym said vaguely. Rodrick was never sure how much Hrym remembered about his long life. The sword claimed to have great gaps in his memory, and sometimes seemed to possess residual memories both from the dragon and from some of his earlier wielders, but he was also known to lie about almost anything when it suited him.

"I am a student of the wonders of the past," the Specialist said. "Very few thinking beings are as long-lived as you, Hrym. I'd be most pleased to hear any details you can recall of ages long past."

"Do you have any gold?" Hrym said.

"I . . . why do you ask?"

"Because I like gold. I remember things better when people give me some."

The Specialist rubbed his ragged gray beard. "You propose an exchange of coins for knowledge?"

"Why not?" Hrym said. "Anything of value can be bought and sold."

"That's fair," the Specialist said. "I have a small quantity of coin—must it be gold?"

"The fairest of all metals."

"Very well." He plucked a coin from his purse. "Will this do?"

"That will, indeed, buy you an hour of conversation on any subject of your choice," Hrym said.

The Specialist winced, and Rodrick suppressed a grin. "Very well," the old man said.

"Hand it to my manservant for safekeeping," Hrym said. "I'm temporarily embarrassed when it comes to having pockets."

Rodrick accepted the coin—inspecting it to make sure it wasn't some base metal covered in a thin coating of gold, because the Specialist seemed a sharp sort—and tucked it away.

"Tell me," the Specialist said. "What do you know of your origins?"

"I was forged some seven thousand years ago by a Shory blade-mage named Malik the Lame, so called because his left foot was crushed in an accident in his youth . . ."

Rodrick turned his chuckle seamlessly into a cough. Hrym hadn't become truly sentient until he'd absorbed the dragon's essence, and certainly didn't remember anything from as far back as his forging. Besides, Malik was the name of a jeweler they'd worked with years ago in Almas, who had a technique for plating lead bars in gold, which Rodrick could then sell to unsuspecting fools as the real thing; exactly the sort of dodge he'd suspected the Specialist of perpetrating. Hrym was spouting great geysers of bullshit . . . but he'd found a way to make a little money on this venture, which was more than Rodrick had managed so far.

Hrym kept up his patter, full of grandiose and illogical tales of the wonders of his early life, wielded in battles between the famed flying cities of the Shory. The Specialist asked occasional questions, and nodded a lot, and made many fascinated noises. Hrym's tale was quite lively, even the parts that didn't make much sense. Rodrick had heard worse stories out of bards in common rooms. The Specialist was getting his money's worth in terms of entertainment, anyway.

The Fangwood went from being a distant brownish-green blur to a nearby brownish-green blur, and soon the horses were carefully picking their way along what was either a very well-traveled animal trail or a sorely neglected human path. They'd pause occasionally so Merihim could consult the maps, marked with the locations of sightings of Bannerman. She had some notion of plotting those points through time to somehow deduce where Bannerman might be *now*, which Rodrick didn't think was likely to succeed, though the Specialist commented that such techniques were used in some of the more enlightened cities to track habitual thieves and other criminals to their lairs.

They had to move single file, which at least cut down on conversation. "Probably aren't any carnivorous lizards in these woods, at least," Hrym said as they moved carefully through the gloomy forest. The rain didn't fall straight down among the trees, but came in great plops as it gathered on branches and then fell all at once.

Rodrick barked a laugh. "That's something to be grateful for."

"Hmm?" the Specialist said from behind them. "Have you traveled in the Mwangi Expanse, to see such things?"

"Jalmeray." Rodrick didn't bother trying to suppress a shudder. "A remarkable place, beautiful cities, but the jungles . . . giant man-eating lizards were the least of it."

"You've really been, then?" Eldra twisted on her saddle to look back at him. "I thought you were just making that up as a way to flirt with me."

"I find the best flirtations are rooted in the truth. We weren't on the island long, but the visit was . . . memorable."

"You are a man of unexpected depths, Rodrick," Eldra said.

"And entirely predictable shallows!" Merihim called from the front. She laughed at her own joke, a sound rather like rusty hinges squawking. Rodrick liked her less with every passing moment.

They reached a clearing, about as large as the main room in their headquarters, with a huge oak tree standing near the center, proud and alone. Merihim called the halt. The remains of an old campfire rested in a rough circle of stones near the tree. "Bannerman camped here, so it should do for us, too. Tether the horses.

They dismounted and started to lead the horses toward the edge of the clearing. "No, not all together," Merihim said. "If Bannerman creeps up on us I'd prefer it if he can't set *all* our horses loose to trample through the camp at once."

Rodrick shrugged and walked his mount to the far side of the clearing near a clump of shaggy undergrowth, tying it to a tree and patting its flank. "That Specialist," Hrym said from Rodrick's back. "Did you see him swallow up that swill I served him? We could sell him a cow bone and tell him it was a sacred relic of

Aroden himself! He may know his cookery, but he's outclassed in this crowd."

"Mmm. Maybe. What do you think of the rest?" Rodrick busied himself with unsaddling the horse and spoke in a low voice. He didn't think anyone could hear them at this distance, but better to be safe.

"Prinn is some kind of murder-maniac, by the look of him, but Merihim's got him on a leash of some kind. She seems to know her business, though she's not as funny as she thinks she is. Eldra . . . well, if you'd asked me before I saw her throw a knife, I would have said she'd be deadly dangerous in a palace or boudoir and not much to worry about out here, but now . . . I'd say keep an eye on her."

"Oh, I intend to. At least she's easy to look at."

"She doesn't even have a *pommel*," Hrym said. "I'll never understand human ideas of beauty."

Once the horse was settled Rodrick turned back to camp—and saw Prinn crawling on all fours, his nose inches from the ground, eyes closed, bony rear stuck up in the air as he slowly scuttled about. The others were regarding him with interest (the Specialist) or amusement (Eldra) or both (Merihim). Rodrick joined them, walking the long way around to avoid stepping into Prinn's path. "What is he *doing*?"

Merihim showed her teeth. "Prinn is very attentive, very detail-oriented. He's looking for some sign of Bannerman that we can use to track him more effectively. The Fangwood's big, and after plotting Bannerman's movements, I've been forced to conclude that he's moving around almost at random. He's crossing running water a lot, creeks and small rivers, probably to avoid being tracked by dogs, or even in order to disrupt divination spells—some of them are ruined by water. I can narrow his likely location to the southeastern part of the forest, but beyond that . . ." She shrugged.

"One man on the alert for pursuit will see us coming easily. If Prinn can give us an edge, I'll take it."

"This campsite is a week old, at least." The Specialist sucked his teeth—a repulsive sound—as he gazed around. "It's been disturbed by animals, too. I don't see any definitive sign to indicate which direction Bannerman was going when he left—not that knowing that would tell us much about his current whereabouts. I'm not sure what Prinn—"

The—What was Prinn? A sorcerer, as Temple suspected? People that strange were often sorcerers or oracles, in Rodrick's experience—suddenly rose and hurried to Merihim, holding something so small it was invisible in his hand.

"Aha," Merihim said. "Look at that. A bitten-off bit of fingernail, still with a shred of flesh attached. Looks like Bannerman snagged a finger on a bit of firewood. Foolish of him to leave it behind."

"What good will a bit of flesh do?" the Specialist said. "A sufficiently powerful wizard could make use of something like that, I suppose, but if any of us were *that* strong, we'd be flying over the forest and controlling Bannerman's mind."

"I've got this bracelet." Merihim held up her arm, which held many bracelets, but she was indicating one in particular, a hammered bronze thing forged of several interlinked arrow-shaped segments. She opened a tiny compartment in one of the arrowheads and put the ragged bit of fingernail inside. She snapped the lid closed, and the metal arrows began to glow with a faint light. "I can find anyone, if I can get my hands on a piece of their body. The bracelet glows more brightly when you move in the right direction, and begins to pulse when you're *very* close."

"Did Temple give you that bracelet?" the Specialist said.

"No, I acquired it some time ago, for an unrelated purpose."

Eldra cleared her throat. "You were captured snooping around the Whispering Tyrant's dead city. Were you looking for someone *there*?"

Prinn, who'd stood by silently, curled his dead-looking lips in a smile.

Merihim sniffed. "I told you, I was just out for a walk in the country. I didn't realize I'd strayed into a restricted area. I know the crusaders of Lastwall are largely an illiterate lot, but they could have put up a sign with a skull on it, or something."

"There are walls, fences, and sentries," Eldra said.

Merihim shrugged. "Clearly not enough of them." She looked at the sky. "I'd rather not track our quarry in the dark. He can't escape us now, anyway—we could track him to Tian Xia if it came to that. We'll camp, eat, get some sleep, and go after him fresh in the morning. We'll be done with this business by noon, I'd wager. Hrym, I assume your sight is magical, since you lack eyes. Can you see in all directions at once?"

"Among my many other talents," the sword said.

"How's your night vision?"

"I see as well at night as you do in the day." Hrym did like boasting, but in this case Rodrick knew it was true.

Merihim nodded. "Would you mind taking watch, then? The rest of us will take shifts, too, but I'd be more comfortable with you stuck up in that tree, keeping watch from on high."

Rodrick grunted. He usually just jammed Hrym point-first into the ground when he needed the sword to keep watch, but giving him a higher vantage point wasn't a terrible idea.

"Always delighted to be of service." Hrym's tone didn't match the words, but Merihim pretended not to notice.

Prinn clambered up the tree's trunk as deftly as a lizard, barely pausing to find handholds. When he reached a thick branch thirteen or fourteen feet off the ground, he swung out, hand over hand, until he was some distance along the branch away from the trunk. As he moved, dry dead leaves showered down on the others. Prinn swung his legs up, hooked his feet over the branch, locked his ankles, let go of the tree with his hands, and in another moment was dangling completely upside down by his feet. He reached one long arm down and gestured impatiently.

Rodrick was loath to hand Hrym over to this creature, but he walked until he was standing almost directly under Prinn, reversed his grip on the sword, and held Hrym up, hilt-first. Prinn's hand closed on the hilt, and for a moment, his face contorted in a flash of terrible rage, as it had when he'd watched Merihim walk away at dinner. Then all was blank again, and the man bent at the waist in a sudden fluid motion, folding himself nearly double as he jammed Hrym point-first into the bottom of the branch. Then he grabbed the branch with his hands, released his foothold, let his feet fall, and dropped, crouching where he landed for a moment before rising.

"How's your view, Hrym?" Merihim called.

"Unless Bannerman has the wit to keep the tree trunk between himself and me, I should be able to see him coming."

"We'll post a guard on the other side of the tree, just to be safe," Merihim said. "I think we're reasonably secure, though."

The Specialist circled the great tree, peering at the trunk. "This tree is dying," he said. "If not already dead. It's infected with a peculiar sort of blight. These greasy black patches on the trunk? I've never seen their like before. They seem almost like . . . flesh." He leaned forward, sniffed, then turned his head away. "Bah. That's foul. Like a sewer full of corpses." He twiddled a finger in his ear, which Rodrick had come to realize indicated deep thought on his part; it was still disturbing to watch, though, especially when the Specialist did it while cooking. "I read something about a dark blight that infects some trees, deep in the Fangwood, but only in Nirmathas, on the other side of the river. I've never heard of it happening here—"

High up in the tree, something moved, sending more leaves falling down. A high-pitched, strangely echoing, somehow *inhuman* voice tittered, like something from a nightmare about a deranged child.

"Oh." The Specialist turned his face upward. "That's not good at all."

8

The Deep Woods

The thing in the tree tittered again.

"What is that?" Merihim said. Prinn whispered in her ear. She frowned. "Some kind of fey? A dryad? But do dryads continue to live in dying trees?"

"We should move away, *quickly*." The Specialist joined words to action, and the others followed after him—except for Rodrick, who stood looking at Hrym embedded in the tree branch above. Rodrick was about six feet tall; Hrym was about four feet long. The space between them was less than a yard. If he reached up, and *jumped* . . .

His fingers brushed the edge of Hrym's hilt but couldn't quite close on it.

"Rodrick, come on!" Merihim shouted.

"Not without Hrym!"

"Dryads have to stay within three hundred yards of their trees!" the Specialist shouted. "Which means we should get about three hundred and *ten* yards away!"

"So it's a dryad," Rodrick muttered. Why was everyone panicking? Dryads were supposed to be quite beautiful, and less murderous than their cousins the nereids. In fact, now that Rodrick thought about it, dryads were probably one of the few good reasons to wander around in forests. Who didn't like a woman with flowers in her hair?

A humanoid figure emerged from the tree trunk, as if stepping through a waterfall made of bark. She looked more or less like a woman, albeit one with skin made of wood, but she wasn't beautiful, and she didn't have flowers in her hair. She *did* have great blooms of mold in her hair, and also on her face, and liberally splotching the rest of her petite form. Black thorns protruded from her skin all over her body, and when she smiled, her teeth were thorns, too. She reached out with long briar-patch fingers and Rodrick stumbled backward. How did you hurt the fey? Fire? No, cold iron—which he'd always ignored in the shops because it was twice as expensive as *regular* iron, and anyway, steel knives held their edges better.

There was a loud *crack* from above, and an immense irregular block of ice with Hrym at its center landed on top of the blighted dryad's head, driving her to her knees, or whatever dryads had instead of knees. The thick icy shell Hrym had spun around himself cracked apart on impact, and the sword shouted, "Pick me up!"

Rodrick dove for the weapon just as the dryad rose swaying to her feet, snatching up Hrym from the chunks of ice and rolling away. He got to his feet in time to see the dryad come at him, claws extended.

The Specialist shouted unintelligibly, then flung something underhand at the tree. A great burst of flame and smoke exploded, and the dryad screamed, spinning on one foot to stare at the burning trunk of her tree. The fire climbed up the immense fir, the dry dead and dying branches bursting into fiery torches. The dryad rushed toward the Specialist, but Rodrick blasted her in the back with a cone of ice, freezing her in place.

Merihim and Prinn approached—now that the danger was past, Rodrick thought—and stood staring at the frozen dryad and the burning tree. "Do you want to put that out?" Merihim pointed at the flaming branches overhead. "I'd rather not burn down the whole Fangwood."

The fire was already guttering out as it reached the higher branches, recently dampened by the rain, but Rodrick shrugged and walked around the tree, pointing Hrym upward and spraying ice. The wood groaned, sounding eerily like a moaning old man, as the temperature suddenly shifted.

A pall of smoke drifted over the clearing as dusk began to fall. Eldra walked around the outskirts, trying to calm the horses, who'd reacted to the fire with varying degrees of panic, only Merihim's warhorse standing entirely unperturbed.

The Specialist tapped a fingernail against the sheet of ice covering the dryad's face. "Fascinating. I've heard of blighted fey, but never seen one. They're said to be corrupted by demonic influences, you know, some lord of parasites and fungi exerting influence in our plane of existence."

"This was a trap," Merihim announced. "There's no way Bannerman camped here peacefully in the shadow of that tree all night. He left the signs of a camp, knowing his pursuers would pause here, and be attacked." She smiled. "I like this man. His mind works the way mine does." She nodded toward the dryad. "Is she—it—secure? I don't want her melting and getting free in the night."

"Hrym's ice is more durable than most," Rodrick said. "I don't know if dryads need to breathe, but if they do . . . she isn't doing much breathing in there. She'll be frozen long enough for us to get well away, at least."

Merihim shook her head. "If we keep moving into the forest, in the dark, who knows what other ambushes we might blunder into? There's no safer place to rest than in the middle of a trap that's already been sprung. I say we keep camp here. We'll just watch our frozen friend."

"Oh, good. Sleeping in a clearing full of smoke, beneath a half-burned tree infected with demonic mushrooms, will be very restful."

Merihim shrugged. "You can take first watch with Hrym, if you aren't feeling sleepy."

Rodrick opened his mouth, but couldn't think of anything to say that wouldn't seem childish, churlish, or pointlessly contrary, so he just shrugged.

The Specialist squatted, squinting through a milky expanse of ice at the dryad's hands. "Did you know that sometimes when you see a vast field of mushrooms, they aren't really hundreds of individual growths, but actually a single organism, linked by a sprawling underground root system called a mycelium?"

"I did not know that," Rodrick said. "I feel so much less ignorant now."

"You aren't suggesting this dryad could be linked to *other* blighted fey?" Merihim said.

The Specialist shrugged. "Why not? If so, I suspect that such creatures can sense one another—that, in a way, they are parts of a single organism, just as a vast field of mushrooms or forest of aspen trees share a single root system. But as long as this is the only corrupted tree in the vicinity—"

Rodrick had, once or twice in the past, heard horses scream, and as a result, he recognized the sound instantly. Eldra's pretty white high-stepper howled as it sank to the ground, and though the fog of smoke made it hard to see, there seemed to be two or three pale, human-sized creatures attacking it, and other figures emerging from the trees in the same direction.

"Run!" the Specialist shouted.

"Kill them!" Merihim shouted.

"My horse!" Eldra shouted.

Rodrick swung Hrym around, intending to blast the approaching fey and the fallen horse both—the latter was doomed anyway—but Merihim was in the way. He was tempted to let loose a blast regardless, but worried Prinn would set upon him if he hurt Merihim, even "accidentally." The Specialist looped around to the west, bringing objects the size of apples out of his bag—more firebombs? But he didn't have a clear line of attack, either, because Eldra was shrieking in fury and hurling knives at the fey attacking her horse. Prinn ran off into the trees to the east, where there were no fey at all, and Rodrick wondered if he was fleeing or circling around to ambush their attackers.

He didn't get to wonder for long, though, because two dryads rushed at him, their white-bark bodies splotched with fungus, their snarling mouths and outstretched hands bristling with thorns.

Hrym had a great many powers that could aid in escape, which was Rodrick's preferred method for dealing with conflict. He could summon a freezing fog to blind his enemies, and make the ground so slippery the dryads would have trouble walking, let alone pursuing. But those environmental attacks would work against his allies, too, and Temple was unlikely to greet him warmly if he returned with news that the other Volunteers had died.

Hrym got tired of waiting for instructions and flung yard-long spikes of ice at the approaching dryads. The icicles pierced them through the chest and abdomen, respectively, but they didn't slow down in the slightest. Tree spirits didn't have the same sort of internal organs humans did, apparently. Rodrick stumbled backward, swinging Hrym toward their thorny feet, freezing them in ice.

Before he could fully encase the blighted fey in ice, though, three more dryads were upon him, so close he was reduced to using Hrym as a *sword*, swinging wildly and without finesse. He knew a few showy sword flourishes, suitable for impressing watchers on a parade ground, but when it came to practical fencing skills he'd never learned more than the bare minimum necessary to avoid cutting off his own feet—and even those skills tended to leave him when he panicked in the heat of battle.

Hrym was a magical blade, though, so even wild swings were successful in lopping off blighted limbs, sealing the edges of the wounds in ice, and making the fey monsters howl as the frost climbed across their bodies, transforming them into statues of themselves. Rodrick spun, arm extended, and Hrym's blade passed easily through the two dryads frozen by their feet, their upper bodies falling to the ground. Like chopping firewood, Rodrick thought wildly. At least there wasn't blood from the slaughter, just sap and slime from the burst fungi.

He turned, trying to see if he could help anywhere else, but the clearing was a scene of madness. Eldra had run out of knives and was slashing at dryads with her folded parasol, which had bizarrely sprouted a foot-long silver blade from the tip. The Specialist was loping around, tossing objects that exploded in gouts of flame or sprays of acid, maiming and infuriating and occasionally even killing the dryads. Merihim rode her warhorse, the great stallion rearing up to smash the fey down with its hooves. Prinn emerged from the forest, carrying a severed dryad head in each hand, dangling by their mossy hair. He tossed them onto the flaming corpse of another dryad the Specialist had struck directly, then leapt, a blade in each hand, to take down the fey closing in around Eldra.

"I think we're winning," Hrym said.

Rodrick nodded tiredly and staggered around the clearing, lopping the heads off any fallen dryads that showed signs of life. After a while he looked around and didn't see any more of the fey moving. Night had fully fallen by then, though the burning remnants of dryads still lit the clearing, and filled the air with a fungal stench. Eldra sat slumped with her back against the central tree. The Specialist knelt in the grass sorting through his pack, muttering to himself. Prinn collected fey corpses and tossed them onto what was becoming a reeking bonfire. He dragged Eldra's horse over, too—there were blackened blotches on its white hide as the fungi spread on its dead flesh—and it began burning as well, which didn't improve the overall scent of the clearing. It was only after staring dully at the burning horse for a moment that Rodrick realized the titanic strength Prinn must possess in order to drag the beast single-handed.

Merihim touched Rodrick's shoulder, and he turned his head, blinking at her. "That was terrible," he said.

She nodded, her usual smirk gone, face grim. "Yes. Let's have a family meeting."

Rodrick went to the central tree and sat beside Eldra, who smiled at him weakly. A smear of soot smudged her cheek, and he reached out unthinkingly to wipe it away. Her hand shot out and grabbed his wrist in a shockingly strong grip.

He winced. "Sorry. You've got some dirt on your cheek there."

Her sharp gaze softened, and she released him. "Go ahead."

Rodrick wiped at her cheek with the edge of his sleeve, then laughed hollowly. "That would work better if my clothes weren't filthy. Sorry about that."

She shrugged. "I've been dirtier."

The Specialist closed up his pack with a sigh. "I used up most of my supplies in that battle. If we have to fight again, I won't be quite as useful."

Prinn walked over and squatted in the grass some distance away and just sat, unmoving as a gargoyle. Merihim stood looking down at them all, her arms crossed, and then sighed heavily. "I blame myself."

That's a good start, Rodrick thought.

"We're supposed to work as a team, but we're not a team yet. So when trouble came, we all fought individually, with no thought about coordination. The fact that all of us are still alive, and all these mushroom maidens are dead, proves we're pretty formidable individually. But imagine if we'd worked together? How could things have gone differently?"

Rodrick frowned. He'd avoided schooling as much as possible, and this felt very much like a teacher quizzing her students.

The Specialist spoke up. "If Rodrick and I had stood back to back, flinging ice and fire outward from a fixed position, we could have destroyed most of the blighted fey as they initially approached. As it was, neither of us had clear lines of attack—we couldn't strike effectively without risking hurting the rest of you."

Rodrick nodded. That was true enough.

"I should have done as Prinn did," Eldra said. "Slipped into the trees and tried to take any stragglers unawares. My skills aren't as well suited to frontal assaults."

Merihim nodded. "Very good. I propose that, in the future, if we find ourselves under attack, Rodrick and the Specialist form the front line, and Prinn and Eldra make sure we aren't flanked or attacked from behind."

"Where will you be in this scenario?" Rodrick said.

"Where a general should be: in a position to see the battle as a whole, and make adjustments to our strategy as necessary."

Rodrick grunted. Oh, to be a general. He'd never aspired to be infantry. Then again, being in charge of others in the midst of an attack didn't appeal to him, either. He was more of a deserter by nature.

Merihim went on. "It seems obvious now we were led into a trap, following trail signs deliberately created to bring us to a place where we were likely to be ambushed. We might as well have blundered into a pit full of spikes. Bannerman could be out there, waiting for us, even watching us, and if so, I'm sure he enjoyed the show." Rodrick looked at Merihim's wrist, where the glowing bracelet should have been, but it was gone. Interesting. "We'll take precautions," she said. "Two of us will be on guard while the others sleep, with a shift change halfway through the night. I don't like the idea of sleeping beside a campfire made of fey corpses, but at least in this clearing we can see danger coming. Tomorrow, when we proceed, we'll go on a *lot* more cautiously. All right?"

"You're in charge," Rodrick said. "So I suppose it must be." He yawned. "I'll take first watch."

"I'll join you," Eldra said.

Merihim nodded. "That's fine. Wake me and the Specialist in the small hours."

"What about Prinn?" Rodrick looked around, realizing the man had slipped away at some point.

Merihim's haughty smirk was back. "Prinn has his own mission. Don't worry about him. He'll rejoin us in the morning."

9

An Island in a Lake

Rodrick's watch passed uneventfully. He jammed Hrym point-first into the dirt on one side of the clearing, and he and Eldra sat together on the other side of the great tree, watching the west. He'd hoped for a few stolen kisses, but when he made an attempt she put her hand on his chin and turned his face away. "Really, Rodrick. I've just seen my horse set upon by monsters, and then burned. The air still stinks of burning horsehair. There's a time and place for romance, and this is neither."

She was willing to chat with him, though, and that helped keep them both awake. He probed her in his usual ways, trying to find out about her background, her upbringing, her social class, her connections—all the levers and buttons and soft spots that were so crucial to learning how to manipulate a person. She was adept at turning his questions back on him, deflecting without seeming to do so, and giving airy and amusing answers that nevertheless failed to provide any real substance. He *did* ferret out that she'd been trained at the Conservatory of Jalmeray, the elite school for diplomats, musicians, and courtesans, which Rodrick suspected was secretly a training institute for Vudrani spies—their graduates went on to serve foreign kings and queens and tyrants all over the Inner Sea, after all. He shared that theory with Eldra, who chuckled musically. "If that's the case, I never got the class on spycraft. I left the school a bit earlier than most, though, to seek my fortune."

"Oh?" Rodrick said. "Did you find it?"

"Let's just say I haven't stopped looking yet."

The hours passed companionably. Against all his instincts, Rodrick found himself liking Eldra. He knew intellectually that she was probably using him, cultivating an air of mystery and then letting a few little details drop so that he could feel like her special confidante. She was grooming him, so that, if the time came, he would move just a *bit* faster to save her, or that he would prioritize protecting her over, say, Merihim or the Specialist. (He couldn't imagine going out of his way to save Prinn; then again, he couldn't imagine Prinn needing him to.)

Rodrick had used his own not inconsiderable charm in similar ways in the past, forging bonds of fellowship that seemed solid but were actually as ephemeral as spiderwebs . . . but Eldra was so *good* at it, she almost made him believe her. Maybe if she pretended affection long enough, it would become true? Or maybe she'd decide that to well and truly wrap him around her finger, she should actually sleep with him at some point. Conservatory-trained courtesans were supposedly proficient in arts he'd never experienced, but only seen in salacious illustrations, and though Rodrick was generally a lazy student uninterested in learning, he was willing to take instruction along those lines.

Eventually they judged it was the dimmest watches of the night and went to rouse Merihim and the Specialist. The latter was rather groggy until he lifted a vial of something to his nose and sniffed the vapors, and then he sprang to his feet as if he'd been poked in the nethers with a needle, eyes wide and body positively vibrating with energy. Alchemists were such strange folk, and he was at least an alchemist, even if he was other things, too.

Rodrick rolled out his blanket, then opened his coin pouch. His total net worth, in gold, was a mere three coins, including the one Hrym had extorted from the Specialist. Rodrick scattered the paltry array on the ground before resting Hrym atop the gold.

"What a pitiful hoard," Hrym muttered. "Why do you have to spend our gold all the time? I don't go around bartering away your mattresses."

Rodrick ignored him, turning his attention to more interesting sleeping companions. "Want to huddle together for warmth?" he whispered to Eldra.

"We both know we wouldn't get any actual *rest* if I nuzzled up against you. Save it for a night when we're not on a mission, hmm?" She rolled herself up in a blanket a decorous distance away.

She's really very good, Rodrick thought, and then went to sleep.

He woke to birds singing in the grayish half-light of dawn. The fire was cold, having reduced the horse and dryads to a pile of ashes and bones and unidentifiable lumps. Merihim and the Specialist were up, saddling the mounts that hadn't died yet. Rodrick rose and yawned, and Eldra rolled over and smiled up at him, blinking her long eyelashes prettily.

Prinn walked into camp, limping slightly, his face covered in scratches, his expression as impassive as ever. Merihim raised a hand and beckoned him over. Prinn removed the glowing bracelet of linked arrows and handed it to his mistress, who slipped it over her wrist. Prinn then murmured into her ear at some length, and the devilkin scowled as she listened. She patted him on the shoulder—he stiffened as if she'd threatened him with a whip—and said, "Gather round, children, for the good news."

Rodrick picked up Hrym and the gold and wrapped up his bedroll, while Eldra yawned and stretched most fetchingly, then they ambled over to join the others.

"Prinn scouted ahead. There's a very obvious trail, which he followed, and it led to a concealed pit full of spikes smeared with animal dung, because apparently ordinary wooden spikes aren't unhygienic enough. He found a much less obvious trail, and followed *that*, thinking it would lead us to Bannerman . . . but instead it led to a series of traps made with vines and bent-back limbs and more wooden spikes smeared with *more* dung. He had to dive into a briar patch to avoid being impaled, which is why he's all scratched up. Two other likely trails led to similar sets of traps, but he was prepared for those, now, and managed to set them off without being caught himself. Beyond the most treacherous set of traps, though, he found a hillside with a dry creek bed full of boulders, the sort of thing that doesn't leave any sign of tracks, and scurried up it . . . and on the other side of the hill, there's a pond, and in the midst of the pond a rocky island, and in the midst of the *island*, a small opening in the rocks that leads to a cave. That's where Bannerman is hidden. The bracelet flashed and pulsed like mad when Prinn got close."

"Assuming we're operating from correct foundations," the Specialist said. "The bracelet will lead us to whomever left that shred of fingernail in the clearing, but we have no proof that was Bannerman."

"There could be another wily ex-crusader hiding out in the forest laying traps, I suppose," Merihim said, "but I'm willing to bet it's our man."

The Specialist shrugged. "I'm merely pointing out that few things in life are certain."

"That's what makes it exciting," Eldra said.

They led the horses to a grassy clearing Prinn had found, where a flowing creek belled out into a pool before continuing on its course, so they could eat and drink in pleasant surroundings. Prinn and Merihim did something magical, driving stakes into the ground in a loose circle around the horses, apparently setting up some kind of sorcerous perimeter, presumably to protect their mounts from fey or other monsters. Rodrick appreciated the precaution. Not enough horses was better than no horses at all, and he didn't relish the idea of returning to the Bastion on foot.

Once the animals were as safe as possible, the party moved on. Prinn led the way, since he'd scouted beforehand, followed by Merihim. Eldra was in the rear, keeping her keen eyes on their back trail, leaving the Specialist and Rodrick to walk together. The Specialist handed over another gold coin and listened solemnly as Hrym spun the most outrageous nonsense about being taken on a Shory expedition to a blasted temple in what was now the Sodden Lands, where an enclave of serpentfolk plotted to restore the supremacy of their race. The Specialist was rapt. At least Hrym's blather kept the Specialist from educating Rodrick about the economic importance of the Fangwood or the social organization of woodland fey and their demon-corrupted counterparts. He'd have preferred chatting with Eldra, though.

Before noon they found the first of the traps Prinn had triggered, nasty and inventive things set off by tripwires and loose stones. Who knew you could achieve such terrible effects with the odd bit of rope, vines, branches, heavy logs and rocks for counterweights, and gravity? Their progress slowed a bit as the forest grew more dense, the underbrush thicker, the trees here younger and closer together, mostly firs bristling with needles and oozing sap. Prinn was content to slither and crawl beneath branches, but Merihim laid about her with a heavy blade, hacking out a path. They skirted a pair of five-foot-deep pits bristling with spikes, which had been covered with thin latticeworks of branches covered with fir boughs until Prinn found them. Rodrick watched the ground very carefully, and made a point of following as precisely in Merihim's footsteps as possible.

They made it through the traps safely, and reached the rocky hillside with its dry creek bed. Calling it a "hill" wasn't quite descriptive enough, Rodrick thought. If the incline had been just a bit steeper, it would have been more properly termed a cliff wall. You could climb it without ropes and spikes, probably, if you went slowly. The stones scattered on the hill ranged from pebble-sized to wheelbarrow-sized to one high up near the ridge that was nearly as big as a carriage. The Specialist started talking about glaciers and geological forces and Rodrick let the words wash over him without bothering to take in their meaning.

"Prinn will go up ahead and make sure the path is clear," Merihim said. "I don't like how exposed we'll be on that hillside. Bannerman could be watching."

The pale sorcerer scuttled up the steep hillside, finding hand- and footholds with impressive dexterity. He was halfway up when the immense boulder Rodrick had noticed before started to shift forward. "Look out!" he shouted, and Prinn stopped and looked back at him, which was entirely the wrong thing to do, as the boulder began to roll ponderously toward him.

But it was only ponderous at first. The combination of weight and gravity caused the boulder to speed up rapidly, and when Prinn finally looked the right way he flung himself to one side and rolled, bouncing, down the hill. Fortunately, the boulder bounced along a different route, hitting the creek bed and then rolling as smoothly as a ball dropped down a chute.

Right toward the rest of them. They broke in different directions, and all managed to get clear in time, watching the boulder hit the level ground and actually *bounce* before caroming off into the underbrush and coming to rest.

Prinn didn't seem troubled by his brush with death-by-crushing. He resumed his climb, pausing often to look up occasionally this time, and reached the ridge, peeking over the top. He turned and beckoned, and the rest of them began to make their way up the hillside. Rodrick stuck to the creek bed, since it seemed to offer the most handholds, grunting with effort and trying not to slide backward with every step. His calves burned with effort. "You're lucky you don't have legs, Hrym."

"I do have legs. They're called 'Rodrick.'"

When they reached the top, Prinn was crouched down examining the place where the immense boulder had been. Merihim and the Specialist joined him. "Yes, I think it was deliberate," the Specialist said. "You can see where the hillside was undermined, here and here, to make the boulder more precarious."

"Also there's a six-foot-long branch on the ground," Merihim said dryly. "Looks a lot like a lever to me. Bannerman's definitely keeping an eye on us." She held up her wrist, and the bracelet was pulsing with light faster than the heartbeat of a running man. "Rodrick, you and the Specialist are going over the top first. Blast ice, throw fireballs, make a lot of noise. Rodrick, when you get close enough, use Hrym to freeze the pond. Eldra and Prinn will flank and approach from either side, crossing the ice to the island proper, to see if they can catch Bannerman unawares. All right?"

They all gave their agreement, none with great enthusiasm.

"Go on, then."

Rodrick and the Specialist leapt over the top of the ridge and raced down the gentler slope on the other side. There was a miniature valley below, dominated by a large, algae-slimed pond with a small rocky island in the center. The word "valley" was too idyllic, though: the area around the pond was full of shaggy, knee-high grass and large mounds of rotting vegetation. The Specialist threw a pair of small clay bulbs overhand at the island. Both fell short, landing in the water, but seconds later erupted with loud booms and sprayed geysers into the air. Hrym spat long spears of ice before them, which landed in the water harmlessly or shattered on the rocky island. There was no sign of Bannerman or any other life.

The Specialist howled something as he ran down the hillside, maybe an orc battle cry, and Rodrick yelled right along with him, feeling rather ridiculous. They were supposed to make noise, though, so make noise they would. Rodrick pointed Hrym toward the pond, and once they were in range, the slimy water began to freeze, tendrils of ice racing out and meeting to connect until a solid sheet of ice filled half the pond, connecting the shore to the island. Prinn and Eldra appeared from either side, moving low and fast—though Prinn was rather lower and faster; the man moved like a lizard—and slowing down only slightly when they hit the ice.

The Specialist kept hollering but stopped throwing bombs, and Rodrick didn't bother to yell anymore. If Bannerman was here, he'd certainly noticed their arrival. Rodrick noted a shadow among the cracked stones of the island that was probably the cave mouth Prinn had mentioned. Maybe Bannerman was holed up in there, pointing a crossbow at the opening, waiting for them to cross in front of it, silhouetted nicely and turned into appealing targets.

"See how I made the sheet ice uneven?" Hrym said. "All rippled? That's to help Eldra and Prinn walk across it without slipping. Something like that deserves praise, I think. My teamwork is exemplary."

"Well done," Rodrick said distractedly. He and the Specialist stopped at the edge of the iced-over pond, both scanning the rest of the valley while Prinn and Eldra crawled all over the island, carefully avoiding the cave mouth, to make sure Bannerman wasn't crouched in some other crevice. They both came together at the highest point on the island, just a few yards above the cave opening, and shook their heads.

Merihim joined Rodrick and the Specialist, looking at the even-more-rapidly-pulsing light of the bracelet on her wrist. "He's very close. Must be in that hole."

"I could toss a bomb into the cave mouth," the Specialist said. "I have a few left."

Merihim sniffed. "We're supposed to bring Bannerman back alive and unharmed, not a charred corpse."

"There are *other* sorts of bombs." He reached into his pack and took out a bulb of reddish clay, about the size of an apple. "This is a concussive, not an explosive, and it makes a bright flash, too, to blind anyone who looks in its direction. We can throw this into the cave, wait for it to go off, and then rush in. If Bannerman is there, he'll be dazed and easily taken." The Specialist paused. "Unless it's a *deep* complex of caverns, and he's hidden off in some side tunnel, but I don't think that's likely given the prevailing local geographic factors—"

"All right. Drop your bomb. Then you and Rodrick and Hrym will go in to subdue Bannerman."

"Can we hit him just a *little*?" Rodrick said. "He dropped a demon-tainted dryad on our heads, after all."

"Don't hurt him unless it's necessary to subdue him." Merihim grinned. "But I'll let you be the judge of what's necessary or not. I have total faith in the rightness of your choices."

They walked across the ice, leaving Merihim on the far side, watching over the valley in case of surprise attack. Rodrick waved jauntily at Eldra, who waggled her fingers at him in a friendly wave. He was careful not to cross directly in front of the cave mouth, which was about four feet wide and three feet high and as black as a slaver's heart. He'd had some experience crawling around in caverns and barrows, and wasn't eager to add more.

Rodrick and the Specialist flanked the hole, and the Specialist tossed in the reddish bulb before turning away, squeezing his eyes shut, and putting his hands over his ears. Rodrick followed suit hastily, as well as he could with a magical longsword in one hand. The noise was shockingly loud, a boom that reverberated through the soles of his boots and into his bones, and the blast of light from the cave mouth was so bright he could see it clearly even through his eyelids.

After a moment he blinked, caught the Specialist's eye, and they ducked and headed into the cavern. The Specialist drew a tube that glowed yellow as the sun from his pack, and it illuminated a small space, barely a hole in the ground, with a fallen figure on its back, unmoving, next to the shards of the Specialist's bomb. "He's in here!" Rodrick shouted.

Eldra entered the cave. "Merihim's on her way."

After a few moments the devilkin descended as well, bracelet flashing brightly in the dimness. "Ha! Excellent. Drag him out. We can give him one kick *each*, all right? Just be careful not to rupture anything vital."

The Specialist knelt by the form on the cavern floor. "This isn't Bannerman," he said.

Merihim stiffened. "Who is it, then?"

The Specialist shrugged. "An old man. I'd guess some kind of forest hermit, by the state of his beard and teeth. He's been dead . . . oh, a few weeks, at least. No signs of murder. Probably just passed away naturally."

Merihim held up her bracelet, which flashed wildly. "Then where's Bannerman?"

The Specialist held up the dead man's arm, and then straightened one of his fingers. "Look here. The fingernail was ripped off, probably after death."

Merihim groaned. "It was a *trap*. We have to get out of here—"

Outside, beyond the cavern mouth, someone screamed.

10

BANNERMAN

They rushed out of the cave, Rodrick going first with Hrym outstretched, though he hated to lead. There was only the one scream, which was either comforting or terrifying, depending on *why* the screaming had stopped.

Prinn was kneeling on top of a prostrate man, twisting his captive's arms up behind his back as the man tried without success to heave the pale sorcerer off him.

Rodrick lowered the sword. "I think Prinn caught Bannerman."

The renegade crusader was a huge man, dressed in green and brown and gray, garments ideal for blending into the forest. A quiver of arrows and a large bow lay on the ground beside him.

"It's good we didn't *all* rush into the cave," Merihim said. "What was the plan, Bannerman? Shoot us with arrows as we emerged?"

"Don't know any Bannerman," the man said gruffly. "I'm just a huntsman, out looking for deer. I heard some kind of a boom and came to see what it was, and *this* fella jumped out and knocked me down and *sat* on me."

Merihim squatted, grabbed him by the hair, and twisted his head so she could get a good look at his face. "Looks like the sketch of Bannerman to me."

Rodrick had to agree, and the Specialist said, with his usual certainty, "It's either Bannerman, or a doppelganger, or a totenmaske who stole his face, or someone using an illusion to disguise themselves—"

"Yes, it's Bannerman, I agree, too." Eldra crossed her arms, looked to the cave, and shuddered. "Can we get out of here now?"

Merihim reached into her pack and brought out a pair of black iron shackles. "Temple gave me these. Get him upright, Prinn." The sorcerer unfolded himself and dragged Bannerman to his feet. The former crusader towered over Rodrick by at least a foot, and Rodrick wasn't a small man. The top of Eldra's head would have barely come up to Bannerman's breastbone.

The fugitive tried to do some sort of clever move, twisting his body and moving his feet and trying to lift his arms, but Prinn adjusted his grip on the man's elbow minutely and made Bannerman bite back a cry of pain and drop to one knee.

"We'd be just as happy to bring you back dead," Merihim said. "Keep resisting, and we will. The reward's the same either way."

Bannerman snorted. "Temple needs me alive. There's knowledge inside my head she *needs*."

Merihim shrugged. "It was worth a try. We were told not to kill you, or permanently break you, but that leaves a wealth of other options to make you behave, doesn't it, Prinn?"

The sorcerer, without changing expression in the slightest, dislocated Bannerman's left shoulder. The fugitive's face instantly sheened with sweat, and he gritted his teeth, but didn't cry out. Rodrick winced with involuntary sympathy.

"Be a good boy and we'll pop that back into the joint later." Merihim clasped the shackles around Bannerman's wrists, behind his back, which must have been excruciating with the knob of his shoulder joint out of place, visibly pressing against his skin. The ex-crusader bore it stoically, though.

The Specialist bent to look at the shackles. "Mmm, magical— they tighten to fit. That's marvelous. Suitable for binding everything from ogres to gnomes, I would imagine."

Merihim took a rough hemp rope from her pack, made a slipknot, and tossed the loop over Bannerman's head, drawing it snug around his neck without making it tight. "Don't go running away, now." She put the end of the lead in Prinn's hand.

She looked around the valley. "Let's get out of—" She stopped, frowning. "Are those heaps of leaf mold *moving*?"

Rodrick looked, and yes, the piles of rotten leaves and old branches that dotted the valley were now in motion, moving slowly but implacably toward the island at the center of the pond. Some of them rose up on what looked like stumplike legs, while others seemed to drag themselves forward with viny tendrils.

"They're carnivorous plants!" Bannerman said. "I was hoping you idiots would trip over one and wake them up. They've noticed us now. Quick, let me loose, I know how to avoid them, I'll show you how to escape."

"Shut up." Merihim turned to Rodrick, then nodded at the Specialist. "Gentlemen?"

Rodrick hefted Hrym, and the Specialist delved into his bag, and they began to calmly and efficiently lay waste with fire and ice.

When they were done, and the mounds were lumps of ice or smoking piles of fire or both, Bannerman let out a long, low whistle. "All right, then," he said. "I'll go along quietly."

The horses were all still alive, which was another bit of luck. They hung Bannerman over the back of Merihim's warhorse, and the animal didn't seem bothered a bit by the extra weight. Rodrick was hoping Eldra would ride pressed up against his back, but his skittish horse wouldn't hear of it, and she ended up sharing the Specialist's plodding mount. What a waste.

"I can get you money," Bannerman said as they moved along the forest paths, watching for blighted fey and carnivorous mounds and other dangers. "Just tell Temple you couldn't find me, or that you found me dead in a cave, I don't care."

"We're not above being bought, usually," Merihim said. "And your offer would be tempting, if you hadn't tried to feed us to poisonous dryads and murderous compost heaps or drop us on spikes covered in dung."

"Oh, that? It's not as if the traps were personal. I would have done that to anyone Temple sent for me. Who are you, anyway? You don't look like her usual crusaders."

"We're freelance," Merihim said. "Doing a job for money, and more money than you can afford to match, believe me. What did *you* do, anyway, to get the likes of us sent after you?"

"Oh, the usual dark deeds. I picked up a few valuable secrets along the way. I knew those secrets would keep me alive . . . but, unfortunately, they also made me a target."

"Swords do usually have two edges," Rodrick said.

"Not scimitars," the Specialist said. "Or scythe-swords, falchions, sabers—"

"Yes, all right, I was being *metaphorical*," Rodrick said, and Eldra laughed at him, or the Specialist, or both.

They camped outside the forest, taking turns watching Bannerman and the camp. Their prisoner seemed content enough once Eldra popped his shoulder back into place and fed him some bread and water. She paid entirely too much attention to him, actually, in Rodrick's estimation, even making the man laugh several times in a gruff way.

As they were settling down for their turn to sleep, side by side but with a good two feet of bare earth between them, Rodrick said, "Why show Bannerman so much kindness? He's a treacherous bastard who tried to kill us."

Eldra reached out from bedroll and patted him on the cheek. "It's much easier to deal with a prisoner when they like you, Rodrick. It's a good principle in general when dealing with hostile people, even those in your power. If you want to get answers from someone, you can beat them with a stick, and good luck to you—or you can make them think you're their friend, their *only* friend, a confidante and potential savior. Build a rapport. They won't struggle as long, they'll confess just because confessing feels good . . . and, if the worst happens and they manage to escape their bonds and steal a sword, they'll hesitate a moment before striking you down as they make their escape. There are carrots, and there are sticks. I like to think of myself as a carrot."

"Don't say that around Prinn," Rodrick said. "He'll eat you for dinner."

It was an objectively terrible joke, but she laughed that musical tinkle and patted his cheek again, a bit more lingeringly, before rolling over and going to sleep.

Rodrick lay on his back, looking at the stars, Hrym beside him on his pile of gold, which had grown to five coins thanks to the lies he told the Specialist. "She's showing you the carrot, too," Hrym said in his best approximation of a whisper. "But it's *always* going to be dangled just out of reach."

"Since when are you a student of human nature?"

"You've taught me a great deal about how to take advantage of people, Rodrick. Have you remembered any of your own lessons?"

"Oh, go to sleep, or whatever it is swords do," he muttered.

They made it back to the Bastion well in advance of their deadline, taking a roundabout route and avoiding the main thoroughfares. Temple hadn't been keen on the idea of parading a fugitive crusader through the streets, according to Merihim. Probably bad for morale. Being a knight of Lastwall meant having unshakable bedrock faith in your own moral superiority, and seeing one of your own fallen into disrepute and villainy could only serve to shake one's unshakable convictions.

A guard opened up the high wooden gate in the back of the Bastion and let them into the stable yard. Surly grooms took their mounts from them and led them away to be fed and watered and brushed. The head of the stables inquired after the missing white horse and scowled and walked off muttering after Merihim said, "Killed by dryads. These things happen."

A stiff-faced crusader who made a point of not looking directly at Bannerman told them Temple was waiting to receive them. He led the way into the Bastion, down echoing hallways of dark stone with arrowslit windows, and threw open a heavy wooden door. "Wait there with the prisoner."

They went in, Merihim holding Bannerman's leash. The room beyond was large and spare: a vaulted ceiling with a battle scene painted on it arched over the bare stone floor, and a few wooden chairs of ancient provenance stood arrayed along the walls; they looked so uncomfortable that Rodrick's ass felt numb at the thought of sitting on them. Eldra dropped into one anyway, lounging with one leg kicked over the arm, and began peeling an apple with a knife. Where had she even *gotten* an apple?

The Specialist gazed up at the painting on the ceiling, and Rodrick took a closer look himself. There were massed ranks of armored knights on horseback facing off against their foes, an undead horde clad in black with skeletal arms and weapons that were all hooks and spikes and barbs, with a black and foreboding tower looming in the background. Some ancient scene from the glorious history of Lastwall, no doubt. Rodrick lived a life devoted to making sure he never ended up in a situation that could someday be commemorated in a mural like that one.

A small door on the far side of the room opened, and Temple came through, dressed in unassuming brown robes. She didn't say anything, just walked slowly toward them, looking at Bannerman all the while. "Unshackle him," she said.

Merihim glanced at Rodrick, who drew Hrym and held him ready. The devilkin did something to the magical shackles that made them fall away.

Bannerman grunted, then rubbed wrists.

"Crusader Bannerman," Temple said gravely.

"Underclerk Temple," Bannerman replied, stone-faced.

Then Temple's face broke into a breaming smile, and she threw her arms wide, wrapping Bannerman in a welcoming embrace.

11

Rousing the Rabble

Temple thumped Bannerman on the back, and he hugged her back warmly. She stepped back, smiling up at him, and said, "How are you, soldier?"

"Just fine, boss. They banged me up a little, but all within acceptable bounds. I was prepared for a few more boots to the ribs, honestly."

"What's going on?" Rodrick looked at the other Volunteers. The Specialist was shaking his head ruefully, Merihim was glaring at Temple, Eldra was laughing behind her hand, and Prinn might as well have been a statue carved out of soapstone. "Are you . . . wait . . . he's not a fugitive?"

"Not at all," Temple said. "He's my most trusted lieutenant."

"No, no, no." Rodrick shook his head. "You said you'd never lie to us, that honesty was the bedrock of our relationship, and then you sent us under false pretenses after a supposed fugitive—"

"She didn't lie." Merihim sat down in one of the chairs. "We're idiots."

The Specialist's tone was faraway, distracted, as if he were only halfway paying attention to what was happening in the room. "True. I remember what she said, verbatim. I have a great memory for such things. She never said Bannerman was a fugitive. She said he was a trained crusader of Lastwall, that he was in the Fangwood, and that we were to bring him back unharmed. When asked why she wanted him, she said only that she needed him, alive and unharmed."

Temple nodded. "Indeed. I said I'd never lie, Rodrick—I didn't say I'd spell everything out for you. That said, there was a certain level of omission in this case that I won't bother with in the future. Though teaching you to listen carefully is a good lesson all on its own."

"So, what, this was an initiation?" Rodrick said. "Like the knight who sends his new squire to the armory to ask for a left-handed lance?"

"Not at all," Bannerman said. "Or not entirely, anyway. Before we sent you on a real mission, we needed to see how you'd behave when you thought no one was watching. If you'd scheme, connive, try to weasel out of your situation, break and run, seek out a wizard to save you . . . or if you'd actually work as a team and get the job done."

Rodrick shook his head. "This still seems awfully treacherous for a noble paladin of Lastwall."

Bannerman chuckled. "I'm no paladin. A crusader, yes . . . but there are more ways to serve the forces of good and order than shining up your armor and riding into the teeth of an assault."

"Lastwall needs people like Bannerman and me," Temple said. "People who can do . . . unorthodox things . . . in the interest of the greater good. Do you know how Bannerman got his name?"

"Oh, now, there's no need for that," the crusader said.

"It's because he's carried quite a few banners in battle." Temple smiled at her lieutenant. "He fought in more than one army before seeing the light and joining the crusaders in our great endeavor—he used to particularly enjoy border skirmishes among the nobles in Taldor. Sometimes, in all the confusion, he'd accidentally find himself in possession of an enemy banner . . . either stolen from one of their soldiers or brought along in a pack until the moment seemed right."

"It's remarkable where you can go if you're carrying the right flag," Bannerman said.

"There were times when he carried an enemy banner into the heart of their camp, walked right up to a commanding officer, and stabbed them in the back."

"Or the neck. I wasn't picky."

"Definitely not a paladin, then," Merihim said.

"The tactic doesn't work as well with orcs, unfortunately," Bannerman said. "Somehow, even when carrying one of their ragged flags, I don't quite blend in with their soldiers. Fortunately, Temple has found other uses for my talents in recent years."

"How nice for you," Merihim complained. "What about using our talents? We were sent into the field to chase wild geese. We went to all that effort for an exercise? A test?"

"Don't be stupid." Temple's voice was a lashing whip. "It would have been a waste to send you chasing a fugitive who wasn't really a fugitive, but you had a secondary mission, too. I just didn't bother to tell you about it. How did that go, Bannerman?"

"The operation wasn't clean or neat, but they managed to kill that cluster of blighted fey, down to the last dryad. I'll send in a few of the new recruits with torches and axes to bring down the infected trees before the corruption can spread further, but they're just sick trees, now, not sick fey, too. With luck we can keep the infection away from this side of the river, and leave it in Nirmathas."

"All right." Rodrick could be gracious when the situation called for it. "That was neatly done. I can admire efficiency. It would have been nice to have some warning about the blighted fey, though."

"Nice for you. Not so nice for me." Temple sniffed. "I needed to see how perceptive you were. Did they pull together as a team, Bannerman?"

"The blighted fey seemed to shock them into camaraderie. I'm not saying they're a dedicated band of brothers and sisters and whatever Prinn is, but they've learned to watch one another's backs. I'd be willing to take them out into the field."

Merihim straightened. "Hold on there. I'm the field leader."

Bannerman nodded. "You seem like a capable one, too. Think of me as your . . . liaison. I'll guide you to your mission destinations, provide a little support, cover your escapes, give you intelligence when you need it. Keep you on point if you start to . . . drift."

Temple clapped her hands. "For now, you can return to your quarters, get some rest, and clean up. Bannerman will be in touch in a couple of days with your next mission."

Merihim cleared her throat. "Sorry about your shoulder."

Bannerman chuckled darkly. "I would've done worse to you if our positions had been reversed, Merihim." He and Temple strolled out of the room, arm in arm, chatting companionably.

Their quarters had been improved when they arrived. There was a shelf holding a few books, and a better class of food in the larder (or so the Specialist said), and dice, a deck of cards, and game boards with polished stones for markers. There were even more cushions on the chairs, and nicer blankets in the bedrooms.

Merihim scowled at the gifts. "Oh, look, the good dogs have been rewarded with nice new bones to gnaw."

"Woof, woof." Rodrick looked through the cupboards. "Still nothing to drink though. Just water. How disgusting. You don't even want to know what fish do in water."

Eldra said, "I'm going to freshen up," and vanished into the bedroom, shutting the door.

Rodrick drifted over to examine the bookshelves, but there were no illustrated tomes to his liking, just dry histories of Lastwall and neighboring territories, and a slim volume of more recent vintage that seemed to be a screed about how the foundation of the nation of Nirmathas was a chance for the oppressed and downtrodden people of Molthune to boldly forge their own destiny, and other such twaddle.

"Put me down on my gold," Hrym demanded, and Rodrick obliged, setting him up with his hoard on the settee. Rodrick wandered into the kitchen, where the Specialist appeared to be inventorying jars of dried spices.

"Your sword tells the most outrageous lies." The Specialist shook some whitish flecks onto his palm, touched the tip of his tongue to them, and made a thoughtful face.

"Ah. You noticed that. Why did you pay him for more lies, then?"

"Because, every once in a while, he lets slip something real—the name of a Shory city that appears only in a single fragment of a manuscript that, forgive me, I doubt you've ever read. Or one of his false tales of adventure will glancingly intersect with the fragmentary account of a real hero's adventures from thousands of years ago. I'm not sure Hrym even realizes he's embroidering his lies with truths. I think when he's wildly inventing these tales, old memories bubble to the surface. It makes me wonder, though—what else might he know, that he doesn't even know he knows?"

"He doesn't know the location of any large caches of undiscovered gold, I can tell you that much." Rodrick affected an airy tone, but he was troubled to hear that Hrym had old memories even the sword himself didn't realize were real.

"That's a shame," the Specialist said. "Such a trove would be helpful. I don't know how long I can afford to keep paying Hrym to talk."

After a peaceful—which was to say, tiresome and boring—interval of two days, Temple and Bannerman finally called and had the Volunteers gather in the common area to be briefed on their next mission.

"You'll be going to Molthune," Temple said. "I'll assume total ignorance of our local history, shall I? Just south of us is the young and rather . . . underdeveloped . . . nation of Nirmathas, and south of that is Molthune. Before you can understand the nature of your mission, I need you to understand something of the complex history between Molthune and Nirmathas and, to some extent, Lastwall itself."

Rodrick groaned. "Politics. Must it be politics?"

The Specialist clucked his tongue. "Everything is politics, Rodrick. Every relationship, every conversation. They're all just politics writ small."

Temple said, "I trust you've all read *A Vindication of the Rights of the Downtrodden,* by the revolutionary philosopher and poet Zumani? I left a copy there on the shelf for you, along with some books on the history of the region."

"The Specialist read them, I'm sure." At Merihim's glance, the man nodded. "For the rest of us, you may have to summarize."

Temple sighed. "I suppose I should have left copies under your pillows if I wanted you to pay attention. Fine. Zumani's book is the usual sort of revolutionary fare, with a local emphasis. Seventy years ago, Nirmathas didn't exist—the country was just part of Molthune. Not a very well-loved part, either—widely considered a backwater full of ignorant provincials, of value chiefly because they occupied the Southern Fangwood, and had all the very valuable lumber there. The people in Molthune's capital weren't very kind to their northern countrymen, and governed with, shall we say, a heavy hand. After wriggling under the boot of their southron masters for too many years, the brave people of northern Molthune finally rose up and seized their own destiny, rebelling and declaring their independence. Thus, Nirmathas was born.

"Zumani grew up in the midst of that revolutionary zeal, and his book adds more fuel to the fire. Zumani does his best to remind his countrymen that they are the vanguard of a great human experiment in self-government, free from the prejudice and nepotism and small-minded short-sightedness of the Molthuni government. The people of the nascent nation of Nirmathas—that's poetic, isn't it? It's Zumani's phrase—must never stop fighting, never stop resisting, never stop battling the rapacious selfish monstrosity that is Molthune. The book is written with great flair, mostly in a vernacular the average citizen of Nirmathas can easily understand, and the literate ones read it aloud to their less educated friends and family at meetings in the forest and under canvas tents and in rude wooden halls." She smiled to herself. "His words fill his countrymen with the will to fight on, against difficult odds. Zumani has really done great work for us."

Merihim sat up in the armchair. "I'm sorry. Are you saying Lastwall employs revolutionaries from Nirmathas?"

Temple seesawed her hand. "Not so much Lastwall in general as the Bastion of Justice, and the odd high-ranking officer among the crusaders who recognizes the importance of our work, and can be trusted not to get bogged down in the tedious particulars of how our work gets done." Temple took out a wooden pipe and began to fill it, paying careful attention to packing in the herb as she spoke. "Molthune is an ambitious country, you see. They have territorial desires, very profound ones, but the countries around them are mostly too powerful to be gobbled up. They find this very frustrating. More than a hundred years ago, it became apparent that Molthune was looking to Lastwall as a possible conquest."

"That's insane," Rodrick said. "You're a country made up almost entirely of hardened veterans of assorted wars against unspeakable monsters. You're a—I don't know, a paladin-ocracy. How could Molthune hope to conquer you?"

"Because we're a nation of divided attention, Rodrick. We formed to watch the remnants of the Whispering Tyrant's empire. That might seem like a ceremonial duty to you, like sentries watching over a graveyard, but let me assure you, there are still very real and present dangers in the ruins of that old regime. There are forces at work inside those blasted, blighted lands, and there are outsiders who seek to rekindle those terrible flames." Did Temple glance at Merihim then? For just an instant? Rodrick couldn't be sure. "The bulk of our forces, though, are focused on the Hold of

Belkzen, and the orc hordes there who want to trample all over the lands of the Inner Sea, pillaging and looting as they go."

"Orc culture is unfairly maligned," the Specialist said in a musing tone. "They are widely perceived as bestial monsters, but they have a complex and beautiful culture based on honor, family, and obligation. Oh, from the outside, I'll grant you, some of their traditions seems a bit, er, rustic, but—"

"They are our greatest living enemy." Temple stared the Specialist into silence. "So you see, our attention is split between the orcs to the west and the legacy of the Whispering Tyrant to the north. If Molthune chose to attack from the south . . . let's just say it's our least-well-protected border. The Molthuni could at the very least manage to seize some of our border villages, and use that as a foothold to annex us further, or force us to divide our attention, leaving us vulnerable to the depredations of the orcs or even a resurgence of the undead and evil forces in the Hungry Mountains. So when, many decades ago, the oppressed Molthuni of the Southern Fangwood decided to rise up against their masters in the capital, the powers that be in Lastwall weren't entirely displeased. In general, we frown on chaos and instability, but I have no doubt many in the government were quietly wishing the great freedom fighter Irgal Nirmath luck in his noble struggle."

"Ah," Rodrick said. "Nirmath. Like Nirmathas."

"You're so observant," Merihim said. "Truly, your mind is a thing of wonder."

"Yes, well," Temple said. "Nirmath's forces did well during the Freedom War. Alas, Nirmath himself was slain by an assassin, and the fledgling country that took his name has been looking for comparable leadership ever since, without notable success. Even without a strong hand to guide them, though, Nirmathas has proven an admirable buffer zone between Molthune and Lastwall. Molthune can hardly contemplate attacking us when they have those rebellious former territories standing between us. They can't possibly threaten Lastwall until they get Nirmathas under control, and that country has been independent for sixty years now—Nirmathas has been its own nation for longer than it was part of Molthune at this point, though that hasn't stopped Molthune from trying bring the lost sheep back into the fold. There are always new, fiercely independent rabble-rousers rising up to make sure Nirmathas fights the good fight and resists Molthune's ongoing territorial aggression." She gave a small cough. "I have taken it upon myself to assist some of those freedom fighters, here and there, in my own small way, to make sure the instability in Nirmathas continues to protect Lastwall."

"Remarkable." Merihim whistled in appreciation. "So you're covertly funding fighters in a neighboring nation to protect your own interests."

"Everything is politics," the Specialist murmured. "Sometimes writ large."

Temple puffed her pipe. "You're all so cynical. I shouldn't be surprised, since the whole reason you're valuable to me is because of your naked self-interest, but I work for the greater good. Lastwall exists to protect the entire world—including those childish, squabbling nations to our south—from threats too dire for most mortals to contemplate. If aiding unrest in Nirmathas spares the entire Inner Sea from being overrun by orc hordes, I can do it without so much as a twinge of conscience."

Merihim snorted. "Do you think the Watcher-Lord would agree?"

Rodrick's grasp of local government was hazy, but as he understood it the Watcher-Lord was the crusader-in-chief.

Temple sighed. "Naturally, some of my superiors have a more black-and-white view of the world, but the Bastion is given a degree of independence precisely to deal with situations like this. The generals are good men and women, clever tacticians, indescribably brave . . . but they don't all have the subtlety of mind necessary to handle problems that can't be solved by hitting someone over the head with a warhammer. For that, they need the Bastion, and I am honored to serve."

"This Zumani, then," Merihim said. "He's the Bastion's latest puppet in Nirmathas?"

"He is a man of deeply held convictions," Bannerman said. "Who is always happy to accept large sacks of gold from anonymous benefactors. He's a pretty decent field commander, too, and he's been instrumental in keeping Molthune busy, pushing back their attempts to reclaim territory in Nirmathas. We've urged him to take more of a supervisory role, but he has the true courage of his convictions, and believes in fighting on the front lines with his people."

"Aha," Merihim said. "He got himself captured, didn't he?"

Bannerman nodded. "That he did, just a few days ago. He's been taken to a prison in Molthune. They probably think he's a common soldier, but it won't take long before someone mentions that he's one of the leaders of the revolutionary forces. Once the Molthuni realize he's a man who matters, they'll start to work on him, and try to find out his secrets. He's strong, he's brave, he's even a zealot . . . but everyone breaks eventually."

"Oh no," Eldra said. "He doesn't know the government of Lastwall was paying him, does he?"

Temple took her pipe out of her mouth, looked at it for a moment, then sighed. "We kept it secret for a while, with Bannerman approaching him covertly, hiding his connection to the government . . . but Zumani is a smart man, and eventually one of his operatives managed to track Bannerman back to the Bastion after a meeting."

"I am very good at skulking around," Bannerman said. "But even I can't compete with some of these trackers in Nirmathas. Their founder was a woodsman, and the true patriots try to follow in his footsteps. They can slink unseen across a freshly burned field. They can hide in a rock crevice almost as well as Prinn here does."

Temple puffed contentedly at her pipe, smiling as if reminiscing about a pleasant vacation. "Zumani let Bannerman know he knew the Bastion was secretly supporting him. He threatened to expose our involvement to Molthune, to let them know we were meddling in their sovereign affairs. We thought he was going to make some outrageous, impossible demand, and that we'd have to assassinate him."

"But after all that threat and bluster, all he demanded was more swords, and better armor, and alchemical explosives." Bannerman shook his head. "We would have given him those things anyway. That's patriots for you. I got the sense he didn't like being used . . . but he liked having access to our resources too much to stop, so he wanted to give himself the illusion of control."

"But now he's been captured," Merihim said. "So you need us to go assassinate him after all, before he can tell his captors he's an agent of Lastwall."

12

A Voyage to Tamran

Ha." Temple shook her head. "You'd like that, wouldn't you? A simple little murder. No, we don't want you to kill him. He's valuable to us. We want you to break him out of prison and bring him back here. Think how his legend will grow, when word arrives that he escaped from a prison in the very heart of Molthune! With a little care, we could have another Nirmath on our hands."

"I hope not," Eldra said. "If he's *too* effective, there might be some risk of him turning Nirmathas from a chaotic mess into a fully functioning country, and then you'd have to assassinate *him*—just like you did Nirmath."

"That is a scandalous accusation." Temple's bland voice gave nothing of her thoughts away. "But if you want to believe we killed Nirmath in order to keep his fledgling nation from growing too strong and stable, please do. I support anything that makes you respect and fear my office."

"Another retrieval," Merihim said. "At least we've got some practice, and this target won't try to stab us with shit-covered spikes."

"True, but the entire nation of Molthune, or at least those portions you encounter, will be against you," Bannerman said. "Still, it shouldn't be too difficult for people with your resources."

"What do we know about his situation?" Merihim said. "I'd rather not charge in blind."

Temple shrugged. "We have some sources in Molthune, though none in a position to help us directly. We know Zumani is being held in a prison not far from the border with Nirmathas. It's basically a fort, but it's a convenient place to hold captured Nirmathi for interrogation and execution."

"So we're supposed to break into a prison and mount a daring rescue?" Rodrick said.

"I don't care *how* you get him out. Loud or quiet, it's your choice, as long as the operation can't be traced back to Lastwall. We can't be seen to take sides, or Molthune *will* try to attack us—they're a prideful bunch. If you can get Zumani out of Molthune, Bannerman has some contacts who are less motivated by zeal and more motivated by gold who'll help you on the journey back."

"A jailbreak and then babysitting. Delightful." Merihim tapped a fingertip against her pursed lips for a moment. "We could ask Zumani a few pointed questions, you know—find out if the Molthuni got anything out of him. There's no need to drag him all the way back here."

Temple raised an eyebrow. "How thoughtful of you. I prefer to handle discussions with my agents personally. Even if I were to delegate the responsibility, you aren't the person I'd choose to speak for me, Merihim."

The devilkin sighed. "Fine. It doesn't matter how you choose to use my year of service, though I'm wasted on trivialities likes this. All right. It's a journey of, what, two hundred miles?"

"A bit more," Temple said. "Bannerman will take you. He'll also send me regular updates. You should have plenty of time to plan your plans and plot your plots before the time for action arrives. Let Bannerman know if you need anything in particular before you go." She gathered her files and strolled out.

Bannerman smiled at them toothily, peering at each of them in turn from beneath his lank hair. "It should be a relatively peaceful journey, at least until we get close to the border with Molthune. We'll leave tomorrow."

"Can we take some liquor on the trip?" Rodrick said. "If it's going to be peaceful anyway, we should be able to drink."

Bannerman ignored him. "We're going to travel fast, because time is limited. They've only had Zumani captive for a few days, and he was taken with a number of other fighters, so with luck the Molthuni have no idea yet that he's a man of importance. That's one advantage to the . . . informal fighting style . . . the Nirmathi use. No one down there wears rank insignia, so it's possible for leaders to remain anonymous. We want to get there before they realize what they have and move him to a more secure location, or put in better safeguards. We're in a hurry, so I'm requisitioning a longship with a crew of rowers. Be glad you lot have skills that Temple considers worth using—less useful prisoners will be heaving the oars on our trip. I do reserve the right to chain any of you down in the galley if you misbehave, though. Any questions?"

Merihim held up a finger. "Not so much a question as a demand. The Specialist will need access to alchemical supplies. If we're going to break someone out of jail, we need to be able to blow things up. Prinn might also need some items—amulets and such—I'll have him draw up a list. Eldra? Rodrick? Any requests?"

"The aforementioned liquor."

"I could use new shoes. My best pair got ruined in the Fangwood."

"Gold," Hrym said. "Not that anyone *asked* me."

Bannerman grunted. "I'll provide anything that seems plausible. We sail in the morning. I'll be around to collect you a bit before dawn."

"I'm beginning to develop an aversion to travel by water." On their last day aboard ship, Rodrick stood in the bow, leaning on the rail, the wind blowing into his face, hair streaming from his brow. It was an impressive pose, and Eldra *seemed* duly impressed, standing close to him, her head resting on his shoulder as they watched the waters of the lake shimmer in the sunlight. There were fishing boats off in the distance, and birds flying low, and all in all, it was an idyllic scene. You'd never know they were sailing through war-torn Nirmathas, gliding smoothly across the water, their ship driven alternately by the rowers below and the odd favorable wind billowing the sails and giving the prisoners in the galley a rest.

Eldra traced her fingertip in a small circle on his forearm. "Why's that? I like the air and the breeze."

Hrym spoke up, voice muffled in the sheath at Rodrick's hip. "Last time we were on a ship, we were sailing *away* from trouble. It's not the water's fault."

Rodrick shook his head. "Let's just say I've had some bad experiences in lakes. I spent some weeks living on an island in one, doing hard manual labor every day."

"That explains these." She gave his bicep a squeeze. "The result of good honest labor."

"Ha!" Hrym said. "A phrase to make Rodrick tremble."

He sighed. "I wish I were stupid enough to believe you felt genuine affection for me, Eldra."

"Mmm. I'd assure you it *is* genuine, but you wouldn't believe me." She went up on tiptoe and pecked him on the cheek. "Such a shame, to see such cynicism in one so young."

Rodrick leaned away and looked into her entirely open and guileless face. "Young? Eldra, you're probably a decade younger than I am. If I were even a few years older, I suspect I'd have fatherly impulses instead of . . . the impulses I actually have."

She chuckled. "It's possible I'm older than I look."

"I've seen the magic women can do with a bit of paint and powder, and a judicious understanding of where to stand in relation to light sources. But I've *also* seen you just awake, sleeping in the dirt in a forest, and you didn't look noticeably older then."

"There's the magic of cosmetics, Rodrick, and there's *actual* magic." She leaned her head back against him. "Would you like to know a secret about me? One almost no one knows? Apart from Temple, who dragged it out of me with spells that compelled truth. And Bannerman, I suppose."

"You want to take me into your confidence in order to strengthen our bond and enhance the likelihood that I'll step in front of a spearpoint to save you at some point?"

"No, silly. I just like to brag. The other things are just happy side effects."

"By all means, do go on."

"I must swear you to secrecy. And you, too, Hrym. There are those who hold terrible grudges, you know, and I'd rather they didn't hear about my current name and location, even third- or fourth-hand."

"I promise not to tell unless I'm offered enough money to overcome that promise," Rodrick said. "But it would take a *lot* of money, and no one has any reason to ask me, so I think you're safe."

"What he said," Hrym added.

"Who would have expected an honest oath from a thief? Good enough." She took a breath. "I am, as of my last birthday, eighty-eight years old."

Rodrick turned his head and squinted at her. "If you're dressed in an illusion, it's a good one. I've seen you move, too—you don't move like someone the age of my dead great-grandmother."

"It's not an illusion. Have you ever heard of the sun orchid elixir?"

"Of course," Hrym said. "Magical potion that restores youth, made by alchemists in some awful desert land to the south."

Eldra nodded. "Only a few vials are produced each year, sold for extraordinary sums. They tend to be purchased by the most wealthy families in the world."

"Am I to assume you're a dowager duchess or something, then?" Rodrick said. "Spent your fortune on the elixir of youth, and turned to crime in your impoverished desperation?"

Eldra laughed. "Not exactly. I *am* a Conservatory-trained courtesan. I moved to one of the great capitals—I won't say which one, a girl needs some secrets—and began my career. I was the adored mistress of several high-ranking nobles, and even the occasional artist—I have a weakness for musicians, they often have such gifted hands—and I did quite well for myself. My lovers tended to be generous, and I'm exceptionally good at investing. But, of course, youth and beauty fade, so before I could lose those assets, I moved to a neighboring country, reinvented myself with a rather less colorful past as a fresh émigré from Jalmeray, chose a young noble, and manipulated him into pursuing me until I agreed to marry him." She sighed, wistfully, and Rodrick wondered if the wistfulness were genuine. "Eobard was good to me, a devoted husband, and a doting father to our children. He never had the sort of ambition I did, though, and was content to putter around the ancestral family estates. Marrying me—the 'exotic' Vudrani woman, as his family called me—was a wildly rebellious and scandalous thing for him to do . . . but it seemed to fulfill his allotted lifetime desire for scandal. He was never unkind to me, but eventually his ardor faded, and we essentially led separate lives. I kept myself busy, running the house, exerting an iron grip on the society of our village, raising up and dashing down hopeful social climbers as the whim took me, but it was all so petty. Eventually my husband died as he'd lived, wandering aimlessly around the countryside, hitting the long grass with a stick, his health sapped by a lifetime of eating heavy puddings and fatty hams. I never could get the cooks at the house to learn how to make good Vudrani cuisine."

Remembering the oddly spiced dishes he'd alternately enjoyed and been terrified by in Jalmerary, Rodrick murmured, "I expect not."

"It was then that I took stock of my life. The estates passed to me when my husband died, but I didn't want them. My children were grown, with children of their own, settled in their own lives. They visited for the funeral, of course, and wrote slightly more letters than usual in the months following Eobard's death, but we'd never been close, not since they were young. I was, in short, *bored.* I still maintained a secret correspondence with some of my old friends, from my previous life as a courtesan, and a letter reached me with a bit of interesting news: a man I'd once known, and with whom I'd parted on bad terms because he was something of a brute in his personal affairs, had successfully bid on the sun orchid elixir. The thought of that pig having his youth and vigor restored was appalling to me. I resolved to prevent it."

"How did you manage that?"

"Oh, I was trained in all sorts of arts at the Conservatory. They follow what you might call an interdisciplinary approach to education. I had, in my former life, occasionally needed to steal things from the guilty, or plant incriminating things on the innocent, and I'd developed certain contacts among unsavory portions of society. Of course, all my contacts were quite old and retired themselves by then, but they were able to put me in touch with conditionally trustworthy members of the new generation."

"Ha. Conditional trustworthiness. 'If you pay me more than anyone else does, you can trust me.'"

"Exactly so." She squeezed his arm. Was she *really* almost ninety? It seemed outlandish, but he'd been visited by a dark goddess and stared a demon lord in the face in the not-so-distant past, and his best friend was a talking magical sword, so he was hardly one to dismiss outlandish claims just on the basis of their outlandishness.

Eldra went on. "I left a note saying I couldn't go on living without my Eobard, and left certain signs to make it appear I'd drowned myself in a lake not far from our estate. I left a scarf in the mud on the shore, things like that. There was no body to recover, of course, but it's a very deep lake, known to be home to a family of aquatic ogres, so no one was likely to look very hard, and even if they did, they would assume the lake-ogres ate my corpse. I took my secret store of jewelry and gold and returned to the capital where I'd once made such an illustrious career, and put together a team. It cost me almost everything I had, but my plan worked: we intercepted the heavily armed caravan delivering the sun orchid elixir, and swapped the potion for a vial of colored water that appeared identical. I think one of my crew intended to betray me and take the elixir for himself, but he never had the chance: as soon as the vial was in my hand, I uncapped it and drank it, right there in the forest by the road. I was instantly transformed." She shuddered. "The process of aging in reverse is not *entirely* pleasant—your skin and every muscle tightening, your body purging itself of toxins—but the end result was most acceptable. I still like to imagine the look on my old acquaintance's face when he realized the potion he'd sold off most of his estates to purchase didn't have any effect."

"So you mean to tell me you've got the mind of a ninety-year-old in the body of a twenty-year-old?"

She slapped him lightly on the arm. "Oh, stop. You don't think I look twenty."

"Perhaps twenty-three," he conceded. "Sorry. The flattery is habitual."

"You're still wrong. It's hard to be sure, but I think the elixir restored me to about eighteen years of age, physically. That was ten years ago, so this body is probably about twenty-eight. I've always aged well."

"What have you been doing for the past ten years?"

"Trying to make a fortune sufficient to bid on another batch of the elixir in, oh, another twenty or thirty years? Or else enough money and information to stage another heist . . . though it's a trick I'd hesitate to repeat often. The man I stole the elixir from has since died, and good riddance, but the alchemists of Thuvia are rich and influential and probably don't like people stealing their elixir. It's bad for business if the bidders think they'll be robbed, after all. It's possible they're still looking for me."

"What makes you think I won't write them a letter offering them information about your whereabouts in exchange for a hefty purse?" Rodrick said.

She stroked his arm. "The fact that we're both slaves to the Bastion of Justice, mainly. We've got other things to keep us occupied, and if you can get a message to a foreign power while you're under Temple's thumb, I'll be the first to applaud your ingenuity. After our year of service is over, I'll disappear like a bit of dandelion fluff on the wind . . . or a corpse sinking into a lake full of ogres." She leaned over and breathed in his ear. "Besides, after a few more months together, you'll be so devoted to me you'd never even consider turning me in to my enemies."

"You sound awfully sure of yourself."

"I've been doing this since before your father was born, Rodrick."

"It'll take more than stroking my arm and murmuring in my ear to win my devotion, Eldra."

"Ah, but making you *wait* for it means you'll appreciate it that much more."

"Yes, but now that I know you're a grandmother . . ."

"Rodrick, Rodrick. You said it yourself: a lifetime of knowledge in a young, strong body. The perfect combination of experience and . . ." She pressed her body up against his. "Capability."

"When you put it that way." Rodrick's voice was a bit hoarse.

"Humans are disgusting," Hrym said.

Eldra clucked her tongue. "I thought you'd appreciate the presence of an old woman, Hrym. I must make a nice change from all these impetuous youngsters."

"Ha. You're all children as far as I'm concerned. What's ninety years? I'm thousands of years old."

"Hrym, you weren't even conscious for most of that time," Rodrick objected. "And much of it you can't even remember."

"What do you expect?" Hrym said. "They say the memory is the first thing to go."

Bannerman strode toward them across the deck. "No fraternization among the Volunteers."

Eldra gave him a lazy salute. "Sir, yes sir."

The crusader pointed across the water. "You see that?"

Rodrick squinted. "I see the shore, and maybe some shacks and piers."

"Yes, indeed." Bannerman clapped him on the shoulder almost hard enough to make him stumble. "That is the mighty city of Tamran, capital of the great nation of Nirmathas, and most likely your last chance to sleep on anything resembling a bed for a while."

13

A Border Crossing

Tamran looked like an overgrown fishing village. If this is the capital, Rodrick thought, what must the hinterlands look like? Of course, he'd seen a map of Nirmathas, so he knew the answer: it looked like a huge forest full of valuable natural resources, and probably lots of monsters.

Eldra stood on the dock, wrinkling her nose as she looked around. "Bannerman, are you sure this is the right city? Half these buildings are made of new wood. The place looks like it's only been here a few months."

Bannerman nodded. "Tamran has been occupied half a dozen times by Molthune's armies in the past century. The Molthuni can never hold it for long, though. The citizens don't resist, they let the occupiers settle in without a fight . . . but then, at night, guerrillas sneak in and slit throats, and poison food, and make people disappear. The army always retreats eventually. One time they burned the whole city to the ground first." Bannerman chuckled. "If there's one thing the people of Nirmathas have, besides a sheer bloody-minded refusal to be conquered, it's *wood*. When your whole nation is built around a huge forest, rebuilding isn't a particular hardship, so they just put up new houses on the ashes of the old."

"They should build a wall," Eldra said. "It would be cheaper than rebuilding a whole city."

No they shouldn't, Rodrick thought.

Merihim wandered over, shaking her head inside the recesses of her cloak. She was entirely covered with cloth, and wearing gloves as well, because her devil-touched nature was too obvious to easily disguise. Devilkin were hardly unknown in the region—long ago Molthune and Nirmathas had both been part of devil-worshiping Cheliax—but she preferred to avoid the attention her red skin inevitably drew. "No they shouldn't," she said. Rodrick glared at her for voicing his own thought, but she didn't notice. "A wall is a terrible idea. Build a wall and you're in a siege situation. Sieges are all about time and resources. You can win a siege behind city walls if you've got the time and resources to outlast your opponents, but in that case, you want the besieging army to come from far away. The way you win is, you make it too *expensive* for them to keep besieging you. Molthune has more resources than Tamran, though, and their supply lines are short because we're so close to their border. The Molthuni could blockade the docks, and keep supplies from getting into the city by land, and starve the city out. No, a wall's a losing proposition here. The way they do it's better: let the enemy come in, don't give them a force to fight, and then pick them off with small raids. It's your basic asymmetrical warfare, and it's the only way an outmatched ragtag bunch of rangers and hunters can hope to fight an actual military force."

Bannerman looked at Merihim with something like respect. "All true. Tamran used to have a wall, but they tore it down ages ago, for just those reasons."

Rodrick tried not to grind his teeth. Bad enough Merihim was in charge. Did she have to go around proving how qualified she was to be in charge all the time, too? He could have spoken up and said the same thing, but he hadn't wanted to contradict Eldra when she was being so warm toward him.

"That's how we're going to get Zumani out, too." She caught Rodrick's eye and smirked at him. "A small, flexible force can do disproportionate damage to a larger and better-provisioned enemy."

"Flies can irritate an elephant," the Specialist said. "But it's surprisingly hard for an elephant to kill flies."

"It's easy for soldiers to kill people, though," Hrym said. "But maybe I'm being too literal. I've never quite gotten the hang of metaphors."

Bannerman led them inland, past houses on stilts and over rickety, haphazard piers and bridges across the marshy land. Eventually they reached streets of packed dirt, and he took them to a small cottage with an incongruously solid door and stout lock. Bannerman unlocked the door and ushered them into a dim, fish-smelling, single-room dwelling. "Our safe house."

"I've never felt safer." Eldra nudged a filthy pallet with the toe of her shoe.

Bannerman lit a lantern—burning some kind of fish oil, apparently, based on the increased stench. He rolled back the pallet, brushing aside a scattering of straw, and revealed a trapdoor set into the floor. He hauled the hatch open and descended the stairs he revealed, lantern in hand, and the others followed.

The basement was three times the size of the cottage above, with walls of mortared stone. Bannerman went around the room, lighting other lanterns. "No one looks for a basement this close to the lake, because any hole you dig tends to fill with water. We used some magic to keep that from happening here, I'm told. We called ahead with all your special requests. You should find everything you need for your excursion into Molthune."

The Specialist rushed to a long table against one wall, set with a wide array of beakers, tubes, retorts, alembics, and vials, near an apothecary cabinet. Merihim lifted the lid on a crate, said, "Ooooh," and lifted out a pair of daggers. Eldra opened up a wardrobe and made a noise of amusement or pleasure or both and ran her fingers along a row of dangling gowns. Prinn started knocking spiderwebs out of high corners and then shoving the sticky filaments into a pouch, but that was sorcerers for you, assuming that's what he even was.

Rodrick went over to the Specialist and looked glumly at all the glassware. "I don't suppose you can use any of this stuff to make something good to drink?"

"Mmm? Alcohol, you mean? Alcohol is easy. It's just sugar and time, really. But we don't have much of the latter."

Bannerman clapped Rodrick on the shoulder, which was a bit like having a tree fall on you. "I've got a flask in my boot, Rodrick, full of the finest corn liquor in Lastwall. Which, given that our patron nation is full of abstemious crusaders, isn't high praise, but it's better than the nothing you've been drinking otherwise. Temple doesn't want you to have so much as a nip, on the principle that if you *want* some you probably shouldn't be *allowed* any, but I've got a certain amount of discretion as field commander. I'll tell you what: If we get Zumani safely away, and you help the mission more than you hinder it, we'll celebrate in the safety of the Fangwood and I'll let you get so drunk we'll have to tie you to your horse the next morning."

"Are you trying to motivate me?" Rodrick said. "Do you think I can be manipulated that easily?"

"For you, Hrym, I've commissioned a scabbard of solid gold as a reward for successfully completing this mission."

"So I'd be . . . *surrounded* by gold?" the sword said.

"It's impractical for carrying every day," Bannerman said, "because it's rather heavy, but I thought you might enjoy resting in it when you're not on duty."

"Surrounded. By *gold.*"

"Assuming we succeed in our mission and make it back to the Bastion safely, yes, I'll present it to you personally. And as Temple told you: we don't lie."

Rodrick scowled. "Hrym gets gold, and I get whatever liquor is left in your flask? Doesn't that seem a bit unequal to you?"

"Perhaps you should have negotiated better," Hrym said. "Besides, I do all the work. You just carry me around."

"And make tactical and strategic decisions about how best to deploy your powers!"

"No, that's what you *used* to do," Hrym said. "When we were carefree travelers. Now Merihim does all the deciding—and for a scabbard of gold I would follow her to the gates of the Abyss."

Bannerman gave Rodrick another staggering shoulder-slap. "I like to see my people happy in their work." He went to consult with Merihim, who was hiding an alarmingly growing number of knives about her person.

"Traitor," Rodrick said conversationally.

"At least it takes more than a flagon of wine to buy my loyalty."

"I don't even think the Abyss has gates. I mean, why would it?"

"Just as well," Hrym said. "I don't have legs, so I can't actually follow anyone anywhere anyway."

Crossing the border into Molthune was a disappointingly simple affair. Rodrick had hoped for secret tunnels, or maybe hiding in a concealed compartment in the back of a cart—he'd had good luck with that approach before. But instead they loaded horses with their supplies, dressed in cloaks of dirt brown and leaf green and stone gray, and set off for the Southern Fangwood, which filled the entire interior of Nirmathas.

As they entered the forest, Rodrick eyed the trees nervously, looking for telltale blooms of mold. "Are there blighted fey here, too?"

"Oh, yes." Bannerman nodded. "They say there's a demon-tainted dryad queen deep in the heart of the forest, spreading her corruption. Quite far from here, though, fear not."

"We're not expected to kill *her*, too, are we?" Merihim said. "Just in a casual way, as we pass by?"

Bannerman shook his head. "We were troubled when her influence crossed the river into Lastwall, and wanted the blighted fey there eradicated, but having her here . . . It's a problem for Nirmathas, not us. Some hero or another will doubtless saunter into the woods and face her down at some point. In the meantime, having a forest full of monsters *and* evil fey as a buffer zone between Molthune's territorial ambitions and our southern border isn't the kind of problem we're in a hurry to solve."

"Some paladins you are!" Rodrick said. "You've got a demon-haunted forest next door, and you think of it as a strategic buffer zone?"

"*I* think of it that way. Temple does, too. Some of the more traditional crusaders are extremely concerned about the demonic taint, though, and as soon as they've decisively defeated the orc hordes they'll doubtless send a party to root out the demon queen. Of course, we've been fighting the orcs for centuries now, and neither side seems close to overwhelming the other, so in the meantime, I find it's best to look for the good in a bad situation." He glanced sidelong at Rodrick. "Though if you're that bothered about the situation, I can ask Temple to consider sending you—"

"No, no, I'm just the muscle here, don't mind me."

After a few hours on a well-traveled forest trail, they reached a broad and slow-moving river, where the burned remains of a bridge stood. Bannerman looked at the charred timbers and sighed. "They think they're *helping.*"

"Who's helping?" Eldra said.

"The revolutionaries of Nirmathas. If you can call them revolutionaries when their revolution was won ages ago, more or less. Loyal sons and daughters of Nirmath, anyway. Molthune's borders tend to shift as they gain and lose ground, but basically, Molthune is on the other side of this river."

"It just looks like more forest over there," Rodrick said.

"The last straggling bit of the Southern Fangwood, yes. Amazing they haven't cut down every tree for timber yet. The Molthuni build bridges so they can march their armies across when they try to invade, and the Nirmathi destroy the bridges."

"They should leave the bridges," Merihim said. "Or even build their own, and then set watchers and ambushes on this side."

"Oh, they do that sometimes, too. But it's not as if the forces in Nirmathas are all that well organized. It's more a bunch of loosely cooperating militias, led by assorted zealots. There's always *some* group that sees a bridge and can't think of anything better to do than tear it down. Ah well. I suppose that sort of thing keeps them occupied. Makes it a bit difficult to get across the border, though. There's a place we can ford some distance to the west—"

"Rodrick?" Merihim said. "Would you mind?"

"You speak, and we obey." Rodrick drew Hrym and pointed the glittering blade at the river, where a crust of ice began to form, slowly extending a bridge of white frost across the span.

Bannerman whistled. "I saw you do that to the pond up north, but I didn't realize you could freeze a flowing river this wide."

"Everyone underestimates me," Hrym said. "Do you think white dragons who *look* like white dragons get treated that way?"

"If you were more dragonish it would inspire a different reaction, it's true," Rodrick said.

"Draconic," the Specialist said absently, and tested the ice with his foot, first tentatively, then stomping, then jumping up and down with both feet. "Seems solid enough." He mounted his horse and persuaded it across, muttering to himself about temperature differentials and energy expenditures as he went.

The others followed, and once they were all across, Rodrick gestured with Hrym, and the icy bridge started to break up, chunks of frozen river floating and bobbing gradually downstream. "So that's it? We're in Molthune? I can't say it's any worse than

Nirmathas, but at the same time, it's not any better." That wasn't entirely true: the dirt trail Bannerman led them to was wider here, and meandered through the trees rather less.

"Borders are just lines drawn on a map." Eldra rode up alongside him. "The land doesn't know anything about them."

"Not *just* lines. Sometimes they've got walls, and armed guards, and gates and things."

Bannerman nodded. "They've tried that sort of security along this border, but the forts all get burned down, torn down, or undermined. Any time the Molthuni move a sizable force into any sort of permanent emplacement too close to the border, they become a target of hit-and-run raids. Doesn't stop them from trying. The dance goes on and on."

Prinn suddenly pulled his horse up short, leapt from the saddle, and ran some distance down the trail. Merihim raised a hand to call a halt, and even Bannerman obeyed instantly.

The sorcerer returned and went to Merihim, who leaned down in her saddle to hear his report. Rodrick had still never heard the man's voice, but he imagined it sounded like wet maggots writhing and dry paper crackling all at once. Merihim straightened up. "We've got a problem."

14

A Red Plume

Merihim spoke in a low voice, but Rodrick could hear her well enough. "Prinn says there are people hiding in the forest up ahead, at least a dozen of them, and well armed." She gestured, and the sorcerer slipped off into the trees on foot.

Bannerman drew his sword, which was short and heavy and looked very sharp. The Specialist slid down from his horse, and after a moment's thought, Eldra did the same. Merihim nodded at them, and Eldra handed the bridle of her horse to the Specialist and then went into the woods, on the opposite side of the trail from Prinn. They probably had special standing orders and things. Merihim hadn't bothered to give Rodrick any instructions. He knew his role if things got violent: knock people down or freeze them in place or both.

"If they're with the Molthuni military, killing them could be a bad idea," Merihim said. The fact that they were outnumbered two to one, minimum, didn't seem to concern her. Which Rodrick supposed was fair. He could handle four or five without much trouble, with Hrym in his hand, assuming they didn't come prepared with spells to neutralize Hrym's powers. Prinn looked like he could kill a legion without even having to think about it much. The Volunteers *were* a formidable lot. Rodrick thought, briefly, of the sort of things they could accomplish working as a team *without* the interference of Lastwall—the thefts they could pull off!—but then dismissed the idea as foolishness. He'd operated in crews before, but it was hard to imagine this particular group working together if they weren't forced to do so.

"Agreed," Bannerman said. "We may need the element of surprise to break into the prison, and if the local forces are on alert, that becomes much more difficult."

"We—" Merihim began, but was interrupted by a short man with a wide-brimmed hat sporting a long red feather.

The man bowed, sweeping off his hat and flourishing it, replacing it at a rakish angle when he straightened. "Welcome to Molthune, weary travelers. My name is Karstan, and I'm delighted to meet you."

"We're not all that weary," Bannerman growled.

"Nonsense. Your horses must be exhausted, too. Those saddlebags are bulging, and I'm sure the weight is terrible. I've come to help lighten your load."

Merihim swept back her hood and smiled a terrible smile. "Are you a bandit, then?"

The man shook his head, seemingly unimpressed by her crimson skin. "You wound me. Have you heard of privateers? Captains of sailing ships given a commission by the government to commit blatant acts of piracy—as long as they commit them against the enemy? I have a similar arrangement with the leaders of Molthune. The regular military has a . . . less than successful track record when it comes to dealing with the rebels in the forest. I persuaded them that a small force composed of men loyal to Molthune but unsuited for traditional military service could be useful. My men and I are a sort of . . . pilot program. Call us privateers of the wood."

Bannerman leaned forward on his horse and looked down at the man. "So you get to prey on any Nirmathi who cross the border. Fascinating. Of course, we're not Nirmathi."

"You're wearing cloaks that blend in with the forest. That's a very rebel sort of thing to do."

"Nevertheless. We are simple travelers, and uninvolved in your local squabbles. Will you let us pass?"

The man shook his head, almost sorrowfully. "Would that I could! But I just don't believe you. You just have that Nirmathi *look* about you."

Merihim snorted. "*I* look Nirmathi?"

Bannerman objected, too. "When have you known a Nirmathi rebel to pretend to be anything else? Screaming defiance in the face of death is more their style."

The bandit shrugged. "Perhaps you're a particularly crafty rebel. I will say, it's difficult to tell a dead civilian from a dead rebel. Let's put it this way: My worldview is simple. You're either filthy rebels, or loyal Molthuni. If you're the former, then I have every right to kill you and strip your corpses. If you're the latter . . ." He spread his hands and smiled. "Then you'll willingly donate all your worldly goods to the cause, and leave here alive and well. I'll even let you keep a couple of horses. You can always ride double. I'll lose out on the bounty Captain Lewton pays me for bringing in captive rebels, but it's a long ride to the fort, and I'm not in the mood to deal with a lot of prisoners. It's such a lovely day."

"How formal do you think their relationship with the government is?" Merihim said.

"Do you mean will anyone miss them?" Bannerman shook his head. "I doubt it. The Molthuni are very regimented. Employing roving bands of privateers is hardly their usual approach. If Karstan's story is true at all, I think he's just made an arrangement with some lower-level officer with local authority."

Karstan clucked his tongue. "I see you're contemplating violence. I really wouldn't recommend it. I have a force of twenty men, you see, including some perched in trees with bows trained on you at this very moment—"

An arrow struck him in the neck, and he gurgled—the expression on his face would have been *almost* comical, if it hadn't been for the spurting blood—and fell to his knees. Bannerman spurred his horse forward, disappearing around a bend in the trail. Screams echoed on both sides of the forest.

"Did you want us to . . . do anything?" Rodrick said.

"Against a dozen bandits?" Merihim shrugged. "I suppose if any of them stagger past in their panic to escape Prinn and Eldra and our fearless liaison, you can cut them down."

The Specialist took a book from his saddlebag and started reading.

After ten minutes, Prinn came back, wiping his hands on the shredded remains of someone else's shirt. Eldra returned soon after, carrying a bow. She looked down at the dead bandit chief, then turned a dazzling smile on Rodrick. "Not a bad shot, was it? I would have put an arrow through his eye, but the angle was wrong." She picked up the dead man's hat and put it on her head, feather poking up jauntily. It looked quite fetching on her.

Bannerman rode back to the party, his boots and the flanks of his horse speckled with blood. He'd had heavy cavalry training, Rodrick suspected. Crusaders were murder on horseback. "Took a few of them down. The rest broke and ran."

Merihim nodded. "I think Prinn finished off the ones that tried to hide. Did they have anything worth taking?"

"I'm not a corpse-picker," Bannerman growled.

The Specialist didn't look up from his book. "It's an honorable profession."

The crusader snorted. "Judging by their weapons, they weren't very successful privateers. I think we were the richest pickings they've encountered in a while."

"I suppose it's good we got a bit of exercise," Merihim said. "Though when I think what I could accomplish with this crew, if I had my own way . . ."

Rodrick scowled at the echo of his own thoughts.

LIAR'S BARGAIN 133

"Perhaps you'll forge bonds of fellowship and continue to work together after your year of service is done," Bannerman said. "I only ask that you try to commit your crimes within the borders of Lastwall so we can arrest you and press you into another term of service."

"It's so nice to be appreciated," Merihim said.

The Specialist handed his spyglass to Rodrick, who peered through the tube at the distant fort. The prison was walled with timber poles sharpened to points, with guard towers at each corner and foot patrols on the outside. There was only one gate, heavily guarded. The area around the prison was scoured, every tree uprooted, so the soldiers had clear sightlines in every direction. The Volunteers were lined up on their bellies behind the ridge of a low hill about five hundred yards to the east, the only thing approximating cover anywhere in the vicinity.

"It would be helpful if we could fly," Merihim said.

"Difficult," the Specialist said. "Not *impossible*, but . . . difficult."

"We could tunnel in," Eldra said. "By 'we' I mean . . . someone. I don't shovel."

"They send out patrols at regular intervals," Bannerman said. "I suspect they'd notice an extensive mining operation in the vicinity, and also it would take too long."

"I know I'm the brute force here," Rodrick said, "but I don't think charging in with magic blazing and bombs flying is the right approach, due to all the snipers and the fact that we'd have to do the charging over a rather large distance, giving them ample time to shoot."

"Subterfuge it is, then." Merihim rolled on her side and looked them over. "Bannerman, I'll need you to—"

He shook his head. "I'm your escort, not part of your team. If you go in there and never return, I'm the one who goes back and tells Temple we need to assemble another batch of Volunteers. I'll be back in the woods waiting for your triumphant return."

Merihim sighed. "The Specialist looks too old, I'm too red, Eldra is too pretty, and Prinn is too . . . Prinn-ish. It'll have to be you, Rodrick."

"Naturally. I am, as always, the best choice. But what am I the best choice *for*?"

"That hat looks better on Eldra." Merihim reached out and adjusted the feather while Rodrick stood stoically. "But you'll do. Try to look dashing and disreputable."

"So he should just be himself, then." Eldra chuckled.

"No, I said *dashing*. All right. Prinn, Specialist, are you ready?"

The old man nodded dolefully. His hands were bound with rough rope, and another loop went around his neck. Prinn was similarly tied, and a rope around his waist connected him to the Specialist, and from there, to the back of Rodrick's horse.

"Are we sure this is the right fort?" Rodrick said.

Merihim shrugged. "Bannerman said it probably was—it's the closest to the area where the bandit was operating." The crusader had taken his horse and gone, telling them to meet him near the site of the bandit massacre when they had Zumani in their hands. "If we're wrong, and it doesn't work . . . I'll have to trust you to improvise. Temple will be cross if the man we're supposed to rescue dies in the fighting, though, so try to follow the plan, all right?"

Rodrick drew himself up to his full height, back straight. "I am very good at pretending to be things I'm not."

"Like a warrior, and a leader of men, and a hero, and—"

"Thank you, Hrym, I think you've made your point." Rodrick unbuckled his sword belt, reluctant to part with Hrym, but knowing he wouldn't be allowed to carry such a weapon into the fort, even if the plan went perfectly.

"I'll take good care of him." Eldra accepted the belt and buckled it around her own waist, resting her hand on Hrym's hilt.

Rodrick mounted his horse and took the rope attached to Prinn and the Specialist. "Try to look like unhappy captives, gentlemen."

Their expressions didn't noticeably change: the Specialist looked a bit gloomy and preoccupied, and Prinn looked like a murderous rodent.

"Excellent work."

Rodrick rode for the fort at a walking pace with his "prisoners" in tow, watching the tiny figures in the guard towers grow incrementally larger. He could practically *feel* the arrows pointed at him; they made his eyeballs itch. He kept smiling, though, and sat relaxed in his saddle, and rode up to the gates without being shot. One of the two foot patrols approached him, crossbows trained on him and his captives.

A small panel slid open on the heavy gate, and a pair of rather suspicious-looking eyes peered out. "What do you want?"

"I've come with gifts for Captain Lewton: a pair of captured rebels."

The man frowned. "You're wearing the right hat, but you've got the wrong face. Where's what's-his-name?"

"I'm afraid our valiant leader Karstan was . . . unavoidably detained. I'd be happy to tell the captain about it."

The man sighed. "Irregular. Very irregular. I hate irregular. Hold on. Boys, don't kill him yet."

The Specialist sat down in the dirt and began drawing with his fingertip. Prinn stared at everyone like a bird of prey would stare at a field mouse, which wasn't a bad look for a defiant captured revolutionary, actually.

"Nice weather, eh?" Rodrick said. The patrolmen stared at him, crossbows unwavering. "The farms could use some rain, I suppose, but I like it dry. I'm sure you're the same, you work outside too.

I like the fresh air, myself. Say, do you happen to have any dice? Since we're waiting anyway, we could play a game . . ."

The panel slid open. "The captain says disarm them and send them in."

"I've just got this sword here." Rodrick patted the scabbard lashed to the saddle, which held some sort of saber he had no idea how to wield with any finesse. "I disarmed these gentlemen already and distributed their paltry arms among my men."

"Dismount," one of the patrolmen barked. The other had chivvied the Specialist to his feet and was patting him down. Prinn began to struggle wildly, attempting to *bite* through the ropes with his teeth, and the patrolman turned to him, wrestling him down, while the other tried to find a clear shot with his crossbow.

15

PRIVATEERING

Rodrick shouted in alarm and dismounted, then waded in to help the patrolman wrestling with Prinn. He had the pleasure of punching Prinn in the jaw, making the man rock back on his heels. Prinn held up his hands and ducked his head in submission. All part of plan, but there was glittering hate in the sorcerer's eyes when he met Rodrick's gaze. That was hardly fair. Rodrick had seen Prinn shake off blows from monstrous fey without breaking stride, and it would have taken *ten* men to hold him down if he'd been determined to escape, rather than merely causing a distraction. Nevertheless, Rodrick felt himself the target of a grudge.

As they'd hoped, once Prinn was restrained, they patted him down rather viciously and, when they found no weapons, seemed content, and didn't go back to finish checking the Specialist— which meant the vials and small bits of metal hidden under his clothes in the vicinity of his crotch went unnoticed.

"Clean!" a patrolman called.

A small door in the larger gate swung open, big enough to lead a horse through, but not to ride through. Rodrick guided his horse, trailing the restrained captives, inside. The interior of the fort was vast and sprawling, with several low buildings made of timber, a smithy, storehouses, stables, and training grounds where entirely too many soldiers were drilling and practicing archery and swordplay. The general impression was that of wood and dust and smoke and horseshit, and it all struck Rodrick as immensely dreary.

He couldn't imagine what would cause people in full possession of their faculties to sign up for the soldiering life. Most people who lived lives more conventional than his own baffled him, but to become a soldier seemed especially lunatic: if you were a tanner or a cooper or a hostler your life might be boring, but at least people trying to kill you wouldn't be a regular part of your duties.

Then again, people tried to kill Rodrick as a regular part of *his* duties, so perhaps he was in no position to judge. At least his job paid well. When it paid at all. Which it didn't at the moment. How depressing.

The guard controlling the gate was older, more grizzled, and more competent-looking than the patrolmen outside, and he examined the prisoners with occasional grunts of disapproval. "All right, then." He took the rope from Rodrick and gave it a jerk, making the Specialist stumble and Prinn tense up. "One of the grooms will see to your horse. The captain's office is just there." He nodded toward a sturdily built structure of wood flying a flag that Rodrick supposed must be that of Molthune: a red field with a sword crossed by a hammer. Ah, well, *that* explained it. If you grew up seeing a flag like that flapping all the time, no wonder you'd think a life of blood and blade and toil was a fine aspiration.

"Where are you taking us?" the Specialist said.

"Shut up, rebel."

"Nirmathas has been independent for sixty years," the Specialist said. "It's older than *me*, though not by much. Referring to me as a 'rebel,' therefore, is inaccurate and—"

Rodrick smacked the Specialist on the back of the head, earning a sullen glare and a mumbled complaint in reply. *He'd* probably hold a grudge against Rodrick, too, even though he'd only smacked the Specialist to keep the guard from hitting the old man a whole lot harder. "This one doesn't know when to shut up," Rodrick said. "I'm sure your interrogators will have a fine time with him."

"He'll have to wait his turn." The guard sighed wearily. "We caught a whole raiding party a few days back and we're still trying to find out if any of them have information worth hearing, or if they're the usual run of idiots. Go on and talk to the captain." The guard jerked the rope and the Specialist and Prinn followed him. Rodrick watched long enough to see where they were going—a large and heavily guarded structure well away from the fort's walls, with steps leading down, suggesting there was a cellar or basement underneath, too. Well, why not? When you had prisoners to do the digging for you, such construction was very cost-effective.

Rodrick strolled through the fort, whistling, nodding to passing soldiers, making his way toward the command center while trying to get a sense of troop strength at the same time. A guard at the door nodded at him without making any demands or objecting to his entrance. Once you were inside the walls, you were assumed to be friendly, unless there was a rope around your neck. The interior of the building was well made, almost more house than fortlike, and Rodrick grabbed a harried-looking aide on the way past and asked for directions to the captain's office.

Captain Lewton was about the Specialist's age, with a fair bit of gray in his beard and his drooping mustache, but he was broad across the shoulders and still looked fit and hale. He wore a neat uniform with rank insignia on the shoulders, and worked with his head bent over a sheaf of papers spread out on a desk covered in files and scroll cases. He glanced up when Rodrick entered, gestured vaguely at a hard wooden chair—the Molthuni were not a people known for their embrace of creature comforts—and then returned to his files. Rodrick was used to petty displays of power, and didn't object to being kept waiting. The longer he sat here, the more time Prinn and the Specialist had to find Zumani.

Eventually Lewton put his folder aside, sat back in his chair, and laced his fingers over his stomach. The way he looked at

Rodrick made it clear he wasn't impressed by what he saw, but Rodrick didn't mind. Some people just had terrible judgment.

"What happened to Karstan?" Lewton said eventually.

Rodrick put on a sorrowful face. "I'm afraid our fearless leader should have been a bit more fearful. He swaggered up to a rebel group to give them the bad news about their impending massacre, but they killed him before he finished gloating over our impending victory. We engaged the rebels, of course, but it was a bit chaotic, and both sides withdrew bloodied but undefeated."

The captain nodded, as if the news didn't surprise him at all. "Karstan always did have a flair for the dramatic. That made him a terrible soldier, but I thought being something of a peacock could be an asset in a bandit. He could be persuasive, too—he talked me into letting him be a 'privateer,' didn't he? Ha! The others made you the leader after he died, then?"

Rodrick nodded. "It's possible I have a small flair for the dramatic myself." He tilted his hat to a more rakish angle. "I just know there's a proper time and place for such things."

"Mmm. And you expect me to continue the arrangement I had with Karstan with *you*? He served under me—not well, it's true, but I knew from experience that Karstan was a loyal son of Molthune. I don't know you at all, and by your accent, you're from somewhere off east."

"Well spotted! I hail from Andoran. I came west, as so many have before me, in search of new frontiers and opportunities."

Lewton grunted. "And signed up with a bandit troop, even if it was an authorized one. That last part is the only thing that keeps me from simply hanging you."

"I'm always pleased to hear I won't be hanged. It never fails to brighten up my day. I can be of service to you, Captain. Indeed, I have been already. I brought two prisoners, both leaders of the resistance."

The captain looked like he might spit, if he hadn't been sitting in his own office, so he settled for a sour face. "How can you tell who's a leader, in that filthy rabble?"

"One of them is an older man, and his people fought fiercely to protect him. Once we caught him, he went on at great length about the nobility of the human spirit and how all men and women are born free only to be enslaved by tyranny and circumstance . . . and other such claptrap."

"Ah, one of the philosopher types. A few of those always spring up, even among the dirt and rocks and trees. What about the other one?"

"I'm not sure he's a leader, exactly, to be honest. But he killed four of my men and fought like a demon possessed before we brought him down, so he's certainly *dangerous*, and if he's locked up here, he's not murdering good soldiers of Molthune in midnight raids."

The captain nodded and rose. "All right, let's see what you brought me—"

A bell began to ring in the distance, a wild tolling, and the captain's gaze snapped toward the door. One of his aides leaned in and said, "There's an attack on the south wall!"

"Stay here, and don't let this man leave," Lewton snapped, pointing at Rodrick, who held up his hands to show how harmless he was.

Rodrick half-rose from his chair. "Lend me a sword instead, and I can help you repel the invaders—

"Ha!" Lewton stalked out of the office. Ah, well. He was smart enough to be suspicious of a stranger who arrived immediately before an attack on his fort. A pity, but not entirely unforeseen.

Rodrick finished rising from the chair, extending a hand and smiling widely at the young and panicked-looking aide. The man didn't take Rodrick's hand, just stared at him, so Rodrick patted him on the shoulder instead. "What kind of attack was it?" he asked.

"I—some sort of explosion, and smoke."

"That would be the bombs," Rodrick said. "Eldra's got marvelous aim."

"What are you talking aboughhrr . . ." The aide's eyes glazed over and he slumped down, Rodrick catching him and lowering him gently to the floor. The trick ring Rodrick wore, with a hollow needle on the underside, had delivered a single dose of the Specialist's sleeping potion through the aide's shoulder. The man would be under for ages.

According to Merihim's plan, all Rodrick was supposed to do now was get out of the fort, perhaps causing a few minor distractions and sowing acts of sabotage if the opportunity arose. Merihim clearly didn't want to assign him any more crucial duties—she must think that, in the absence of Hrym, Rodrick wasn't worth much. That annoyed him.

Rodrick looked at the fallen aide critically and decided he would do, though the uniform would be a bit tight across the shoulders.

Dressed in the unconscious soldier's uniform, Rodrick ran through the halls and out of the building, trying to look like he was on an important mission. There was a delightful amount of chaos in the fort: the wall was broken by bombs and ice on one side, and an impenetrable freezing fog hovered over a large portion of that area, with soldiers running into the haze and occasionally sliding back out again. Rodrick seized a passing soldier by the arm and shouted, "What's going on?"

The man wrenched free and kept running, but shouted, "Rebel attack!" as he went.

How gratifying. Eldra and a sack of bombs and Merihim and Hrym had managed to successfully impersonate a full-scale attack by the Nirmathi. All this fuss was supposed to cover the escape of Prinn and the Specialist and the rescued revolutionary leader, but Rodrick didn't see his compatriots or their charge anywhere. He moved purposefully toward the long, low building where the other Volunteers had been taken. Rodrick nodded to the guard on the door, who gripped his polearm with white knuckles. "Captain Lewton sent me to secure the prisoners," Rodrick said.

The guard, who was a head taller than Rodrick and had the flattened nose of a man who got into a lot of fistfights and didn't always win, scowled. Rodrick got the sense he was the type who'd taken up soldiering because it was a way to hit people without getting arrested for it. "They're already secure. They're in cells down there."

"Yes, but the captain thinks this is an attempt by the rebels to rescue their captured comrades, so I'm supposed to make them *even more* secure—and execute them if the attacking rebels manage to murder you and force their way in."

The man's eyes went wide. "They're coming *here*?"

Rodrick nodded. "Looks that way. They've got some kind of filthy nature magic, too—fire and ice and things. Nasty stuff."

Rodrick half expected the guard to drop his polearm and flee, but the Molthuni clearly beat serious discipline even into their more brutish recruits, because the man swallowed, put his back against the wall, and held his weapon higher. "I'll hold them off as long as I can."

"Good man." Rodrick gave him a firm handshake, very brothers-in-arms, and a moment later, the guard slumped against the wall and slid down to sit in the dirt. That was it for the Specialist's lovely potion. Rodrick should have worn more rings—he'd have to knock people out in a cruder fashion from now on. He took the guard's keys and opened up the heavy door, stepping into the gloom.

16

A Political Prisoner

Prinn was just inside the door, standing over the *very* fresh corpse of a soldier. The Specialist stood nearby, the unconscious body of a man dressed in brown rags thrown over his shoulder—the old fellow was deceptively strong. He also had the beginnings of a black eye. "Oh, hello," the Specialist said. "Glad you came. I was wondering how we'd get out—only the guard outside has keys to the outer door. I thought Prinn would have to chew through the wall."

"Always happy to be of service," Rodrick said. "Who's that sack of potatoes you've got draped over your shoulder?"

"The great revolutionary poet Zumani."

"Where are the other prisoners?" The plan had been to release everyone imprisoned here, and let that addition to the chaos help cover the escape of the Volunteers.

The Specialist shook his head dolefully. "Still locked up, and it's better that way. I'll explain later. Let's escape, hmm?"

When they emerged, there was a lot more chaos than before in the fort, and an ice-crusted hole in another wall. The freezing fog Hrym had created was confusing matters wonderfully, but eventually the soldiers were sure to realize they hadn't actually made *contact* with any enemies, and Lewton would start to figure things out. The thing about people who worshiped military order was that they seldom stayed panicked for long enough.

"Carry him." The Specialist all but tossed the revolutionary at Rodrick, who hoisted him over his own shoulder. Zumani was a slight man, almost willowy, and he smelled of dirt and sour, stale body odor. The Specialist looked around the fort, closed his eyes for a moment, nodded, and then strode off purposefully around the side of the jail. Rodrick looked at Prinn—and, to Rodrick's shock, the man gave a little shrug, as if to say, "Who knows?" before following the Specialist. Was the mad silent mage actually becoming companionable? Maybe the Volunteers *were* becoming a team, despite themselves.

Rodrick followed them, lugging Zumani, and his stomach churned as he realized they were walking across an execution ground. A gibbet stood in the center of a cleared area, with four ropes dangling over the platform, for those times when killing prisoners one by one was simply too time-consuming. Rodrick wondered what the Molthuni did with the bodies of the condemned. At least there wasn't an open mass grave next to the gallows.

"Here." The Specialist went toward the wall, waving his arms wildly at the lone guard on the gate there. "Excuse me! We've got a body to take out for burial!"

"We're being *attacked*," the guard began, but Prinn was on him in an instant, wrenching his head around on his shoulders and dropping his corpse to the ground. Rodrick winced. He never liked killing, if he could avoid it. Ending someone else's life seemed a rather extreme way to further one's agenda.

"You have keys?"

Rodrick tossed the ring of keys he'd taken off the jailhouse guard to the Specialist, who clucked his tongue. "Very poor security protocols." He opened a heavy iron padlock and dropped it into the dirt, pushed open the door, and poked his head out. "All clear," he said, opening the door.

Rodrick surveyed their path to freedom. They would have to cross a large expanse of open ground, dotted with fresh grave mounds, before they reached the concealment of the trees. Rodrick didn't relish running with an unconscious zealot over his shoulder as snipers shot arrows at him. He glanced up at the nearest watch-tower, though, and was relieved to see it was actively on fire. One of the Specialist's incendiary bombs had made that position an inhospitable one to hold.

They went through the gate, and didn't see another soul in the vicinity. Eldra and Merihim had shifted their attention to the other side of the fort, and the soldiers had turned their focus that way as well. The Volunteers rushed past the graveyard, then through a field of stumps, the trees cut down to remove cover for any approaching enemy forces.

They made it halfway to the trees before the first arrow fell. It was almost as if it magically appeared, a feathered shaft suddenly there, sticking out of a stump, alarmingly close to Rodrick. He swore, shifting Zumani around on his shoulder, hoping the man draped over his back would catch any arrows that would other-wise hit Rodrick. Sure, Temple would be displeased at the poet's death, but if Temple was shouting at Rodrick, that meant Rodrick was alive to be shouted *at*.

Suddenly something lifted Rodrick off his feet, and he began to move very quickly. After a moment of intense confu-sion he realized Prinn had picked him up, carrying the weight of Zumani and Rodrick both, and set off at a rapid clip, weaving through the stumps and avoiding falling arrows with a terrifying economy of motion. Soon they were beyond the tree line, but Prinn didn't put them down until they reached a small clearing where Merihim, Eldra, and Bannerman were waiting with their mounts. Hrym hung in a scabbard dangling from the saddle of Rodrick's horse.

Way off in the distance, there was a noise that sounded a bit like a horde of giants roaring, but even more like a very loud explosion.

As the echoes rolled away, Merihim said, "There go the delayed bombs we planted. The Specialist does good work. Where is he?"

As if summoned, the Specialist limped in, clutching his left arm close to the shoulder and looking even more doleful than usual. "An arrow grazed me. I doubt it was poisoned. If I'd been loosing arrows, they would have been poisoned."

"Why is Zumani unconscious?" Bannerman demanded, taking the man from Rodrick.

The Specialist sighed. "That is something we will have to discuss once we have made our escape."

Prinn nodded, once, sharply.

Bannerman quickly tied Zumani to the back of his horse, then mounted. "All right, let's go. We need to put some distance between ourselves and that fort. I've made arrangements to meet up with a group of Nirmathi fighters just this side of the border. They'll help us make our way north."

Before climbing on his horse, Rodrick paused beside Prinn. "Thank you for that. Saving me from the arrows, I mean."

Prinn looked at him for a long moment, and then his lips moved, transforming his face into a grim rictus. Was he trying to *smile*?

Just to be safe, Rodrick smiled back, then hurried to his horse. "Did you have fun, Hrym?"

"Oh, it was all fog, fog, fog. My talents were wasted."

"On the bright side, it wasn't hard work."

"It was still *work*, though. I'd better get that scabbard of gold at the end of all this."

"It's certainly something to look forward to."

After that, there was no talking for a while, as Bannerman pushed them at a fast pace along a fairly well-maintained trail that cut through the forest. Judging by the heaps of horse apples everywhere, mounted people used this route often, and Rodrick hoped they wouldn't run into anyone wearing Molthuni uniforms. After a while they slowed and took a less traveled path, one that meandered with the contours of the landscape rather than imposing order upon the resistant terrain.

Bannerman called a halt in the middle of nothing at all, just bushes and trees and so on, as far as Rodrick could see.

"Is this the Nirmathi camp?" Rodrick said. "They must be *very* good at camouflage."

"The soldiers will hesitate to follow us this far into Nirmathi territory, wary of an ambush—that's if they even realize we went in this direction," Bannerman said. "The camp isn't far, but before we get there, I need to know why Zumani is on the back of my horse groaning with a lump on the back of his head?"

The Specialist shrugged. "We were taken into the prison. Prinn disabled the guards easily. We announced that we'd come to save Zumani. He asked if Temple sent us, and I admitted that she had. And then . . ." The old man sighed. "He said he wouldn't come with us unless we met his demands."

Bannerman frowned. "What do you mean?"

"I mean he insisted we meet certain conditions before he would allow us to rescue him."

"That's asinine," Bannerman said.

"That's idealists for you."

"What were his demands?"

"Apparently a few elder statesmen of the movement have been captured recently. The Molthuni realized they were valuable targets, and took them to a special facility farther south for interrogation. The sort of interrogation that involves hot knives and pincers, I would imagine. Zumani insisted we rescue *them*, too, or he wouldn't go with us—he would rather, he said, be a glorious martyr to the cause. I told him it would be better to save himself now, and deal with other issues later. Zumani then threatened to reveal all his dealings with Lastwall to the Molthuni authorities if we didn't agree to his scheme."

Bannerman pinched the bridge of his nose between his thumb and forefinger. "All right. What did you do?"

"*I* wanted to lie to him, and tell him we'd be delighted to save his compatriots if he'd come along with us. Prinn, however, elected to take a more direct approach, and bashed Zumani over the head to subdue him. The other prisoners were unhappy about that— one of them struck me in the eye, which means I've been injured *twice* on this operation—so we had to push them back into their cells, lock them in, and leave without them."

"Oh, this is *marvelous*," Bannerman said. "This operation was meant to enhance Zumani's reputation, you know—the stories would have made *him* the leader of a daring prison break."

"We were told to retrieve this man, and we did," Merihim said. "It's not our fault he was uncooperative."

"Yes, but it changes our situation. We were supposed to meet up with Zumani's people, let them know he was free, and start building him up as the brave new leader of their movement, before taking him back to see Temple. Now . . . He's not likely to be very cooperative, is he? If we meet with his men, they'll almost certainly *help* him be uncooperative." He sighed. "I've got to contact Temple and see how she wants us to proceed."

"How long will *that* take?" Merihim said.

"Not very. I have a magic scroll—I can write a few words, and they'll appear on a scroll in Temple's possession, and she can write back. It's a one-use spell, unfortunately, for emergencies only . . . but I'd say this qualifies. Take a rest, eat something, make sure Zumani doesn't have permanent head trauma, and I'll see how Temple wants us to proceed."

They all dismounted, Bannerman going off to find a flat rock to write on, the others patting their horses and breaking out rations, except for the Specialist, who examined their unconscious revolutionary. The rest sat along the trunk of a fallen tree while they ate.

"Prinn tells me you improvised a bit in there," Merihim said. "Came to help them get out of the stockade."

Rodrick shrugged. "I saw an opportunity to be of assistance, and took it."

"Right. I disapprove of the show of initiative, but appreciate the apparent competence. I'll keep it in mind when I deploy you in the future."

"Oh, good. I strive to impress."

Eldra leaned her head on his shoulder and made a contented noise, which cheered Rodrick up despite himself.

"Good work throwing bombs," he said. "If you hadn't taken out that guard tower, I'd be feathered with so many arrows I'd look like a chicken."

"There was a game we played in the Conservatory, throwing a small ball at moving targets. I was champion three years running. The watchtower just *stood* there. It was easy." She had a smear of soot on the end of her nose, and Rodrick wiped it off, feeling a surge of tenderness for the ninety-year-old brazen thief of a great-grandmother. "This job isn't so bad," she said. "I'd prefer it if it paid in something other than threats, but the work itself isn't objectionable."

"Except insofar as it's *work*," Hrym said. "I'm an immortal sword of living ice. Why do I need to work at all? It's not like I need food or shelter."

"Gold, though," Rodrick said.

"Gold, though," Hrym agreed glumly.

Prinn leaned over and whispered into Merihim's ear, and she chuckled. "Prinn says to remind you that the love of gold is the wellspring of all trouble."

"True, true," Hrym said. "But what else am I supposed do? It's *gold*. The heart follows its own dictates."

The revolutionary woke up, groaning first, and then struggling. "What is this? Let me go!"

Merihim rose and went to him. "Shh, Zumani, please, you're among friends."

He looked at her and shrieked. "Devil-creature, get away from me! Are you one of the Molthuni's monstrous recruits?"

She sighed. "I work with Temple. I'm one of the people who broke you out of the fort."

"You stole me away from the struggle! I am just one man among many, and my brothers and sisters still languish in chains. I demand that you free—"

"Can we knock him unconscious again?" Merihim interrupted.

"I wouldn't hit him on the head again," the Specialist said. "We might damage him permanently. I could dose him with something, but that can have deleterious effects, too. He is ostensibly our ally, after all."

"Gag him, then, if he won't be quiet," Merihim said wearily.

Zumani declined to be quiet, so the Specialist used a few strips of cloth to gag him. The poet still struggled and complained, but it was a lot less noisy.

"Nothing's ever easy, is it?" Rodrick said.

Eldra put her hand on his knee and smiled, her cheeks dimpling fetchingly. "Nothing worth doing, anyway."

17

AN EXCESS OF CONSCIENCE

The revolutionary poet eventually settled down enough that they took out his gag, let him off the horse, and sat him down on a log to eat, though they kept his legs tied. He complained between bites, though in a more level voice. "My captivity serves to symbolize the bondage of all the Nirmathi people, who must struggle against the territorial ambitions of the Molthuni oppressors."

The Specialist chewed a bit of bread thoughtfully, then said, "You've got that wrong. This captivity doesn't symbolize anything—this is literal captivity. That other kind of captivity, the kind where you live free in the forest in the independent nation of Nirmathas, *that's* the symbolic sort of captivity. It's important to keep such things straight. Confusing the real for the symbolic is a good way to get killed."

"I knew someone who was eaten by a symbolic dragon once," Hrym said.

The Specialist cocked his head. "Do you care to explain that?"

"If you've got the gold."

Bannerman joined them, nodding to Zumani. "How are you doing?"

"I was dragged away from my compatriots, who are doubtless being tortured by the enemy."

"So you're doing better than *they* are, anyway." Bannerman took a swig from a canteen. "I don't understand you, Zumani. My people come to save you, and you make demands?"

"Some things are more important than the freedom of one man."

"The freedom of four other men, apparently?"

Zumani lifted his chin. He did look very poetic, Rodrick had to admit: sort of pale and slender and delicate-looking, despite the fact that he lived and fought in a forest. Though who knew how much he really fought? Perhaps he was just adept at encouraging others to fight. "They are leaders of four of the major militias, Bannerman. They were having a secret meeting to coordinate a large-scale operation against certain Molthuni fortifications near the border, and someone betrayed them."

Bannerman nodded. "They were taken the day before you were, Zumani. They're probably dead already. You must know that."

"If they can't be freed, we can at least liberate their bodies and make sure they're buried in the soil of Nirmathas, the land they fought and bled for!"

Bannerman squinted at him. "You want me to deploy a highly trained team of mercenaries to retrieve some corpses? Admittedly, it would be good for your image—Zumani, the man who gave the fallen heroes a proper burial. It would play well with the people. But I'm not sure it's the best use of my resources."

"Have you forgotten all the things I know?" Zumani said. "Names. Places. Times. Transactions. I have proof that Lastwall has secretly supported Nirmathas for years. If Molthune found out . . ."

"Threatening to betray your allies to your enemies isn't usually a good tactic," Merihim mused. "I'll grant there could be *some* circumstances where it's the right choice, but this doesn't seem like one of them."

"Threatening Temple and the Bastion of Justice is *never* a good tactic," Bannerman said. "You've been useful to us, Zumani. If you stop being useful . . ." He shrugged.

"I don't fear death."

Rodrick shook his head. "Why in the world *not*?"

"It's not my decision anyway, Zumani." Bannerman unrolled a scroll and looked it over. "Temple replied to my message. I told her your demands and asked if we should try to free your compatriots."

"Another prison break?" Merihim looked at Prinn, who shrugged. "How boring."

"Temple replied, 'No. Return to the Bastion by fastest route.' There it is. From here on out, it's just down to me following orders."

Zumani lifted his chin even higher. "Am I to be executed, then? Because I will not collaborate with you under these conditions."

Rodrick wondered the same thing. At least he wouldn't be expected to do the killing, if so. There seemed to be a general understanding among the group that if cold-blooded murder needed to be done, that was Prinn's department.

Bannerman shook his head. "Zumani, don't be so dramatic. Temple would greatly prefer to have you alive—she wants the opportunity to convince you of the stupidity of your ways. That said, I have a certain amount of discretion. If you slow us down, or work to inhibit our swift departure from Nirmathas, I am authorized to do what's necessary to pacify you, even if it's the sort of pacification that involves leaving you in a shallow grave. Do you understand, Zumani? Just don't make a fuss. If you cooperate, you might even end up leading your people again. We're on your side, you know. Treat us like allies, not enemies."

"I'm tired of being Lastwall's pawn."

Bannerman snorted. "Pawn? It's a partnership. True, one partner is a nation and the other is a poet, so there's a certain power imbalance there, but we've treated you fairly, and will continue to do so. Come to Lastwall peacefully and talk to Temple. Maybe the two of you can come to some accommodation that satisfies everyone."

Rodrick wasn't so sure. Temple didn't strike him as the nego-tiating type, and zealots were very difficult to threaten. Even implanting a gem in Zumani's chest and ordering him to obey could fail—the man seemed to value honor more than he feared death. The reason the gems worked so well on the Volunteers was because they were all criminals, and criminals could generally be counted on to act in their own best interests, barring a few lunatics with peculiar personal codes.

"Will you come willingly, or do we have to keep you bound and gagged the whole way back to the Bastion?" Bannerman said.

"Did you hear that birdcall?" the Specialist asked, his head cocked.

Rodrick listened, but there were lots of birds calling, and branches creaking, and leaves rustling in the wind, and all the usual noises of the forest.

"What about it?" Bannerman said.

"Oh, nothing. I'm just surprised to hear that particular birdcall in this part of the country. A fluted warbler. They have a distinctive cry, but they're mostly found much farther south."

An arrow streaked out of the forest and struck Prinn in the right shoulder, knocking him off the log. He sprang up instantly and streaked off into the woods. Eldra dropped to her belly and went slithering into the trees, Bannerman leapt up and drew his sword, Merihim jumped to hide behind a horse, and the Specialist sighed and put down his piece of bread. "That arrow looked home-made, not the standard issue produced for the Molthuni military, so these are probably Nirmathi here to liberate Zumani. Adjust your tactics accordingly."

Rodrick picked up Hrym and swung him in the direction the arrow had come from, sending out a flurry of icicles, and was rewarded with a scream and a thump as someone fell out of a tree.

"I'm here, brothers!" Zumani cried. "They have me—"

The Specialist cracked Zumani on the back of the head with the hilt of his dagger, making the poet's jaw clack closed, then thumped him again to make him fall down. The old man knelt, listened for a moment to Zumani's breathing, then joined Rodrick. "I wouldn't want to throw firebombs around here. Conditions are dry. We could easily become caught in the resulting conflagration."

Merihim reappeared, deciding that hiding behind Rodrick was better than hiding behind her horse, apparently. "We need to get Zumani out of here. Bannerman!"

The crusader was still holding his sword, looking around for someone to hit, but he joined them when Merihim beckoned. "We should have posted sentries."

"Agreed. That was my mistake."

Rodrick was astounded. To hear Merihim matter-of-factly admit she'd done something *wrong* . . . It was as unbelievable a second time as it had been the first.

"But now we need to get away," she went on. "Eldra and Prinn are out there picking off anyone they can find, but even Prinn might be outmatched by people who know the terrain. The mission is to get Zumani back to the Bastion. I say you, me, and the Specialist get on our horses and ride out of here while Rodrick and Hrym cover our escape."

"I do not approve of this plan," Rodrick said.

They ignored him as Bannerman nodded. "All right. Help me load up Zumani. We're making our way back to Tamran. Meet us at the safe house, Rodrick. Try to meet up with the others, but don't dawdle too long—we won't stay in Tamran longer than overnight, and if we get to the Bastion without you, I imagine Temple will consider you a deserter and let the gem in your chest do its work."

"There, in the trees!" Hrym shouted, and Rodrick turned his attention to swinging the blade and sending more ice shards into the branches above them, praying—to no god in particular, just in general—that he wouldn't hit Eldra. Prinn, of course, would probably be fine if a few spikes of ice hit him. An arrow in the shoulder certainly hadn't slowed him down.

The Specialist and Bannerman got Zumani onto a horse, and without so much as a fond farewell or a "Good luck," they left.

Rodrick moved hunched through the trees in the opposite direction until he could put his back against a nice wide tree. Once his rear was covered, he basically just swung Hrym in an arc, spraying ice, with occasional upward swings to pepper the tree branches with frozen shards. Leaves, needles, trees, and branches came down like hail, among bits of ice, which were even more like hail. Rodrick doubted he was inflicting much damage on the enemy . . . but no one was even *trying* to get close to him.

"Ease up for a moment!" Eldra called from somewhere to the right, and Hrym stopped spewing ice without waiting for Rodrick to ask. Eldra rose from the underbrush and hurried toward him. She'd acquired a magical cloak at some point, doubtless stripped off a foe, and its shifting patterns made her almost disappear into the trees around her, her lovely oval face seeming to float in isolation.

"Where are the others?" she said.

"Escaping. We're supposed to make our own way to the safe house in Tamran."

Eldra sighed. "That's just where we'll go, too. They have us on a long leash, don't they? I killed a few, and I think Prinn did what he usually does. I saw several men flee while shouting about ice elementals and nature magic."

"Why don't people ever assume it's a white dragon attacking them?" Hrym complained. "Ice elemental? Pfah."

"We don't spend enough time in the frozen north, Hrym," Rodrick said. "We could spend more time in dragon country, though I see certain downsides to the idea. Do you think it's safe to flee, Eldra?"

"I'd rather call it retreating than fleeing, but yes. I don't know if the Nirmathi are all gone, but I think it's harder to hit someone riding a horse with an arrow than it is to hit someone standing around debating whether or not to leave, so we should risk it."

"Should we wait for Prinn?"

Eldra shook her head. "If anyone can take care of himself, it's Prinn."

"Right. We'll just head for Tamran then." He looked around the forest. "Er. Which way is Tamran, do you think?"

"East . . . and north . . ." She squinted at the sky. "Where's the sun? We could tell directions with the sun, right?"

"Yes. The sun is behind those clouds." The whole sky was a blanket of pale gray.

"Isn't there . . . something about . . . moss? It grows on the side that gets the most sun, which around here would be . . . um . . ." Eldra squinted at the base of a tree.

"I have noticed, in the past, that moss seems to grow all over trees, without regard for cardinal directions."

Eldra chewed her lower lip, which was adorable, and meant she was worried. "Now that I think about it, Merihim or Bannerman always led us. I'm sure the Specialist knows what direction everything is. He probably knows all sorts of interesting facts about compasses and moss and the stars and things."

"How about you, Hrym?" Rodrick said. "Do you have a secret affinity for the north, or something else that can help guide us?"

"Walk, and if you hit snow, you've probably gone north."

"Very helpful." Rodrick leaned against the tree. "You know, I never thought I'd die in a forest."

18

A Dialogue

M aybe the horses know the way back home?" Eldra gestured
to the remaining animals, who were stamping nervously,
aware of all the commotion but not entirely panicked. At least the
Nirmathi hadn't managed to put arrows in *them*. That was the nice
thing about fighting a disorganized rabble. The revolutionaries
weren't as systematic in their ruthlessness as more well-trained
forces would have been.

"I suppose that's an option." Rodrick had visions of them
riding aimlessly on their horses as the beasts followed the smells of
grass and water and eventually led them either to a camp of angry
Nirmathi or a settlement of equally angry (for different reasons)
Molthuni.

"It will do in the absence of an actual plan, anyway. Perhaps
we'll meet a kindly woodcutter who can give us directions."

Rodrick opened his mouth to say something scathing, but
then realized that Eldra, despite being foreign and entirely too
fancy-looking to fit in among these coarse forest folk, probably
could charm someone into giving her directions, and possibly an
armed escort, too.

Prinn dropped out of a nearby tree, landed in a crouch, then
slowly rose and walked toward them. His shoulder was seeping
blood, but not badly, and he'd managed to get the arrow out, the
gods alone only knew how. Since Rodrick hadn't seen him *climb*
that particular tree, that meant he'd been traveling among the

treetops themselves, going from branch to branch through the forest. There was no denying the man had talent. It was a shame his personality alternated between "crazed mink" and "plank of wood."

"Prinn!" Eldra said. "Merihim and Bannerman escaped with Zumani. We're supposed to meet them in Tamran. I don't suppose you know the way back?"

Prinn stared off in the distance, and after a long moment, nodded. He swiftly packed up his belongings, and Rodrick and Eldra followed suit, though not as rapidly: cleaning up a campsite while warily trying to watch the forest in all directions in case of ambush was a complicated affair. Once they had their gear stowed on the horses, Prinn mounted and took the lead. He didn't seem in any great rush, his horse proceeding at slightly more than a walk, as Prinn swiveled his head left and right in endless arcs, watching for enemies, or omens, or who knew what.

After a time the trees thinned out and they reached a better-maintained path, and Eldra nudged her horse up to ride alongside Prinn. "May I ask you a question?" she said.

He shrugged.

"Is there a reason you only speak to Merihim, and never say a word to anyone else?"

Prinn looked at her for a prolonged interval, then nodded.

"Aha." Eldra smiled. "Did you make . . . some sort of a vow?"

Another long look, then a shrug.

"Hmm. But you don't mind *communicating*, clearly, so perhaps we can still talk, in a way?"

Shrug.

Rodrick tried to decide if what he was feeling was incredulity or jealousy or both. Was Eldra trying to charm *Prinn*? If so, would she actually succeed? Maybe he should insert himself into the conversation. He nudged his horse up closer. "Are you a sorcerer, Prinn?"

The man looked a trifle alarmed at all the attention, but he shrugged, which was as good as no answer at all. Rodrick said, "What were you and Merihim doing in—wait, sorry, we have to ask yes-or-no questions, don't we?"

"Do you have any gold, Prinn?" Hrym said, getting into the spirit of the thing, though they all ignored him.

"Unless Prinn is willing to do elaborate pantomimes, simple questions are probably best," Eldra said. "But you aren't much of an actor, are you, Prinn? Have you and Merihim been together for long?"

Prinn shook his head.

"Really! You seem so . . . strongly connected. I'd assumed it was a partnership of long standing, like Rodrick and Hrym. Have you been together for . . . five years?"

No.

"Two years?"

No.

"One year?"

Yes.

"Does she pay you well?"

No.

"Do you owe her a debt?"

No.

"She has some other sort of hold on you?"

Yes.

Rodrick was impressed. Eldra was seeking out fault lines, places where a wedge could be driven between Prinn and Merihim, and probably for no particular reason, other than the fact that knowledge was valuable. She continued in this vein for a while, asking broad questions and then narrowing them down, and determined over the course of a long ride that Prinn came from Cheliax; that Merihim was a treasure hunter; that Prinn couldn't count how many people he'd killed; that he ate so strangely because he had poor digestion, not because of any sort of ascetic vow; and that he worshiped no gods. Rodrick relaxed as he listened to her patient, chatty, but relentless interrogation technique.

She must have been an extraordinary spy; Rodrick had seen no reason to update his operating theory that all Vudrani trained at the Conservatory were spies. Imagine how much information she could get out of someone she was *sleeping* with!

Of course, he was making the assumption that Prinn was actually telling the truth. Temple said Prinn was a master of infiltration, and he'd demonstrated a great affinity for sneaking and crawling on his belly and stabbing people in the back, so that was a large assumption. The usual cues that gave you some hint about whether someone was lying or not were largely absent when you were dealing with someone who was habitually blank-faced and who only nodded, shook his head, or shrugged in response to queries.

Finally Eldra said, "Do you *like* working for Merihim?"

Prinn didn't shake his head. He didn't nod. He shuddered, and then spat off the side of his horse. He dug in his heels, driving the horse forward, and Rodrick and Eldra matched pace to keep up, which put an end to their conversation.

Soon it was too dark to ride, and they stopped at a place of Prinn's choosing, in a little depression in the forest near a creek, to make camp. Eldra kept up a bright line of chatter, but the sorcerer ignored her completely, either regretting his earlier communicativeness or simply having reached his limit of conversation. She gave up when Prinn climbed a tree and disappeared into the branches while she was in mid-sentence.

Eldra sighed and joined Rodrick, who was sitting on the ground gnawing on some jerky and trying not to think about what kind of animal the meat had come from. "I thought having an opportunity to talk to Prinn alone might yield some useful insights, but I barely scratched the surface."

"Who cares?" Rodrick said. "I mean, yes, he's a fascinating if disturbing enigma, but it's not as if he's a target you can shake down for personal profit."

"We're all stuck on this team together for the next year, Rodrick. I'd like to know who I'm working with, and where possible points of failure and disaster might be. I also have some interest in creating connections with my teammates—"

"So they'll be inclined to save your life if it ever needs saving, yes. You really think you can befriend *Prinn*?"

"He clearly needs a friend. I don't understand his relationship with Merihim, but she treats him like a well-trained dog. You and Hrym have a more equal relationship, and Hrym is *literally* an object."

"I object to being called an object," Hrym said.

"A wondrous and wise object, of course," Eldra said. "Prinn clearly hates working with Merihim. I rather think he'd prefer working with *me*, and having him as a personal bodyguard would increase my life expectancy a lot. I just have to figure out what kind of hold Merihim has on him, and how to loosen it."

"Stealing away her pet sorcerer would not be good for group cohesion," Rodrick said.

Eldra nodded. "Do you think he's a sorcerer? I've never seen him do anything that was definitely magical. Anyway, I didn't say I was going to implement the plan. But working through the possibilities keeps my mind active. Prinn acts as though he's enslaved by Merihim, and I think she's forbidden him to talk to anyone else, but how does she *enforce* that? He could clearly kill her in seconds if he felt like it, so there's some reason he doesn't. Is he doubly enslaved? Does Merihim have some magical hold over him, in addition to the hold Temple has over *all* of us? I was going to ask Prinn if he was magically compelled somehow, and if he wanted my help *breaking* that compulsion, but he stopped answering me before I could get around to that."

Rodrick chewed thoughtfully, swallowed, and said, "I don't think Merihim would hesitate to use any means at her disposal to further her goals, *whatever* those are, so you may be right. But you should keep in mind: Merihim is, somehow, formidable enough to enslave a sorcerous murder savant like Prinn . . . which means she might not be someone you want to cross, *especially* when she's in a position to choose what you do and where you go during missions."

"Oh, of course, Merihim would have to be eliminated." Eldra said that almost absently, and followed it up with a dazzling smile. "Then we could make you the tactical leader of the team. You clearly have the necessary abilities."

"Getting rid of Merihim would certainly make the next year more bearable," Rodrick allowed.

"Something to consider, hmm? A lot of angles to examine, and such a coup may not be feasible, but as a mental exercise it could help pass the time and keep our minds sharp, don't you think?"

"I think you're a very dangerous woman."

She nuzzled up against him. "I can also be very generous to those who help me achieve my goals."

"Ah, so that's it. I collude with you to overthrow Merihim, let you install me as puppet team leader, and *then* you'll let me into your sweet embrace."

"Isn't it elegant? And everybody wins."

"That woman is going to get you in trouble."

"You don't sound worried about that, Hrym. Just amused." They were on guard duty in the deep dark watches of the night, and Rodrick shifted his weight from foot to foot, trying to stay awake. Eldra was bundled up asleep by the dim remnants of the campfire, and Prinn was up in a tree, either sleeping too or keeping his own watch, Rodrick didn't know.

"You just can't relax and take things as they are, can you?" Hrym said. "Just put in a year of service and then go on your way. You've got to get drawn into *plots*."

"Temple put together a team of treacherous, duplicitous, selfish criminals. This was *bound* to happen. I think I'm the most open and honest of the lot."

"No, that would be the Specialist. I don't think it occurs to him to lie."

"Ha. You've certainly been lying to *him*. He knows it, too."

"What?" Hrym was all outrage. "Why does he keep paying me if he's realized I'm selling him dirt and calling it diamonds? I've made *seven* pieces of gold off him so far!"

"He says there are little grains of truth in the river of nonsense." Rodrick paused. He and Hrym had a long partnership, and in truth he had no better or closer friend, but there were certain subjects they seldom broached. "How bad *is* your memory, really?"

Hrym was silent for long enough that Rodrick didn't think he would answer. At last the sword said, "I don't think about the past much. I mostly think about gold, and ice, and about the incomprehensible actions of the humans in my midst. I remember clearly everything from when you found me in that barrow, in the linnorm's hoard. I remember *most* of the years before that, back to when I was taken from the white dragon's cave. And before that . . . I don't dream, exactly, but I understand sometimes humans wake from a dream and can't tell right away if the dream was real or not?"

"True," Rodrick said.

"There are a lot of things floating around in my mind that might be memories . . . or they might be dreams, of a sort, from the long years I spent under a dragon in the dark, absorbing his essence. I have a clear memory of looking at clouds—but looking *down* on them, seeing them from above. And I have visions, sometimes, of a room full of gold, in a *temple* made of gold, guarded by inhuman soldiers made of gold—but that's probably just a fantasy? I don't know. Maybe I took some of the memories of the men who wielded me, all those long centuries ago."

"Do you think you're absorbing something from *me*? That might explain why we get along so well."

"Ha. I absorb *magic*. I was once taken into battle by warrior-mages, men and women infused with arcane power, so it's natural I picked up some of their power. What could I possibly absorb from you? An inflated sense of your abilities? Hmm, that *would* explain why I keep working with you. No, if I'm becoming anything like you, it's just because we've been together so long, the same way old married couples sometimes come to resemble one another."

"Wonderful. My life partner is a curmudgeonly old sword."

"You seem to have a taste for the elderly, judging by the way you pant over great-grandmother Eldra there."

Rodrick groaned. "Don't remind me. I'm entirely aware of how she's manipulating me. She doesn't even try to hide it, and it *still* works."

"It's *because* she's honest about it. You're a confidence trickster, suspicious and cynical by nature, so she knows there's no point in trying a more subtle approach on you. Instead she pretends you're equals, and lets you in on the secrets of her technique, knowing you'll admire her as a fellow professional, as well as a confidante. When she does all that and occasionally presses her bosoms up against you too, you're *lost*."

"It's good to have allies, though."

"You're *her* ally, but she might not be yours. I suppose she's made an investment in you, so she might make some small effort to keep you around, but not if it actually *costs* her anything."

"You're very cynical, for a sword."

"Swords are realistic. It's our nature."

"You know, I think this is going to be a very long year, Hrym. I'm in a pit of snakes with no way out."

"The worst thing is, you're not even the biggest and most dangerous snake."

"More's the pity."

19

DISSENTING VOICES

They finished the journey to Tamran the following day, the weather growing gloomier as they went, crossing the river into Nirmathas at what looked like exactly the same point they'd crossed before—Prinn's sense of direction was uncanny. They made it to the safe house, leading the horses to the dilapidated stable in back, where the mounts the others had ridden were already taking their ease.

Bannerman opened the door at their knock and beckoned them into the darkness. "Any problems on the way?" he said.

"Prinn didn't have to kill anyone at all," Rodrick said. "Once we got on the road, anyway."

"How disappointing for him. Come on downstairs."

The basement was the same as before, except for Zumani sitting glumly in a corner, flipping through the pages of a book with occasional pauses to look up and glare at everyone. The Specialist glanced at them distractedly from the alchemy table, where he was distilling something, and didn't bother to say hello. Merihim leapt to her feet when they entered and crooked a finger at Prinn. The sorcerer went to her obediently, and they retreated to the most distant corner of the basement, Merihim whispering intently into Prinn's ear and then listening with a scowl to his responses.

"Oh dear." Eldra's voice was breathy and amused in Rodrick's ear. "I think Prinn is telling on me."

Rodrick turned and put his mouth close to her ear. "Whisper, whisper," he said. "Secrets, whispers, etc."

Eldra giggled and went to greet the Specialist. She was still intermittently trying to charm the old man, too, for all the good it did.

Merihim left Prinn, stormed over to Eldra, and shoved her, making her bump into the table and rattle the beakers and vials. "What are you doing, interrogating my partner?"

Eldra rubbed the spot on her shoulder where Merihim had pushed her, then smiled sweetly. "Do you mean 'conversing with my teammate'? I'm a friendly and inquisitive person, interested in the thoughts and feelings of those around me. Prinn is a fascinating person. I'm not sure you appreciate him properly."

Merihim moved closer, putting her red face inches from Eldra's. "You don't need to talk to Prinn. No one does."

"It wasn't much of a talk, really, since you've forbidden him to *speak* to anyone else. How did you do that, by the way? And more importantly, why?"

"I've been curious about that, too." Bannerman leaned against the wall with his arms crossed, watching them with a half-smile.

Merihim growled. "There's no conspiracy here, Eldra. Prinn is very shy. Painfully so. That's all. We're old friends, so he's comfortable with me."

Eldra tapped her finger against her lips for a moment. "Funny, he told me he's only known you for a year, and I don't think he'd describe *you* as a friend."

"You stay *away* from him." Merihim punctuated her demand with another shove—or tried to. Eldra stepped smoothly aside, grabbed Merihim's arm, and wrenched it up behind her back in a particularly nasty joint-lock. The devilkin started to struggle, then stopped, realizing that any attempt at moving would dislocate her shoulder. "Let me *go*," she said.

"Apologize for your rudeness." Eldra's voice was still sweet, but there was steel underneath us.

"Prinn!" Merihim cried out.

The sorcerer blurred across the room toward Eldra—and without even thinking about it, Rodrick stepped into his path, bringing Hrym up sideways, the flat of the sword smacking Prinn right in the face. The sorcerer—or whatever—reeled backward, blood spurting from his nose, and Rodrick aimed Hrym's point in his face before he could recover. Prinn *howled*, the first real sound he'd heard from the man, a noise of pure anguish, and Merihim shouted, "Prinn, stand down!"

Prinn slunk back to the corner and sat on a crate, his hands shaking.

"I apologize for my rudeness." Merihim's voice was flat. "Now please release me."

"See?" Eldra said. "Everything is so much *nicer* when people are polite." She let go of Merihim, who walked with exaggerated dignity to join Prinn.

"You children had better work out your personal issues," Bannerman said. "You've got most of a year left to spend together. The Specialist and I are going to arrange transport back to the Bastion. Don't kill each other while I'm gone, if you can help it. Or if you do, leave at least one of you alive to watch Zumani."

The Specialist put down his beaker and trailed after Bannerman up the stairs, muttering to himself about unstable compounds and volatile chemical combinations. Rodrick couldn't tell if it was a commentary on the altercation or just coincidence.

Zumani started talking the moment the trapdoor shut behind the Specialist. "You should let me go."

They ignored him.

"I fight for a cause greater than myself!" he said. "Can any of *you* say the same?"

"Hmm. First I'd have to believe there *was* a cause greater than myself," Rodrick said. "Can't say I've ever noticed one."

"I fight for gold," Hrym said.

"Do you dream of ruling an empire, Zumani?" Merihim said.

"I dream of a world where every man and woman is *free*, devilkin."

Merihim snorted. "Ha. That's a wild dream, especially here— no one in this *room* is even free. Not a single one of us. As long as one person is stronger than another, the weaker will never be free. The key to freedom, then, is to be the strongest. And you . . . perhaps you're an excellent poet. I'm not qualified to judge. But you are not strong."

"Ah, but the weak can join *together* to overcome the strong, and good people can cooperate in a way that evil ones cannot." Zumani was clearly warming to the argument, which was a terrible thing to contemplate—what if he started quoting his own poetry?—so Rodrick lay down on the ground and put his fingers in his ears and hummed to himself.

There were no further outbursts or arguments in the hour that Bannerman was gone, though when Rodrick couldn't avoid listening he did hear a spirited discussion among Eldra, Merihim, and Zumani about the nature of personal freedom and the responsibilities of government. Rodrick's preferred method for dealing with governments was to keep as far away from their representatives as possible, so it wasn't a discussion he wanted to join.

Bannerman and the Specialist eventually returned. Their liaison said, "There's a ship heading to Vellumis tonight, and I've booked us passage. Zumani, will you be quiet, or do we have to stuff you in a trunk and pretend you're luggage? The journey takes a few days, so you wouldn't like it in the trunk."

"I can suffer the indignities of your outrageous crimes against my person in silence."

Merihim shook her head. "Zumani, we saved you from prison. They were going to hang you soon, and that's if they *didn't* realize how important you are in Nirmathas—if they figured out you were a man of renown, they would have tortured you. How can you still be angry with us?"

He punched the wall beside him. "I'm tired of being a puppet, devil-woman! Lastwall is useless to me if it won't help me save my comrades, and they're taking me away from the battle I need to wage. You aren't a patriot. You don't care about anything but yourself. You couldn't possibly understand. My own life doesn't matter when the fate of my nation is at stake." He nodded at Bannerman. "*Him*, though, he *is* a patriot, and he does this to me anyway."

"True, but I'm a patriot of Lastwall, and we're *much* better organized and armed than your lot, so I win. If you'll be reasonable, Temple might even provide you with the resources you need to achieve your goals."

Zumani shook his head. "Temple doesn't want my people to win. I was desperate for help, and made a deal with a devil. Her only interest is in keeping Nirmathas and Molthune locked in conflict, in chaos, forever."

Rodrick couldn't help but nod. All true, as far as he knew.

Bannerman sighed. "I'm just a soldier. The philosophical and strategic discussions happen above my rank. Let's go get on the ship, all right?"

There was only one cabin available on the trading ship for passengers, and Bannerman took it, keeping Zumani confined with him. That left the Volunteers to sleep in hammocks strung belowdecks, or up on the deck of the ship with the sailors. Eldra increased her flirting with Rodrick exponentially on the voyage, which initially delighted Rodrick until he realized she was doing so because there was nothing resembling privacy on the ship, so she could tease without worrying that he'd expect her to follow through. He did get a few very satisfying kisses in the cargo hold, but when he pressed for more she told him she didn't intend to take their relationship to that level on the floor between forty barrels of salted fish and a hundred sacks of flour; what kind of a woman did he think she was?

The experience was a bit frustrating, but it helped pass the time.

Bannerman watched over Zumani, and didn't do much else. The Volunteers mostly avoided one another, outside their factions: Merihim and Prinn kept to themselves, as did Rodrick, Hrym, and Eldra, with the Specialist spending most of his time with the ship's navigator, bonding over their shared love for charts and things.

Merihim did join Eldra and Rodrick one evening, crouching on her heels near them on the deck. She wore her gloves and her deep-hooded cloak, hiding her hands and face. "I hope I'm not interrupting?"

"Of course you aren't." Eldra showed her teeth. "That would be rude, and I know you would never be rude to me."

Rodrick knew there were some men who found the prospect of two attractive women getting into a hair-pulling, face-scratching, clothes-ripping fight strangely erotic, but he just found the idea distressing. He was pleased when Merihim chuckled in what seemed a genuine way.

"Yes, you taught me that much. I keep underestimating you—which, I suppose, is one of your great talents. I've been thinking about our . . . disagreement . . . and I'd like to make things up to you. I have an idea about how to improve our situation, and if it works, I'll include you in the plan, all right?" She glanced at Rodrick, and Hrym at his belt. "All of you."

"Mmm," Eldra said. "What plan is that?"

"I'd rather not say more until I work out how feasible it is, but if my idea works . . . I could shorten our tenure in the Volunteers considerably."

"I'm open to the idea of getting on with my life, and accept the gesture of goodwill," Eldra said.

Merihim smiled. "I'll keep you informed as the situation warrants." She rose and sauntered off.

"What do you think *she* has in mind?" Rodrick said.

"Who knows? She's a good planner, though. Maybe she does have a worthwhile scheme. It must be something she needs our help with—or at least our complicity—or she wouldn't have offered to include us."

"I just hope she doesn't get us all killed."

"That's always a good minimum to hope for, yes."

Just hours before they were due to reach Vellumis, Zumani hit Bannerman over the head with a heavy ceramic pitcher and escaped the ship, stealing a rowboat and setting out for the nearby shore.

20

Taking Initiative

Rodrick and Eldra were leaning on the railing, watching the land slide by in the distance, when they saw Zumani in his boat, furiously working the oars. He wasn't a strong man physically, but he was putting on a decent bit of speed, driven by fear and zeal and haste. "That's not good," Rodrick observed. Hrym was resting on a meager bed of gold in their cabin, having pronounced himself disgusted with Rodrick and Eldra's flirtations, so Rodrick couldn't freeze the boat in place.

They rushed to Bannerman's cabin, where the crusader was just sitting up, groaning and rubbing the back of his head.

"Your poet has fled," Eldra said. "Should we go get him?"

After a great deal of cursing and some unsteady stumbling around, they gathered Prinn and Merihim and the Specialist and paid the captain for one of his other rowboats—Bannerman had to pay for the one Zumani had stolen, too, which put him in an even fouler temper. Their rowboat was made to hold four people comfortably, so five people fit rather *uncomfortably*, but Prinn worked the oars fiendishly as Merihim scanned the shore with her spyglass. "I see his boat by the shore, but there's no sign of Zumani. He must be among the trees already."

Bannerman cursed again. "He's a woodsman as well as a poet. If he wants to lose himself in the forest, he probably can."

"Good thing I had Prinn pluck a few of his hairs while he was unconscious." Merihim shook her wrist, rattling the bracelet they'd used to try to track Bannerman on their first mission, and gave a sharp-toothed grin. She reached into her cloak and withdrew a vial that held a few hairs, and put them into the small compartment in the bracelet. The arrows pulsed as they approached the shore, which at least indicated she had the right person's body parts this time.

Prinn rowed a lot faster than Zumani had, so they got to the shore in good time. The poet hadn't bothered to drag his rowboat out of the water, so it was drifting back away into the lake. Merihim led the way through the trees, with Prinn darting ahead and returning periodically to report.

Rodrick was growing heartily sick of the Fangwood. The trees here were almost all the sort with needles, dense and green, and there was a disturbing stillness. Didn't a lack of birdsong mean something bad? The presence of predators, or something?

Merihim's bracelet began to flash faster, and they hurried, dodging among the trunks. At least there wasn't much underbrush here, just a carpet of slick needles. They caught sight of Zumani's back up ahead, and Prinn pushed forward, lips peeled back in a silent snarl, covering the ground in great leaping strides.

The rest of them stopped hurrying. They strolled easily to the spot where Zumani sprawled, held down by Prinn.

"Why?" the poet sobbed. "Why did he chase me? He *told* me to escape—he said I could take a boat and get away, that I could find safety in the forest!"

Prinn frowned, looked at them, and shook his head. "Prinn doesn't talk to anyone but me," Merihim said.

"Zumani, you were never out of my sight," Bannerman said. "Prinn didn't tell you anything—believe me, I would have noticed." He glanced at the Specialist. "Could the pressure of his situation . . . affect his mind?"

"That is one possibility," the Specialist said. "Perhaps it was a dream he had, or a fantasy."

"Get him to his feet." Bannerman sighed. "It's back to ropes for you, I'm afraid, Zumani. I'll have to tell Temple about this. She won't be pleased. Being an ally of the Bastion is far better than being a prisoner."

"Truer words were never said," Merihim murmured.

Bannerman looked around the forest. "We're only about a day's walk from Vellumis. We can survive another night sleeping rough. This isn't such a bad patch of the woods, either."

"Prinn and I camped in this part of the forest before we were invited to join the Volunteers, I think." Merihim looked to her— partner? slave?—and he nodded. "Do you think you could find the place where we camped last time, Prinn? It was near that nice stream, against those rocks, out of the wind."

Prinn nodded, and Bannerman grunted. "Sounds fine. Let's get moving." He slapped Zumani across the back of the head, though not hard. "Really, what were you thinking?"

"I . . ." Zumani shook his head, glaring at Prinn, then subsided into sullen silence.

They trudged through the woods, lugging their packs, with Prinn and Merihim in the lead, Bannerman holding Zumani's leash, Rodrick and Eldra side by side, and the Specialist walking along behind them, occasionally scribbling in a small notebook and peering at the trees around him as if they exhibited some wondrous novelty or variety, instead of all being boring, green, and needle-ish.

After a few hours they reached the campsite, which was as good as Merihim had suggested: a pile of boulders provided a natural windbreak, and there was clean, fresh water nearby, and a circle of stones with the remains of a campfire inside. They drew lots to see who would do guard duty. Rodrick, Hrym, and Eldra drew lucky and got the first watch, with the Specialist and Bannerman taking the middle-of-the-night hours, and Prinn and Merihim the last hours before dawn.

"Do you think Prinn really told Zumani something, somehow?" Eldra asked as they watched the forest, where not so much as a bird stirred.

"I don't see how he could have. As Bannerman said, he was always there."

"Some wizards can speak to you in your dreams," Hrym said. "Even if Prinn isn't a sorcerer, he and Merihim seem to have an array of magical items. Several of her bracelets look like more than jewelry to me."

Eldra nodded. "I was thinking the same thing. I'm not sure Zumani is all that good at telling dreams from real life *anyway*, given how resistant to reality his worldview is, and if Prinn created a particularly convincing dream . . ."

"But what's the point? To get us out here in the woods, for what?"

"Merihim said she had a plan. Perhaps whatever that plans is requires privacy. And if she knows the area . . ." Eldra frowned. "I find it all very suspicious. I don't mind plots—I just prefer to be the one *plotting* them."

Rodrick nodded. "I suppose we'll find out in good time."

"How reassuring. I hate waiting."

"Ha! Really. You don't seem to mind making *other* people wait."

"Oh, well, *some* things—"

"—are worth waiting for, yes, I know." Rodrick sighed. "It's hard to know for sure if they were worth it until after you're finished with the waiting, though."

"If we were closer to civilization I could provide references. For now, you'll just have to take my word for it, darling."

They woke Bannerman and the Specialist at the appointed time, or their best guess, and went to sleep. Rodrick was exhausted by a day of tramping through the eerily silent forest, and fell into a deep sleep. He kept Hrym close by, sleeping with his hand on the sword's hilt, just in case Merihim *did* have something in mind, and that something required fight or flight.

He woke, yawning, when someone shook him by the shoulder. The Specialist crouched over him, frowning, looking even more lost in thought than usual. "What's going on?" Rodrick said.

"Bannerman and Zumani are gone," he said. "Merihim and Prinn, too. And a vial of my sleeping potion is missing."

Rodrick groaned and shook Eldra awake. She stretched fetchingly and smiled up at him until she saw the expression on his face. "What happened?"

The Specialist repeated his revelation. Rodrick stood up, lifting Hrym. "Did you see anything, Hrym?"

"Hmm? No. My view was of the trees above and of you and Eldra on either side of me. There were some sounds of movement in the night, but I didn't think much of it—I just thought it was the guard changing. Nothing that sounded like a fight or a struggle or people being eaten by ravenous forest monsters. I had other things on my mind. Temples full of gold, mostly."

"There's no sign of any violence here," the Specialist said. "But if someone used my potion to knock them out, there wouldn't be."

Eldra walked around the campsite, poking through bags and packs. "Everyone's things are still here . . . except Bannerman's pack. A lot of the food is missing, and several canteens and water skins, too."

"What *happened* here?" Rodrick said.

Pine needles crunched, and they turned to see Merihim enter the campsite. She waved jauntily, grinning. "What happened is, I've saved us all."

"Where are the others?"

"Oh, Prinn is . . . around." She gestured vaguely at the trees. "As for Bannerman and Zumani, they're in a safe place. I *told* you I had a plan."

Rodrick put his hands over his face. "No. You're not planning to ransom them?"

"It's beautiful, isn't it?" Merihim beamed.

"Temple is going to kill us *all*," Eldra said.

Merihim waved that away. "Nonsense. I'm very good at reading people. Temple and Bannerman have a bond—I bet she thinks of him like a son. She obviously wants Zumani very badly, to go to all this trouble for him. But the rest of us—what are *we* to her? Just some unlucky people who wandered into her vicinity and got tangled in her plans. I put Bannerman and Zumani somewhere secluded and secure, with enough food and water to last them a week, if they aren't greedy. We'll return to the Bastion and give Temple a choice: remove the gems and set us free, or kill us and let Bannerman and Zumani starve. She'll *have* to meet our demands. The Fangwood is vast, and she won't be able to find them in time without us. We even set up a few wards to disrupt attempts to locate them through magical means— Temple shouldn't have let me keep so much of my equipment, but I convinced her the charms could be useful in the field if we needed to hide out. My plan is perfect. And, because I am a kindhearted and benevolent leader, and have enjoyed our time together, I'll make Temple set *you* free, too."

Rodrick rose, Hrym in his hand. "What if it doesn't work? What if Temple gets angry and kills us all?"

"Don't point your friend at me, Rodrick." Merihim leveled her finger at him. "Prinn is out there in the trees, watching, and if any harm comes to me . . . Well, you wouldn't like what happens next, let me put it that way. Temple is an intelligent woman—a prag- matist, not an idealist. If she loses *us*, she hasn't lost very much—a group of malcontents who would have caused her almost as many problems as we solved. If she loses Bannerman, her right hand? And Zumani, when she has such plans for him? This will *work*. Temple will let us go, and we'll give her back her men. Of course, we'll all have to leave Lastwall at great speed, and never return, but are any of us eager to spend more time here?"

Eldra touched Rodrick's forearm, and he lowered Hrym until the sword was pointed at the ground. "It *could* work," Eldra said. "It's a bit more . . . brute force . . . than I'd like, but it's not necessarily a bad plan."

"I would estimate our chances of success at . . . slightly more than fifty percent," the Specialist said. He sighed. "But I'm not confident that I have a complete grasp of all the variables. Temple in particular is quite hard to read."

"We could be in the Bastion by this afternoon," Merihim said. "We could be free of these cursed gems by nightfall. Are you with me, or do I have to unleash Prinn on you, and go on alone?"

"It's worth a try," Eldra said. "Though I intend to let Temple know this wasn't *my* idea."

Merihim shrugged. "I'm happy to take all the blame."

The Specialist stroked his mustache, then nodded. "There's no real alternative. We can't very well knock you down and torture their location out of you, not with Prinn out there, ready to strike."

Rodrick sheathed Hrym. "You're supposed to be a good planner, Merihim. I hope your talents haven't deserted you now. I'm in."

"Where Rodrick goes, I go," Hrym said. "But if this doesn't work, I'll freeze you until you turn blue."

"Hmm," the Specialist said. "I wonder if she'd turn more of a purple?"

"Let's hope we don't have to find out," Merihim said.

They traveled quietly, Merihim leading the way. They never even caught a glimpse of Prinn until they reached the edge of Vellumis proper, when he appeared from an entirely unexpected direction. The Specialist, Eldra, and Rodrick *could* have tried to overpower Prinn and Merihim at that moment, but none of them made the effort. Rodrick was beginning to feel the faint stirrings of hope. Merihim's plan was an ugly way to escape their situation . . . but it was an ugly situation. Maybe it *would* work.

They reached the Bastion in midafternoon, and were not welcomed warmly, presumably because Bannerman wasn't with them. A heavily armed contingent of crusaders herded them into a courtyard, leveling polearms and crossbows at them, and a wizard wandered among the crusaders, muttering spells and touching each soldier in turn. Doubtless imbuing them with magical protection, probably against ice magic. Always a prudent move when Hrym was in the vicinity.

One of the crusaders strode forward, holding the strange scabbard Temple had used to neutralize Hrym. His voice was an unhappy growl: "The sword goes in here."

"Are you all right with that, Hrym?"

"It's no scabbard of gold, but it's restful in its way. Hand me over. Just get me *out* again sometime soon, all right?"

Rodrick handed over the sword, and the crusader jammed Hrym into the scabbard, then tied the hilt to the sheath with leather cords. He handed the sheath to another soldier and it passed hand to hand until it vanished into the building, out of sight.

"The rest of you hand over your weapons, too."

Eldra gave up her parasol with the hidden blade and assorted throwing knives, Merihim handed over her daggers—she'd never even stabbed anything as far as Rodrick knew; Prinn was really her weapon—and the Specialist gave up his satchel of explosives.

Prinn handed over a bow and clutch of arrows, but of course, he couldn't *really* be disarmed short of dismemberment.

"Also the jewelry."

Merihim rolled her eyes, but removed several bracelets and her earrings, handing them over. The wizard peered at her for a moment, probably looking for hidden magic, then nodded.

The guards behind nudged the Volunteers with the butts of their polearms, and they were directed to the meeting room where Bannerman's true identity had been revealed, the one with the mural depicting a great moment in Lastwall's history.

The guards didn't withdraw, and entirely too many crossbows were pointed at them for Rodrick's comfort. The far door opened and Temple shuffled in, her brow furrowed, her mouth set in a frown. She glanced at the guards, then waved her hand at them. "This is under control. You can go."

The leader of the soldiers, the one who'd taken Hrym, said, "Underclerk, I don't think—"

"They won't hurt me," she said. "If I die, they die. These crusaders aren't authorized to hear what my Volunteers have to say anyway." She crossed her arms and glared until the guards left the room.

Once she was alone with the Volunteers, Temple barked, "Report."

"Bannerman and Zumani are alive," Merihim said. "And they can stay that way, if you'll make a few small concessions."

Temple nodded. "Ah. I see. Extortion. Are you all in this together?"

Rodrick, Eldra, and the Specialist all took a step back. "We couldn't stop her," Eldra said.

"We had no idea she was doing this until she sprung the news on us," Rodrick said.

"No," the Specialist said. "We are not all in it together."

Merihim glared at them. "*Despite* that craven display, my demands remain the same. If you want to see Bannerman and Zumani again, you'll deactivate the gems and let us *all* go."

"Oh, how generous," Temple said. "Of course you want me to let the others go too—if I just freed *you*, Merihim, you know I'd send the rest of the Volunteers to collect you." She shook her head.

"I'm very disappointed. I thought we had an understanding. I even made you team leader."

"You chose me because I show initiative and make plans." The devilkin shrugged. "This is my initiative. This is my plan."

"And if I don't agree?"

"Bannerman and Zumani will starve to death."

"If I torture you to get the information out of you?"

She snorted. "You tried that when I wouldn't tell you why I was exploring the Whispering Tyrant's ruins, and it didn't work then. You might make me say *something*, but it would be a lie, and you'd waste time following up on my lies, and your friend would die."

"I see," Temple said. "You won't change your mind?"

"When I'm holding an unbeatable hand? Of course not."

"Very well. If you can't be persuaded to give up this course of action . . . I'm afraid my answer is no. *Tekritanin*."

Merihim gasped as Temple uttered the last word, but she didn't have time to scream before her chest exploded in a pulse of red light and a spray of blood, meat, and bone fragments.

Rodrick stood, stunned. He looked down at his chest. Something from inside Merihim had *splattered* on him.

Prinn began to laugh. The sound began as a chuckle and grew to a roaring belly laugh, until he was doubled over, clutching his stomach, howling with mirth.

Temple and the Volunteers stared at him as he straightened, wiped tears from his eyes, and smiled. Then Prinn spoke, and his voice wasn't the rasping nightmare Rodrick had imagined, but cool, deep, and almost mellifluous.

"You fools," he said. "You've killed my captor. And now I am free."

21

TOTENMASKE

It's nice to hear your voice, Prinn," Temple said dryly. "I'm afraid you're not entirely free, though. I still have a gem embedded in your chest." She looked at Merihim and sighed. "Foolish woman. I *told* her I wouldn't lie to her, didn't I? She should have known disobedience meant death. Losing Bannerman would be a terrible blow, but if I gave in to the demands of criminals like her, if I demonstrated that sort of weakness, everything I've built here would crumble." She lifted her eyes to Prinn. "I assume you know where Bannerman and Zumani are hidden? You can save yourself if you confess their location now."

Prinn chuckled, still full of dark delight. "You have no idea what you've done. How amusing. *Of course* I know where the crusader and the poet are being held, but why would I tell you? I have no interest in them." He looked at the broken body of the devilkin on the floor and guffawed. "Merihim. She laid a compulsion on me, forced me to serve her. Helping with her petty tricks and treacheries. Furthering her mad dream of finding artifacts from the Whispering Tyrant's realm and using them to take over some small corner of this filthy world. I had no choice to obey her whims . . . but now I am my own master again."

"Except, as Temple pointed out, for the gem," Rodrick said. "Listen, Temple, if Prinn won't tell you, the rest of us can lead you to the spot in the forest where we camped. Bannerman and Zumani can't be *too* far from there, and with a contingent of crusaders to comb the forest we can locate them, I'm sure."

"There will be no rescue," Prinn said. "You will all die. The only reason you aren't dead already is because it will amuse me to watch all your hopes crumble."

"Ah," Rodrick said. "How disappointing. I thought we were becoming friends."

"Are you ready to die, Temple?" Prinn's voice was low and self-satisfied. "To die knowing you brought this doom upon yourself? To die knowing that I will ruin your country, that I will destroy Lastwall from the inside, and only because it pleases me to do so? That the Bastion of Justice will become the rot at the center of your nation, under my command?"

Temple sighed. "This is tiresome, Prinn."

The pale man took a bow, then straightened up—and the skin on his face began to melt and run like bacon fat heated in a pan. Rodrick wondered if Prinn was suffering some strange attack from Temple, except she looked alarmed, too, as did Eldra. The Specialist just leaned forward, eyes wide, mouth open, taking it all in.

Globs of flesh dripped off Prinn's face and spattered on the floor, revealing a layer of festering, moldy-looking green skin underneath. Prinn's head began to bulge, as if inflating, and his mouth grew wider, and wider, and wider, until his maw was vaster than a shark's, and seemed to take up most of his head. The teeth in that huge mouth were the gray of tombstones, all triangular and sharp, and his breath was like low tide, exhalations of rot and death. Prinn's fingers lengthened and twisted into claws, and he tore open his shirt—and started to claw a hole in his own chest.

"He's trying to dig out the gem!" Eldra shouted.

Prinn laughed—the laugh was the same as before, though the mouth it emerged from was now altogether monstrous—and ripped great hunks of green flesh from his body, flinging them toward the Volunteers, who scattered to avoid the filth. Prinn prised open his ribs and began digging in the vicinity of his own heart . . . assuming he even *had* one in his true form.

Tampering with the gem was supposed to set it off, but apparently Temple wasn't willing to count on that. She took a breath and shouted, "*Ceratioidi!*"

Rodrick averted his eyes, expecting an explosion of negative energy to rip off the monster's fingers and blow apart his chest, but after the burst of red light there was only Prinn's ongoing laughter and Temple's moan of dismay. Rodrick looked back . . . and Prinn's chest was closed up again, healed. The gem nestled in his monstrous green palm. He turned over his hand and the gem fell, tinkling when it hit the floor.

"Ah," the Specialist said softly. "Just as I thought."

"Kill it!" Temple shouted, taking a step back as Prinn advanced on her.

"You took our weapons," the Specialist said, almost apologetically.

She looked at the door, and looked about to run for it, but the monster reached out with one long, thin arm and *caressed* her face with his talons. She screamed, and her cheeks hollowed out, as if Prinn were stealing her flesh. She sagged to the floor, if not unconscious then at least weakened, and Prinn crouched over her, chuckling to himself and continuing to caress her face.

Rodrick picked up a chair and charged forward, intending to smash the monster over the head, but Prinn lashed out at him, one long arm slamming into Rodrick's chest with inhuman force, sending him sprawling and gasping to the floor. Prinn returned his attention to Temple, cooing and stroking. Eldra was trying to edge around toward the door, but hesitantly, clearly afraid to pass by the monster Prinn had become. The Specialist was, strangely enough, ignoring the creature entirely, and creeping slowly toward Merihim's corpse.

Rodrick hauled himself upright, and got a good look at Temple's face. He shuddered. Under Prinn's touch, Temple's flesh moved like clay, easily shaped, and where her mouth had been, he left just a smooth patch of skin: no lips, no teeth, and no way to speak. Her eyelids fluttered, and she made a voiceless moan.

Prinn rose, leaving Temple on the floor, still alive, but sweating, shivering, and convulsing. The monster turned to face his former compatriots, and when he saw the Specialist moving toward Merihim, he snarled and stomped toward him, making the old man scuttle backward. Prinn stood between the three of them and Merihim's corpse, his baleful head swinging back and forth as he regarded them . . . and then his features transformed again, his mouth shrinking, his skin changing color, his face returning to that of a human's.

But not the human he *had* been. Now the monster looked exactly like Temple, though dressed in the rags of Prinn's old clothes. "That's better," Prinn said in Temple's voice. "It's been ages since I wore the face of someone in authority. I love having power. It's so much fun to abuse. Merihim knew I loved the pleasures of the flesh, and so she denied me all of them, made me eat raw vegetables and sleep on a stone floor." Prinn turned and spat on Merihim's corpse. "That all changes now." He—she—it cracked its knuckles and smiled at them. "What are you three still doing here? This is your chance to escape. Your captor is in no position to hold you . . . and I have no interest in running a nursery for you mewling infants."

"But—the gems—" Eldra said.

Prinn cocked its head. "My gem didn't cause me any trouble. But if you don't have my talents . . ." It gave an awful smile, the sort of gloating grin that Temple would never have turned on them, because Temple didn't bother to gloat. "I suppose you should run along and enjoy your last night of life before your gems kill you in the morning. Temple said some magic words to keep you from dying every day, but I don't have any interest in keeping up that tradition, if I even knew the words. Or I could kill you *now* . . ."

Eldra plucked at Rodrick's sleeve, and he turned to see the Specialist already disappearing through the door. Eldra went after him, and Rodrick reluctantly followed, casting a last glance at Prinn, and Merihim's dead body, and the still-twitching Temple.

All he could think was: *Hrym*. Hrym was in the Bastion, somewhere, and Rodrick couldn't leave him with that monster.

Out in the hallway, Eldra was following the Specialist, who seemed to be going *somewhere* with purpose. They went down a few deserted corridors until they reached an ironbound door. The Specialist reached into his boot, drew out two slender pieces of metal, and began working on the lock, popping it open in less than a minute and throwing the door wide. He went into the room and emerged with his pack. Eldra darted in after him and came back with her traveling gear, too, and her parasol.

Rodrick hurried in, looking around for Hrym . . . but though Rodrick's pack was there, his sword wasn't. "Hrym's not here!"

Eldra patted him on the shoulder. "Come on, Rodrick. We should get away."

"But—without Hrym—how can we fight that thing? How can we save Temple? How can we save *ourselves*?"

"We can't," the Specialist said. "Let's go. We have problems to discuss."

Rodrick considered that something of an understatement, but he was too numb with horror and fear to think of anything else to do, so he followed.

Even a city like Vellumis, home to noble crusaders, had taverns, and the Specialist found the darkest, dimmest, most disreputable one available, less than a mile from the Bastion. They took a table in the far corner and hunched over their drinks. This was Rodrick's first time with access to liquor since he couldn't remember when, and he couldn't even enjoy it. His thoughts ran along two tracks, incessantly, over and over.

One: He had to rescue Hrym.

Two: It didn't matter if he rescued Hrym, because he was going to die horribly in the morning, his chest burst open by an evil gem.

Eldra sat beside him with a goblet of wine, and the Specialist sat across from them, calmly sipping ale. "You know things," she said. "That . . . monster. Do you know what it is?"

The Specialist nodded. "Oh, yes. It's called a totenmaske. I've read about them, but had never seen one before—at least, not in its true form. I suppose I might have seen dozens of them, disguised as their victims, and never realized it."

"Are they some kind of demon?" Rodrick said. He had a particular antipathy toward demons.

The Specialist shook his shaggy gray head. "No, no. Prinn used to be human, and now he's undead. Particularly sinful mortals, those dedicated to the pleasures of the flesh, sometimes return to life as totenmaskes, driven by all the same appetites they had in life, only more twisted and perverse. Of course, their rotting bodies, their monstrous mouths, their terrible claws—these things make it difficult for them to acquire such pleasures. They use their powers to shape and steal flesh to take on the identities of others, infiltrating the lives of the living—and using those lives to gratify their corrupt desires." He sipped his drink. "Sometimes totenmaskes just happen, and sometimes very powerful clerics of dark gods make them, from the corpses of evil mortals."

"You're saying Merihim was some kind of . . . evil high priest?" Rodrick had encountered an evil god once—she'd even *touched* him—and had no desire to get close to any sort of divinity ever again.

"I doubt it. She didn't exhibit any priestly powers. I think she was more of a treasure hunter. Somehow she gained the power to command the undead—she clearly had a fondness for magical items, and I suspect she found something that allowed her to enslave Prinn." He sighed. "Alas, we have no such item—the solders must have taken her jewelry wherever they took Hrym, and I didn't get to search her body before Hrym chased us away."

Eldra drummed her fingers on the tabletop. "So we . . . we'll hire a priest, and—"

The Specialist shook his head. "Gaining access to Temple—and remember, Prinn now *is* Temple, as far as the Bastion knows—won't be that easy. We escaped without much trouble, but gaining entrance to a fortress is usually much harder than getting out. Moreover, with all the resources of the Bastion at his disposal, I'm sure Prinn will ward himself against being controlled in the same way again."

"Is Temple still alive?" Rodrick said. "The real Temple, I mean?"

"I don't know. I've heard tales of totenmaskes keeping their victims alive for years, taking more flesh from them to renew their disguises periodically, but who knows? Prinn is hardly short of other identities to steal. We know Temple sometimes meets with at least one high-ranking crusader leader, Andraste, the one who came to inspect us—maybe Prinn will move on to bigger and better things the next time they're alone together."

"We need to do *something*," Eldra said. "If we don't rescue Temple before morning, she can't say the words that will keep us from dying."

"Why didn't the gem kill Prinn?" Rodrick demanded. "We know they *work*—one of them certainly turned Merihim's chest into wreckage—but Prinn's didn't seem to harm him at all."

The Specialist nodded. "The gems work by releasing bursts of negative energy. *Death* energy. That energy is a terrible force, inimical to life."

"But we *saw* Prinn heal— Wait." Rodrick slumped. "It's because he's undead, isn't it?"

Eldra said something in the Vudrani tongue that was probably a curse. "Of course. Healing magic *harms* the undead, so this death magic, it heals them. Right?"

The Specialist nodded. "Totenmaskes are not creatures of illusion, but of transformation. When Prinn wore his human disguise, he *was* human—his body was human, his heart beat in his chest, his flesh was like our flesh, and as such, he was vulnerable to the gem. But once he transformed himself back into his true form, he could remove the gem without fear. And you're right—by activating the gem, Temple actually healed the wounds Prinn had inflicted on himself."

Rodrick rubbed his chest. The gem lurked inside him, waiting to burst. "So . . . what do we do?"

Eldra sighed. "I suppose we stage a desperate suicide attack on the Bastion of Justice to try to kill Prinn and rescue Temple before morning. Or else we make peace with our gods. I can't think of any other options."

"I know one other," the Specialist said.

22

THE NECKLACE

The Specialist blinked as they stared at him, seemingly taken aback by the sharpness of their focused attention. "When we met—or, rather, were *presented* to—General Andraste, did you notice the necklace she was wearing?"

Rodrick frowned. He'd mostly noticed her very large sword and her dyspeptic expression, but, yes, there'd been a glimmer at her throat he'd thought seemed out of place. "I think so."

Eldra nodded. "I did, but just a glimpse—most of the necklace was hidden under her clothes. I thought it was a peculiar choice considering that the rest of her ensemble was mail and leather."

"That necklace is the key to our freedom . . . and we won't have to face a totenmaske to get it."

"Please explain," Eldra said.

"As I believe I mentioned right after the rat incident, I was researching the Whispering Tyrant's reign before I came here," the Specialist said. "In a forgotten codex, I came across a reference to a 'necklace of terrible gems,' also called 'the Tyrant's Collar.' The Whispering Tyrant's lieutenants used the necklace to compel the loyalty of nobles and aristocrats, forcing them to betray their people at the Tyrant's command. 'The gems burrow like insects and nestle next to the heart, to rend the flesh of those who disobey. So long as the necklace is clasped, the gems pulse with dreadful light and the promise of death, but unclasp the necklace, and the gems return harmlessly home.'" He shrugged. "It seems clear that

Temple got her hands on one such monstrous artifact and decided to use it to compel our service. It would be dangerous to keep the necklace on her own person, where we might get our hands on it, so Temple gave it to her patron to wear instead. I don't know if deactivating the gems is really just a matter of undoing a clasp, but if we get our hands on the necklace, I suspect I can figure out how to use its powers."

"So all we have to do," Eldra said, "is steal a piece of jewelry from around the neck of one of the leading generals of Lastwall."

"Before morning," Rodrick said.

"We could just go to Andraste and tell her what's happened," Eldra said. "That Prinn was a totenmaske, that he's taken over Temple's identity, that the Bastion has been corrupted from the inside . . ." She sighed. "Of course, we're notorious liars and thieves and confidence tricksters, and judging by the way she looked at us when she met us, I can't imagine she would believe us."

"Totenmaskes are adept at deception," the Specialist said. "They have magical abilities designed to let them step seamlessly into the lives of their victims, and they can be *very* convincing. I don't think the direct approach would do us much good. Besides, putting ourselves in Andraste's hands wouldn't free us from our predicament—even if she believed us and moved against Prinn, we would still be prisoners. I was willing to endure my year of service in the Volunteers, as it seemed there were some interesting learning opportunities involved, but at this point . . . I would rather gain my freedom."

"It's a shame we don't have Merihim here to plan something for us," Eldra said.

Rodrick scowled. "We don't need her. We've got *me*."

The Specialist didn't have the book about the necklace anymore, of course, but he claimed to have a memory so perfect he could recall every page of every volume he'd ever perused, and it didn't take him long to duplicate the drawing he'd seen of the "necklace of terrible gems": a doubled strand of gold, with a dozen dangling fittings that held the teardrop-shaped red gems. Rodrick sent the Specialist with almost the entirety of their combined funds to find a goldsmith. The sword would not be pleased by that . . . but the alternative was never *seeing* the sword again, so the opportunity to face Hrym's displeasure was actually a fairly rosy prospect.

Rodrick sent Eldra on a mission to gather intelligence. If Andraste was off at the front, or attending high-level meetings, or otherwise surrounded by her highly armed compatriots and subordinates, they would have a hard time pulling this off. Fortunately, Eldra returned to the tavern beaming.

She slipped into the chair beside him. "We're in luck. General Andraste has just returned from the front. Everyone's talking about it. She won a great victory against some formidable orc chieftain, and her deeds are on everyone's lips. In a few days she's being honored with a great feast, to be attended by various high-ranking figures, including the Precentor Martial for Cavalry—I even heard rumors Andraste is being groomed to take over that position herself in time."

"Knowing where she'll be in the future doesn't do us much good," Rodrick said. "Because of the fact that we'll be shredded corpses by then."

Eldra tapped him on the end of the nose with her forefinger. "Patience, Rodrick. I just enjoy gossip. Overhearing one such conversation, I wondered aloud why they didn't honor her right away, and was told that Andraste is very devout, and prefers to spend the days immediately following a battle alone at home, observing private devotions in the chapel to Iomedae in the center of her house. Rededicating herself to her goddess, thanking her for the opportunity to serve, and so on. Doubtless she scourges her flesh and harrows her soul and cleanses the soles of her feet and so forth, too. Religious people always find interesting ways to pass the time. The *point* is that even the servants leave Andraste alone during these rituals, so the general should be home alone, and deep in contemplation. I'm beginning to think our luck is changing for the better."

"I should hope," Rodrick said. "It doesn't really have much room to get *worse*."

The Specialist returned after nightfall, as Eldra and Rodrick were picking at the last remnants of a roasted chicken at their table, and beginning to worry.

"This was very expensive, because of the rush, but it looks right." The Specialist unfolded a black cloth on the table and revealed a necklace just like the one he'd sketched. Rodrick suppressed a shudder at the sight of a full dozen duplicates of the red gem in his chest, each one dangling from the necklace like a blood-filled tick. "I wasn't sure how many gems are missing from the necklace," the Specialist said. "At least five, but possibly more, since Temple had one on hand to demonstrate on the rat. These false ones are easy enough to pop out, so we can make the fake necklace match when the time comes. Assuming this wasn't a waste of time and gold?"

"Not at all," Rodrick said. "We're going to wait until it's properly dark, and then we're paying a visit to the general's estate."

"I wish I had access to an alchemy lab." The Specialist sighed. "If everything goes *perfectly*, I've got what we need in my pack. But I prefer having more options."

"Options are in short supply all around," Rodrick said. "But look on the bright side: if we're captured, what's the worst that can happen?"

"They can torture us," Eldra said.

"Ah, but not for long," Rodrick said. "Since we'll die at dawn regardless."

"When you put it that way," Eldra agreed.

Rodrick had expected an ostentatious estate, but he'd forgotten the essentially pious nature of the crusaders. The house was *nice*, certainly befitting Andraste's rank, but it was no palace: just a big house in the locally popular Chelish Old White style, all gleaming pale stone walls and immense arched windows, many filled with stained-glass windows depicting various triumphs by paladins. The big windows on the higher floors were particularly lovely from a burglar's point of view, as they were large enough to walk through upright. The whole house was surrounded by a wall of white stone, but the wall wasn't topped with spikes or shards of glass or anything. There probably weren't a lot of burglars eager to rob the home of a highly ranked crusader. Rodrick wasn't too keen on the idea himself, but their circumstances were dire.

The house was on a large lot with a lot of privacy, on a hill overlooking the harbor, so they didn't have to worry much about passing traffic or overly observant neighbors. There was one soldier ambling in a desultory way around the perimeter of the wall, occasionally poking his pike into bushes and sighing a lot: this was probably a low-status punishment detail. He clearly wasn't expecting any trouble, and the remaining Volunteers had no desire to give him any.

The Specialist counted quietly as the soldier made two slow circuits of the wall, then nodded. "Plenty of time." They waited until he vanished out sight around the near corner and then started after him, keeping their distance. Eldra peered around the corner, and after a moment beckoned to them. "He's rounded the other corner."

Now they were on the deepest-shadowed side of the house, where several tall trees blocked the moonlight, though none grew close enough to the wall to provide a handy branch to climb across—the security wasn't *that* sloppy. Rodrick boosted Eldra up to the top of the ten-foot wall, and she scurried over. A moment later a rope, with fat knots tied every foot or so, flew over the wall toward them. The Specialist skimmed up the line quick as a spider, and Rodrick clambered up after him and descended to the interior, pulling the rope after him and coiling it up to stow in his pack. They were all dressed in blacks and grays to blend in with the dark, and they moved low and quietly across the expanse of lawn, avoiding puddles of moonlight. They were alert for guard dogs or other security, but encountered nothing. Andraste probably didn't have any real enemies apart from the orcs of Belkzen, and Vellumis was a long way from the front, probably the safest city in Lastwall.

The windows on the first floor were all stained glass, but they climbed up a pillar—helpfully carved with ornamental hand- and footholds—to reach a ledge on the second floor. From there they moved, backs pressed against the wall—Rodrick, at least, wishing he was wearing white for this part—until they reached a window that actually opened. The Specialist slipped a bit of wire through the crack in the window to lift the inner latch, and just like that, they were inside.

The room beyond the window was a library, with some uncomfortable-looking chairs and high wooden shelves full of books and scrolls. The Specialist looked in danger of losing himself entirely, squinting in the darkness at the spines of the books until Eldra kicked him in the ankle and he remembered himself. He sighed, almost too softly to be heard, and continued on his way. The doors here had nice big keyholes, the kind servants and spies could peer through, so Eldra took a look out and then signaled the all-clear. They eased open the door and went into a dark hallway.

The house was sparsely decorated, with no carpets on the stone floors and empty niches that held no bits of ornamental statuary or war trophies. They hadn't been able to find floor plans of the house—there were ways to do so, but not in such a short amount of time—but they'd heard the chapel was in the center of the house, so they made their way down a wide staircase, testing each step carefully to make sure it wouldn't creak.

Downstairs, there was almost no furniture, which was good, since it was so dim they would have endlessly cracked their ankles and barked their shins against tables and chairs. They found the kitchen, with a cold store and a wood stove and a well-stocked pantry, along with a wooden table and straight-backed wooden chairs. The only thing of interest at all was a jug of wine on the counter, which Rodrick wanted to sample but didn't. This was a stealth mission, and they were meant to leave no sign of their presence.

Rodrick had never been a great fan of sneak-thieving. He preferred to be loud and charming, because why rob someone when it was possible to convince them to just *hand* you whatever you wanted? Still, he'd crept through his share of dark houses, and he'd never liked it. The only thing worse than the oppressive silence was the possibility of hearing a *noise*—or making one.

They finally found a door that led to a central room, and he knelt to look through the keyhole. A flame burned in a bowl, illuminating a tall statue of Iomedae, resplendent with a silver shield and golden-hilted sword, surrounded by stone benches . . . but there was no one inside. They eased the door open anyway and looked around, in case there was some alcove where Andraste might be abasing herself, but the place was deserted.

"Maybe she went to the privy," Eldra whispered. "Even the most rigorous religious devotions have to be put on hold when nature demands."

The Specialist shook his head. "That flame is fed by alchemical fuel, and will burn for ages without being replenished. Look at the benches. They're covered in dust. There's dust all over the floor, too, apart from our footsteps." He sighed. "We'll have to scrub those away, or risk being noticed. Andraste hasn't been here in a long time."

They walked backward through the dust, sweeping at the mess with the hem of the Specialist's cloak to quite literally cover their tracks. Back in the hallway, they stopped to consider their next move. "If she's not devoting herself to her god, then what *is* she doing?" Rodrick said.

"Indulging some other impulse, I would imagine," the Specialist said. "Perhaps one that isn't seen as befitting the dignity of a holy crusader of Lastwall. Perhaps even something Temple could use to blackmail her into supporting her plan with the Volunteers?"

"Aha," Eldra said. "Now we're into *my* territory."

23

A Desperate Offer

They went back upstairs, this time taking a different hallway, in search of a bedchamber—and they found one, at the end of the hall, the door standing slightly ajar, light spilling out. There were voices beyond the door, too: gasping in pain, or pleasure, or, Rodrick supposed, in both at once.

Eldra crept forward and risked glancing into the room—and then looked for a long moment before returning. She beckoned them through the open door of another room halfway down the hall, some sort of study with a meticulously neat desk and a map of the area around Lake Encarthan tacked up on the wall. "Well. We were right. Andraste's in there with three healthy-looking young people, two men and a woman—if any of them is older than twenty I'd be very surprised. We were right about there being some scourging, but I don't think it's for religious purposes, and everyone seems to be having a good time." She shook her head. "I don't think Andraste is devoting herself to a god. There are some Vudrani gods who look kindly on such activities, but I've always found your Inner Sea deities to be a bit more prudish. Even Cayden Cailean might disapprove, what with all the people being tied up."

"What now?" Rodrick said. "There are four people in there. How are we supposed to sneak up on *four* people unawares?"

"We could just barge in and make threats and steal the necklace, I suppose," Eldra said. "They're not armed, unless you count the whip, and it's not meant to be a serious weapon. We can tie them up and flee the city. With luck, we could get a long way off before Andraste freed herself and raised the alarm. If she raises the alarm at all—she might prefer to be discreet about the whole affair."

"That plan doesn't work for me," Rodrick said. "I still need to get Hrym."

"It's good you're loyal to your friend, but our alternative is *death*."

"I'm afraid she's right," the Specialist said.

A voice—probably Andraste's—boomed, "You, fetch more wine! No, not *him*, does he look like he can walk anywhere? I'm talking to *you*!"

The moment she said "wine" the Specialist darted from the room without a word of explanation, and Eldra and Rodrick looked at each other and shrugged. They settled back into the shadows, sitting on the floor beneath a window, and watched a very attractive young man wearing a small amount of military gear—some of which Rodrick thought was meant for warhorses, not humans— go padding barefoot down the corridor. They waited, listening to the noises drifting from the bedroom, Rodrick at least wondering what acts those sounds corresponded to. Eldra had been trained at the Conservatory, so she probably had an encyclopedic knowledge of such things. Not that he expected to ever find out firsthand, even if they lived. Alas.

Eventually the youth returned, carrying the jug of wine they'd seen in the kitchen, and a few minutes after *that* the Specialist returned and sat beside them. "It all depends on whether or not she shares the wine," he muttered.

Aha, Rodrick thought. The man was a quick thinker.

The noises stopped, and there was the low murmur of chat and laughter. They moved closer to the door so they could hear better. After a few minutes a woman said, "She's fallen asleep!"

"She did have a lot of wine already," a male voice said.

"Does she usually do this, Janna? You've been here before."

"She wears herself out, sure, but usually closer to dawn. Ah well. Anyone want to try the wine? I don't think she'll miss it."

Some time later, when the only sounds to be heard were faint snores, they risked going into the hallway. Eldra looked through the gap in the bedchamber door, then pushed it open. "Come on, they're all passed out."

The rest of the house was austere, but only because all the opulence had been piled in the bedroom: it was all velvet and cushions and four-poster feather bed and crystal chandelier . . . plus a fair bit of rope and some furniture that had obviously been custom-built by very discreet leatherworkers and carpenters for reasons Rodrick could guess at, and did.

Andraste was sprawled on the bed dressed in a version of a crusader's uniform that would most assuredly not have passed a military inspection, and the youths were attired even more outlandishly. Various implements were scattered on the floor, some familiar, some merely intriguing. Rodrick couldn't help but take in the view, and Eldra looked around knowingly, but the Specialist was all business. He tilted Andraste's head, making her snore more loudly, and removed the necklace from around her neck.

Eldra gasped and bent over, and a moment later Rodrick experienced a burning sensation, deep in his chest. *No no no.* They'd misjudged it, bungled it, the Specialist had misunderstood the passage he'd read or the person who'd written it hadn't known what they were talking about, they'd set off the gems, they were all going to *die* in this ridiculous room—

Rodrick coughed as something stuck in his throat, and then spat out a gleaming red gem that landed on the bedclothes and bounced.

Relief flooded him, like a cool wave washing through his body from the pit of his stomach up through the top of his head. He fell to his knees, looked at the gem, and then grinned at Eldra, who was smiling at him. They fell upon one another in an embrace, and suddenly she was kissing him, her mouth warm and wet and wonderful, and all the kisses before had *obviously* been pretense, because this was the real thing—

The Specialist cleared his throat, and Eldra pulled away from Rodrick. The old man knelt and picked up their gems—touching them fearlessly, which was more than Rodrick would have been able to do—and pressing them to a few of the half-dozen empty clasps on the necklace. The gems attached themselves firmly, and he put the necklace in his pocket.

Ah. They'd never discussed who'd get to *keep* the dangerous artifact. Then again, what good was it to Rodrick? He didn't want to sell it to anyone, because they would be inclined to use the horrible thing. The Specialist would probably just keep it as an object of study, at least. He probably had the wit to conquer the world, but he lacked the interest.

The Specialist took out the fake necklace they'd commissioned, carefully plucked out false gems until the new necklace matched the old, and carefully clasped the fake around Andraste's neck. He surveyed his work, gave them a nod, and strolled out of the room.

Rodrick picked up a particular item from the floor and showed it to Eldra, raising one eyebrow. "Do you have any idea what this is for?" he whispered.

"I mastered it fifty years ago, my boy," she said. "Maybe I'll teach you someday. Come on. Let's leave before the sleeping potion wears off."

They sat on a low stone wall by the harbor, watching the lights of distant ships twinkle on the water.

"What happens to the necklace now?" Eldra said.

The Specialist said, "I'd like to keep it."

"And *I'd* like a large quantity of money," Eldra said.

"Oh?" the Specialist said. "You'd prefer to sell it, then?"

They sat silently, and if the other two of them were anything like Rodrick, they were considering the nature of the necklace, and the sort of people who might buy it.

"All right, fair enough. But what are you going to do with it?" Eldra said.

"Study it, for a bit," the Specialist said. "See if there's a way to destroy it. If not, I'll drop all the gems in the middle of Lake Encarthan, and the necklace itself in the Obari Ocean. I don't like the idea of this thing continuing to exist."

"Huh," Rodrick said. "You never struck me as the type to believe there are forces humankind shouldn't meddle with."

"I wasn't, until someone used one of those forces to meddle with *me*. I usually don't take things personally. For the necklace, I will make an exception."

"Fair enough," Eldra said. She gazed at the harbor.

"It's been very educational, working with you," the Specialist said. "Why, just the things I saw in the general's bedchamber were immensely instructive."

Eldra snorted. "We've opened up a whole new avenue for your researches, I'm sure." She stretched her arms into the air and rolled her head around on her shoulders. "I feel almost free. This is where we part company, I suppose? Where are you headed next?"

The Specialist sighed. "I had business in Vellumis . . . but my last attempt to do that business led to my capture by the Bastion, so I'm afraid I'll have to give it up. If Prinn discovers we're still alive, he might perceive us as a threat, and act accordingly. I think it's time to move on and leave Vellumis behind. I may make my way to Kyonin. I don't know much about elves. They're interesting . . ."

"There are things you don't know much about?" Eldra said. "I'm astonished. I had a reason for visiting Vellumis, too, but like you, it didn't work out for me. I could take passage to Druma. There's always money to be made there, if you're savvy. What about you, Rodrick?"

Rodrick scowled. "What? I can't go anywhere. Hrym is still in the Bastion."

The Specialist shuddered. "A totenmaske with the resources of the Bastion at his disposal, *and* a sword like that . . ."

"Hrym would never help Prinn. He'd freeze him to death first."

"Oh, I don't know about that. As far as Hrym knows, Temple is still in charge. If someone who looks just like Temple says, 'Do as I say, or Rodrick will die,' Hrym might obey." Eldra shook her head. "That sword is very fond of you." She patted his hand. "I hope you get him back, Rodrick, but I wish you wouldn't try. You'll almost certainly die in the effort."

Rodrick had a scant bit of gold, and his wits, but he didn't have a lot of other resources. His chances of recovering Hrym were much better with these two on his team, and the three of them had already proven their ability to work well together. "Listen, both of you, there's a *monster* in that fortress. He wiped away Temple's mouth and stole her life. He's an abomination. What if he gets alone in a room with the Watcher-Lord and steals *his* identity? Prinn could bring down Lastwall entirely, release the orc hordes on the rest of the Inner Sea, break the seals on the Whispering Tyrant's prison. What then?" Appealing to their better natures was a risky move, since they were just as selfish as Rodrick himself, but he'd been stirred once or twice in the past by fate-of-the-world situations, if only because the destruction of the world would make life in general a lot less pleasant overall.

The Specialist stroked his mustache. "Prinn may be an abomination . . . but he's an abomination who did us a favor, in a way. We escaped our indentured servitude much earlier than I'd anticipated. As for the rest of it, I wouldn't worry. Totenmaskes aren't the world-conquering sort. It's not as if Prinn is a lich, or one of those vile undead sorcerers with a body composed of a swarm of writhing insects. Prinn is probably most interested in food, torture, and sex—not conquest."

Rodrick turned to Eldra, who looked at him with fondness and concern, but nothing like agreement. "Rodrick, really. If you had Hrym on your hip right now, you wouldn't be asking us to fight Prinn. You don't care about killing him any more than we do. Oh, if I were in front of him with a sword and had the opportunity to strike, I'd take it, just as I'd kill a venomous snake or stomp on a scorpion, because such a creature might hurt me later. But I don't go out of my way to *hunt* scorpions. You care about rescuing Hrym, and that's admirable, but it's not realistic." She put her hand on his knee. "I've grown rather fond of you, you know. We could go to Druma together."

He picked up her hand and put it back on her own knee. "I can't leave Hrym. We're . . . we're family."

Eldra shrugged. "Oh well. I tried. Good luck." She stood up, and the Specialist rose too.

"Wait!" Rodrick said desperately. "I don't think I can get Hrym back alone. What would it take to make you help me?"

"To go *back* into the Bastion, and face a totenmaske?" The Specialist shook his head. "Nothing you can provide, I'm afraid. As much as I enjoyed talking to Hrym, it would be best if you consider him lost, Rodrick. Move on with your life."

"No, listen, we don't *have* to face down Prinn. You're right, it's true, I don't really care if he rots out Lastwall or not. If we can avoid Prinn entirely, so much the better. How much to help me sneak into the Bastion and retrieve Hrym? He's probably still in that cursed sheath, hanging from the back of a chair in Temple's office, or down in our quarters, or tucked away in the armory. Surely the price for a simple *theft* is within my power?"

The Specialist *hmm*ed. "No," he said finally. "I don't see how."

Eldra nodded. "Sorry, darling. I'm sure you have the talents necessary to lay your hands on some gold, but I do, too, and can do so without getting within miles of Prinn." She turned away.

"Wait." Inspiration struck Rodrick, as it so often did when times were desperate. "You both came to Vellumis with missions in mind, didn't you? Missions that failed. How about this: I'll help you fulfill your goals, and in return, you'll help me fulfill mine."

"Mmm. You don't even know what those goals *are*," the Specialist said.

"It doesn't matter. There's not a job in the world I can't plan. Temple was a fool to put Merihim in charge—*I'm* a mastermind. You saw how smoothly I pulled off the theft of the necklace."

"It was the Specialist who thought to race ahead and put the sleeping potion in the wine," Eldra pointed out.

"Yes, of course, I'm not disparaging his talents, *or* yours, but the original plan to switch the jewelry and escape undetected was mine, wasn't it? The Specialist knows everything, but he's not a planner, and I have nothing but respect for your abilities, too, Eldra, but this is what I do: make plans and execute them. Let me do it for you."

"*If* you can get me what I came for . . . then I'll help you retrieve Hrym," Eldra said.

"Hmm," the Specialist said. "I suppose another few days in the city won't hurt, if we're discreet. I agree."

"You won't regret this." Rodrick stifled a yawn. It had been a long day and a longer night. They'd have to find a place to hole up and sleep soon. "Tell me what you want, and I'll figure out how to get it."

"I want to steal a book," the Specialist said.

"I want to steal a ring," Eldra said.

"That should be easy enough," Rodrick said, inaccurately.

24

A Family Heirloom

It's called the Interdicted Library," the Specialist said. He and Rodrick sat in the common room eating bowls of nutritious mush. They were sharing a room with one narrow bed, which meant Rodrick, who'd lost the coin toss, had spent the night on a hard stone floor. As a result, he was rather less cheery than the Specialist. "Interdicted means prohibited, or forbidden," the Specialist went on.

"Yes, I know *words*," Rodrick said. "That one, anyway."

Eldra joined them, looking fresh and lovely, and one of the serving girls brought her a plate of fried eggs, the yolks golden and shimmering, along with toasted bread and a slab of ham glistening with delicious grease.

"How did you get that?" Rodrick said. "They didn't even *offer* me that, at any price!"

"I make friends easily," Eldra said. "What's this about you knowing words? That sounds implausible."

Rodrick reached for a piece of bread and she slapped his hand away with enough force to keep him from trying again, so Rodrick returned to his mush. "The Specialist was telling me about the book he wants to steal. Or, I guess, the place he wants to steal it *from*."

The Specialist nodded. "It is a library, of sorts, though the librarians are heavily armed, and don't read the books on the shelves. No one reads them, which is the worst thing that can happen to a book, really. It's like unplayed music or uneaten food."

"Or unspent gold." Rodrick glanced at Eldra. "Or unkissed lips."

"Quite." The Specialist stirred his spoon around, looking down at the bowl of mush as if it were a scrying bowl showing him secrets. "When the Shining Crusade defeated the Whispering Tyrant, they found his collection of magical volumes. Being defenders of righteousness and honor . . . they burned them all." He sighed. "I can understand why, of course. These were books bound in the skin of intelligent creatures, some of them still alive and suffering due to dark magic. Books that screamed when you opened them. Books with words that could climb inside your eyes and repeat themselves in your mind until you went mad, books with pages that drew blood, books with portals to the Abyss embedded in their footnotes. They were *bad* books. Still, they contained much knowledge, and wisdom, and much of value was lost. Of course, some books are so magical they *can't* burn, or be torn to pieces, or be blotted out by ink. So potent that even throwing them into a pool of lava doesn't do anything but warm them up. *Those* books cannot be eradicated, so they have to be hidden away, instead. Lastwall created a secret library, the *Interdicted* Library, to store those volumes—and, over time, the collection grew as the crusaders added any other rare, dangerous, heretical, or simply *alarming* volumes they came across. Now in addition to books of dark magic, the library holds the private diaries of people who became gods—complete with unsavory secrets—and *true* histories of nations that reveal the recorded histories to be lies, and books written in the forgotten tongues of lost races. Basically, when any crusader finds a volume that's too disturbing to leave alone and too dangerous or interesting or powerful to destroy, it goes into that library." He paused. "I should clarify that when I say 'library,' I do not mean a single room full of books, or even one building.

There is danger in putting too many magical volumes together, and so there are caches scattered throughout Lastwall, some hidden in plain sight, others buried deep in unknown places. Even an enterprising and ingenious thief could never hope to plunder even a fraction of them."

"How do you know all this?" Rodrick asked.

"I met a beggar in Cheliax, a man with no eyes. We became friends, and he told me he'd been a librarian—which is to say a guard, really—in a Vellumis branch of the Interdicted Library. He was actually illiterate when he took the position, but all those long hours with the books made him curious, so he learned to read, and he *did* read, in stolen moments when the other guards weren't looking, for a few months, until he was discovered."

"They blinded him when they found out he'd been reading the books?" Rodrick was aghast. That seemed uncharacteristically vicious by Lastwall's standards.

The Specialist shook his head. "No. He opened the wrong book one day, and the words he saw seared his eyes right out of his head. He was found on his back with smoke rising from his eye sockets. Somehow, he survived, and escaped the asylum where they put him after he wouldn't stop gibbering, and eventually drifted to Cheliax. As far as I know he lives there still . . . and in rather better circumstances than he used to, given how much I paid him to tell me everything he knew about the library."

"You tried to break in?" Rodrick said.

The Specialist nodded. "I did. The former guard told me about a back entrance, accessible through an old tunnel, forgotten and never guarded." He sighed. "At some point since the blind librarian's exile, they started guarding it. I wonder what other security measures they might have put in place, after his accident. I didn't get far enough to find out."

Rodrick whistled. "What were you hoping to get your hands on?"

"Oh, there are a few volumes I've heard about. I'd like to cart off the whole place, of course, but I'd settle for an hour to peruse the stacks and choose a few indispensable items."

Rodrick nodded. "All right. We'll do it tonight."

"Why does he get to go first?" Eldra objected.

"He doesn't," Rodrick said. "We're going to do yours *today*."

She smiled, dipped her toast in her egg yolk, and offered Rodrick a bite.

"Why do you want this ring anyway?" Rodrick said.

"Would you believe it's a family heirloom?"

They were lounging on the grass in a shady park, with a good view of a parade ground where a group of infantry crusaders were drilling marching maneuvers, moving in matched step with their pikes held at the ready, periodically dropping to their knees to create a wall of spikes in a maneuver designed to impale charging enemy cavalry. What did orc cavalry even *ride*? Dire wolves? Carnivorous horses? Big lizards? He hoped he never had to find out.

"I might believe it's a *valuable* family heirloom," he said.

She chuckled. "It's not, particularly. A signet ring that belonged to my husband's grandfather, and was passed down through the generations, son to son. It features the family crest, a sort of stylized blackbird. I always thought it looked like a bird with its head bent to pick lice out of its own armpit, or wingpit, but that wasn't an observation I ever shared."

"So one of those, ah, fine young men of Lastwall over there is, what, your grandson?"

"Close. I'm almost ninety years old, Rodrick. True, I started having children a bit late, but my progeny didn't. My oldest grandchild is nearly forty now, and *his* son, my great-grandson, is an idealistic youth of eighteen. Firstborn, too. Renounced all claim on his family titles in order to fight for righteousness and glory. The only reason he's not already a corpse being eaten by demons at the Worldwound is because the family convinced him there was more honor in joining the crusaders of Lastwall. Since the demons began erupting from the ground up north, Lastwall's had trouble getting as many recruits, you see. The really war-crazed zealots with dreams of glory all go to Mendev to die in the killing fields there. The family convinced young Tobern there that it would be more meaningful to come here, where the help is more desperately needed. Also, of course, it's a *bit* safer in Lastwall, though they didn't mention that part. Tobern has the signet ring. I doubt anyone else in the family even remembers it. Why would they? No one's used it for anything but putting a mark on blobs of wax on parchment in generations."

"Are we going to have to pluck it off his finger?" Rodrick said. "We've already stolen one piece of jewelry off a crusader, so I don't see why we can't do it again."

"Ha. No, he doesn't wear the ring, and that ploy wouldn't work on him anyway. Tobern isn't as susceptible to the distractions of the flesh and adulterated wine as Andraste was. He's celibate by choice—though I suppose he might make an exception if Iomedae herself appeared before him and loosened the straps on her armor—and has never touched a drop of alcohol. He came into Lastwall with a great deal of money—his personal inheritance—and he donated all of it to the cause. As a result he was given a commission as a junior officer, and gained his very own tiny room adjoining the barracks where some of the regular soldiers are housed. I have reason to believe the ring is in the chest at the foot of his bed, in a small box of keepsakes and souvenirs—a few letters, a cameo that belonged to his mother, that sort of thing. He's just a *tiny* bit sentimental—it's an occasional weakness in warriors for the cause of good."

"You *think* the ring is there? You don't know for sure?"

"I didn't get close enough to confirm, I'm afraid. I was caught just before I could break into his room. I got unlucky, and was noticed by a crusader who couldn't be charmed. Warrior ascetics can be *so* unreasonable. But I was told about the box of keepsakes by a reliable source, and there's hardly anywhere else in that tiny room where he could keep the ring."

"What source? You left your family ages ago."

"Oh, some of the maids are still paid to send me letters, though they think they're sending the notes to business rivals looking for some advantage to exploit. I've remained curious about the family fortunes, though less so than I used to be, since most of my relatives are strangers to me now."

Rodrick sighed. "Then why do you want the ring? *You* don't have much of a sentimental streak."

"Nonsense. If I weren't a little bit sentimental, I wouldn't be here with you. Let's just say the ring is the key to something more."

"Let's just say you *tell* me what the ring is the key to. Surely we're close enough for that?"

She chuckled. "Fine. The founder of my husband's family, the one who made it into a force to be reckoned with, was something of a scoundrel. Indeed, his line of work wasn't that different from *ours*, though he plied his trade with less finesse. He was a pirate, with the good sense to take his ill-gotten gains and move them into legitimate businesses once he'd amassed enough of a fortune. He didn't have any great romanticized love for the outlaw life, you see, unlike *some* of us: he just knew thieving was the fastest way to gather a great deal of capital. He started as a homeless wharf rat who learned to sail, gathered a group of black-hearted villains who *also* learned how to sail . . . and then stole a ship. They were one of many scourges of the sea for a few years, and then he retired. Whether he paid off the rest of his crew, or passed the business to them, or left them all to drown, no one seemed to know. The family didn't like to talk about their origins."

"If I ever have descendants, I'm sure they'll be similarly ashamed of me," Rodrick said. "What does this have to do with the ring?"

"It was our founder's ring, of course. There was a story in the family, only it was more of a joke, that the old pirate had hidden away a great treasure of gold and jewels in a safe place, in a vault sealed by magic and guarded by monsters, just in case he ever needed to abandon his new, respectable life and start over again. No one really believed it—those who spoke of the treasure said it was a story the old man liked to tell when reliving his glory days, and by all accounts the size of the hoard and its location changed from telling to telling."

"Aha," Rodrick said. "But you have reason to think differently?"

"I started thinking about it after I took the sun orchid elixir and became young again—because when you become young after being old, Rodrick, you immediately start thinking about how you can *stay* young. As I've said, stealing the elixir again would probably be a bad idea, but if you can amass a nice big fortune . . . So I became curious about those stories about the vault. It seemed improbable, but worth investigating. In my newly young form, I went to the family estate and claimed to be my own cousin. I was incredibly sad to hear of my own recent death. I had letters—from myself—to prove my identity, and so they welcomed me and let me stay at the estate for a few months. I claimed to be a student of the history of the Inner Sea, and was given free run of the family library and archives by my not-very-bookish descendants. I burrowed through the dust and found ledgers and journals no one had looked at in a century, if not longer, including the personal writings of our piratical family founder. They were in a cipher, but you learn to break codes at the Conservatory right along with how to play the harp and snap necks and make men and women go weak in the knees with a look, so it was the work of only a few days to unravel his mysteries."

"And the stories were true." Rodrick shook his head. "Remarkable. Was there a map with a big X drawn on it, leading you to the treasure?"

"Nothing so traditional, but in between the lists of grudges and vendettas—and the horrible truth about what he'd done to the rest of his crew—the old man did talk about building a vault, and hiring a wizard to secure it, and then killing the wizard so no one would know *how* he'd secured it, and keeping the key with him always, and so forth. He was a bit coy about the location of the vault—or else, he just didn't bother to mention it, because he didn't expect anyone else to read his journals, and he *knew*—but I pieced together the details of his journey and figured out where it must be, under a hill near a remote farm we own where the people grow spelt."

"I don't even know what spelt *is*."

"A sort of wheat, I gather. You can eat it or make beer from it. At any rate, I took a trip to the farm . . . and it turned out to be all hills. Hills upon hills. Why anyone would farm at all in such hilly country is beyond me. I spent the next *year* poking around hills, trying not to be noticed, looking for traces of magic, or for places where digging had been done, but the vault had been built many years earlier, and all the traces were gone. I'm nothing if not persistent, though, and eventually I found what looked like an old dry well, descended into it, knocked down a crumbling stone wall, and there it was: a little round door, just like the one our great-pirate-father had written about. I crawled down a short hallway, and the passage opened up into a corridor high enough to stand in." She spread her hands. "There was the vault door, etched with mystic symbols. And utterly indestructible and immovable."

"Because you didn't have the key."

"I didn't. I hadn't worried about it. I just thought, if there's a key, there's a lock, and a lock can be picked . . . but it wasn't that kind of lock."

"Aha. A magical lock. Which is where the ring comes in."

"In the center of the door, right at my eye level, there was a little circle, and inside it, indentations shaped like a blackbird pecking at its own lice. I recognized the design instantly."

"So the signet ring is the key. Lovely."

"Exactly. I filled the well with rocks to keep anyone *else* from stumbling upon it, and set out for Lastwall to find my great-grandson Tobern, and here we are."

"You know, after we rescue Hrym, if you need help *retrieving* that treasure . . ."

"You sweet, sweet boy." Eldra patted him on the cheek.

"Your mistake was trying to break into Tobern's quarters," Rodrick said. "When, after all, you could have been *invited.*"

She opened her mouth, then closed it, then frowned, and then smiled.

25

A Family Reunion

Cousin Ashima?" Tobern said, bewildered. "Is that really you?" He was young, earnest-looking, and handsome, apart from his jug ears and terrible haircut. He was also large, heavily armed, and standing on the edge of a parade ground with many other large and heavily armed men, so Rodrick decided to keep any observations about ears and grooming to himself.

Eldra leaned forward and kissed the young crusader on both cheeks, then stepped back, beaming at him. "Tobern! What a fine figure of a man you've become! You were, what, a boy of fourteen when I saw you last?"

"Thirteen." He stared at her, a smile that wavered between bewilderment and delight on his face. "I—I'm sorry, I just wasn't expecting . . . What are you *doing* here?"

Rodrick tried to imagine what it would have been like to have Eldra wandering the halls of *his* house when he'd been thirteen, and knew immediately what sort of impression she'd probably made on Tobern.

She twirled her parasol prettily and laughed. "Oh, I know, I'm sorry, I didn't mean to *accost* you in public this way, and when you're busy training besides. I've just had the hardest time getting in touch with you!" She wrinkled her nose. "I know you must be terribly busy, but I thought you'd at *least* visit the inn where I'm staying. I know I arrived a few days early, but I thought by *now*—"

Tobern frowned. "Cousin, I had no idea you were staying anywhere! I haven't heard from you in years."

Rodrick snorted a laugh and tried to look like a crass hireling. "Told you, ma'am."

Tobern gave him a speculative look, and Rodrick ducked his chin and knuckled his forehead. Perhaps that was a bit much, but the boy *was* an aristocrat by breeding, and if you bowed and scraped the way they expected, they tended to stop looking at you closely.

Eldra frowned. "You mean didn't get my letter?"

Tobern shook his head, the very picture of bafflement. Rodrick thought rather unkindly of the confused way puppies looked if you hid their toys under a blanket. "No, I didn't, but sending messages can be unreliable. What did your letter say?"

"Oh." She pouted. "Many things, of course—but mainly that I was visiting Lastwall, and hoped I'd be able to see you."

He shook his head. "This is an odd place to come for a holiday, Cousin. I thought you'd returned to Jalmeray?"

"I did indeed, to write papers on what I'd learned about the history of our family in the Inner Sea. Even on my faraway island I received the occasional tidbit of news, though, and when I heard you'd joined the crusaders of Lastwall I realized how little I knew about the place. I began doing research, and, well." She beamed. "It's fascinating. Such a grand and glorious tradition you've joined, protecting the world from the restless spirit of that monstrous conqueror!"

Tobern blinked at her. "Ah. Yes. It's—yes. Mostly these days we're concerned with the orc threat, of course, but many of us spend at least some time watching over the Whispering Tyrant's tomb."

"Oh, I'm sure there are all *sorts* of nuances that escape me— there's only so much that books can tell you, which is why I'm here. I want to bring word of the glory of Lastwall's crusaders back to Jalmeray." She lowered her voice to a conspiratorial whisper. "There are those among the Vudrani who think the denizens of the Inner Sea are barbarous, devoid of fine feeling, nobility, and virtue. I want to show them how wrong they are. If I write an account of the crusaders of Lastwall, the most noble and honorable people on the entire continent, I think I could change their minds. It could create a new atmosphere of warmth between the nations, and perhaps even inspire Vudrani fighters to join your cause here! What a coup! And you, Tobern—you could be the key to the whole thing." She squinted at the sky, or rather, at the underside of her parasol. "It's terribly hot in the sun—could we go to your rooms and discuss this further?"

Rodrick suppressed a chuckle at her wilting-flower routine. Jalmeray was orders of magnitude hotter than this for most of the year, but her credulous "cousin" didn't seem to realize that.

Tobern glanced at the parade field, where the crusaders were packing up their gear and departing, with much gruff rumbling and manly camaraderie. "I—I have a bit of free time, yes." He glanced at me. "Who's your, ah . . ."

"Hmm? Oh, that's just Rodrick. He's very reliable, and he's kept me out of trouble more than once."

The crusader looked relieved. "That's good. I'm glad you have someone looking out for you. Vellumis is very safe, but some of the countryside hereabouts is . . . less secure."

"Oh, you must tell me *all* about it, back in your room . . ."

They'd discussed what to do once they were within reach of the signet ring. A *normal* happy reunion would have involved drinking, and they could have slipped the last precious drops of the Specialist's sleeping potion into a glass of wine and stolen the ring once Tobern passed out, but of course he never touched the stuff. For much the same reason, seduction was out, even though it was easy to steal from a man sleeping naked beside you. Tobern might certainly *think* impure thoughts about her—"I'd be insulted if he didn't," Eldra noted—but he was sufficiently young and idealistic and iron-willed that she didn't think he'd give in. She also vetoed Rodrick's second-best idea, hitting him over the head with something heavy and stealing *lots* of things. "He *is* family, you know."

They finally settled on a more straightforward approach, with the bashing-over-the-head idea as a fallback.

Tobern's rank was high enough that he had a small stove in his quarters, and so they were able to drink tea, which Rodrick had always considered a foul concoction. Eldra loved it, but only proper Vudrani tea, not the "vile piss-water" they served on this continent. The two of them both made appreciative noises as they sipped what Tobern gave them anyway.

Eldra chattered away about her imaginary experiences as a scholar in Jalmeray, and Tobern gradually opened up and talked about his motives for coming to Lastwall, which was all the usual idealistic twaddle about giving something back to society and the importance of leading a life with real meaning and so on. If he'd said, "I'm bloodthirsty and want to lop off orc heads by the score," Rodrick would have found it equally distasteful, but at least that would have been *comprehensible.*

Eldra and Tobern sat together on the bed—as the hired help, Rodrick made do with a stool in the corner—and she reached over and touched his face. "Do you know," she said softly, "I hope my son grows up to be a man as noble as you."

Tobern blinked. "You have a son?"

She sighed. "Not yet, but soon, I hope. I have been promised to a fine young man—a distant relation of the thakur, in fact—and we're to be married in the fall. This is likely my last trip to the Inner Sea for some time. I *am* eager to start a family, of course, but I'll miss the opportunity to travel." Eldra twisted a ring on her finger; it was a nice touch, Rodrick had to admit, and he saw Tobern glance down at her hand and notice. "I'd hoped to stop by your family's estates to see if perhaps there was some little keepsake or heirloom they'd be willing to part with, that I could give to *my* son someday, to let him know he has a connection to your people. I know it's silly, but I just love this land so much, and I'm afraid he'll grow up without that fondness. I wouldn't ask for anything valuable, of course—something of purely sentimental value, perhaps one of those little silver figurines your great-grandmother collected, or one of the books I so enjoyed when I stayed that summer, or a piece of jewelry—"

"How about a ring?" Tobern went to the footlocker at the end of the bed and lifted the lid, rooting around inside for a while.

Eldra looked at Rodrick, raised one eyebrow, and kissed the air at him.

Tobern returned to the bed and held out . . . a chunky silver ring, but not a signet. "This is an old family heirloom, and I would be honored if you'd take it to give to your son, or daughter, when the time is right."

"Oh, Tobern, you're *so* generous." She clasped his hands in hers, warmly, and then took on an abstracted expression. "Is this—this isn't *the* ring, is it? The one the founder of your family passed down from son to son to son? My great-grandmother told me about it once in a letter—

He laughed. "You mean the signet ring? No, nothing like that. This was my grandfather's ring, a gift from my grandmother, but he couldn't bear to wear it, after she passed—too many memories—and he gave it to me. No, the signet . . . Well, in truth I should have left it back at home for my brother, since I'm unlikely to ever have children."

"Oh, well, if you'd like to give it to *me*, I was going to visit the estate anyway . . ."

Nicely done, Rodrick thought.

Tobern shook his head. "That's kind, but that ring . . . it's the one connection we have to our family's founder. I know it's a bit ridiculous, but it's sort of a *solemn* thing, passing it from hand to hand, man to man. My brother plans to visit me in a few months, and I'm going to give it to him then. Did you know, there's even this old story—almost a family legend—about the ring. They say it's the key to a vault full of treasure. Have you ever heard of such a thing?"

Eldra listened to him avidly, focusing her full attention on him, and he gave his full attention back to *her* as he spoke. Rodrick rose, stretched, yawned, and reached into the pocket where he'd concealed a length of leather wrapped around several bits of lead. Eldra narrowed his eyes at him, then suddenly bent double, retching horribly.

Tobern leapt up. "Cousin! Cousin, are you all right?"

"I—I just— Air, I need air. Please, help me out."

The crusader put his arm around her and helped her to her feet, and Eldra contrived very naturally to knock over both their teacups in the process, retching and gasping all the while. Rodrick leapt to his feet and opened the door for them. "You tend to her, good master, and I'll just clean up that mess."

Tobern ignored him as thoroughly as a king would ignore a sparrow, all his attention focused on his sick relation

When they were gone, Rodrick went and rifled through the chest at the end of the bed until he found a small box full of letters bound with ribbon, colored stones, locks of hair—and, yes, an ancient signet ring bearing the distorted image of a crow. He pocketed the ring, put everything back as he'd found it, then picked up the cups and dabbed a bit at the puddle of cold tea with one of the crusader's shirts.

When Rodrick got outside, Eldra was clearly much better, leaning against the wall of the adjoining barracks with a wan smile on her face. "I'm so sorry. It's the foreign water, you see. I'm not entirely accustomed to it yet, and sometimes my stomach . . ."

"Are you sure you're all right? I could find a healer . . ."

She patted Tobern's cheek. "You're too good to me, Cousin. No, I think I should go back to the inn and rest. Perhaps I can call on you tomorrow?"

"I've got sentry duty tomorrow, but the next day? I can try to arrange some leave, and show you some of the sights of Lastwall."

"*Nothing* would please me more." She squeezed his hand, then leaned on Rodrick. "Take me home."

As they walked out of the crusader compound and onto one of the well-maintained streets of Vellumis, she said, "Give me the ring *now*."

He sighed and passed it over. "As if I'd steal it from you. I don't know where the vault is, except for someplace with hills, where they grow spelt."

"And even then I could have been lying. Maybe it wasn't a hill at all, but a rock wall. Maybe it wasn't spelt, but millet. I still feel better with it in *my* hand."

"You reminded him of the ring, you know. He might go looking for it. When he realizes it's missing, he might suspect you."

She shrugged. "We won't be in Vellumis long. The inn where I claimed to be staying isn't the place where I *am*. He won't think I stole the ring, anyway, though he might think you did. Even if he does suspect me . . . He's a young and idealistic crusader. A little disillusionment will do him a great deal of good. He might even live longer."

26

The Interdicted Library

They met the Specialist in a row of market stalls, where he was happily arguing with a pottery seller about various methods for firing and glazing pots. When Eldra and Rodrick arrived he looked at them blankly for a moment, as if unsure who they were, then said, "I found a room for us."

They followed him through the orderly streets of Vellumis until they reached an unassuming house of stone and timber, leading them around the back to a cellar door. "The place is owned by an old blind woman living on a widow's pension—her husband died in some battle long ago, and while the Crusaders give her enough to live on, she was happy to take some extra coin to rent out her basement."

They followed him into the dark, where he lit a lamp, and Rodrick grunted. The Specialist was good at procuring and facilitating, he had to admit. For a root cellar, it was almost cozy, with three cots and blankets—and, of course, an array of glassware and vials on a wooden table in the corner. "We needed a base of operations if we're going to free Hrym," the Specialist explained. "This place is conveniently located between the Bastion of Justice and the Interdicted Library." He frowned at Eldra. "I assume you succeeded in your mission?"

Eldra nodded. "If we'd failed, I wouldn't be here."

"Did you get the items we discussed?" Rodrick said.

"Yes, and I did the necessary forging, too. Come see."

Rodrick examined the Specialist's work. "I have no idea what the real thing is supposed to look like, but this is certainly impressive. The seals, and the calligraphy . . . this paper is more substantial than some clothes I've owned. You've got a real gift for this sort of thing. Why didn't you try to trick your way into the library like this in the first place?"

The Specialist smoothed his mustaches. "I am not as skilled at imposture as you and Eldra. I have no natural talent for pretending to be something I'm not, and while I've always thought I should study acting, there are only so many years in one's life. Besides . . . I thought I had a secret way in. If I'd been faced with no approach but the direct approach, I'm not sure *what* I would have done."

"Fortunately, for this operation, you can just be yourself: inscrutable and distracted. I'll be in charge of pretending to be someone else. Should we go now?"

The Specialist shook his head. "Better to wait a few hours, until it's later in the guards' shift, when they're more bored."

"Right. Of course." Rodrick looked around the cellar. Spending the next several hours just sitting here would be intolerable. The only reason he wasn't going mad with worry over Hrym was because he was keeping busy, exercising his mind and occupying his body. The others didn't really understand. They heard Hrym speak, but they still thought of him as an *object*, a sword with peculiar magical properties.

But Hrym was more than a wondrous item to Rodrick. He was more, even, than a friend, or a brother-in-arms. Sometimes Rodrick thought he and Hrym were in some way two halves of a broken circle, made whole only by their partnership. Rodrick had never felt complete until his hand first closed on Hrym's hilt. He'd lived a life before the sword, and in that life he'd been so alone he hadn't even recognized his solitude. His life had always been devoid of trust, but with Hrym, there was someone he could count on completely, without question, or hesitation, or misgiving.

Of course, he'd never tell Hrym any of that—the sword would mock him relentlessly—but those were the facts. Prinn would either abuse Hrym's powers for his own gain, or keep the sword in the antimagic sheath that kept him unconscious, and Rodrick couldn't leave his partner to either fate.

"Could you stop pacing?" the Specialist said from his alchemy table. "It's making me very nervous."

Rodrick stopped. He hadn't even been aware of his own relentless motion, his brain full of *Hrym Hrym Hrym*.

Eldra seemed to understand, and put her hand on his arm. "You know, I didn't have a proper breakfast, and it's past time for lunch. Come with me to get something to eat? Then you'll be properly fortified for your next mission." She snorted. "'Mission,' did you hear me? I wasn't in the Volunteers for long, but it was long enough for their nonsense to rub off on me."

"Yes, that's a good idea. We'll walk around a bit, clear my head, feed the body."

They went into the open air and strolled down the street arm-in-arm. "Though it pains me to suggest obscuring your gorgeous face," Rodrick said, "you should probably put up your hood. It's a big city, but it would be awkward if your 'cousin' caught sight of you."

"Why don't you have to hide *your* face? He saw you, too."

Rodrick shook his head. "He *met* me, but he didn't see me. He just saw a servant. He was too busy gazing at you to notice anything else."

"He did seem a bit smitten, poor boy. As far as he knows we're only just *barely* related by blood, the thinnest of trickles, and in his experience even first cousins sometimes get married. Did you see how his face fell when I told him I was to be wed?"

"I did. And then he immediately felt guilty and became *more* chivalrous to make up for it. You really are very good at what you do, Eldra. Now, hood up, please."

She sighed, but complied. "I feel like Merihim, hiding in this damn cloak."

"Oh, now. You're slightly prettier than Merihim was."

Eldra scowled. "*Slightly?*"

"She had a nice face, even if it was the color of fresh blood, and apart from the way she smirked all the time. She had a *very* good body. Before it exploded, anyway."

"A good body! You shouldn't talk this way to a woman you love, Rodrick."

"Oh, don't worry. I wouldn't."

"Fair enough. You shouldn't talk this way to a woman you lust after, either."

"I know what we have, Eldra. You flirt, you joke, and you insinuate, but I realized about two days after I met you that I'd have to enjoy the banter and flirtation on their own merits, because you were never going to follow through."

"Oh, I don't know about *never*. The time hasn't seemed quite right yet, though. When we shared our room in the Bastion, I honestly thought it was inevitable, but now . . . those cots the Specialist got don't look too comfortable, and there's a certain lack of privacy."

"Let me rephrase," Rodrick said. "It's better for me to assume that there will never be anything more than flirtation between us, because otherwise, I would spend all my time wondering and hoping, and in general being distracted from my other duties." He paused. "Besides, you're old enough to be my great-grandmother."

"You have to admit, I've held up well, though." She patted his arm. "Maybe I'll bake you some cookies, then, or knit you a scarf."

After a pleasant meal at a chophouse, where Eldra's sparkling conversation *almost* made Rodrick stop thinking about Hrym for whole minutes at a time, they returned to their basement. The Specialist was waiting, already dressed in the dull garb of a soldier, complete with mail shirt. Rodrick hurriedly dressed in similar garments, procured by the Specialist, who'd managed to acquire clothing that fit Rodrick better than many garments he'd picked out himself.

They grabbed a handle on either side of a heavy metal box, about two feet on each side, and wrestled it out of the cellar and into a wheelbarrow. After a glance at the Specialist, who just looked at him expectantly, Rodrick sighed, grabbed the handles, and began to wheel their burden forward. The Specialist had planned a route that stuck to alleyways and little-traveled side streets, and while they saw a few people, they didn't encounter any crusader officers who might ask pointed questions.

The Vellumis branch of the Interdicted Library was a dilapidated stone building in a row of the same, so obviously abandoned that small plants were growing from cracks in the walls. "Very convincing," Rodrick said. "Aren't they afraid the walls will come tumbling down?"

"They're *very* solid on the inside," the Specialist said. "And fortified with magic, too. I think I know what to expect in there, but if things become . . . complicated . . . you still have my special ring, yes?"

Rodrick held up his hand, displaying the hollow ring loaded with the sleeping potion. "I do indeed. But I thought we wanted to do this *quietly*?"

"We do, but in case things get . . . loud . . . be prepared to disable the nearest guard, hmm?"

"I'm always prepared for treachery. Present situation excepted."

The Specialist led Rodrick around the back of the building, then hammered his fist on a stout wooden door.

A panel in the door slid open, and eyes appeared. "What do you want?"

The Specialist held up the document he'd forged, its parchment and seals so official-looking that Rodrick felt an elemental variety of fear every time he glanced at it. "We've got a new addition to the collection."

"Let me see the documentation."

The Specialist slid the parchment through the opening, which slid shut. After a full five minutes, the panel slid open again. "This all looks to be in order. Let me unlock the door."

That was apparently a laborious process, with many bolts sliding free, before the door opened silently on well-oiled hinges. The Specialist went in first, and Rodrick pushed the wheelbarrow after him, grunting at the effort.

The guard, a sandy-haired fellow about Rodrick's age, whistled. "Must be a bad one." He nodded at the metal box. "Haven't seen one *that* heavily sealed more than once or twice before."

Rodrick put down the wheelbarrow and mopped his brow, looking around. There was a desk, a chair, and a small woodstove in this dim and windowless room, and beyond that, a fence of iron ran from wall to wall and floor to the ceiling, the bars so close together it would have been hard even to wriggle a finger through the cracks. It was impossible to see what lay beyond the wall of iron. A gate in the door was heavily chained and barred, almost as if to keep something inside locked up. The gate glimmered with bluish light, probably some sort of magical ward.

"You been on this duty long?" Rodrick said as the guard resealed the door behind them.

The man grunted. "Two months, this time, but I've done two other rotations. Most people don't manage more than one."

"Huh. Why's that? Seems a little dull, but I've met plenty of soldiers who'd appreciate a nice quiet posting."

The guard shook his head. "Ha. You might think it's quiet. Most of the time it is. But sometimes the books make *noise*. They whisper, sort of, and while I can't ever make out the words, some people can. Depends on what kind of mind you have, or so they say. I've never been much for daydreams and flights of fancy, and that's the best kind of guard for this place. Practical, down to earth. Even so, nobody's allowed to do more than three months at a stretch anymore. There have been . . . incidents."

Rodrick looked appropriately worried. "Magic. Never liked the stuff."

"You and me both, brother."

"Are you all alone in here?"

"Nah. Always at least two of us, since some . . . mishaps . . . in the old days. Now they station one out front here, and one back in the cage."

"The cage?" Rodrick glanced at the warded iron wall again.

"Where the books are locked up. They're more dangerous than any wild animal. My partner's a spellcaster, in case there's a problem a sword can't solve." He nodded to the Specialist, who was fussing with the bolts and chains holding the metal box closed. "He doesn't talk much, does he?"

Though that was a hilariously inaccurate statement, Rodrick just nodded. "Doesn't seem to. I don't know the man well. He's an expert in these sorts of things, apparently."

The guard nodded sagely. "Sure. You can't let just anybody handle these books and scrolls and things. You have to know what you're doing. That's my partner's territory, though, and he's welcome to it. I'm just here to stab anyone who tries to break in. Where'd this new book come from?"

"I was with General Andraste's division, up in the Hold," Rodrick said. "We took down an orc camp, and found a whole cache of magical artifacts, including this book. One of the shamans fought to the death rather than surrender it."

The guard grunted. "Say what you will about orcs, they aren't afraid to die. Didn't realize they were much for reading, though. I'll call my partner, so he can examine the book and see where it needs to be shelved."

Rodrick kept a bland expression. "No need to go to all that trouble. I'm sure my friend here can put it away."

The guard shook his head. "Doesn't work that way. You can't just shove the book on a shelf—you have to do tests and make sure there won't be any negative interactions." At Rodrick's questioning look, he said, "You know how, when you mix the wrong chemicals together, you can make a poisonous cloud? Or mix together the right powders, and you can make something that explodes?"

"Or mix wine and liquor, and get a nasty headache the next day?"

The guard chuckled. "Exactly. The books are a bit like that. Put the wrong magical books together, and they might feed on each other, or fight each other, or suck all the air out of the room, or who knows what. My partner has all manner of wands and crystals and such to measure the magic and keep things from going bad. Besides, we can't just open up the gate and let you wander back there. The wards prevent people from passing through, and we only deactivate them during shift changes or emergencies. We'll pass the book through a slot in the gate, and you can be on your way. My partner will make sure your prize has a good home."

Rodrick's heart sank. How was the Specialist going to get into the stacks?

"How's it coming there?" the guard called to the Specialist.

"Just about ready," said the Specialist, and then he opened up the metal box. Great gouts of white smoke poured out, and something inside began to howl.

27

A Special Collection

R odrick spun around, hand going to the sword at his waist, and the guard leapt back and swore.

The Specialist backed away from the box, holding up his hands as if to ward off an attack. The horror on his face was so convincing it made Rodrick nervous; maybe the old man was better at acting than he let on. Rodrick hoped so.

The Specialist whimpered. "No . . . oh no, it's waking up! The wards have failed. We're doomed—we're *dead*." He looked at the guard, wild-eyed. "Get help!" He had to shout to be heard over the howling. Light began to flash from the open box in bright pulses.

The guard swore and rushed to the gate, pounding on the metal. A much older man with a hedgerow of a beard appeared on the other side. "What's all this commotion?" he bellowed.

"A new book!" the guard screamed. "It's active!"

The gate flashed blue, brightly, and then went dark, and the iron door swung open. The spellcasting guard hurried out, moving toward the Specialist. "What are we dealing with here?"

The first guard stood beside Rodrick, looking at the box, scowling. "*Magic*. I hate it."

The Specialist cast a meaningful glance toward Rodrick. "I'm not sure, but it's certainly *loud*, isn't it?"

Oh. *In case things get . . . loud.* That was what the Specialist had said. Rodrick grabbed the guard's hand, the ring's tiny needle piercing his flesh. The guard looked at him strangely for a moment, swayed, and then fell.

Rodrick shrieked and pointed at the fallen man. "What happened? Did the book kill him? Is he *dead*?"

The spellcaster looked around in alarm, raising his hands to do something arcane, and the Specialist stuck him in the side of the neck with a needle. The spellcaster stumbled, sank to his knees, and collapsed on the floor.

The Specialist reached into the box, and the screaming stopped abruptly. He waved tendrils of white vapor away from his face. "They should be asleep long enough for us to finish our business."

Rodrick shuddered. "You might have warned me about the screaming."

"Oh, it's just a little charm I had laid on the book, to make it howl and smoke and flash when touched in a particular place. If you'd known about it, you might not have reacted so strongly. Your surprise was very convincing."

"Because it was genuine." Rodrick let his tone turn sour. "It was a neat contingency plan. Well done luring the spellcaster out of the cage. You might have discussed the idea with me, though."

"I wasn't sure what we would encounter here, but I thought it best to have a distraction available, just in case. I didn't want you to think I doubted *your* plan. It would have worked, if not for the warded gate and their protocols."

"You're so considerate."

The Specialist took the now non-screaming book out of the box and tucked it under his arm. They went to the gate, and looked into the stacks. Shelves and shelves of books and scrolls stretched into the dark. Some of the scrolls rustled, like birds, and there was a dull pink glow from somewhere deep in the stacks. If he listened closely, Rodrick thought he could hear something like breathing. Rodrick had seen the thakur's library in Jalmeray, and while this wasn't nearly as grand, the concentrated magic here was even more impressive in its way.

The Specialist rubbed his hands together and went among the shelves, scanning the rows of books with his sharp eyes. Rodrick followed, a bit reluctantly. Books shouldn't make *scuttling* noises. "Is this going to take long? Those men won't be unconscious forever."

"Mine will be out longer than yours. I only gave you my second-best sleeping potion." The Specialist gazed upon the shelves with the sort of acquisitive look Rodrick reserved for wine, women, and wealthy fools. "I wish I could fill the wheelbarrow with books, but I'll have to make my selections more carefully. Fortunately the old guard in Cheliax gave me a partial inventory . . ." He plucked a slim volume from the shelf, then vanished into the dark, having a conversation with himself.

Rodrick went back to the front, checking on the slumbering guards. He and the Specialist could still possibly get out of this without being hunted by crusaders afterward. He looked through the slot in the main door, but didn't see Eldra anywhere out there. Of course, he wouldn't be able to, not unless she wanted him to.

He paced around the front room, thinking about Hrym, trying not to think about Hrym, and then thinking about Hrym some more.

After about ten minutes, the Specialist returned with an armload of books and scrolls. Rodrick opened the front door, closed it, and opened it again—the prearranged signal—and Eldra appeared from the shadow of a neighboring building. She opened a satchel as she approached, the Specialist placed the books and scrolls inside, and she darted back to the darkness. The whole exchange took rather less than a minute, and Rodrick closed the door again.

"Will anyone notice the missing books?" Rodrick asked. "We might be able to squirm out of this, but if they notice the theft . . ."

"Doubtful, though there are periodic inventories that come at random intervals. Unless we're extraordinarily unlucky, there's no reason to think anyone will notice right away."

"You found a home for the fake book, too?"

"It's not fake. It's a real book. A book of recipes for assorted puddings with a charm of random screaming laid on it, yes, but a book nonetheless."

"Can we wake them up?" Rodrick said. "Or at least one of them?"

The Specialist nodded. "The one who doesn't know as much about magic, I think."

"Just a minute." Rodrick lowered himself to the floor beside the other guard and took up a sprawling pose.

The Specialist knelt, opened the lid of a small vial, and held it under the slumbering guard's nose for a moment, then tucked it away.

The guard sat up with a jolt, as if electrified, hand going to his sword. "What happened?"

"The book." Rodrick raised himself up on one elbow, affecting vast weariness. "It woke up, and knocked all of us unconscious except for my friend here. I guess he managed to quiet it down."

The Specialist slammed closed the gate, and it flashed blue again, the wards reactivated. "I took the liberty of calculating a safe location and putting the book away," he said. "I know it's not my place to do so, but I thought it best to lock the foul thing away behind the wards."

The guard got to his feet, prompting Rodrick to follow suit, then looked at the spellcaster. "Is he . . . ?"

The spellcaster snorted, rolled over, and then began to snore.

"Should wake up in a moment, I expect," Rodrick said. "He was standing closer to the book, so I think he got the worst of the effects."

"I was behind him," the Specialist explained. "Shielded from whatever power the book unleashed. That gave me time to renew the wards. We're lucky the orcs didn't use the book against us on the battlefield. Perhaps it's too hard to control."

"*Magic.*" The guard looked like he wanted to spit, but then thought better of it. "We'll have to alert our superiors, fill out an incident report . . . I hate it when things like this happen." He frowned. "Hold on, though." He pointed at the Specialist. "You, hold out your arms. You were unobserved for at least a few minutes. No offense, but I need to search you."

The Specialist nodded affably. "Naturally. There are books back there that could *convince* someone to take them out, even against their will."

The guard thoroughly patted down the Specialist, then glanced at Rodrick, and said, "Sorry, but . . ."

"Oh, I understand." Rodrick said.

After the guard finished checking Rodrick for hidden scrolls, he opened up the metal box, which was half full of sand. He drew a knife and poked at the sand, stirring it around thoroughly, then nodded, satisfied. "Good enough. I guess if you were thieves you would have run away while I was unconscious anyway."

Rodrick adored people with linear, straightforward minds. The rank and file of military life seemed to suit such souls. "We need to report back to our commanding officer," Rodrick said. "We'll have to fill out some reports of our own, I'm afraid."

"That's military life," the guard agreed, and Rodrick let himself relax. He'd been afraid the man would insist they remain here for an investigation, but apparently the guard was convinced they were fellow crusaders, and thus beyond suspicion.

"Do you need us to send help?" the Specialist said.

The guard shook his head. "This location isn't widely known. You can't go mentioning it to just anyone. We've got magical protocols in place for contacting our supervisor. They might have some questions for you if there's an inquiry, but they can reach you through the usual channels."

"What I said about this being a nice, quiet posting?" Rodrick said. "I take it back."

"Ha. Let me know if you'd like a turn guarding the cage. I'll put in a good word for you." The guard checked the view through the door's slot to make sure there was no one lurking, then unbolted the door and waved them out.

As they strolled away from the library, Rodrick turned his mind to their next problem: how to rescue Hrym. He had the Specialist and Eldra, and the element of surprise, since Prinn probably thought they were dead . . . but any plan necessarily involved infiltrating the Bastion of Justice—a daunting prospect. Rodrick was hoping inspiration would strike, but so far, inspiration had missed badly.

They walked a block, then abandoned the wheelbarrow and the metal box in an alley where it was likely to be welcomed as salvage by the locals, and continued on to their basement lair.

They found Eldra sitting on her cot, glaring at the satchel of books, which she'd shoved into the corner farthest away from her. "Something in that sack *whispered* to me, and called me by the nickname my mother gave me. No one's called me that since I was a girl."

The Specialist nodded. "Yes. I'm not surprised. Some of those volumes are very treacherous. They want you to read them. There's a reason they're locked up. I wouldn't trust them with anyone other than myself." He went to the satchel, rooted around inside, and removed a book bound in leather so black it almost hurt to look at it. "Did we intend to storm the Bastion tonight, or can I do a bit of research first?"

"I, ah . . . don't have all the details of our approach worked out yet," Rodrick said. "We could use a night to rest, too, I'm sure."

"Mmm." The Specialist was already ignoring him, sitting on the edge of the cot, peering into the pages.

"What's that book?" Eldra said. "Should I be worried?"

"No, no. It's just a bestiary, of sorts. I'm interested in, ah . . . exotic animals."

Rodrick wondered what sort of bestiary would be locked up in the Interdicted Library, and decided he didn't want to think about it.

While the Specialist mumbled to himself and occasionally jotted notes, Rodrick and Eldra sat on crates against the far wall, sharing bread and cheese and the single bottle of wine that Rodrick felt he could safely allow himself without risking a debilitating hangover.

"The problem is getting into the Bastion without being noticed," he said.

Eldra nodded. "Which is difficult, since it's a fortress."

"We could just brazen it out. We're not entirely unknown there. What if we simply stroll up to the gates?"

"Last time we walked in without an escort, we were ringed with steel and crossbows in moments, and promptly escorted to Temple. I don't really want to see Temple again, especially now that Temple isn't Temple."

Rodrick nodded, conceding the point. "Then there must be another way in. There are tunnels, aren't there, underneath the place, leading in and out and all over the city?"

"Probably, but we don't know how to get into them or where they go, and crawling around in the depths beneath the Bastion, without guide or map, sounds like a good way to get lost. The place is probably full of traps and other nastiness, too, knowing Temple."

"Yes. Probably." Rodrick put his elbows on his knees and his head in his hands and thought as hard as he could. He could imagine ways to get into the Bastion, but ways to get in undetected, and creep around until he found Hrym, and get out again? Ideas for *that* were in short supply.

"You could just . . . move on." Eldra's voice was kind. "Hrym is a good sort—I don't know a lot of talking swords, I admit, but it's hard to imagine one better. But . . ."

"You said you'd help me."

She nodded. "I did, and I will. If you come up with a plan, I'll do my part. I have great faith in your problem-solving skills. You've shown wit, and cunning, and ingenuity today, and I concede you're every bit the tactician Merihim was. But if it looks like you're going to die in the course of your plan, I don't intend to stay there and die with you. I can't imagine the Specialist does, either."

"A certain amount of risk is inevitable, Eldra."

She nodded. "Of course. But a good planner takes steps to mitigate that risk. If your only idea is 'try to find a tunnel and hope for the best'. . . I won't be comfortable taking part."

"I think I can do better than that." He slumped further. "At least, I hope so. If only we had someone who *knows* the Bastion, who could tell us its secrets. We could try to gather intelligence, but how long would that take?"

"Longer than I want to spend in Vellumis," Eldra said.

"It's a shame we don't have Bannerman anymore," Rodrick said.

Eldra nodded. "For a tool of our jailers, he wasn't such a bad sort."

"What? Bannerman?" The Specialist looked up from his book. "Did you say you wanted Bannerman?"

"I want lots of things," Rodrick said. "The ability to turn invisible and pass through walls. An army of my own. Prinn's head in a box. But, yes, I'd add Bannerman to that list."

"Mmm. It's possible to turn invisible and pass through walls, of course, though probably a bit outside the reach of our current circumstances." The Specialist coughed into his hand. "But, if you like, we *could* go and get Bannerman."

28

A Rescue

A re you saying you know where Bannerman is?" Eldra said.
The Specialist nodded. "Certainly. I've always been a
light sleeper, and it's even worse as I get older. I heard Prinn and
Merihim drag Bannerman and Zumani away that night. Merihim
carried a rucksack full of food and water, and Prinn carried one
man over each shoulder. A remarkable feat of strength, I thought
at the time, though it's less remarkable now that I know he's an
undead monster. I followed them, naturally, at a discreet distance.
They took their prisoners a mile or so through the woods, to the
remains of an old stone fortification, and when they emerged
some time later, they were without their burdens. I hurried back to
camp and went to sleep."

Rodrick rubbed his temples. "You knew where they were. You
knew. Why didn't you tell us when Merihim sprang her ridiculous
plan on us?"

The Specialist cocked his head. "To what end? If I'd said, 'I
know where they're being held captive,' don't you think Prinn
would have popped out of the trees and killed me then and there?
Besides, I was curious as to whether or not Merihim's plan would
work. I reasoned that, even if it failed, Merihim would be the one
immediately punished. In that case, I could give the information
about Bannerman's whereabouts to Temple, and gain her favor.
Once Prinn revealed himself to be a totenmaske, however, the
subject was moot."

"You were just going to leave them to starve to death?" Eldra said.

The Specialist shook his head. "No. Before I left town, I was going to leave an anonymous note outside one of the barracks houses, letting them know where to look. Merihim left them enough water for a week, and food for longer than that. I considered freeing them myself, on my way out of the country, but . . ."

"Bannerman would have tried to take you into custody. Hmm. He might do that to *us*, if we save him."

"We do outnumber him," Eldra pointed out. "We'd also be negotiating from a position of strength, which is to say, he's chained up in some fort, and he doesn't want to be, and we could let him out. Once we tell him what Prinn did to Temple, how Prinn has *become* Temple, I think he'll have other things on his mind besides forcing us to become servants of Lastwall again."

Rodrick nodded. "He would be a formidable addition to the team, even apart from his knowledge of the inner workings of the Bastion. He's a tough fighter." Rodrick allowed himself a grin. "I've been thinking, what we're lacking so far is pure brute force *muscle*."

The Specialist went out at dawn and acquired four horses, somehow. They were running low on funds, but apparently the Specialist had acquired one "relatively harmless" volume "of merely historical interest" from the Interdicted Library, and sold it to a buyer he'd lined up ahead of time. The resulting money wasn't a king's ransom, but after deducting the cost of the horses, he divided up the remaining coin and doled it out equally, as recompense for their help with the heist. Even though it was rather more silver than gold, Rodrick was still delighted to get *some* material gain out of his criminal activity. He'd almost forgotten what that felt like.

They rode out of Vellumis and into the countryside, and eventually into the forest. Eldra and Rodrick would have gotten lost in the woods, wandered in circles, and eventually been eaten by whatever local monsters enjoyed human flesh, but the Specialist's memory of their route was eerily perfect, as always. He led them back to the place where they'd camped, and they left the horses there, since the journey to the old fort took them through a denser part of the woods.

"This part of the forest is young." The Specialist slashed away at brambles and branches with a heavy stick as he walked. "There must have been a fire not too many decades past. That's why it's so overgrown. The trees and bushes and weeds and vines and briars are all still fighting for supremacy. Not like the deeper forest, where the battle was settled long ago, and the victorious trees block out the sun with their reaching branches, and keep the undergrowth from getting so untidy."

"I like it." Eldra kicked a branch out of her path. "It's hell to walk through, of course, but I love the sense of *life* I get out here."

Rodrick ducked to avoid a tree limb. "I prefer the sense of life I get in a tavern, with a willing wench on my knee and a tankard in my hand."

"That also has a certain appeal," Eldra said cheerfully. She'd given up on pretending to be jealous when he mentioned other women, apparently. He couldn't decide if that disappointed him or not.

"It's just there." The Specialist pointed his walking stick at an overgrown mass of stones and old timbers. Parts of it had clearly been made by human hands, but since then it had been left in the hands of nature for a very long time.

They made their way through the thorn vines to a formidable door made of thick wood that had practically petrified, reinforced with rusty black iron and chained shut. "Well?" the Specialist said. "Go ahead. You're the leader here."

"If we open that door and walk in, I bet Bannerman will throw a rock at us, or try to strangle us with his chains, or something. May I?" Rodrick took the Specialist's stick and pounded it against the door. "Bannerman!" he called. "Are you alive in there? It's Rodrick. We've come to save you." Silence. "All right? I'm coming in. Don't kill me."

He unwound the chains and eased open the door. The interior of the fort was dark and windowless, but a shaft of light illuminated Bannerman, who looked grimy and annoyed, seated on the floor. His hands were bound with the same manacles they'd used when they apprehended him in the forest, and a chain connected them to the central timber that held up the fort's stone roof. He scowled at them ferociously.

Zumani was there, too, with a chain looped around his neck and waist, also tied to the central post. He leapt to his feet, or tried to, but the chain wasn't quite long enough, so he strangled himself briefly and then sat back down. "I demand you set me free immediately!" he said. "I am a free man of Nirmathas!"

"Shut up, Zumani." Bannerman's tone was weary. Rodrick suspected he'd said the same phrase quite often since his imprisonment. He looked at Rodrick. "Did Temple send you to free me? I knew she wouldn't give in to Merihim's plan. Only why did she take so long?"

Rodrick and the others went into the fort. He wrinkled his nose. The inside smelled the way you'd expect it to after a few days holding prisoners who couldn't go farther than the end of their chains to relieve themselves. "How about we unchain you and then we can explain everything in the fresh air?"

"Just unchain *me*," Bannerman said. "I could use a break from the poet there."

"This is outrageous!" Zumani shouted.

"Shut up, Zumani," Bannerman and Eldra said simultaneously.

They told Bannerman everything, apart from the theft of the signet ring and the raid on the Interdicted Library. Rodrick did most of the talking, with Eldra interjecting at certain points, and the Specialist making the occasional technical or purely pedantic clarification.

Bannerman listened to them with obvious impatience, arms crossed, frowning and squinting and sucking his teeth, but he let them get through it all.

"That's a remarkable story," he said at last. "I don't believe it, of course."

Rodrick had considered any number of possible reactions, but somehow outright disbelief hadn't been among them. "Ah. Well. It's true."

Bannerman shook his head. "You're liars, every one of you. Even the Specialist—we *still* don't even know his real name!"

"If you knew my name, you might be able to find out things *about* me," the old man said, in the tones of one explaining an everyday mystery to a confused child.

Eldra frowned. "What could we possibly gain from making up a story like this?"

"Apart from goading me into murdering my employer?" Bannerman shook his head. "You know Andraste had the necklace, and you also know about her . . . predilections . . . so I believe *that* part. Her debauchery is a well-kept secret, and knowing about it has helped Temple a lot politically. I believe you stole the necklace from her, and freed yourself from our hold. As for the rest of your tale, though—no. You're just afraid Temple will chase you down and press you into service again. So instead you come and rescue me, hoping to make me feel *indebted* to you, and then tell me, 'Oh, by the way, your beloved friend and mentor is actually a monster in disguise, even though she looks and sounds exactly like she always does, and you should really help us sneak into the Bastion and deal with her.'" He turned his head and spat onto the forest floor. "I won't be your dupe, Volunteers."

"Why wouldn't we just *run away*?" Eldra said.

Bannerman showed his teeth. "Run? From the crusaders of Lastwall? We're very good at chasing down deserters, and that's what you lot are trying to be."

Eldra shook her head. "I'm sorry, Rodrick, I agreed to help you, but if he's going to be like this, I don't see how we're going to proceed." She turned back to Bannerman. "We don't even want you to kill Temple, you stupid man, we just want to get Hrym out of Prinn's clutches!"

"You don't have to ask me to kill an undead rot at the heart of the Bastion of Justice. Obviously duty would compel me to do such a thing. I don't claim to have a mind as cunning as any of *you* treacherous scum, but even I know it's not necessary to ask someone to do something you know they'll do anyway."

"You give us too much credit—" Rodrick began.

"We checked Prinn out." Bannerman stepped forward, his fists clenched. "Our chirurgeon looked him over, just like he looked over the rest of you, and he was as human as you or me. He wasn't some undead monster then, so he's not one now."

The Specialist bent down and reached into his pack, and Bannerman was on him in an instant, knocking him flat on the ground and pinning him down. Rodrick didn't see what the Specialist did, exactly, but there was a flurry of movement, and suddenly Bannerman was facedown, with one arm wrenched behind his back, and the Specialist kneeling beside him, holding the crusader's wrist almost delicately. "Bannerman, I was going for a book, not a weapon," he said mildly. "Eldra, if you'd be so kind?"

She reached into his bag and took out the slim black volume the Specialist had been studying the night before. "Turn to the marked page, please," the Specialist said.

Eldra flipped through until she reached a page marked with a bit of string, read it, then grunted. She put it on the ground right under Bannerman's nose. "Can you read, crusader?"

"Of course I can." He squinted, at the book, lips moving slowly, and finally sighed. "All right, let me up."

"That must be some very persuasive writing," Rodrick said.

The Specialist released Bannerman, who stalked a few feet away and began to pace back and forth, fists clenched, brow furrowed in thought. Eldra picked up the book and handed it to Rodrick. He'd never enjoyed reading, but he could do it well enough when he had no choice. The book *was* a bestiary, of sorts—but devoted to accounts of the undead, including totenmaskes. He scanned the page until he reached the relevant passage. "Ah, yes," he said. "The Specialists told us about this. When a totenmaske steals someone's identity, they become fully human, indistinguishable from the real thing. Your chirurgeon wasn't incompetent after all."

"This doesn't prove anything," Bannerman said. "What if you're just claiming Prinn is a totenmaske *because* those can't be distinguished from humans?"

"Your suspicion is understandable," Eldra said. "When dealing with people like us, it's even a survival trait. But we aren't asking you to walk into the Bastion and put a sword in Temple's heart. Why don't you go and talk to her? Tell her you escaped from the fort, and feel her out, and see if she seems like the real Temple to you. While you're in there, you can figure out where Hrym is, too, and maybe contrive to carry him out again, once you realize we're telling the truth."

The Specialist cleared his throat. "The totenmaske also drains memories from its victims, though, so it could be a very convincing impersonation. Prinn may know everything Temple knew."

"Oh, isn't *that* convenient," Bannerman said. "So if I ask Temple questions, and she answers exactly as I expect, that proves she's a totenmaske, does it?"

Rodrick closed the book. "Well," he said. "There is one question you could ask, that would prove whether or not we're telling the truth."

29

THE CONVINCER

They left Zumani chained up, to his loud and vocal dismay. Bannerman wasn't even remotely convinced by their story yet, but if Temple *was* an undead monster in disguise, he didn't want to risk bringing her the revolutionary.

If Rodrick hadn't been worried for Hrym, the whole situation would have been amusing. Usually, in his life, if he told a lie and put the full force of his charm behind it, people believed him. Now, for once, he was telling the whole truth (more or less), and he *wasn't* believed. There was probably some morally instructive lesson there, but he wasn't in the mood to learn it.

They returned to the horses and rode back to Vellumis. Bannerman didn't talk much, just glowered and muttered. They didn't reveal to him where they were staying, but made arrangements to meet him at the harbor the following morning, after he'd had a chance to talk to "Temple." At the edge of the city, they parted ways, Bannerman promising swift vengeance if they weren't at the appointed meeting place when the time came.

Back in the basement, Rodrick fretted, and paced, and was generally miserable and distracted. The Specialist kept going through his books, talking to himself and jotting notes, and then announced he had to run an errand. Eldra stopped him before he left, whispering something in his ear, and the Specialist whispered something in return—then chuckled, a rare sound from the old man. He disappeared into the night, and Eldra walked over to Rodrick, smiling in her adorably dimpled way.

"What was all that about?" he said.

"Oh, I just asked him how long he was going to be gone."

"Why's that?"

"Because I don't want there to be any rush, silly." She leaned in and kissed him. Rodrick was briefly surprised, but insofar as he had any success at all in life it was because he tended to seize opportunities when they arose, so he put his arms around her. She melted into him, and for the next hour, he didn't think even once about the fact that she was actually an octogenarian.

Afterward, they lay side by side on their cots, which they'd pushed together to make something resembling a bed, for all the good it did. Rodrick didn't feel any cause for complaint, though. He'd spent far less pleasant evenings in featherbeds and on piles of furs. "That was amazing," he breathed.

"Thank you, darling. You were better than I expected, for someone your age. Imagine how good you'll be after a few mores years of practice."

"I'm insulted," he said. "But, strangely, I don't mind."

She rolled over toward him, putting her cheek against his. "I did enjoy it, darling. I didn't plan to grow fond of you, and yet, somehow, here I am. You're a liar and a thief and a confidence trickster, but your heart's not as black as some."

"I'm touched by your high opinion of me. But I have to ask—why *now*?"

"Two reasons." She traced her fingertip in little circles on his chest. "First, I couldn't stand how sad you looked. You're just eaten up by worry for your friend, and the misery was written all over you. Distracting you for a while seemed like a kindness."

"I applaud your philanthropy. What's the other reason?"

"I don't *want* anything from you now," she said. "I don't need you as an ally in the Volunteers, because the Volunteers are no more. I don't need you to help me steal a signet ring—it's already done, and I have it. Indeed, now you're the one who needs *me*, not vice versa."

"Oh." Rodrick felt a peculiar sensation of warmth in his chest, a tightness in his throat, perhaps even a stinging in his eyes, quickly blinked away. "So you could sleep with me now, and I'd know it was just because you *wanted* to, and not because you needed me for something."

"Exactly. I spent the early years of my career, back before you were born, using sex as a way to get what I wanted and needed. In my old age, I have no patience for that sort of thing. Old habits are hard to break, so I still use the *promise* of sex, and the hint of sex, and the suggestion of sex, when the situation merits—but actually going through with it? I reserve that strictly for people I want to be with."

"Eldra. I just. You. You've been. I want to tell you—"

"Stop, stop!" she cried. "Don't go all hearts and flowers on me now, Rodrick. You'll ruin my good opinion of you. We did a nice thing together, because we wanted to, and because we needed something good in the midst of all this misery. Let's leave it at that."

"Does that mean . . . you don't want to do it again?"

"Hmm," she said. "The Specialist *did* say he'd be gone for at least two hours . . ."

The next morning, they all rose with the sun—even the Specialist, who'd been gone rather longer than two hours, and barely even got home before dawn—and trekked down to the harbor. Rodrick and the Specialist sat on the same low wall where they'd contemplated their future prospects after their escape from the poisonous gems. Eldra was off on her own, watching and armed, just in case Prinn had managed to fool Bannerman after all, and they needed some help making a hasty escape.

The crusader appeared at the appointed time, plodding toward them, either truly disconsolate or pretending to be in order to catch them unawares. The constant vigilance of suspicion could be exhausting, Rodrick thought.

Bannerman sat on the wall next to them and stared at the ships. "You're right," he said. "It's not Temple. I went to the Bastion, and told them I'd escaped, and she—he, Prinn, damn him—met with me right away. I asked what became of you . . . and he said you'd all been killed by your gems as punishment for your treachery."

Rodrick exhaled. That had been his idea: ask Prinn what happened to the Volunteers, and hope the totenmaske would be caught in an obvious lie. It wasn't a perfect plan, though. The totenmaske might have said, "I killed Prinn and Merihim, and the others escaped, so I let the gems kill them." That would have been problematic, but it would have also caused Bannerman to ask other questions, like, "Why did you let them escape?" and "Why didn't you try to drag them back?" and such, so Rodrick had figured it was worth the gamble.

"Besides, I asked around, and everyone agrees Temple has been different the past few days," Bannerman said. "She never drinks, usually, but she's been going through gallons of wine. She's been demanding rich food, when she's normally so focused on work she barely remembers to eat. She's even going to the feast to honor General Andraste tonight, when she makes a point of avoiding functions like that. She's apparently made crude and suggestive remarks to men and women in her employ, too. The Bastion has been taken over by a monster."

Wine, lust, and gluttony? The new Temple certainly sounded more fun than the old one. If she weren't an undead monster, Rodrick would probably enjoy her company.

The Specialist made a hand signal, and a few moments later, Eldra strolled down the waterfront, twirling her parasol, and joined them.

"Did you happen to see Hrym?" Rodrick said. "I can't help but notice he isn't on your hip."

Bannerman shook his head. "No. I know where he is, though. Prinn said he hadn't decided what to do with Hrym yet—to try to convince him to serve Lastwall, or to lock him up in some vault somewhere. He's still sheathed in that antimagic scabbard, in Temple's office. There was no chance for me to grab him, though." He sighed. "I considered lying to you—telling you I had him hidden away, and that if you helped me expose and defeat Prinn, I'd give him back—but I'm so weary of deceptions, I couldn't bring myself to do it. I will make this offer, though: if you agree to help me kill Prinn, I'll show you a secret way into the Bastion and help you get Hrym back while we're there."

"No thank you," the Specialist said.

"Yes, I'll decline," Eldra said.

Rodrick scowled at them. "Both of you promised to help me."

"Help you get *Hrym*, yes," Eldra said. "I have no interest whatsoever in having my flesh shaped or my memories drunk. I do not ever even want to *see* Prinn again."

"Agreed," the Specialist said.

"Okay." Rodrick held up his hands. "All right. This is my proposal, Bannerman. You help us *all* infiltrate the Bastion. The Specialist and Eldra will lend us their skills for that part. We'll get Hrym *first*. Then, their debt to me discharged, those two can slip out again . . . but I'll help you stop Prinn before I leave. Having Hrym in hand will make that easier anyway, don't you think? But I also need you to agree not to consider *any* of us deserters, and let us have our freedom. I think we'll have earned it."

"What's to stop you from blasting me with a spray of ice and running away with your friends after you get Hrym?" Bannerman demanded.

Rodrick shrugged. "Nothing. Just my word that I won't. Along with the knowledge that I'd rather not have angry crusaders from Lastwall chasing me for the rest of my life. It's the best I can offer."

Bannerman stared at the lake for a while, then nodded briskly, and shook each of their hands in turn, starting with Rodrick. "We go in this afternoon," he said.

"Isn't the dead of night more traditional?" Eldra said.

"For sneak thieves like you, yes. Agents of the Bastion of Justice aren't afraid of the light of day."

"The problem with the light of day is that your enemies can *see* you," Rodrick said.

Bannerman shrugged. "It's also when the guard shift on the lower levels changes, so we can slip in through the tunnels when there's a gap in the patrol schedule. I also want to kill Prinn before he goes to the feast. What if Prinn finds some excuse to speak to general Andraste alone, and steals *her* face?"

"Andraste does have access to a better class of pleasures of the flesh," Rodrick agreed. "I defer to your expertise. Though I get credit for the brilliant idea to recruit you to my cause."

They made their preparations, which in Rodrick's case consisted mostly of worrying about everything that could go wrong. At least when he was busy planning an operation he had something constructive to occupy his mind. Bannerman was running point on this, though, and all Rodrick had to do was whatever he was told. He was even too distracted to flirt with Eldra, who spent the time sharpening her knives, adjusting the spring-loaded spike in her parasol, and helping the Specialist put together a few useful concoctions. Rodrick tried to help with that too, but he was inattentive, and was forbidden to step within five feet of the table after he spilled a beaker of something that ate away a small portion of the table and a larger portion of the floor.

At the appointed time they returned to the outskirts of the harbor, where Bannerman lurked near a dilapidated pier. He led them underneath the pilings and instructed Rodrick to clear away a heap of stones and other rubble. *Back to brute force duty.*

He soon realized the point of the exercise, at least, when the removal of the rocks revealed a narrow opening, big enough for a grown man to crawl through. The Specialist went first, because crawling into dark places was a hobby of his, and he'd probably accidentally eaten so many spiders in his life that a few more wouldn't make any difference. Bannerman went next, then Eldra, wrinkling her nose in distaste, with Rodrick in the rear.

The Specialist had a lantern with a blackout panel, and he slid the cover aside to dimly illuminate the room. It was a slimy hole just deep enough for all of them to crowd into, and not quite high enough for anyone but Eldra to stand upright. "Charming place," Rodrick said.

Bannerman went to the stone wall at the rear of the hole and pressed on something. A section of the wall slid back with a grinding noise and the sound of shifting sand. "This is the far end of an escape tunnel that leads from the Bastion," he said. "Meant as an emergency egress if the fortress were ever overrun."

"I thought crusaders never ran from a fight?" Eldra said.

"We prefer to call it falling back and regrouping prior to a renewed assault," Bannerman said. "Or a strategic movement to the rear. The tunnel wasn't even made to open from this side, but Temple, bless her twisty mind, thought there might someday be a situation when one of us might need to get *into* the Bastion unobserved. Come on."

"If Temple knows about this tunnel, then Prinn might know, too," the Specialist pointed out.

"Fortunately Prinn doesn't know you lot are alive, or that I know his true identity. As far as he's concerned, I'm out sniffing around for leads on another batch of Volunteers." Bannerman took the lantern from the Specialist and slid through the gap in the wall. The others followed. The brick-lined tunnel on the far side was dryer, cleaner, and more obviously wrought by human hands, and Rodrick straightened his spine gratefully.

They proceeded down the dark corridor, so narrow they had to walk one abreast, for a distance of at least two miles. There was no sign of life apart from the occasional rat and beetle. The peace and quiet were maddening. Rodrick's nerves felt like lute strings pulled too tight: another half-twist of tension and he might snap. Hrym was off in the distance somewhere, almost in reach, and until Rodrick held him once more in his hands, he wouldn't be able to relax, not really.

He probably wouldn't be able to relax then, either, since he was obliged to go help kill a totenmaske immediately afterward, but he'd feel better anyway.

"Here we are." Bannerman shone the lantern's light on a metal ladder bolted into the wall, leading up to a trapdoor. He went up and lifted the hatch an inch or so and looked through the crack. "Seems clear, come on." He climbed out, swinging the hatch wide open, and the others followed. They emerged in a small storage room stacked with dusty crates—clearly not a place visited often. Once they were all above the floor, Bannerman closed the hatch again. "All right," he whispered, "We'll have to go down a well-lit hallway for about twenty yards until we reach a secret passage that will take us to Temple's office, but we shouldn't run into any guards, if we've timed this right. Once we've got Hrym in hand, Rodrick and I will go totenmaske hunting."

"I'm not even sure why I'm here," Eldra said. "It doesn't sound like there's much for me and the Specialist to do, apart from escape down this same tunnel in half an hour or so."

"You're here in case we *haven't* timed it right," Bannerman said. "Also because I hope you'll reconsider your cowardice."

"I prefer to think of it less as cowardice and more as 'strategic courage,'" Eldra said.

"Cowardice is an excellent survival strategy," the Specialist said. "Though I would argue that a reluctance to engage in unnecessary battle with a monster that can shape flesh like clay and eat memories is perhaps better described as 'wisdom' than 'cowardice.'"

Bannerman sighed and opened the door onto an empty stone hallway lit by wall sconces. He beckoned them forward, and they moved at a swift walk toward the secret passage.

They made it almost ten yards before crusaders poured into the hallway from both ends.

30

THE WRONG SIDE
OF THE BARS

The Volunteers, if they could still be called that, were all experienced fighters. Rodrick knew his compatriots would look around them at the rapidly approaching hordes of armed men and women and make the same determination he did, which was: there are too many here to even bother *trying* to fight. Desperate flight was really the only plausible response.

The Specialist lobbed a bomb toward one end of the corridor, and Rodrick braced himself for an explosion that would cause the ceiling to cave in and kill them all. Fortunately, it was only a smoke bomb, sending out a billowing cloud. The Specialist vanished into the black smoke, fleeing for the storage room and the hatch to the escape tunnel, no doubt. Rodrick thought that was a marvelous plan, and did his best to follow suit. Eldra was ahead of him. Bannerman seemed to be more interested in standing his ground and shouting, which was a peculiar way to respond to an assault by an overwhelming force, but what did Rodrick know? He wasn't a crusader.

Rodrick actually got through the door of the storeroom. The Specialist was there, but he was pushing a crate across the floor instead of jumping down the hole, which was baffling. Eldra threw open the trapdoor, though, and started down it.

That was the last thing Rodrick saw before something heavy hit him on the back of the head and drove him down into the darkness.

"He's waking up," a woman's voice said.

Rodrick blinked up at a dark stone ceiling. "He is? Who is?"

"You are." That was the gruff voice of . . . what was his name . . . Bannerman? Oh. Yes. Rodrick's memory of recent events came trickling back. He groaned and rubbed his head, sitting up.

They were in a dungeon cell, a larger one than Rodrick had been held in during his first day at the Bastion. This one was darker, and windowless, on some deep dark level, no doubt. Not one of the *best* dungeons, then. The Specialist was there too, sitting against one wall, and Eldra was on the floor beside Rodrick. She patted his knee. "Good," she said. "You're awake. Now we can go."

"Oh, good." Rodrick looked around. The door looked very solid. The walls looked even more solid. "Where are we going?"

"*Out*," Bannerman said. "This was a disaster. I'm going to have to find another approach."

"We think Prinn got suspicious after meeting with Bannerman," Eldra said.

Bannerman stood up and punched the wall. "One of the men who captured us—I used to serve with him, and he told me Temple quadrupled the guard on the lower levels, and told them to detain anyone who came out of that storage room. They were pretty confused when they saw *me* coming out, and I might have talked my way out of trouble, if you lot hadn't tried to run away."

The Specialist shook his head. "Even if you'd convinced them that we were allowed to be there, we would have shortly found ourselves alone in a room with Prinn, and shortly after *that*, we would be dead. Escape was the only approach that made sense."

Bannerman sighed. "At this point, I agree. The crusaders in the Bastion won't kill us without an investigation, but Prinn could creep down here anytime and murder us in a number of ways. Come on."

"Come on *where*?" Rodrick said.

"I was Temple's right-hand man for a long time," Bannerman said. "It occurred to me that her . . . flexible . . . approach to problem-solving might someday put me in conflict with her, and it didn't seem impossible that I'd end up on the wrong side of a cell door. This is the dungeon where they keep the *really* dangerous people, you see, and I thought if she ever locked me up anywhere, it would be here." He shrugged. "So I made provisions. I could get just about anything done in the Bastion, claiming Temple's authorization, so I had some modifications made to this cell." He brushed aside some of the straw on a floor, revealing a rusty metal grate. Bannerman pried at a large stone in the floor next to the grate, and it lifted cleanly away, revealing a hole. He moved on to the adjacent stone, and then Rodrick got the idea, and started prying up another. In a few moments they had a heap of large flat stones and an opening in the floor just big enough for a man to slip through.

The Specialist descended first, and the others followed. They were in a dank, piss-stinking sewer hole, but at least the ceiling was spine-curvingly low. Bannerman handed the flat stones down to Rodrick, then descended himself. Rodrick handed him the stones one at a time while Bannerman reached up and put them back in place, sealing them into the dark. "There," Bannerman said. "A nice disappearing trick, and with luck, they won't notice we're gone for a while. Standard protocol for dealing with prisoners like us is to leave them alone to stew in their own guilt and terror for a while."

"Where do we go from here?" Eldra said.

"This sewer connects to the main escape tunnel, not far from here. We can go out the same way we came in."

Rodrick followed Bannerman and the others, thinking furiously. Hrym was up there, above them. "Are we going to try again?" he said.

"Try *what* again?" Bannerman said. "To sneak into the Bastion? That didn't work so well last time. I'll reach out to some of my old friends in the ranks, or try to find a sympathetic officer who'll believe my story. Though after tonight, Prinn could be living *Andraste's* life—if totenmaskes lust for the pleasures of the flesh, Andraste has a lot more money, power, and prestige to burn through than Temple does. How can I possibly be sure where the monster is?"

"Well, if Temple disappears *entirely*, that means Prinn has moved on—" the Specialist began.

"I don't care about any of that," Rodrick said. "I only care about getting Hrym back."

"Then our interests don't align much," Bannerman snapped. "Piss off, Rodrick, I'm talking about the potential collapse of a *nation* here, not a trick sword." They reached the end of the corridor, and Bannerman activated some particular stones in the wall by punching them viciously, and a secret door slid open. The corridor beyond was black. "Come on," Bannerman said. "This is the escape tunnel. Head to the left, and we'll be back by the harbor soon."

"I'm going back to the Bastion," Rodrick said. "I have to get Hrym."

"You idiot!" Bannerman said. "Being captured once wasn't enough for you?"

"It's possible the guards are less vigilant now that the threat has been dealt with," the Specialist pointed out.

"You don't have any *equipment*," Bannerman said. "They took our weapons, our tools, everything."

"Even my parasol." Eldra sighed. "I had that custom-made."

"I don't need weapons," Rodrick said. "I'm going to rescue my best friend, who *is* a weapon." He was terrified at the prospect of returning to the Bastion alone, but he wasn't at all hesitant. There was nothing else he could do. Hrym was *close*.

"Even if you avoid the crusaders," Bannerman said, "you have to go into Temple's office, and if you run into Prinn—"

"Prinn is surely at the feast by now," Eldra said. "Probably looking Andraste up and down and wondering how it would feel to wear her body."

Bannerman didn't have an answer to that, but Rodrick could sense the crusader seething in the darkness.

"I hid a few things in the storage room," the Specialist said. "Just in case we managed to escape and wanted to retrieve them at some point. There's a knife, a concussion bomb, and one or two other items. They might help."

"That was . . . forward-thinking," Bannerman said.

"I had to stay up all night, spend a lot of gold, and yell at a wizard to have the scroll made," the Specialist said. "I wasn't going to hand it over to Prinn *that* easily."

"Scroll?" Rodrick said. "What are you talking about?"

"I meant it to be a surprise," the Specialist said. "I planned to give it to you after we got Hrym back. The book I took from the Interdicted Library, the one about the creation and compulsion of the undead, included an interesting detail about a spell that can force a totenmaske to reveal its true form, and prevent it from changing shape for a brief period. I thought the spell could be helpful—at the very least, you wouldn't have to worry about Prinn pretending to be someone *else*, and it would be easier to convince the other crusaders to fight an obvious monster than to turn on their leader."

"That was thoughtful of you," Rodrick said.

"Wait," Bannerman said. "*Wait*. I have an idea."

"That's nice," Rodrick said, and set off down the dark tunnel to rescue his one true friend.

Rodrick heard the others following him, but didn't pay any attention. He went up the ladder into the storage room, and shoved aside the crate he'd seen the Specialist moving during their failed attempt to escape. There was a scroll hidden behind it, which he ignored—Prinn was probably at the feast by now, and Rodrick wasn't interested in tracking the monster down or exposing him. He had other priorities. Rodrick took a dagger, and the rough clay orb of a bomb, and a leather-wrapped cosh.

"Rodrick!" Bannerman hissed from the trapdoor, but Rodrick just opened the door a crack and tossed out the bomb. He pushed the door closed, and waited through the dull *thump* and the blinding flash of light that shone through the crack beneath the door. Rodrick opened the door a moment later to find one guard unconscious and the other staggering and dazed.

Rodrick hit the upright guard with the cosh, aiming the blow almost absentmindedly, his attention more on the way forward than the trivialities of the present moment. Once the guard was down, Rodrick walked purposefully along the corridor, counting his steps. Bannerman had said the entrance to the secret passage was about twenty yards down, so at that point Rodrick stopped, examining the wall for a few feet in each direction. Soon he noticed one brick that seemed just a *bit* out of line with the ones around it, recessed perhaps a quarter of an inch deeper than the rest.

Rodrick pressed the brick, and a section of the wall swung back an inch, and even farther when he pushed. He glanced down the hall, where the others were hurrying toward him, and stepped into the dark, not bothering to close the secret door behind him.

He walked briskly along the narrow corridor for a bit . . . until he reached an intersection, where one passage went left, and the other went right. He'd made the choice to walk heedlessly into a dangerous place in order to get Hrym back, but it hadn't occurred to him that he'd have to make any *more* choices, like which way to go.

"I see you've noticed the problem," Bannerman said. "These secret passageways are a maze. You can blunder around aimlessly and hope you stumble upon Temple's office . . . or you can let me guide you straight there, and in exchange, help me with my new plan."

Rodrick looked past him to Eldra and the Specialist. "Why are you here?"

Eldra sniffed. "I told you I'd help you get Hrym in exchange for the signet ring. I'd hate you to think I don't keep my promises. I mean, I *don't*, usually, but for you, I'm making an exception."

"I'd like to get my hands on the antimagic scabbard Hrym is sheathed in," the Specialist said. "That quantity of skymetal is very hard to come by outside Numeria—or even inside it." He paused. "And also, what Eldra said, about promises, and so forth."

"Do either of *you* know the way to Temple's office?"

Eldra shook her head.

"I did not have an opportunity to study the layout of the Bastion in any depth," the Specialist said.

Rodrick nodded. "All right then, Bannerman. Take me to Hrym, and I'll help you do whatever it is you think you're doing."

Bannerman looked at him for a moment, grunted, then led him to the right. He chose without hesitation at two other intersections, and finally pressed against a wooden panel that swung open. They stepped into Temple's small and rather impersonal office. Hrym was sheathed in the skymetal scabbard, hanging on a coat hook on the wall, still bound up with leather thongs.

Rodrick rushed across the room, sliced through the leather bindings, and drew forth the blade, feeling whole and complete for the first time in what felt like ages.

"Hello," Hrym said. "Have I been asleep long?"

Rodrick began to laugh, tears squeezing from the corners of his eyes. "You lazy sword," he said. "You've missed a lot."

"Let's go," Bannerman said. "We shouldn't linger here any longer than necessary."

"Where are we going?" Hrym said.

"To a feast," Bannerman replied.

31

True Forms

They escaped the same way they'd come in, though when one of the unconscious guards outside the storage room stirred, Rodrick gave him a blast of ice to pin him to the floor. Then it was back down the trapdoor and on toward the harbor, with Rodrick filling Hrym in on everything that had happened since he'd been sheathed into oblivion.

"I'm glad I missed all that," Hrym said when Rodrick was done. "It sounds exhausting, and you didn't even make much money. I'm going to need back the gold you borrowed from me, too. Don't worry, my interest rates are very reasonable."

"It's good to have you back, old friend," Rodrick said, with total sincerity.

"Ha. Pining away for me, were you? That's only natural. I'm amazing. Everyone says so."

They all paused under the pier, suddenly awkward at the point of parting. "If you two want to help us, I can offer you gold," Bannerman said. "You can consider yourself freelance agents of the Bastion of Justice."

"Ah, but you'll only be able to pay us if you *win*," the Specialist said. "No, I'm content. I'm actually leaving Lastwall with more than I'd hoped. I think I'll go visit the elves."

"I've got a vault to open." Eldra embraced Rodrick and kissed his cheek, then squeezed him harder and kissed his lips. She pulled back. "You're Andoren, aren't you? There's a place in Almas, the Golden Eagle Tavern—do you know it?"

"I do," Rodrick said.

"The owner is an old friend of mine," Eldra said. "I haven't visited Almas in ages. I think, after I recover the family riches, I might go see the city for a bit, and if I do, I'll probably stay at the Golden Eagle. Stop in to see if I'm there, if you happen to be in the area. Maybe we could help each other out again."

"You'd like to work with me again?" Rodrick said. "After all *this*?"

"I don't know about *work*," she said, giving his bicep a squeeze. She stepped back and linked arms with the Specialist, who seemed surprised but not displeased by the contact. "Bannerman, I assume our deal still holds, and if you find yourself in the position to grant us a pardon, you will?"

"Yes, fine, go." The crusader flapped his hand at them. "Lastwall thanks you for your service."

Eldra gave a little wave, blew Rodrick a kiss, and then she and the Specialist walked off into their own bright futures.

"I envy them *so much* right now," Rodrick said.

"We could just freeze Bannerman, and run away," Hrym said. "We haven't done nearly enough running away lately."

Rodrick shook his head. "I couldn't have saved you without his help, Hrym. Besides, if we betray him now, and he succeeds anyway, we'll be dodging crusaders for the rest of our lives. There are enough countries I don't dare visit already—I don't want to add another one. All right, Bannerman. What's the plan?"

"We storm into the feast honoring General Andraste, and we kill Prinn," he said.

"Ah," Rodrick said. "I can see why you and Temple wanted to recruit people who *actually* know how to plan."

There wasn't much time to spend coming up with a real plan, but Rodrick did what he could. He wrapped Hrym's glittering blade in his cloak so he wouldn't be seen carrying a bare magical sword through the streets, and led Bannerman to the basement room. The Specialist's gear was gone, along with Eldra's, and Rodrick supposed they must have cleared out just moments earlier. Ah well. It was for the best. They'd said their farewells already.

Rodrick tossed aside a mundane longsword and put Hrym in its sheath, belting it on over the military garb he'd worn for the infiltration of the Interdicted Library. Bannerman already looked every bit the crusader, so that was all right. Rodrick took the document the Specialist had forged to get into the library—the one festooned with ribbons and seals and the fake signature of General Andraste—licked his thumb, and smeared the ink strategically.

They strode down the streets with the swagger of crusaders on a mission of righteousness, and after a block or so, Rodrick realized Bannerman wasn't even faking it, which struck him as so funny he had to stifle laughter. It was just possible Rodrick was exhausted enough, and under sufficient stress, that his sense was starting to unravel. He hoped he could keep his faculties about him long enough to avoid catastrophe. Or, rather, *worse* catastrophe. They were already in the midst of a catastrophe, after all.

The feast was being held in one of the marble-clad buildings near the city center, and the festivities—insofar as crusaders could be festive—were already well underway. Bannerman strode up to the pikeman guarding the front entrance and barked, "Straighten up, soldier. You're a disgrace. Open that door, we're here with an urgent message." He waved the official-looking document in front of the soldier's face, not giving him a chance to read it, assuming he even *could* read.

"I—" the soldier began.

Bannerman growled. "Boy, did I tell you to speak? Do you see this seal? This is the *Watcher-Lord's* seal. Do you see this signature? This is *General Andraste's* signature. I work for the *Bastion of Justice*, boy. Do you want to hinder an agent of the Bastion in the execution of his duties?" He really leaned on the word *execution*, which Rodrick thought was a nice touch.

"I—no sir, absolutely, sir, go right in."

Bannerman nodded curtly and walked into the building, Rodrick following. "That was easier than I'd expected," Rodrick said.

"Ha. There are only two of us. I don't know how they do things where *you're* from, but in Lastwall, you don't rise through the ranks without proving your ability to hold your own in a battle. We're walking into a room full of some of the most dangerous people in the country. How much trouble could two men possibly cause?"

"You've got the scroll?" Rodrick said.

Bannerman patted the front of his shirt. "Tucked in here. How much do we trust the Specialist? If this thing doesn't work . . . we don't really have a fallback plan."

"I wouldn't say *that*. If it doesn't work, we quietly leave the room, and I look for a fast ship out of Vellumis, and you sneak back to the Bastion and wait in Temple's office and cut off Prinn's head as soon as he comes in."

"Oh," Bannerman said. "I suppose that's an option. Do you know if totenmaskes revert to their true form when you kill them? Or would everyone think I murdered Temple?"

"Not sure. I never read the Specialist's little book."

"Did you notice how I didn't ask how he came to have a volume from the Interdicted Library?" Bannerman said. "I was very particular about not asking that."

"You are a man of wisdom and good character. Are we going to do this?"

"I'm ready. Are you?"

"Oh yes. Hrym?"

"What?" Hrym said. "Why are you still talking? Am I supposed to kill something now? How much are we getting paid for this again?"

They went to the double doors that led to the feasting hall, Bannerman nodding at the sentry and holding up the parchment as if that explained his presence. You had to love the military, Rodrick thought. Wear the right clothes, walk confidently, and wave around an impressive-looking bit of paper, and you could get things done.

The sentry opened the door and waved them through.

Rodrick had been to more than a few feasts, because rich people enjoyed them, and Rodrick liked being around rich people, because they had the most money to steal. He'd seen grand affairs with jugglers and acrobats and musicians and countless courses of rich food, parties with whole cows roasting in fireplaces. Trust Lastwall to eschew the decadence of a good feast: there were long tables of polished wood, and straight-backed chairs that probably didn't even have cushions, and a whole lot of people eating off plates that weren't even a little bit made of gold. The only entertainment was whatever conversation the crusaders could muster among themselves. The guests all looked like they'd rather be wearing armor and wading through an ankle-deep slurry of blood than wearing formal uniforms and making small talk.

Some of the guests looked up when they saw the doors open, but seeing only a couple of crusaders on some errand, returned to their food or desultory conversation. Andraste was on a raised dais in the center of the room, but there was no sign of Temple.

Bannerman went to a man in gleaming armor leaning against the wall, holding an ornamental mace—some kind of sergeant-at-arms?—and asked him a question in a low voice. The man shook his head and murmured a reply. Bannerman looked stunned, and returned to Rodrick. "Temple's not here. She never showed up." He shook his head. "Of all the ways this could go wrong, I didn't think *this* was one of them."

Rodrick frowned and stared at General Andraste, who was laughing uproariously at something the old man seated beside her had said. Rodrick glanced around, and caught sight of a servant approaching with a tray—not even silver, just some dull metal—laden with glasses full of pale liquid.

Rodrick discreetly put his foot into the servant's path, causing the man to trip and send a torrent of glass and wine crashing to the floor. Everyone in the room looked up, some in alarm, some with laughter, and there was a even a bit of mocking applause. Rodrick kept his eyes fixed on Andraste, who looked up, caught his eyes—and stared murder at him, baring her teeth. They weren't the same eyes, oh, no . . . but it was the same *look.*

"Read the scroll," Rodrick said.

"What?" Bannerman stared at him. Rodrick reached out and tore open Bannerman's shirt, snatching the scroll, as Andraste rose to her feet and began shouting for the guards to seize them. Rodrick dove behind a large ornamental planter with a small tree growing in it, tried not to worry about whether he was in range for the spell to work, and then opened up the scroll. He was never happy using magic, despite having a very magical sword on his hip, but this was an emergency. He looked at the general, focusing on her, then lifted the scroll. The words seemed to squirm into his eyes and emerge from his mouth without bothering to pass through his brain first.

The general hubbub of alarm changed its tone, with a few more screams and numerous profane oaths added to the mix, and when Rodrick peeked from behind the potted plant, he was unsurprised by what he saw.

At some point, Prinn in his disguise as Temple had gotten into a room with General Andraste, and taken on her form instead. The scroll's spell to reveal true forms had ripped the totenmaske's disguise away, though, and now the monster stood revealed in its green-skinned, maw-faced horror, lashing about it with long claws as high-ranking crusaders armed mostly with ceremonial weapons tried to kill it. Bannerman drew his weapon and ran roaring right into the fray. Good for him. Rodrick wished him well. For his part, he slipped back to the building's lobby and started thinking of the most efficient strategy to exit Lastwall entirely, and with all due haste.

"RODRICK!" The roar was guttural, enraged, and most unwelcome. He turned as the doors to the banquet room burst outward and the totenmaske rushed out, swinging its immense baleful head to and fro. Prinn saw Rodrick, roared again, and raced toward him. Rodrick hurried toward the front doors, but there were crusaders in the way raising crossbows and *shooting* them, so Rodrick's well-honed survival instincts advised him against charging into oncoming crossbow bolts. He darted instead for a stairway and rushed upward, hoping the totenmaske would be occupied by the attackers coming at it from behind *and* the front.

But no. Prinn apparently held a particular grudge against Rodrick, which was understandable. He should have made Bannerman read the scroll instead. The beast bellowed as it came up the stairs after him. Were these crusaders *incompetent*?

"How hard is it to kill one undead monster?!" Rodrick shouted as he hammered up the stairs.

"Probably quite hard, since it's already dead," Hrym said from his hip. "*We* could fight it instead."

"Why should we?" Rodrick shouted. "There are soldiers here for that sort of thing!"

There were, but the stairway was narrow enough that the crusaders pursuing Prinn were probably getting in one another's way more than they were damaging the monster.

"I will *eat your mind*!" Prinn shouted from entirely too close behind him.

The stairs reached a landing, switchbacked, and continued to climb, so Rodrick climbed with them. It crossed his mind that running *up* stairs wasn't the best strategy, since he would, inevitably, run out of "up" at some point, and then getting down again would prove difficult.

He passed doors on each landing, every one tempting him with the possibility of escape, but Prinn was so close Rodrick didn't dare stop and try one. Prinn would have those long claws wrapped around Rodrick's face before the door was even half open. Rodrick could only hope the pursuing crusaders would kill the monster before he ran out of stairs.

That didn't happen, though they were at least inflicting a bit of damage on Prinn, based on the howls, and the pursuit slowed down. Rodrick took full advantage of the few steps he'd gained and put on a final burst of speed to rush up the last half-flight of stairs. He reached the landing with the last door, which fortunately opened *outward*, and pushed through it—not into a hallway or room, but into open air.

He hesitated for a moment, surprised by the wind and the star-flecked sky above. They were on the roof. The problem with roofs was, they didn't allow a lot of options for escape, unless you could fly. He kept running anyway, toward the parapet, and looked over the low wall. There was no help there, just a dizzying drop to the stones below, and while there was a neighboring building, it was too far away for Rodrick to leap to its roof.

He spun, then, drawing Hrym. What else could he do?

The totenmaske came through the door, slammed it closed before the crusaders could follow—and threw a bolt to lock it.

32

SHATTERED

Rodrick cursed. He hadn't even thought about locking the door. In his defense, he'd been terrified.

"Rodrick." The totenmaske advanced a few steps, needlelike talons extended, then paused, eyeing Hrym. (Probably, anyway. Prinn had so much mouth, it was hard to tell *what* his eyes were doing.) "You ruined everything. Why did you turn on me? I showed mercy. I let you and the others go."

"You expected me to *die*, Prinn," Rodrick pointed out.

"I had faith in your ingenuity. We're not so different. You want gold, and a life of ease and pleasure. That's all I want."

"We're a little different. For one thing, I'm from Andoran. For another, you're an undead monster."

"How is that my fault? I didn't *ask* to rise from the dead. I'm just trying to make my way." Prinn moved forward in a motion that seemed somehow snakelike.

The closed door shuddered in its frame. The totenmaske looked back, then turned its gaze to Rodrick. Rodrick couldn't read the expression of something that was all horrible mouth, but the totenmaske had clearly gotten over its initial rage, and now it was worried. Creatures like Prinn survived by hiding among humans, and he'd been found out. They might be hard to kill . . . but the crusaders of Lastwall were adept at killing the undead. "*Listen*. It doesn't have to be this way. You can use your sword to make a bridge to the next building—"

Oh. That hadn't even occurred to Rodrick. Well, it was a bit late now.

"We can get away, and I'll steal another identity. Someone rich. I'll give you the gold. You love gold, Hrym."

"I do," Hrym said. "What do you think, Rodrick?"

"Hmm, yes, that's very tempting—" Rodrick swung Hrym's point toward the monster. The totenmaske leapt at him, and Hrym spewed forth a cone of ice and wind, knocking Prinn back—but not knocking him *down*. Apparently the undead could weather attacks of ice magic better than most, which made sense; the grave was reputed to be a terribly cold place.

The monster lashed out with its horribly long arms, and Rodrick moved out of the way, the backs of his knees bumping into the parapet. He waved his arms, terrified he'd lose his balance and tumble over the edge of the low wall.

Prinn howled. "I may die, but I'll have the pleasure of drinking your *face* first, Rodrick of Andoran." Prinn reached out with his claws.

Rodrick thought of Temple, her mouth erased by the monster's touch, and whimpered. Maybe falling off the building to his death would be preferable.

He raised up Hrym, trying to get the blade between himself and the beast, hoping to shear off a few of its fingers, at least. Hrym blasted forth a spray of foot-long spikes of ice, and one of them shot into Prinn's gaping mouth, piercing his green cheek and poking all the way through.

The monster recoiled, and Rodrick flung himself to one side, then scuttled away on the ground, in something between a slither and a crawl. The maneuver wasn't very dignified, but neither was having his face smeared into featurelessness.

He turned onto his back in time to see Prinn running toward him, and sprayed a torrent of ice just as the monster leapt at him. He rolled out of the way as Prinn, partially encased in frost, smashed into the stones where Rodrick had been. The totenmaske struggled to its feet, clawing at the icy encrustations on its body and ripping them away, sometimes taking flesh with them.

Rodrick stepped to one side, putting Prinn between himself and the edge of the roof. He pointed Hrym and said, "Freeze him *solid!*"

The sword unleashed a miniature blizzard on the toten-maske, and still the monster pushed forward, head lowered, feet braced, taking one step after another, reaching out with its claws. One touch from those talons, Rodrick knew, would be the end of him—he would drop Hrym, have his memories and mind sucked out, and the totenmaske would *become* him.

Everything in Rodrick told him to run away.

Instead, he ran forward, right between Prinn's outstretched arms, and plunged Hrym into the monster's chest. Prinn howled, and Rodrick ducked, leaving the sword embedded in the toten-maske, avoiding its claws as he rolled aside.

Hrym knew what to do. His blade radiated a ferocious cold that turned the night air to winter. That cold bit into Rodrick's flesh, now that he was no longer holding onto the sword's hilt, protected from the magic. He shivered as the totenmaske lurched forward two steps, then went still, its vast mouth suddenly exhaling frosty vapor.

"Drink . . . you . . ." Prinn croaked.

Then the totenmaske's open mouth filled with ice as Hrym froze the monster from the inside out. Within moments, the toten-maske was a frozen statue of itself, vapor rising from its form.

Rodrick stepped forward, teeth chattering, and closed his hand on Hrym's hilt. The terrible cold stopped afflicting him immedi-ately. "Ready to come out?" Rodrick said.

"Please," Hrym replied. "It smells *terrible* in here."

Rodrick drew the sword from the bloodless hole in Prinn's chest, and stood regarding the totenmaske. "Huh," he said. "Do you think the crusaders will put it on display somewhere? Maybe in the middle of a fountain? I'm not sure I've ever seen an uglier statue."

Prinn's eyes moved in their frozen sockets. The totenmaske's jaws creaked, and bits of magical ice cracked as it attempted to close its jaws.

"No, no, not happening," Rodrick said. He put his shoulder against the monster's chest, braced his feet, and shoved. The totenmaske slid across the roof a few inches, and Rodrick pushed harder, until the back of Prinn's legs hit the low wall. He leaned back, took a breath, and then *slammed* his shoulder into Prinn.

The totenmaske was top-heavy—its huge mouth was filled with ice, after all—so it tumbled quite easily over the parapet. Rodrick looked over the wall at the falling creature. He had some fear Prinn would survive the fall, leap to its feet, and race off into the darkness

That fear was unwarranted. When the frozen totenmaske struck the stones, it shattered like a crystal vase thrown at a fireplace.

"Did we save the world again?" Hrym said.

"A small corner of it, maybe," Rodrick said.

"We have to stop doing that."

"Agreed. But the important thing is, we saved *ourselves*."

Just then the crusaders succeeded in bashing open the door, and a number of armed men and women flooded onto the roof, most screaming some variation on "Put down the sword or die!"

Rodrick sighed. If he hadn't seen what the fall did to Prinn, he would have been tempted to jump himself.

Fortunately, Bannerman got to the roof before Hrym got annoyed and froze all the crusaders. By virtue of being loud and seeming to know what was going on, Bannerman managed to seize some initiative. He sent someone to make sure the shattered thing on the ground was a monster, and wasn't actually Rodrick, which made sense—you couldn't be too careful when dealing with a creature that stole faces. Once they'd determined Rodrick wasn't an undead imposter, things calmed down a bit, and he and Hrym were escorted to the Bastion as something between prisoners and guests. None of the crusaders tried to take Hrym away from Rodrick, thus sparing themselves a considerable diminishment in their ranks. Neither one of them was willing to be parted from the other again, even for a moment.

Rodrick was installed in the suite where he'd lived with the Volunteers, which seemed terribly sad and empty now, as opposed to terribly sad and crowded. He and Hrym were left alone, with Bannerman promising to return soon with news.

Rodrick slept for a while, and then he woke up, and then he sat on the couch. He bickered good-naturedly with Hrym, who wanted to blast a hole in the door and get out of Lastwall forever. Rodrick convinced him there might be a reward coming, though, which settled the sword down. Rodrick got so bored at one point that he tried to read some of Zumani's poetry, which was worse than boredom, so he stopped.

Sometime late on the morning after the feast, Bannerman returned—with General Andraste, who looked haggard, as if she hadn't slept in days.

"You're alive!" Rodrick said.

The general looked at Bannerman. "Does he always state the obvious?"

"I think he's expressing happiness at an unexpected surprise," Bannerman said, in a generous interpretation.

The woman grunted. "Rodrick of Andoran, and Hrym of Shory, in recognition of your services to our great nation, I hereby pardon you of all crimes committed against and within the borders of Lastwall. Please accept this token of our appreciation." She made a tired gesture, and Bannerman tossed a coin purse.

Rodrick caught it, and, even though it was the height of rudeness, opened it up and looked inside. Gold coins, and lots of them. Not quite the chest full of treasure he'd fantasized about, but more than he'd hoped for. "More than a token would be nice, but I accept."

"Tell him the bad news, Bannerman," she said. "I'm going back to bed." The general plodded out of the room.

"Oh, good," Rodrick said. "*Bad* news."

"There's lots of bad." Bannerman sat in an armchair. He was in better shape than Andraste, but not by much. "Temple didn't survive Prinn's attack. I don't know if he meant to kill her, but he did. We found her corpse shoved in a closet in her rooms. Andraste was locked in a closet, too, but we found her still alive, if only just barely. I didn't tell her you stole her necklace and discovered her . . . indiscretions . . . by the way. That discretion is why you got a coin purse and exile instead of prosecution for the myriad crimes you committed *without* our permission."

"I appreciate the kindness," Rodrick said. "Can I go now?"

"Oh, yes. In fact, you *have* to go now. That's the other bad news: your pardon is dependent on you leaving Lastwall and never, ever coming back. It's less a pardon and more punishment in the form of exile, except you're not *from* here, so calling it exile seemed inaccurate."

Rodrick tried to look crestfallen, though really, as long as no one from Lastwall was chasing him, he was happy to leave. Hrym didn't bother with the pretense. "That's fine," the sword said. "We hate this place. We've been exiled from places we'd actually *like* to go again, and those hurt, but having to leave this place forever? Feh."

"We'll miss you too, Hrym. We've got all your gear waiting for you. I even convinced the general to let you have back your cloak of the devilfish. I told her you might need it, since you annoy people so much you're likely to be thrown overboard on your voyage. I can escort you to the border now."

"So ends the brave saga of the Lastwall Volunteers, eh?" Rodrick said.

"Oh, I don't know." Bannerman gave him a disconcertingly wide grin. "I'm taking over Temple's old position as head of, let's say, 'special projects,' and I plan to put another team together. Which reminds me: if you ever want to ignore that order of exile and stray over the border into Lastwall again, please feel free. I'd be happy to force you into servitude again."

"I enjoyed working with you, too, Bannerman."

Rodrick spent a large quantity of his newfound coin to rent the nicest private room available on a ship heading away from Vellumis, and lay on the narrow bed, looking upward, reveling in the recently all-too-unfamiliar sensation of freedom.

"Where are we going after this?" Hrym said from his scattered bed of coins.

"This ship is bound for Druma."

"Hmm. Lots of money in Druma. Are we planning to stay there?"

"Oh, maybe for a little while. Then, I don't know . . . I was thinking of going back to Almas. It's been a while, and I have fond memories of a particular tavern there."

"Oh?"

"Yes. It's called the Golden Eagle."

"I approve of the first half of its name," Hrym said. "Never had much use for eagles, though. What fond memories are you talking about exactly?"

"I'm not sure," Rodrick said, closing his eyes and letting his imagination fly free. "I haven't made them yet."

ABOUT THE AUTHOR

Tim Pratt is the author of the Pathfinder Tales novels *Liar's Blade* and *Liar's Island* (also featuring Rodrick and Hrym), *City of the Fallen Sky*, and *Reign of Stars*. His creator-owned stories have appeared in *The Best American Short Stories*, *The Year's Best Fantasy and Horror*, and other nice places, and he is the author of three story collections, most recently *Antiquities and Tangibles*, as well as a poetry collection. He has also written several novels, including contemporary fantasies *The Strange Adventures of Rangergirl*, *Briarpatch*, *Heirs of Grace*, and *The Deep Woods*; the Forgotten Realms novel *Venom in Her Veins*; the gonzo historical steampunk novel *The Constantine Affliction* (under the name T. Aaron Payton); and, as T. A. Pratt, eight books in the urban fantasy series about ass-kicking sorcerer Marla Mason: *Blood Engines*, *Poison Sleep*, *Dead Reign*, *Spell Games*, *Broken Mirrors*, *Grim Tides*, *Bride of Death*, and the prequel *Bone Shop*. He edited the anthology *Sympathy for the Devil*, and coedited the *Rags & Bones* anthology with Melissa Marr.

He has won a Hugo Award for best short story, a Rhysling Award for best speculative poetry, and an Emperor Norton Award for best San Francisco Bay Area-related novel. His books and stories have been nominated for Nebula, Mythopoeic, World Fantasy, and Bram Stoker awards, among others, and have been translated into numerous languages.

He lives in Berkeley, California with his wife Heather Shaw and son River, and works as a senior editor and occasional book reviewer at *Locus*, the Magazine of the Science Fiction and Fantasy Field. He blogs intermittently at **timpratt.org**.

ACKNOWLEDGMENTS

Books are written mostly by sitting alone in a room for a long time, but it takes a lot of people to make that sitting alone possible. Thanks first to my wife, Heather Shaw, who supports and indulges me, and to my son, River, who is now old enough to play tabletop games, and will enjoy reading these books before too long, I hope. Thanks to my editor James Sutter for being enthusiastic about my ideas, and to my agent Ginger Clark for making things run smoothly. I dedicated this one to my good gamer friends Jeffrey Martin and Katrina Storey, pirate and sorcerer, who always remind me of the things I love about roleplaying.

GLOSSARY

All Pathfinder Tales novels are set in the rich and vibrant world of the Pathfinder campaign setting. Below are explanations of several key terms used in this book. For more information on the world of Golarion and the strange monsters, people, and deities that make it their home, see *The Inner Sea World Guide*, or dive into the game and begin playing your own adventures with the *Pathfinder Roleplaying Game Core Rulebook* or the *Pathfinder Roleplaying Game Beginner Box*, all available at **paizo.com**.

Absalom: Largest city in the Inner Sea region, located on an island.

Abyss: Plane of evil and chaos ruled by demons, where many evil souls go after they die.

Adamantine: One of the more commonly discovered and used skymetals, known for its incredible strength.

Alchemists: Spellcasters whose magic takes the form of potions, explosives, and strange mutagens that modify their physiology.

Almas: Capital city of Andoran.

Andoran: Democratic and freedom-loving nation.

Andoren: Of or pertaining to Andoran; someone from Andoran.

Aroden: The god of humanity, who died mysteriously a hundred years ago.

Bastion of Justice: Key government stronghold for Lastwall, located in the city of Vellumis.

Belkzen: A region populated primarily by savage orc tribes.

Cayden Cailean: God of freedom, ale, wine, and bravery. Was once mortal, but ascended to godhood by passing the Test of the Starstone in Absalom.

Cheliax: Powerful devil-worshiping nation.

Clerics: Religious spellcasters whose magical powers are granted by their gods.

Conservatory of Jalmeray: Famed school on an island controlled by Jalmeray, officially instructing entertainers and courtesans, but widely reputed to be a training center for spies.

Demon Lord: A particularly powerful demon capable of granting magical powers to its followers. One of the rulers of the Abyss.

Demons: Evil denizens of the plane of the afterlife called the Abyss, who seek only to maim, ruin, and feed on mortal souls.

Deskari: The principle demon lord responsible for the demonic invasion through the Worldwound. Also known as the Lord of the Locust Host.

Devils: Fiendish occupants of Hell who seek to corrupt mortals in order to claim their souls.

Devilfish: Semi-intelligent, seven-armed octopus-like creature with hook-lined tentacles.

Devilkin: Someone with fiendish blood, such as from ancestral interbreeding with devils. Often displayed by horns, hooves, or other devilish features. Rarely popular in civilized society.

Doppelgangers: Humanoid creatures able to take on the physical likeness of other humanoid creatures.

Druma: Shortened name for the Kalistocracy of Druma, a nation built on the tenets of the Prophecies of Kalistrade, a pseudo-religion in which individuals view the accumulation of wealth as the highest possible goal.

Dryads: Fey who bond with trees.

Elementals: Beings of pure elemental energy, such as air, earth, fire, or water.

Elves: Long-lived, beautiful humanoids identifiable by pointed ears, lithe bodies, and pupils so large their eyes appear to be one color.

Erastil: Stag-headed god of farming, hunting, trade, and family.

Fangwood: A large forest that covers much of Nirmathas and Lastwall.

Fey: Creatures deeply tied to the natural world, such as dryads or pixies.

Freedom War: War of independence fought between the nation of Molthune and rebel forces that eventually became the nation of Nirmathas.

Gnomes: Small humanoids with strange mindsets, big eyes, and often wildly colored hair.

Hungry Mountains: Sinister mountain range in southern Ustalav, just north of Lastwall.

Impossible Kingdoms: Another name for Vudra.

Inner Sea: The vast inland sea whose northern continent, Avistan, and southern continent, Garund, as well as the seas and nearby lands, are the primary focus of the Pathfinder campaign setting.

Interdicted Library: Secret caches of dangerous knowledge maintained by the crusaders of Lastwall.

Iomedae: Goddess of valor, rulership, justice, and honor, who in life helped lead the Shining Crusade against the Whispering Tyrant before passing the Test of the Starstone and attaining godhood.

Jalmeray: Island nation in the Obari Ocean, heavily influenced by the customs and cultures of distant Vudra.

Kholerus: Nascent demon lord imprisoned in the Lake of Mists and Veils in Brevoy.

Kyonin: Elven forest-kingdom largely off-limits to non-elven travelers.

Lake Encarthan: Enormous body of freshwater with many nations sharing borders along its shorelines, including Lastwall, Nirmathas, and Molthune.

Lake of Mists and Veils: Vast lake far northeast of Lastwall.

Lastwall: Nation dedicated to keeping the Whispering Tyrant locked away beneath Gallowspire, as well as keeping the orcs of Belkzen and the monsters of Ustalav in check.

Liches: Spellcasters who manage to extend their existence by magically transforming themselves into powerful undead creatures.

Linnorms: Immense, snakelike dragons with two forward legs and rudimentary wings.

Mendev: Cold, northern crusader nation that provides the primary force defending the rest of the Inner Sea region from the demonic infestation of the Worldwound.

Molthune: Young, militant, and ambitious nation along the shores of Lake Encarthan.

Molthuni: Of or related to Molthune; someone from Molthune.

Mwangi Expanse: A sweltering jungle region south of the Inner Sea.

Negative Energy: An opposing force to life energy, used in the creation and sustaining of undead creatures, and able to cause harm to living creatures.

Nereids: Aquatic fey that appear as beautiful women, often attempting to lure people to a watery death.

Nex: Nation in Garund formerly ruled by a powerful wizard of the same name.

Nirmathas: Fledgling forest nation constantly at war with its former rulers in Molthune.

Nirmathi: Of or pertaining to Nirmathas; someone from Nirmathas.

Niswan: Jalmeray's capital city and largest port.

Noqual: One of the rarer skymetals, with magic-resistant properties.

Numeria: Land of barbarians and strange alien technology harvested from a crashed starship near the nation's capital.

Ogres: Hulking, brutal, and half-witted humanoid monsters with violent tendencies, repulsive lusts, and an enormous capacity for cruelty.

Oracles: Spellcasters who draw their power from mysterious divine sources.

Orcs: Race of humanoids with green or gray skin, protruding tusks, and warlike tendencies. Generally hated due to their habit of raiding other races.

Paladins: Holy warriors in the service of good and lawful gods. Ruled by a strict code of conduct and granted special magical powers by their deities.

Precentors Martial: Top government officials in Lastwall, who rule under the oversight of the Watcher-Lord.

Rakshasa: Evil spirits capable of disguising themselves as humanoids in order to sow chaos and destruction. In their natural forms, they appear as animal-headed humanoids with backward-facing hands.

Rangers: Outdoor experts specialized in surviving in a particular terrain; often employed as scouts, guides, hunters, and skirmishers.

Serpentfolk: Ancient race of reptilian humanoids with heads and tails like snakes, who once claimed a vast empire but are now extremely rare.

Shory Empire: Ancient empire, long since fallen to obscurity, which was most famed for its flying cities.

Skymetal: Metal that falls to Golarion as meteorites and has exceptional (and sometimes magical) qualities.

Sodden Lands: A land of constant storms and flooding, where only a few pockets of civilization survive.

Sorcerers: People who casts spells through natural ability rather than faith or study.

Sun Orchid Elixir: An extremely rare potion produced only in Thuvia, capable of partially undoing the effects of age and prolonging one's life.

Taldor: A formerly glorious nation that has lost many of its holdings in recent years to neglect and decadence.

Tamran: The capital city of Nirmathas.

Thakur: Title for the ruler of Jalmeray.

Three Pines Ford: A large town settled alongside the Tourondel River in Lastwall.

Tian Xia: Continent on the opposite side of the world from the Inner Sea region.

Totenmaskes: Dangerous undead creatures capable of stealing the faces of living creatures and shaping flesh like clay.

Undead: Once-living beings who have been reanimated by spiritual or supernatural forces, most often the application of negative energy.

Vellumis: The oldest and largest city of Lastwall.

Vudra: Massive nation far to the east of the Inner Sea.

Vudrani: Someone or something from Vudra.

Watcher-Lord: The ruler of Lastwall.

Whispering Tyrant: Incredibly powerful lich who terrorized Avistan for hundreds of years before being sealed beneath his fortress of Gallowspire a millennium ago.

White Dragons: Savage, evils dragons with a mastery over cold and ice magic.

Wizards: People who casts spells through careful study and rigorous scientific methods rather than faith or innate talent, recording the necessary incantations in spellbooks.

Worldwound: Constantly expanding region overrun by demons a century ago. Held at bay by the efforts of the Mendevian crusaders.

Turn the page for a sneak peek at

Starspawn

by Wendy N. Wagner

Available August 2016

3

TALL CLIFFS AND SEA CAVES

Jendara lowered the spyglass. "So that's our island." She brought the glass back up to her eye. The island looked small, maybe four or five miles across, and every inch of it was covered by the ancient city. She had visited a dozen cities on the mainland, even Absalom, the largest and most beautiful city of all the Inner Sea, but she'd never seen a city like this. It grew from the sea like a spiky sea urchin that winked and glittered under the sun.

"We're going to complete a full circuit of it," Vorrin said. "I want to get a sense of the place." He walked away to go talk to Zuna at the bow.

Jendara lowered the glass again. Even without magnification, the island looked spectacular. She couldn't wait to begin exploring the ruins. Hearing about the island back on Sorind, she'd daydreamed about finding gold, but now that she was in sight of the thing, she found herself more curious than greedy. Who had built this place and where had they gone? How long had all of this lain beneath the sea?

Sarni paused at the railing beside Jendara. "It's something else," Sarni sighed. She glanced pointedly at the spyglass. "Mind if I use your glass for a better look?"

Jendara handed it to the girl. "The more eyes, the better."

"Look at all those statues. That one over there has got to be as tall as the *Milady*." Sarni turned to grin at Jendara. "It's got a lot of seaweed on it, but I'm pretty sure it's got wings and boobies." She went back to scanning the island. "Oh wait, those might be a pair of krakens. Boobies are funnier."

Jendara shook her head. It was good to know that thieves had the same breed of humor as sailors.

Sarni handed the spyglass back to Jendara, her face suddenly serious. "I've never seen anything like this place," she said. "I feel weird about it."

"Well, it's old and it's in pretty rough shape. It's going to be an adventure for all of us."

Sarni shook her head. "It's not that. It's . . . all the gold and the decorations and stuff?" She turned to put the railing at her back and folded her arms around herself. "Can you imagine living like that? The palace in Halgrim ain't even half that fancy."

Jendara shrugged. "We're islanders. If we have money to spare, we find ways to give it back to the community. Not that most of us have money to spare."

"Ain't that right. Down by the harbor, where I grew up, nobody had shit." She rolled her eyes. "Well, shit we had, but that was about it. If we got lucky, there was enough fish to eat and the ice sealed up the hole in the roof."

Jendara searched for the right answer. There had been hard times in her life—more than enough—but at least her family had always been able to live off their land. Her clan had always been able to pull together during hard times, and no one had to suffer on their own.

"The first pair of shoes I ever had? Stolen," Sarni admitted. "My mama wouldn't steal, but I would, and damn it felt good not to walk on ice down by the harbor. Stealing was the only way I ever had anything good."

Jendara put a hand on the young woman's shoulder. "That's behind you now, Sarni. You're not living on the docks and running with gangs. You've got us."

Sarni glanced back over her shoulder at the island. This side didn't look nearly as fancy as the west side of the island. There were no golden towers, but only boxy stone buildings packed in beside each other. "If we get rich, I want to help people living like I used to. I don't know how, but I want to."

Jendara just smiled. That was why she'd taken in Sarni. Beneath the foul mouth and loud voice and the history of trouble, there was a warm, kind human. She had no doubt Sarni would use all of her funds from this mission to help others.

Vorrin returned to Jendara's side. "We've almost circled the island. How in all hells are we going to land and start exploring?"

Jendara took another long look at this side of the island. Beneath the structures, the ground looked hilly and rough, turning into steep cliffs that ran straight down into the sea. She lowered the glass. "Not a harbor or entrance in sight."

"I can only guess the island must have been taller when the city was first built," Vorrin said. "They couldn't make a city like that without a way to load and unload cargo. Let's circle the island again and see if we've missed some kind of cove or sea cave. I don't want to climb the cliffs if I don't have to."

Jendara imagined what a long, muscle-eating climb that would be, and rapped her left hand on the wood deck rail. It was her private good luck ritual, a tiny nod to the ancestor spirits she'd witnessed firsthand last summer. She didn't keep a shipboard shrine or even make offerings to them, but she knew the ancestors were out there, watching over her people. The silver scar was a mark they'd left behind when they'd driven out from her hand both a nasty spell and a tattoo devoted to the pirate goddess Besmara.

The thought made her stretch out her right hand. Besmara's other jolly roger tattoo had faded over the years. The ink was beginning to seep into the white spaces, running the skull's teeth together into a solid bar of gray. Jendara wasn't troubled by the reminder of her old life, but she was glad all that was behind her.

A heavy hand clapped on her shoulder. She glanced up with a ready smile. "Boruc. You look ready for business."

The big man adjusted the sword in his belt. "The sea doesn't usually give up what she swallows. I doubt we'll get our treasure without some kind of fight."

"Then it's a good thing I have my new handaxe." Jendara eased the creation out of the straps that held it on her belt. "Who made the axe head?"

"Corwin, the smith. He's damn good at what he does. I did the etching."

Jendara let the sunlight play over the blade. She'd admired the etching before, a light tracery of brighter steel, but now she could see more clearly how the knotwork formed a stylized wolf running toward the handle. The handle itself was high-polished ironwood. Despite the axe's weight—significantly heavier than the axe she'd carried for years before losing it a summer ago—the weapon balanced perfectly in her hand. "This is the finest weapon I've ever carried."

"It's an honor to have made it for you." The red-headed man looked unusually solemn. Boruc usually played the clown, but Jendara knew there were few keener minds in all these islands. Behind the surface mirth hid a fine mind and a remarkable aesthetic.

"Jendara, Boruc! Come look!"

They quickly joined Vorrin at the front of the ship. He leaned out, pointing at the cliffs ahead. They were close enough now to make out details in the rocks: a waterfall tumbling down from a jutting ridge of stone, a fine seam of some white stone Jendara could not name, and there, down by the waterline and off to the right, the dark maw of what might just be a sea cave.

"That looks big enough to sail inside," Boruc wondered.

"Do you think that's natural or man-made?" Jendara narrowed her eyes at the cave opening, but they were too far away to make out any details. If it had been constructed by anything approaching human size, it must have taken years to chisel out of the rock.

"Why don't you and Boruc take a dinghy and find out? I don't want to risk getting the *Milady* too close until I've got a sense of what's under all this." Vorrin frowned down at the water. "I don't see rocks, but I'd lay money there's plenty down there."

"We'll do a sounding and check out that cave. Might at least offer a place to camp." Jendara gave her husband a quick kiss and then hurried to ready the dinghy.

As she lowered herself into the small craft, she caught herself grinning. It had been months since she'd done anything more exciting than negotiating a trade agreement, and while some of the craftspeople she knew drafted rather severe contracts, it was work that called for wits and pen, not a sword. Now here she was, rowing toward a cave, a new handaxe in her belt, and an unexplored island beckoning at her. It almost felt like a vacation.

"Six fathoms here," Boruc said, dropping their sounding line back into the bottom of the dingy. "Water's clean and clear as far as I can see. No rocks."

On the *Milady*, the others would be taking their own soundings, but the ship was anchored and waiting patiently for Jendara's final verdict. She looked back over her shoulder at the oncoming island. Only a few boat lengths away now—she could no longer make out the tops of the nearest towers, which leaned backward from the cliff's edge.

"Strange buildings, aren't they?" Boruc mused. "None of them look square from here."

"Well, they're old." Jendara grunted as she yanked on the oars. It had been a while since she'd done any serious rowing.

"Slow down now, we're almost inside." Boruc reached for the lantern cached in the bottom of the boat and lit it with his flint striker. Jendara twisted around in her seat, no longer rowing, but just letting the obliging current pull the vessel inside the great mouth of the cave.

"Merciful Desna," Boruc breathed.

Jendara stared around the space. Vast darkness surrounded them. Their little lantern cast a golden circle around them, but it was a firefly's glow inside the enormous blackness, and for a moment, direction became meaningless. The dinghy floated in a bubble of brightness like a star in a limitless sky. A thin keening whistle came from nowhere and everywhere. Jendara's ears hurt from the sound of it.

She lowered her oars to slow the boat. "Can you make out anything? Rocks? Walls?"

Boruc put the light on the seat beside him and reached for the sounding line. The lead made a solemn plunking as it broke the surface of the water, and then silence prevailed, save for that faint whistle.

"Do you hear that?" Jendara asked.

"That wind? Damned annoying, ain't it?" He retrieved the sounding line. "Five fathoms. The *Milady* could sail all the way inside if Vorrin wanted."

He lifted the light again, and this time the flame reflected on something besides the deep waters of the grotto: the amber light flickered on something shiny off to Jendara's right. She began to row toward it.

"Look at that, Dara." Boruc shook his head. "You ever see anything like it?"

She shook her head. The water ran up to what looked like a broad white beach, made of the same strange pale stone she had seen running up the side of the cliff. It could have been granite, she supposed, but it had none of the stains granite showed when exposed to the elements. The stone beach was only about as wide as the *Milady* was long, with either end running into a ridge of darker stone that framed it like the cheeks of some great gaping-mouth fish.

"How in all hells is that dock still whole?" Boruc wondered.

Jendara had to twist to see the dock that stuck out along-side the farthest of the two dark cheeks. She couldn't make out what kind of wood the thing had been made of, but it floated neatly enough. The docks in Sorind had been mangled by a small tsunami, and this creation had been submerged for what had to be centuries. It made no sense.

"Sometimes the salt water preserves wood," she began, and stopped. She couldn't find an excuse for this. However the dock had stayed in one piece over the course of the years was unexplainable, the stuff of mystery. She didn't even want to know. "It may only look safe," she mused. "We should check it before we tie up to it."

"The water's deep enough to dock the *Milady*," Boruc agreed. "We can tell Vorrin that much."

Jendara hesitated. She could go back and tell Vorrin they'd found a safe docking spot—but then what? How could they get from this cavern to the treasures above? She eyed the white beach in its gullet of stone. Did it go anywhere? She had to find out.

"Let's do a little exploring." She turned the dinghy so it slid up beside the dock. They tied the mooring rope to the nearest mooring cleat. She gave the rope a sharp tug and was pleased to feel the dock hold up to the treatment. "You stay in the boat while I take a quick look around."

Boruc did not argue with her, but let her scramble up onto the pier alone. She held out her hand for the lantern and he hesitated a moment before passing her the lantern with reluctance. She wouldn't want to be left waiting alone in the dark, either.

"I'll just be a moment," she reassured him. She bounced on her toes a second and then squatted down on the pier to rap on the decking. Jendara frowned. It felt strong enough, but it didn't sound or feel right. She scraped it with her fingernail. "I think it's bone," she called back to her friend. "Whale, maybe? Only thing big enough I can think of."

Whale bone. It made more sense than wood, she supposed. The entire island was covered by construction, leaving no room for crops or forest. What they needed they had taken from the sea.

She took a few careful steps forward. The pier groaned, a sad tenor to the wind's whistling descant. But it held. She raised the lantern higher and tried to make out the beach ahead.

At first, she saw only darkness. She took a few more steps, still slowly, but more confidently, and then strode faster to reach the end of the dock. The beach proved to be reassuringly ordinary stone. Its surface looked smooth, but time had worn it down in places. Patches were still slick with water, and clumps of weed and foam floated in the deeper puddles. The white stone climbed at a comfortable angle until it met a set of stone stairs.

Jendara paused to study the staircase. It ran inside a narrow tube carved into the dull gray stone wall. Jendara stepped up onto the first stair, and then took another halting step upward. While nearly broad enough for two people to walk side by side, the risers were ridiculously short and strangely deep. Whoever had built this place certainly hadn't walked like a human.

She craned her neck, trying to make out the end of the strange staircase, but it snaked around a curve. It looked sturdy enough. No broken stone to warn of cave-ins ahead, and no debris piled up at the curve. If there was a better way to ascend to the gleaming city, she hadn't seen it.

Jendara ran back to the dock and hurried back on board the dinghy. Boruc snatched the lantern from her.

"Well?"

"Looks like there's a way up," she answered. "Let's get the others and find our fortune."

The wind's whistle grew louder as Jendara rowed toward daylight. She tried not to think of the sound as unfriendly, but found herself rowing faster anyway.

Vorrin passed Jendara a lantern and then lit his own. "This cave was a lucky find. We won't even notice if it rains."

Jendara looked past him to the dock, where the crew milled around sorting out exploratory gear, and then beyond that to the mouth of the staircase. With all their lanterns lit, she could see the neat stonework outlining the opening in the cave wall. Whoever had lived here hadn't simply taken advantage of natural cracks and seams in the rocks; they had crafted this place with care and artistry. She'd never heard of any great cities in the Ironbound Archipelago, though. This place must have been built years before any human set foot on the islands.

History had never been Jendara's strong point. The legends of ancient empires with their secret wealth, the kinds of stories that Vorrin loved, had always just sounded farfetched to her. Here he was, beaming like a kid with a new crossbow, ready to hunt treasure and rob graves. This kind of thing was a dream come true for Vorrin, and she wouldn't let him down.

She checked her belt pouch, and on second thought, rooted in her pack to make sure she had her spyglass. She usually left it on the ship for safekeeping, but it might come in handy. She heaved her pack up on her back and walked down the pier.

She paused a moment when she noticed Zuna standing at the end of the dock. She'd hoped to take point with Sarni or Boruc, somebody she'd fought with and trusted to the ends of Golarion. She glanced over her shoulder and saw the others were busy with gear and lanterns. Vorrin thought Zuna was good, Jendara reminded herself. They've worked together for years.

"Hey, Zuna!" she called out. "Want to help me clear the staircase?"

"Sounds more interesting than helping these slowpokes." Zuna adjusted the straps on her own pack and grabbed up the nearest lantern.

Jendara waited for the Zuna to catch up and then strode up the beach. Zuna didn't bother with small talk as they walked. Her hair bells tinkled softly, a much pleasanter sound than the keening wind.

She stomped on the second riser. "Seems sturdy enough."

"That's what I thought," Jendara agreed.

Zuna moved ahead of her, peering up into the vaulted ceiling. Unlike the grotto outside, this space was a reasonable size, the ceiling only a few feet taller than the women's heads. Zuna stroked the wall. "Barely discernible chisel marks here. And this rock is harder than the rock outside. I'd guess these slabs were brought from someplace else and set into some naturally occurring crack in the bedrock."

Jendara squinted at the staircase wall. "You can tell all of this from one look?"

"My mother was a stone mason. I helped in her workshop."

A tendril of guilt niggled at Jendara. She had never asked Zuna about her family or her background. She'd noticed the woman's Mwangi features and her Chelish accent, and simply assumed that like most sailors, Zuna came from wandering stock. But it sounded as if, like Jendara, Zuna had come to sailing via a circuitous route.

"Hey!" Sarni's cheerful voice echoed in the staircase. She bounded up beside Jendara. "You find anything interesting yet?"

Zuna rubbed her ears. "I was just about to say the stairs seem fairly sound, although I wouldn't *shout* in here or anything."

"Do you think sound could set off a cave-in?" Jendara asked. She squinted up the staircase, trying to see beyond their little bubble of light. She hoped the thing didn't go too much further. Visiting an ancient city was one thing; being trapped underground in an ancient city was an entirely different matter.

"It's always possible, so I'd keep all voices to a dull roar."

"Sorry," Sarni whispered, although her face lost none of its good cheer. Jendara shot her a smile.

Zuna led on. Jendara kept her hand on the staircase wall. The risers were just short enough to catch on the toe of her boot, while their tremendous depth called for nearly two steps. What kind of foot had this staircase been designed for?

Zuna lowered her lantern. "Do you hear that?"

Jendara stopped to listen. The wind whispered behind her. Sarni's jacket rustled.

Then something rasped against the stone wall ahead.

Jendara reached for her handaxe.

The Hellknights are a brutal organization of warriors and spellcasters dedicated to maintaining law and order at any cost. For devil-blooded Jheraal, a veteran Hellknight investigator, even the harshest methods are justified if it means building a better world for her daughter. Yet things get personal when a serial killer starts targeting hellspawn like Jheraal and her child, somehow magically removing their hearts and trapping the victims in a state halfway between life and death. With other Hellknights implicated in the crime, Jheraal has no choice but to join forces with a noble paladin and a dangerously cunning diabolist to defeat an ancient enemy for whom even death is no deterrent.

From celebrated dark fantasy author Liane Merciel comes an adventure of love, murder, and grudges from beyond the grave, set in the award-winning world of the Pathfinder Roleplaying Game.

Hellknight print edition: $14.99
ISBN: 978-0-7653-7548-3

Hellknight ebook edition:
ISBN: 978-1-4668-4735-4

HELLKNIGHT

A NOVEL BY
Liane Merciel

Captain Torius Vin has given up the pirate life in order to bring freedom to others. Along with his loyal crew and Celeste, the ship's snake-bodied navigator and Torius's one true love, the captain of the *Stargazer* uses a lifetime of piratical tricks to capture slave galleys and set the prisoners free. But when the crew's old friend and secret agent Vreva Jhafe uncovers rumors of a terrifying new magical weapon in devil-ruled Cheliax—one capable of wiping the abolitionist nation of Andoran off the map—will even their combined forces be enough to stop a navy backed by Hell itself?

From award-winning novelist Chris A. Jackson comes a tale of magic, mayhem, and nautical adventure, set in the vibrant world of the Pathfinder Roleplaying Game.

Pirate's Prophecy print edition: $14.99
ISBN: 978-0-7653-7547-6

Pirate's Prophecy ebook edition:
ISBN: 978-1-4668-4734-7

PATHFINDER
TALES

Pirate's
Prophecy

A NOVEL BY
Chris A. Jackson

Larsa is a dhampir—half vampire, half human. In the gritty streets and haunted peaks of Ustalav, she's an agent for the royal spymaster, keeping peace between the capital's secret vampire population and its huddled human masses. Meanwhile, in the cathedral of Maiden's Choir, Jadain is a young priestess of the death goddess, in trouble with her superiors for being too soft on the living. When a noblewoman's entire house is massacred by vampiric invaders, the unlikely pair is drawn into a deadly mystery that will reveal far more about both of them than they ever wanted to know.

From Pathfinder co-creator and award-winning game designer F. Wesley Schneider comes a new adventure of revenge, faith, and gothic horror, set in the world of the Pathfinder Roleplaying Game.

Bloodbound print edition: $14.99
ISBN: 978-0-7653-7546-9

Bloodbound ebook edition:
ISBN: 978-1-4668-4733-0

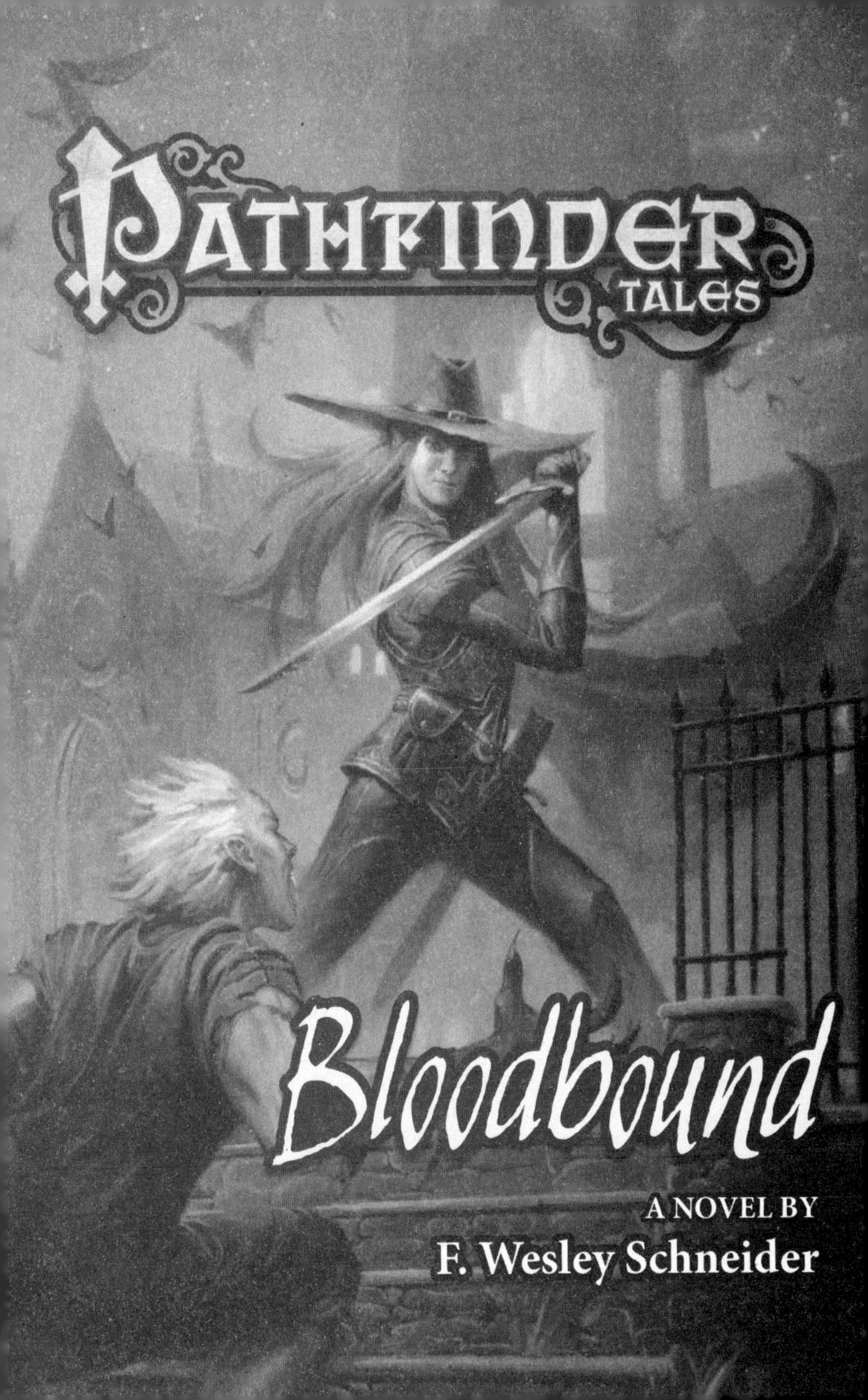
Pathfinder
Tales
Bloodbound
A NOVEL BY
F. Wesley Schneider

M irian Raas comes from a long line of salvagers—adventurers who use magic to dive for sunken ships off the coast of tropical Sargava. With her father dead and her family in debt, Mirian has no choice but to take over his last job: a dangerous expedition into deep jungle pools, helping a tribe of lizardfolk reclaim the lost treasures of their people. Yet this isn't any ordinary dive, as the same colonial government that looks down on Mirian for her half-native heritage has an interest in the treasure, and the survival of the entire nation may depend on the outcome.

From critically acclaimed author Howard Andrew Jones comes an adventure of sunken cities and jungle exploration, set in the award-winning world of the Pathfinder Roleplaying Game.

Beyond the Pool of Stars print edition: $14.99
ISBN: 978-0-7653-7453-0

Beyond the Pool of Stars ebook edition:
ISBN: 978-1-4668-4265-6

PATHFINDER TALES

Beyond the Pool of Stars

A NOVEL BY Howard Andrew Jones

Rodrick is con man as charming as he is cunning. Hrym is a talking sword of magical ice, with the soul and spells of an ancient dragon. Together, the two travel the world, parting the gullible from their gold and freezing their enemies in their tracks. But when the two get summoned to the mysterious island of Jalmeray by a king with genies and elementals at his command, they'll need all their wits and charm if they're going to escape with the greatest prize of all—their lives.

From Hugo Award winner Tim Pratt comes a tale of magic, assassination, and cheerful larceny, set in the award-winning world of the Pathfinder Roleplaying Game.

Liar's Island print edition: $14.99
ISBN: 978-0-7653-7452-3

Liar's Island ebook edition:
ISBN: 978-1-4668-4264-9

PATHFINDER TALES

Liar's Island

A NOVEL BY **Tim Pratt**

Count Varian Jeggare and his hellspawn bodyguard Radovan are no strangers to the occult. Yet when Varian is bequeathed a dangerous magical book by an old colleague, the infamous investigators find themselves on the trail of a necromancer bent on becoming the new avatar of an ancient and sinister demigod—one of the legendary runelords. Along with a team of mercenaries and adventurers, the crime-solving duo will need to delve into a secret world of dark magic and the legacy of a lost empire. But in saving the world, will Varian and Radovan lose their souls?

From best-selling author Dave Gross comes a fantastical tale of mystery, monsters, and mayhem set in the award-winning world of the Pathfinder Roleplaying Game.

Lord of Runes print edition: $14.99
ISBN: 978-0-7653-7451-6

Lord of Runes ebook edition:
ISBN: 978-1-4668-4263-2

PATHFINDER
TALES

Lord of Runes

A NOVEL BY Dave Gross

With strength, wit, rakish charm, and a talking sword named Hrym, Rodrick has all the makings of a classic hero—except for the conscience. Instead, he and Hrym live a high life as scoundrels, pulling cons and parting the weak from their gold. When a mysterious woman invites them along on a quest into the frozen north in pursuit of a legendary artifact, it seems like a prime opportunity to make some easy coin—especially if there's a chance for a double-cross. Along with a hooded priest and a half-elven tracker, the team sets forth into a land of monsters, bandits, and ancient magic. As the miles wear on, however, Rodrick's companions begin acting steadily stranger, leading both man and sword to wonder what exactly they've gotten themselves into . . .

From Hugo Award winner Tim Pratt, author of City of the Fallen Sky, comes a bold tale of ice magic and situational ethics set in the award-winning world of the Pathfinder Roleplaying Game.

Liar's Blade print edition: $9.99
ISBN: 978-1-60125-515-0

Liar's Blade ebook edition:
ISBN: 978-1-60125-516-7

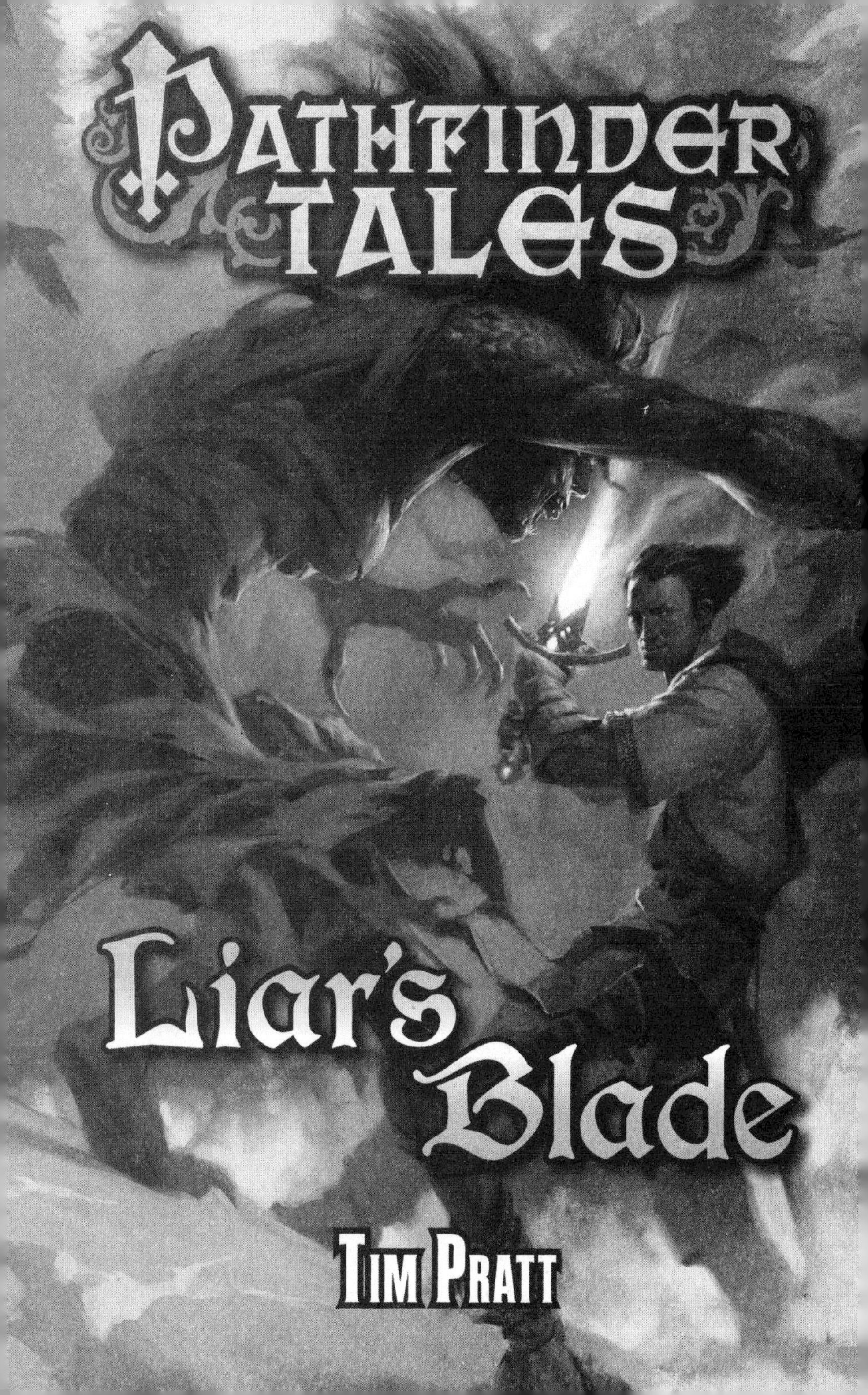
Pathfinder Tales
Liar's Blade
Tim Pratt

Once an alchemical researcher with the dark scholars of the Technic League, Alaeron fled their arcane order when his conscience got the better of him, taking with him a few strange devices of unknown function. Now in hiding in a distant city, he's happy to use his skills creating minor potions and wonders—at least until the back-alley rescue of an adventurer named Jaya lands him in trouble with a powerful crime lord. In order to keep their heads, Alaeron and Jaya must travel across wide seas and steaming jungles in search of a wrecked flying city and the magical artifacts that can buy their freedom. Yet the Technic League hasn't forgotten Alaeron's betrayal, and an assassin armed with alien weaponry is hot on their trail . . .

From Hugo Award winner Tim Pratt comes a new fantastical adventure set in the award-winning world of the Pathfinder Roleplaying Game.

City of the Fallen Sky print edition: $9.99
ISBN: 978-1-60125-418-4

City of the Fallen Sky ebook edition:
ISBN: 978-1-60125-419-1

CITY OF THE
FALLEN SKY

TIM PRATT

PATHFINDER

CAMPAIGN SETTING

THE INNER SEA WORLD GUIDE

You've delved into the Pathfinder campaign setting with Pathfinder Tales novels—now take your adventures even further! *The Inner Sea World Guide* is a full-color, 320-page hardcover guide featuring everything you need to know about the exciting world of Pathfinder: overviews of every major nation, religion, race, and adventure location around the Inner Sea, plus a giant poster map! Read it as a travelogue, or use it to flesh out your roleplaying game—it's your world now!

EXPLORE YOUR WORLD!

paizo.com